☞ Begin story
Give up already

THE

INTEGRITY

OF

THE

SUPER

CLUB

VOL.

1

GERRY

HINES

MY MIDDLE NAME IS "ULTIMATE"

WHEN Rover Chork answered the front door that afternoon, his life was in for a hell of a change. Forever.

The smiling girl at his doorstep—Rover had seen her at school on occasion.

But this was the first time seeing her so close. He had only one thought, and it paralyzed his mind and body:

She's beautiful!

"Good afternoon," the smiling girl said. "May I have a few minutes of your time?"

This was the first time Rover had heard her voice.

"Um, okay."

And this was the first time he had ever spoken to her.

And he was terrified.

"Great!" Her smile widened as she blushed. "I'm doing a fundraiser for [*bleep*]. I'm selling [*bleep*], and it'd be appreciated if you purchased something."

Rover couldn't pay attention to what she was saying, too engrossed in the delicate voice and soft mulberry eyes. Her hair held the colors of rose petal lemonade against a summer sunset, warm and refreshing.

The girl unfolded a brochure for Rover to look at, and it broke his gaze away from her eyes.

Chocolates, he thought as he looked at the ornate pictures on the paper in her hand. *She's selling chocolates.*

"I'll buy a box!" Rover said, more excited than he'd ever been for candy.

"Great!" The girl was overjoyed. "Take a look to see which one you want."

She handed him the brochure, but Rover turned it away.

"D-Don't bother," he said, playing it cool, yet tensing up from head to toe. Using his fingers, he combed his short hair that shared the color and sheen of freshly mined coal. "I'll just take the most expensive one!"

Confused by Rover's sudden insistence, the girl studied him for a second, but then her expression lit up.

1

"Oh, thank you very much! That'll be the *Shamelessly Massacred by Chocolate* airdropped pallet, which comes to,"—she glanced at the brochure— "comes to twenty-six thousand thuggoons."

"More like '*Shamelessly Massacred Our Allowance*,' if you ask me."

Rover's younger sister snuck up unnoticed and seemed to materialize in the doorway, creating a rift between the love-struck boy and the cheery girl. With her brother, she shared the same coal-colored hair (although shoulder-length) and young pine needle-colored eyes (although crinkled with disapproval).

"Adele!" Rover glared at his younger sister. "Wh-What are you doing here?!"

"I live here, duh."

"That's not what I meant."

Adele looked at the teenage girl—the *stranger*—standing on the doorstep.

"You're selling candy?" Adele asked. She looked at the brochure in the girl's hand. "Oh, I know that fundraiser. That's for the Super Club at our high school. Do you go to Southbound Thugwood High School, too?"

Super...Club? Rover thought that club sounded familiar.

"I do!" the girl said with a delighted grin. She adjusted the shoulder strap of her purse shaped like a plushy assault rifle. "I'm the president of the Super Club. My name is..."

Quinn Integrity.

Rover would never forget that name.

1!1@1#1$1%1^1&1*1(1)1_1+1

"Twenty-six thousand thuggoons," Adele muttered, sitting cross-legged on the living room couch. "You're lucky I put a stop to that, or we'd be broke."

Rover had purchased the much more reasonable *Backhanded by Chocolate* box for two thousand thuggoons after Adele coerced him.

"Hey, it's *my* money, too." He stretched out in the reclining chair, staring at the eggshell-toned ceiling. "What would you buy, anyway? Other than *Magical Poodle Snickerdoodle* merchandise. You're only sixteen. The stuff you shop for can't be that important."

Adele's face got hot. "You're only two years older than me." On TV, she searched for a specific ad video and pointed at it. "And we've been saving up for *that*. Remember? We talked about it before summer break."

"The new Anti-Grav skateboard, yeah," Rover mused, looking at the TV. The ad showed a skater punk dude doing anti-gravity tricks on the groundbreaking board while a riffy guitar squealed out a squirrely solo in the background.

"Now we're two thousand thuggoons *back* from that goal. I quit buying *Snickerdoodle* merch, so whaddaya doin' buying *chocolate*? Man, having to share my allowance with you sucks!"

"Whatever," Rover grumbled.

"All because you were gettin' lovey-dovey with that girl."

"I was not!"

"Don't lie." Adele gave Rover a grumpy grimace. "It was pretty obvious. You were practically drooling."

Rover's muscles tightened and cheeks felt warmer. "I...gah, uhh...."

"Honestly, you're pathetic." Adele tilted her head while chastising her brother. "You always try to be so tough, but around girls, your brain just pukes baby noises out your mouth."

"You'd best shut up!" Rover barked. He snapped the recliner upright and glared at his little sister.

"I don't blame you, son."

Much like Adele, the siblings' father arrived from seemingly nowhere. Adele had inherited that trait from him. Also, both siblings inherited his coal-colored hair.

It was the grin on Dad's face that scared Rover.

"Uh, what do you mean, Dad?"

"That girl was quite the looker," Dad said. "I'd be choked up around her, too."

"You saw..."

Dad stood in front of Rover, trapping the boy in the recliner while giving him the classic Dad-is-being-devious smile.

"If you need any advice, you can count on me." Dad leaned in close, making Rover sweat and shrink into the recliner's cushion. "Your mother and I have been discussing *grandchildren*."

"*Huh*?!" Rover's heartrate skyrocketed.

"Geez, Dad." Adele knew it was time to flee the conversation. She stood and walked to the stairs. "Way to crank up the creep factor."

Adele headed upstairs and Dad walked away guffawing. Rover, though, melted into the recliner. There, he decided, he would want to live with the dust bunnies beneath the chair, hiding from the embarrassment until the two thousand-thuggoon box of chocolates would arrive.

1!1@1#1$1%1^1&1*1(1)1_1+1

Satty-*day* classes let out the next day, giving way to the weekend.

That afternoon, Rover occupied his bedroom with his best friend from school, a tall and gangly fellow named Lumpy Freeb who had eyes the color of wet sand and spikey hair resembling exploded pumpkins. The two boys played *Glove Alien Fight*, the hottest new mobile game released earlier that year. It was a mandatory app and pastime for everyone.

Literally mandatory.

The CEO of the Thugwood Governmental Entity (T.G.E.) had fallen in love with the game the day of its release, so he thereby instated a citywide policy.

"All capable residents of Thugwood age ten and older must log at least one hour of *Glove Alien Fight* every day!" CEO Claudius had declared on that fateful midsummer midday during an emergency broadcast across all screens with an internet connection. "I'll know if you don't, because your save data will be uploaded to the Claudius Cloud where all reports of gameplay will be accessed by my mainframe. And if you fail to log a full hour of *Glove Alien Fight* each day between midnight to midnight..."—his grin spread on his face like a piece of paper being torn in half— "...then you'll be *de-rationalized*. Prost!"

Then the broadcast had ended. That was two months ago.

"You remember CEO Claudius' big announcement?" Lumpy asked, sitting in Rover's desk chair as the two boys undertook a quest in the mandatory game. They were playing two-player co-op, each using their own phone. "I still don't know what the heck he meant by '*de-rationalized*.'"

"Huh, I think it means we'll be recycled for parts." Rover was joking, but spoke monotone as he zoned in to the smartphone game while sitting on his bed.

"Yeah, whatever!"

"Or thrown in the Vast Penitentiary. Or put on trial in front of the Substantial Board of Exile."

Lumpy acknowledged that. "I heard you never come back from those places."

Rover squelched a Goblin in the game, earning his character experience points and brass coins, then equipped his character with a different weapon, the Knitted Glove Aliens.

"That's not true," Rover said, looking up from the phone screen. "People come back from the penitentiary."

"But not exile, right?"

"Uh, maybe not from *exile*."

Over an hour of gameplay passed, longer than what was necessary to satisfy CEO Claudius, but the game was fun and engrossing. After a while, though, the boys needed to rest their eyes from the smartphone screens.

"Let's eat something," Lumpy said, plugging his phone into the charger.

"Okay." Rover rubbed his stomach. "We have a bunch of snacks. Mom bought Peanut Butter Dunk Monkeys the other day."

"Those are gross." Lumpy wrinkled his nose. "I'll take some Rocket Rolls if you still have any."

"Yeah," Rover replied. "Pepperoni ones and peach sundae ones."

"Oh yeah!"

Without warning, Rover's 127-cm TV turned on by itself, and the boys' smartphones did the same. All three screens displayed the immaculately groomed face of CEO Claudius, the Chief Executive Overlord of the Thugwood Metropolitan Address. His curly, buttery hair and blocky facial features were impossible for anyone to forget.

"People of Thugwood!" CEO Claudius announced with vigor. "This is an emergency broadcast."

"He looks like a sheep, doesn't he?" Rover commented, looking at his TV screen.

"I think he kinda looks like a piñata," Lumpy said. "It's hard to tell how old he is. Maybe my parents' age...?"

CEO Claudius continued, "There will be an update in the current mandate involving my favorite game in the world, *Glove Alien Fight!*"

"An update?" Rover narrowed his eyes. "Is he making a new rule for the daily quota?"

"As you all know," CEO Claudius said, speaking through every internet-accessible screen in Thugwood, "you are all required to log one hour of the game each day. Beginning now, I am putting another rule into action."

"So, it *is* a new rule," Lumpy muttered.

"There will now be a way to *lift the mandate*," the CEO explained. Every single Thugwood resident leaned in closer to their screens—had they heard correctly? "That means you would no longer be required to log any game time whatsoever. Although, who would want to quit such a fun game?"

Rover and Lumpy nodded.

"Well, it *is* a fun game," Rover said.

"However!" CEO Claudius' voice thundered from the TV and smartphone screens in Rover's bedroom, reverberating through the house infrastructure. "You must *earn* this mandate being lifted. And to do that..."—he pointed at the camera, and any Thugwood residents with 3D televisions had their faces violated by his authoritative finger— "...you must DEFEAT ME IN *GLOVE ALIEN FIGHT*!!!"

Rover and Lumpy jumped back from the TV, feeling assaulted by the intrepid proclamation.

"What?!" Rover squawked. "*Defeat* him?"

Lumpy tousled his spikey, exploded-pumpkin hair. "But...there's no player-versus-player feature in the game!"

"The game's developers," CEO Claudius added, "has just informed me of a new player-versus-player feature in the game."

"Oh, I guess there is now," Lumpy said.

"To summarize," the CEO continued, "if one person defeats me in the game, *everyone* will be released from the mandate. I will only accept challenges from those who have met the prerequisites; you must figure out what they are, though. Doing so is not necessary, but you will still need to meet your daily gameplay quota until then. And remember,"—his bleak grin shone through thousands of screens across Thugwood, reaching the hundred million residents simultaneously— "failure to meet the daily quota will result in *de-rationalization*."

The broadcast cut out.

The house fell quiet.

"Hmm, sounds fun," Lumpy said.

"Noooo..." Rover grumbled. "Sounds like a *pain*."

"Yeah, it *is* a pain, but at least the game's fun."

"I guess." Rover looked at his TV's dark screen. "I'm gonna do it."

"You mean beat CEO Claudius?"

Rover sneered, clenching his fist. "Hell yeah. Screw his stupid daily quota mandate. I love *Glove Alien Fight*, but a lot of people are wasting their time because they have to play it for no good reason...and that pisses me off!"

"He said he won't accept your challenge unless you meet the prerequisites first, and it doesn't sound like he'll tell us what they are."

"Fine," Rover said. "I'll figure it out, then. I'm ending the mandate."

"I wonder why he instated the mandate to begin with. What's the point?"

"For people like me to step up and stick it to him, Lumpy."

Chuckling, Lumpy said, "If anyone can do it, I bet you can, man. You're, like, crazy good at video games. You also know how to do computer codes and stuff." He grinned. "And the mods you've done in games are freakin' awesome!"

"Ha-ha! I know."

"It's too bad *Glove Alien Fight* has super-mega strict rules against modifications." Lumpy sighed. "People could do some cool stuff in that game if they were allowed to."

"Yeah..." Rover shrugged. "Whatever. Let's get some Rocket Rolls."

Rover's parents were still out on their date, and Adele was out with her friends. Standing in the kitchen, the two boys snacked on fresh Rocket Rolls, some pepperoni and some peach sundae.

"I wonder how the player-versus-player thing will work," Lumpy mused, chewing on a Rocket Roll.

"I dunno." Rover washed out the blender and put it away. His least favorite thing about making Rocket Rolls was the unusual preparation, part of which involved a blender and a buggy phone app. "Let's check it out later today."

The doorbell rang. Leaving Lumpy in the kitchen, Rover walked to the living room and looked out the window.

His heart nearly popped.

Quinn Integrity was standing on the front porch.

Swallowing hard, Rover reached for the doorknob. This would be the second time he had ever spoken to her.

And he was still terrified.

His heart pounded in an accelerating rhythm.

Tha-thump, tha-thump

Tha-thump, tha-thump

Opening the door, Rover was met with a rush of warm air and warm sunlight, but an even warmer presence emanated from the visitor herself.

"Hi again!" Quinn's voice was radiant, her beauty unrestrained by any sort of possible hindrance. In both hands, she held a pristine box of chocolates ordained with an outlandish ribbon and presented it with utmost glory. "I'm here to deliver the chocolate you ordered!"

The boy was hypnotized by her captivating smile, but it was her aura that scrambled the circuits in his head, as if the air around her was chockfull of gaga gas.

"Y-You're..." He gulped before continuing. "You're Quinn Integrity."

"Yes! And my middle name is 'Ultimate'!" Quinn giggled. "It's a joke. I don't have a middle name...but if I did, 'Quinn of Ultimate Integrity' would be my title!"

Rover gawked—awkward as hell—confused by the girl's words and astonished by the speediness of his order being fulfilled.

"Um, that was fast," he said, calming down despite his thrashing tides of teenage hormones.

"Of course," Quinn replied. "I work very fast."

"I ordered this *yesterday*, though."

She bowed in apology. "Sorry for the delay."

"*That's* not the issue!" Rover scratched his head, offering a smile. "But, uh, thank you."

"My pleasure."

Quinn handed over the box of chocolates, and Rover's cheeks glowed as he accepted it, like the girl's warmth was conducted through the chocolate and into his bloodstream.

"Huh?" Lumpy came to the door and noticed the ribbon-topped box Rover held. "Girl scout pancakes?"

"No," Rover told him, "a fundraiser for the Super Club."

"Okay, I know which one."

Rover glanced at Quinn and felt a flurry of flittering butterflies in his stomach. "Sh-She's the president."

"Oh, cool," Lumpy said, hardly interested, tapping on his phone screen. "Wanna play more *Glove Alien Fight* now? We can see if that player-versus-player feature is ready yet."

Curious, Quinn looked at the boys.

"You're playing that game?" she asked. "The one CEO Claudius likes?"

Rover nodded. "Yep. You saw the announcement just a little bit ago, right?"

Quinn turned her soft mulberry eyes to the floor.

"I did," she said, "but I don't really understand it."

"Yeah, neither do we," Lumpy said. "It sounds like a new multiplayer component is being added to the game, so we're gonna check it out now."

The expression Quinn wore was dull, almost sullen, and seemed to take the sunlight out of the sky. "Is that so?"

"Hey, if you have time," Lumpy said to her, "we can all check it out together."

Rover panicked, a silent and secretive fit within him. *Why* was Lumpy signing away their time with the girl who made Rover sweat buckets from anxiety?

Quinn smiled. "Really? You'd do that?"

"For sure," Lumpy said.

And why is Lumpy succeeding at this?!

"Ah, gahh...uhhh..."

Lumpy turned to his panting friend. "What's wrong, Rover?"

"N-Nothing a-at all!" Rover turned to Quinn while scratching his sweaty head. "We can check it out together!"

"Thank you, I'm delighted!" Quinn beamed with joy. "I'll gladly accept your offer."

When Quinn entered the house and closed the door behind her, Rover stopped breathing.

ROVER CHORK

AGE... 18
HEIGHT... 173 CM (5' 8")
HAIR COLOR... FRESHLY MINED COAL
EYE COLOR... YOUNG, BUDDING PINE NEEDLES
OCCUPATION... SENIOR AT SOUTHBOUND THUGWOOD HIGH SCHOOL
FAVE FOODS... PEPPERONI ROCKET ROLLS, PEANUT BUTTER DUNK MONKEYS
FAVE HOBBIES... PLAYING & MODDING VIDEO GAMES

HE'S CAREFREE AND STUBBORN, BUT GETS NERVOUS AROUND GIRLS, ESPECIALLY AROUND HIS GIRLFRIEND. HAS GODLIKE ABILITIES WHEN PLAYING *GLOVE ALIEN FIGHT*, AND PEOPLE TEND TO ACCUSE HIM OF CHEATING. WILL OFTEN GET VERY COMPETITIVE, HOTHEADED, AND COCKY. HIS ATTITUDE GETS HIM IN TROUBLE AS HE RUNS HIS MOUTH WITHOUT THINKING.

IS KNOWN TO GET OBSESSED WITH GOALS, AND HE WILL PUSH HIMSELF TO UNHEALTHY EXTREMES TO ACHIEVE THEM. HAS TURNED DOWN MULTIPLE INVITATIONS TO JOIN HIS HIGH SCHOOL'S SWIMMING TEAM, DESPITE BEING A VERY STRONG SWIMMER AND GENERALLY ATHLETIC.

ROVER... Lvl 666

Allowance... {T}38,000

<<EXPENSE GOALS>>

Anti-Grav Skateboard... {T}499,999

<<CURRENT EQUIPMENT>>

Gloves... Knitted
Armor... Brick Jacket
Acc.1... Yeet-Line Skates
Acc.2... Farm Equipment

LEVEL CAP: BUSTED!!!

"THIS is my room."

Rover led Quinn into his bedroom. His legs wobbled from his effort to not sweat, which made him wobble more...which made him sweat more.

Quinn's smile conveyed excessive happiness for merely having looked at somebody's average bedroom. The generic tapestries and burly Chork coat of arms placards interested the girl, and she surrendered control to her eyes as they moved along the marvelous miniature models, somberly silent air purifiers, and humdrum furniture fitted with titanium-xenon lights.

"It's a very lovely room," she said.

The blood ran to Rover's face as he gripped the chocolates in his hands. His room had been painted with the vibrancy of Quinn's compliment, and his nervousness threatened to melt the sweet contents inside the box.

He laughed. "Not too shabby for a bedroom, r-right?!"

"Yes," Quinn said, still smiling and her eyes glittering as she stepped in farther. "A person's bedroom is like a reflection of themselves. I see that you're a very clean, organized, up-to-date person."

"Awww...ya think so???" Rover cooed, scratching his head while the chocolates in the box really did begin to soften from his body heat. "It's important to, um, stay up on things. I'm a good stay-upper, you could call it!"

She gave a thumbs-up. "A fine stay-upper, I *do* call it!"

Lumpy raised his eyebrows. He watched his friend take the long plunge from a levelheaded person to a love-struck chump. It was to be expected, though, and Lumpy was used to this side coming out when Rover was exposed to feminine cuteness.

But...

Something is different this time, Lumpy thought. *Rover's reaction is exaggerated compared to usual.*

"Hey, Rover," Lumpy said, throwing his pal a lifeline. "Let's see that new feature in *Glove Alien Fight.*"

Rover snapped back to reality. "Oh yeah, that's right."

"Wait until you see Rover in action," Lumpy told Quinn. "He's awesome at the game! If video game skills could be measured, Rover's level cap is *busted!*"

Quinn smiled. "I don't know what that means, but it sounds like you're very talented, Rover."

When Rover's speech failed, Lumpy said, "The phrase 'breaking the level cap' means growing a character beyond the maximum level in a game, letting you achieve the 'true' maximum level. So yeah, Rover is quite talented. Ain't that right, bud?"

Lumpy elbowed Rover's ribs, dislodging the nervous boy's words.

"Ha-ha! Y-Yeah, you could say so! All right...let's do this." The two boys started up *Glove Alien Fight* on their phones. "It's supposed to be a player-versus-player feature, but how do you access it?"

"Hmm, I dunno," Lumpy said, moving through the game's menus. "There's no notification. Maybe we have to find it somewhere in the game?"

After about twenty seconds of clueless gameplay, Rover looked at Quinn. She wasn't playing and instead was browsing the PlayBastion IV games on Rover's shelf by his TV, curiosity on her face. The game *Per Sauna 5* was especially interesting to her for some reason. She could sense the funky anime vibe within its programming, and it stole her heart.

"Uh, h-hey," Rover said to the girl. "Are you gonna check out the new feature? Me and Lumpy are kinda stumped. We don't know what the player-versus-player thing is about."

"Well," she said with a slight, embarrassed smile as she scratched her cheek with her index finger, "I don't have a phone, tablet, or video game system to play it on. My phone isn't a smartphone."

Rover and Lumpy gawked at Quinn.

"What?" Rover asked in disbelief. "Then...how do you play it?"

"I don't," Quinn replied, shaking her head.

That statement made no sense.

Therefore, the two boys didn't know what she had said. Her words, in that context, couldn't be used together.

Rover was sweating again, this time more from confusion than hapless hormones.

"Then...how do you play it...?" he asked, desperate that the same question would spur a different answer.

"I don't," Quinn repeated with a smile so innocent that it overrode her impossible statement.

Perplexity socked Rover out of his cupid stupidity, turning him angry.

"There's no way!" he shot back. "Playing an hour of *Glove Alien Fight* each day is mandatory by law!"

"I know," Quinn said, hanging her head.

Rover glanced at Lumpy, but his friend's concerned expression was zero help.

"If you can't play it," Rover said, looking right at Quinn, "then you'll be...be...*de-rationalized!*"

Quinn grinned. "It's no problem!"

"It's a huge problem!!! Right, Lumpy?"

Lumpy nodded, seriously and indubitably in agreement. "A huuuge problem."

"Listen, dude," Rover told Lumpy, "we *need* to buy Quinn a phone or tablet so she can log her one hour of gameplay today!"

"But I'm *broke!*" Lumpy protested. "I mean, she could just sign in on one of our phones. We already logged our hour today."

"Oh. Good point." Rover patted Lumpy's shoulder, grinning. "You're so smart, Lumpy!"

"Actually..." Quinn dropped her voice, tapping the tips of her index fingers together. "I've never played that game before."

The boys did not digest what Quinn had said. They stared at her, their minds shutting down and rebooting to cope with the fact that Quinn had admitted to something that couldn't be something at all.

Rover handed his phone to Quinn.

"Here, use my phone," Rover said, his chest tight, watching the gorgeous girl take his phone from him. Her fingerprints were already contaminating his possessions, which was appealing for reasons he didn't understand.

Quinn looked at Rover's smartphone in her hands, the newest Yonkrin fonePod, unsure of what to say.

"But," she said slowly, "...I don't have an account for the game."

Rover's mind, already freshly rebooted from one inconceivable statement, was unable to discount this new piece of ludicrousness Quinn had tossed his way.

"You...don't have...an account...?"

"No." Quinn frowned. "Sorry for the misunderstanding."

Rover and Lumpy could only stare—they weren't prepared for this particular load of codswallop and malarkey.

"Lies!" Adele declared, pointing at Quinn.

"Ack!" Rover jumped from his sister's appearance. "Where'd you come from, Adele?!"

"Zip yer trap, Big Bro." Adele marched into the room, went right up to Quinn, and stood toe-to-toe with her. "You're lying about not playing *Glove Alien Fight.*"

Unfazed, Quinn said, "No, it's the truth. I've never played it."

"*Lies!*" Adele declared again, stomping her feet like an orangutan doing a rain dance on sunbaked asphalt.

"Look…Quinn," Rover said, "if it's true that you've never logged the mandatory playtime, then…you probably wouldn't be here right now…"

"But I *am* here," Quinn replied, not sharing the confusion, her tone and mannerisms straightforward.

Rover, Lumpy, and Adele exchanged grimace-coated glances.

"So," Lumpy said to Quinn, his eyes widening with curiosity, "does that mean you've been…*de-rationalized?*"

Everyone stared at her, fascinated.

But Quinn smiled. "I'm familiar with that term, but I don't know what that means."

"How can we be sure if you haven't been?" Adele pressed with half-lidded eyes. "How do we recognize a *de-rationalized* person?" She glared at Quinn with a frown so big it hurt her mouth and cheeks. "Big Bro, you let this *intruder* into our home, and now you're accepting her lies at face value! You really *did* fall outta the Idiot Tree and hit *every branch* on the way down!"

Rover shied away. "I…missed a few branches, thank you very much…"

(Fun fact: the Idiot Tree is a real tree in Thugwood, notorious for zapping the IQ out of anyone who fails to climb it without injury…according to rumors on the Craddit *forum website.)*

"But, Quinn," Lumpy argued, "the Thugforce Militia would be all over you! There's no way you can get away with not logging the daily gameplay, because CEO Claudius has access to our save data in the Claudius Cloud! I don't know what *de-rationalization* means, but I know the Thugforce Militia is authorized to arrest anyone who doesn't meet the gameplay quota."

"Lumpy and Adele are both right," Rover told Quinn. "It's really hard to believe you for those reasons."

However, Quinn grinned with her hands on her hips. Her courageousness blinded out the bleakness of doubt bombarding her.

"Have no fear!" she told them with such confidence that the room's soul shook. "I haven't been arrested because…I'M FAR TOO SUPER AWESOME TO BE CAUGHT!!!"

Such radiance! Such heartiness! Quinn dominated the atmosphere without needing proof supporting her intrepid statement. She embedded her truth into the hearts, minds, and even the *spleens* of Rover, Lumpy, and Adele, leaving them in a stupor.

After the echo and aura of Quinn's announcement subsided, Rover was the first to regain his ability to talk, loosening his clenched fists.

"You're being *serious,*" he said, looking at the grinning, valiant Quinn. "But you should've asked someone to help you get a phone or something to play the game. There are a lot of services to help with that because of CEO Claudius' law, and it's gotta be easier to just play the game...instead of running from the law."

"C-C-Criminal!" Adele sputtered, horrified that a lawbreaking person was in her home.

Quinn sighed and shook her head. "It's okay if you think ill of me. It's true that I'm breaking the law, and I'm doing so of my own volition." She looked at Rover with total resolve. "I *choose* not to play the game."

"Why would you choose that?" Rover asked Quinn, studying her. "Especially because you know it's illegal if you don't."

Quinn nodded, somewhat meek, but not quite embarrassed. "I have my reasons."

"Such as?" Rover asked.

She shrugged. "I'm too good for CEO Claudius and his law."

More stares.

"Uh..." Adele shivered and turned to Rover. "...Is outspoken defiance against the supreme leader a crime?"

After some thought, Rover answered, "I believe it is treason."

"*Criminal!*" Adele shouted at Quinn.

KABOOM!!!

An explosion outside rattled the house.

"Wahh!" Rover cried. "I recognized that *kaboom*! The damn paint immobilizer blew up again!"

Adele grabbed her head. "Not again! We told Dad that duct tape won't work forever!"

"The paint immobilizer?" Quinn put her finger on her chin, then smiled when she realized something. "Oh! Is that what was smoldering on the side of the house when I got here?"

"And you didn't tell us?!" Rover barked.

"Hee-hee! Silly me."

Flinging his bedroom door open, Rover shouted, "Adele! Get the fire extinguisher!"

"Y-Yeah!"

"Leave it to me!" Quinn told them, raising her hand with a big grin. "I'll take care of this, no problem!"

Without hesitation, Quinn opened Rover's second-floor window and, with peculiar springiness in her knees and ankles, hopped out onto the roof.

"Hey!" Rover ran to the window to see the girl jump off the roof down to the front yard. "C'mon! Let's get out there!"

He, Adele, and Lumpy dashed down the stairs and out the front door. Around the corner, they saw the damaged side of the house, the burning grass, and the charred tree, all the result of the exploded appliance.

More importantly, they saw Quinn elbow-deep in the paint immobilizer unit (which resembled a central air conditioning unit) as it shot flames and sparks in every direction.

"*Quinn!!!*" Rover could only scream as Adele and Lumpy were too horrified to act.

The girl pulled the defunct unit away from the house, cutting the electrical supply by tearing it from the cement foundation it was bolted into, and she ripped it apart with a single motion, scattering the fiery components to break up the flames.

"No way!" Lumpy gasped, watching Quinn. "That's impossible!"

Kerrr-rAAAKKKkkkk!

Heavy splintering sounds cut through the air. The tall tree that had been damaged by the explosion began to lean and fall toward the Chork's house. As if anticipating it, Quinn leapt up close to the top of the tree (which was taller than the two-story house), and she smacked it aside as easily as spiking a volleyball. The tree trunk snapped along the damaged part near the bottom and crashed into the front yard, harming nothing but the dirt and grass.

Rover's, Adele's, and Lumpy's jaws were already on the ground before Quinn's feet were.

Quinn brushed the soot off herself with a relieved smile. Under different circumstances, Rover would have welcomed the burnt holes in the girl's shirt providing a sneak peek of her bra underneath...but his cowering libido was indisposed at the moment. He huddled with his friend and his sister, stepping backward as Quinn approached them with a bubbly expression.

"Looks like everyone and everything is shipshape!" she chortled. "But, you're gonna need a new paint immobilizer before all the paint melts off your house."

"HOW?!?" Rover's outburst made Lumpy and Adele jump away from him. "Y-You...just...BLARRGGHH!!! *What'd you do?!*"

"She's like a god!" Lumpy fell into a shaky, kneeling position before Quinn. "You're a *goddess!*"

Adele followed Lumpy's lead, falling to her knees as well. "Please forgive me, almighty criminal goddess! Find it within your treasonous righteousness to forgive my mean and true words against you!"

Quinn blushed.

"No, I'm not a goddess!" she said bashfully. "I'm just a Quinn."

Rover gaped at the unbelievable girl...the *unremarkable* Quinn Integrity, stumbling toward her.

"You really don't think *anything special* of what you just did??? You didn't get burned or shocked from the paint immobilizer! You ripped it out of the cement it was bolted into!" He waved his frenetic finger at the fallen tree. "You *slapped a tree aside* like a volleyball!!!"

Quinn's soft mulberry eyes sparkled.

"Thank you for your praise," she replied with a humble bow. "I always try hard. It makes for epic results, if I say so! Hee-hee-hee!"

"Duuuude..." Lumpy's eyes were bugged out and mouth hung open. "Wouldn't you say—?"

"I know what you're thinking, Lumpy..." Rover cut him off, making eye contact with his friend, sharing the same bewildered facial expression.

As if on cue, Rover and Lumpy looked back at Quinn and said in unison, "Level cap: BUSTED!!!"

Feeling touched, Quinn blushed and smiled.

2!2@2#2$2%2^2&2*2(2)2_2+2

Rover and Adele waited for their parents to come home, wondering how they would explain the damage to the property. They sat in the living room, pretending to watch TV, but the shock hadn't worn off, making it hard to focus on anything.

Yet, a news report caught Rover's attention as he searched the channels. He watched the Thugforce Militia footage of an old woman getting arrested, and he twisted his face in disgust.

"All because she missed her gameplay quota by *four minutes*," Rover growled.

Adele remained motionless, staring at the screen with a bored look. "It's too bad. It wasn't even her fault because she had to take her husband to the senior citizen prom, so it's not even fair."

"She'll be *de-rationalized*."

The girl looked at her brother and saw his face rigid and solemn.

"Can't she fight it in court?" she asked. "Because it wasn't her fault."

Shaking his head, Rover replied, "I don't know. I don't think so, though."

"Well, Quinn better be careful, I guess." Adele sighed. "She'll probably get caught if she's missed the quota, and that'll be it."

"Do you really think they can catch her after what we've seen her do?"

"I dunno, maybe."

"Makes me wonder," Rover said, "if I put an end to the gameplay mandate, how many people I would save. It's more than a nuisance. It's getting people arrested and punished!" He fidgeted a bit on the couch. "And...uh, I'd save Quinn, too."

Adele rolled her eyes. "Oh no, don't tell me you're doing it just for her now."

"No! I-It's for a good cause. Besides, she probably made up not meeting the quota. So…I'm doing it for a *good cause.*"

However, Adele noticed the masculine hunger on Rover's face, and she threw a ceramic coaster at him. Lumpy entered the living room with a glass of Sploder Cola to see Rover rubbing his forehead and muttering curses.

Quinn Integrity

AGE: 18
HEIGHT: 178 cm (5' 10")
HAIR COLOR: Rose petal lemonade against a summer sunset
EYE COLOR: Soft mulberry
OCCUPATION: Senior & Super Club president of Southbound Thugwood High School
FAVE FOODS: Cold cut sammiches, sparkling tea
FAVE HOBBIES: It's anyone's guess

The president of the school's enigmatic Super Club. She tasks herself with helping the students and faculty with absurd fundraisers and questionable philanthropy. Known to be optimistic and caring. Although she's popular, nobody seems to know anything about her or her club.

Has superhuman abilities that she (kind of) keeps secret, but she claims to be a normal girl. A fan of funk music and often gets it stuck in her head, but there seems to be a deeper meaning behind that.

ROVER… Lvl 666

Allowance… {T}38,000

<<EXPENSE GOALS>>

Anti-Grav Skateboard… {T}499,999

<<CURRENT EQUIPMENT>>

Gloves… Knitted
Armor… Brick Jacket
Acc.1… Yeet-Line Skates
Acc.2… Farm Equipment

OVER-POWERED BY DEFAULT

"I'M **gonna tell you** this straight, Lumpy."

"What's up?"

Later that evening, Rover and Lumpy were outside Rover's bedroom window, sitting on the roof, playing *Glove Alien Fight*. Dad and Mom were in the front yard, chatting with the tree removal crew who were grinding the fallen tree in a wood chipper while the emergency painter service installed the new paint immobilizer. Adele was getting ready for bed, and Lumpy was on his way out when Rover spoke up.

With a dead serious look, Rover said, "Quinn is...one of the most badass people I've ever met."

"That's an *understatement*! She's, like, insanely strong and stuff!" He glanced around, keeping his voice down. "We shouldn't tell anyone about it...or about her secrets, too..."

"Probably." Rover was quiet for a moment. There was no point preparing himself to say it, so he just said it. "I'm going to ask her out."

"...Are you serious? You feel safe dating someone like that???"

"I don't know, man. She has guts."

"You wanna get involved with her after everything she said about...what she said?"

"She's probably making it up," Rover said with a shrug. "Who knows? It might be fun to date her."

"You're crazy, man. I'll never understand how you're so impulsive."

Rover made a fist, smirking. "Imagine how helpful she'd be for my mission, too."

"To beat CEO Claudius and end the *Glove Alien Fight* mandate?"

"Yes, sir."

Lumpy laughed. "Right on, man!" He gave a double thumbs-up. "I wish you luck!"

"But, I've never asked out a girl before," Rover said, his tone more weary. "I-I don't know...how to do it..."

"Just ask her." Lumpy shrugged.

"But *how*?"

"It depends. That's why I'm wishing you *luck* instead…"

"You're no help, Lumpy."

"Also…she's definitely not a normal girl."

Rover gazed at the darkening sky. "That's another understatement."

"So, the same rules of dating may not apply." Lumpy stood on the roof and watched the tree service workers throw the last chunks of wood into the chipper. "Do you think you can handle her?"

"What's that supposed to mean?"

"She'll snap you like a *twig*!"

"…"

"Anyway," Lumpy said, sliding Rover's window open, "you have my support."

"Thanks, Lumpy." Rover gulped. "I'll…do my best."

Thus, Rover created his foolproof "Asking Quinn Out" list.

3!3@3#3$3%3^3&3*3(3)3_3+3

1) DRESS TO IMPRESS

Sundun-*day* morning, Rover sorted through his wardrobe, trying on dozens of combinations. Polka dot suit? Nope. Silk dress shirt with fluffy ruffles? Nah. Neon high top shoes with automatic laces? Nay.

"Playing dress-up?" Adele stood in her brother's doorway, casting belittling sneers at the foray of clothes scattered about the bedroom.

Rover dangled two different colored socks in front of him to compare.

"If I say 'yes,'" he muttered, "will you go away?"

"Just dress casually."

The boy looked at his younger sister.

"Don't play dumb," Adele said. "I know what you're doing. Just be yourself…with your Moron Metre turned down a tad." She snickered. "Unless the criminal goddess is into that."

"I'll do what I feel like," Rover replied, turning his nose up.

"All righty then." Adele turned to leave. "Hope she enjoys the stench of desperation."

After the girl left, Rover looked back at the socks he was comparing, grinned, and tossed them behind him.

"Being a desperate moron is my specialty! I don't need fancy clothes for that."

The verdict: An outfit that doesn't damper his *natural* desperation with *aesthetic* desperation. Graphic T-shirt, shorts, sneakers, plain socks—the *casual* desperation!

3!3@3#3$3%3^3&3*3(3)3_3+3

2) REHEARSE THE PICKUP LINE

Rover rehearsed his lines to his reflection in the bathroom mirror, saying "Hey, Quinn...(blah blah blah)" a hundred different ways.

"Who are you talking to, Rover?" his mom called from the hallway.

Startled, the rehearsed words got tangled up in his tonsils. "Nobody, Mom."

"Talking to yourself?" She didn't sound convinced.

"Yeah, I am. I'm not replying, so I'm only half-crazy." He smiled to himself at his lame joke.

"I knew it." Now Mom sounded exasperated. "You're practicing to ask out that girl your sister and father told me about."

"*Urrk!*" Rover choked.

"The tree breaker woman. The female fire extinguisher."

"Heh-heh...Adele told you the truth about the paint immobilizer, huh?"

Mom's voice continued from behind the *very securely* locked bathroom door.

"While it's true your father and I have been discussing grandchildren..."

Oh, God, Rover thought, anxiously wringing the hanging hand towel by the sink. *Please don't go there!*

"...I think it's still very important that you wait until marriage."

Rover twisted the hand towel, shaking and grimacing.

"Th-Thanks, Mom..."

"That goes for you too, Adele," she added.

"What?!" Adele's voice echoed from the hallway. "Don't lump me in with that hoser!"

When Rover was almost sure (but mostly hopeful) that Mom had walked away, he dropped the hand towel by the sink and turned back to his reflection in the mirror.

"Hey, Quinn..." His eye twitched. "Wanna...save it for marriage?"

His face turned hot. Unable to look at his reflection any longer, he exited the bathroom. Mom stood outside the door, beaming. Her eyes, the color of budding pine needles that Rover and Adele had inherited, were glazed and teary.

"Spoken like a genuine gentleman," she said with a dreamy voice, clasping her hands together.

Rover's face doubled in temperature, turning his sweat to steam, and he stomped down the hall to his bedroom, slammed the door, and proceeded to die a little on the inside.

The verdict: He will need to improvise his conversation with Quinn, and perhaps...save it for marriage.

3!3@3#3$3%3^3&3*3(3)3_3+3

3) SMELL LIKE A WINNER

The next day, on a cloudy Nundinum-*day* afternoon, Rover sniffed every single bottle of cologne and body fragrance in the house, deciding that the men's ones were best suited (a surprisingly not-so-obvious conclusion to him).

While in his parents' room and sneaking Dad's cologne, Dad seemingly materialized right behind him.

"Rover!"

The boy yelped, nearly dropping the bottle of *Fanci Shite* cologne he held.

"D-Dad!"

"Gwa-ha-ha! You smell like a man-whore, my boy." Dad's face was smiling, but this was a common ruse to hide the disappointment and deviousness. "You don't want that poor girl's nostrils to catch on fire from all that smelliness, do you?"

"No, I-I just ended up this way because I've been sampling everything we have." Rover turned away with a raised eyebrow. "Why do we have *so many* fragrances in our home, anyway...?"

"Did you try on your sister's perfume, too?"

"Uh...when you say it out loud...it sounds reeeeaaally weird..."

"Your best bet is to be subtle," Dad said. "Don't smell too hard."

"...'Smell too hard'?"

"Absolutely." He took the bottle of *Fanci Shite* from Rover. "Things like this are unnecessary. A simple deodorant and fresh breath will do the trick, unless she has a thing for laundry boys who smell like potpourri, then you can add a hint of regular body spray. Don't go full man-whore on the odor."

"I figured that much," Rover said impatiently. "I told you I smell like this because I tried all these samples."

"Even your sister's *Magical Poodle Snickerdoodle* fragrances. The *girl* ones."

"...Y-Yes..." Rover looked at his parents' dresser with the plethora of sprays and cosmetic technology. "So, if all the colognes and stuff aren't really necessary, then why do you and Mom have all these?"

Dad stood proudly. "When you reach a certain point in your life, you need to be prepared for all kinds of occasions. Your granddad used to say to match the smell with the situation! Ha-ha!"

"Ah, I get it." Rover nodded. "You have all these to hide your 'old people smell'!"

"'Old people smell'...?"

Again, the smile on Dad's face belied the thoughts in the man's head, although Rover could see the harshness in those eyes. Dad placed his hand on Rover's shoulder.

"You'll learn someday, son..."

Rover heard his shoulder pop under his father's grip.

"Ow! Dad! That hurts!"

"...You'll learn."

Crack! *Snap!*

"*Owww*!!!"

The verdict: Regular deodorant with a hint of *Championship Night* body spray.

That night, satisfied with his decisions, Rover went to bed, where he lay in anticipation of the big moment the next day.

3!3@3#3$3%3^3&3*3(3)3_3+3

Each of the five Thugwood Metropolitan Address prefectures had only one high school, so Southbound Thugwood High School was the only one in the Southbound Prefecture. Being one of only five high schools, its campus was treated as a neighborhood of its own, being large enough to accommodate for the forty thousand attending students. It was where Rover, Lumpy, and Adele attended.

Quinn also attended it, and she was the president of the Super Club.

Everyone at the school understood the merits and plausibility of the enigmatic Super Club—*whatever* mysterious doings it was responsible for around campus. Although this was only the first year of the club's inception, it was considered "the number one blessing" bestowed upon the school. Only good had happened because of the Super Club, and that was the most everyone knew about it.

However, on that Mondee-*day*, a single student in all of Southbound Thugwood High School was geared up to leverage on the *entirety* of the Super Club...

...Rover Chork was ready for the worst, and all he needed to do was ask Quinn Integrity a few simple questions.

He approached one of the posters on the hallway wall, which advertised the Super Club's current fundraiser, titled "Operation Chocolatier Action Punch," and featured a cartoon of a chocolate tank shooting a heart into a posh, suburban house.

Somehow, Rover thought, looking at the poster, *that seems like something she would actually draw...and do...*

3!3@3#3$3%3^3&3*3(3)3_3+3

Botany class dragged on as Rover couldn't pay attention to the lesson. He mulled over his lopsided strategies for talking to Quinn, rehearsing multiple scenarios in his head. A small trickle of sweat down his back seemed to be constantly present.

"On the board is a generic diagram of a plant's anatomy," Mr. Botany Teacher said to the class, indicating to the image on the touchscreen chalkboard.

Anatomy.

Rover briefly remembered Quinn's beauty, and he had to claw the bottom of his desk to keep his mind from treading into dangerous realms.

Scrape *Scraaape* *Scraaape*

"One must always remember proper sunlight exposure," the teacher explained as the touchscreen chalkboard automatically displayed his words while speaking, "because all plants are different."

Sunlight exposure.

Rover imagined Quinn wearing a bathing suit, giving plenty of sunlight exposure to her skin.

Scrape, scrape, scrape, scrape, scrape

"Hmm?" Mr. Botany Teacher turned and faced the class, looking puzzled. "What sounded like treated wood being whittled away?"

Rover held his breath.

The teacher tapped his ears. "Gah, sorry," he said with a smirk. "Sometimes I'm still haunted by the sounds from the war." His eyes glazed over and his hands trembled. "The plants hide the enemy... They whisper amongst the leaves..."

Mr. Botany Teacher locked himself in a state of traumatic memories. He ended up staring into nothingness, not moving while muttering frightening things to himself. The students recognized this behavior and took the chance to goof off or play *Glove Alien Fight*, and Rover cleaned the wood shavings out of his fingernails.

3!3@3#3$3%3^3&3*3(3)3_3+3

Every year, the five high schools in Thugwood took part in an athletic competition known as the Interschool AthletaCom, where every high school student participated in various competitions. The winning team would receive free tuition for two college semesters, a Certificate of Supreme Bragging Rights, and a personal honorary mention from CEO Claudius.

In preparation for the upcoming Interschool AthletaCom, all Thugwood high school students had the option of skipping a class in exchange for a physical training session. They could do this for one class a day, every day, until the event.

Rover enjoyed the athletic competition and always did well. However, he had opted out of his expressive diagnostics class and gone to the pool area for a very different reason.

"I heard Quinn Integrity was going to be at the pool next period for a puppet show," some boy said in the hall, which Rover overheard.

"That's probably a lie," some girl replied.

Turned out, it was a lie. Quinn wasn't there, nor was there a puppet show.

Fighting discouragement, Rover stood at the edge of the school swimming pool, staring at the other end. He and ten other students were about to do a timed swim to the other end and back. When the coach blew his whistle, Rover dove in and felt the shocking chill from the cold water.

But he had so much energy. His legs felt unrestrained as they paddled.

He pushed and pushed ahead, keeping his mind on victory as adrenaline propelled him.

"Good, Rover, nice one!" Mr. Pool Coach said after Rover emerged from the water. "You came in third."

"Third?"

He looked around to see the rest of the swimmers arrive. Not surprisingly, the two who beat him were a boy named Griff Kellogg in second and a girl named Jinkies Clayfast in first. Griff Kellogg was a diamond medalist in the Youth Division Swim-Off three years in a row. Jinkies Clayfast was a literal mermaid.

"Keep this up," the coach told Rover, "and you'll be a valuable competitor in the Interschool AthletaCom! Just don't eat too much junk food... I know the Super Club is doing their fundraiser."

That gave Rover a thought.

"Hey, Coach," he said. "Do you know if the Super Club has any meetings today?"

"Hmm, possibly. Their president usually takes walk-in appointments with students after last period every day. She should be in the Clubhaus High-Rise building at that time."

"Great. Thanks, Coach!"

Now Rover had a lead.

3!3@3#3$3%3^3&3*3(3)3_3+3

The last class let out. In seconds, Rover was out of the classroom and scurrying past the other students. He was on a *mission.*

Gotta get to the Clubhaus before Quinn leaves!

It was a long walk across the campus to the Clubhaus High-Rise building. Rover jogged across the outdoor Courtmeadows field in the center of the school grounds, a difficult endeavor in the blinding sunlight reflecting off the shiny grass. Thousands of students were going this way and that, and he was hoping to find his target sooner than later.

Walk fast. Scan every face.

Closer to the Clubhaus High-Rise, Rover still hadn't spotted Quinn. He entered the building, didn't see her among the crowd, and headed down the first floor's hallway.

Walk and scan. Walk and scan.

He grew more disheartened with each student who wasn't her.

Until he saw her.

Quinn Integrity was in the hallway, chatting with a few other students from the Cryptozoology Club.

He paused for a moment, the breath coming to a traffic jam in his chest. Shaking his head and giving his cheeks a solid smack, he poured the confidence back into his legs, making his feet carry him in the direction of the gorgeous girl.

His feet fell into a rhythm—a comforting, empowering rhythm.

Step. Step. Step. Step.

The hallway stretched out in front of him. Each rhythmic footstep he took sank into the linoleum. All surrounding students vanished—Rover only saw Quinn now. The nearby doors led to nowhere meaningful, melting into the walls as an irrelevant backdrop.

Step. Step. Step. Step.

Every window reflected the boy as he passed, each a mirror failing to capture the embodiment of his determined and steadfast approach. Sunlight burned through the glass, filling the space between Rover and Quinn with glistening luminescence until his final footstep ended the rhythm.

Yet, the song was not over.

"Hey, Quinn."

Quinn turned toward the voice, landing her eyes upon Rover's. There was utterly nothing else for her to look at, the rest of the world and its inhabitants having dissolved into something that wasn't important at that moment.

It was just the two of them.

"Can I speak with you for a second?" he asked.

The girl tilted her head with curiosity. "Hmm?"

3!3@3#3$3%3^3&3*3(3)3_3+3

Rover met Quinn outside—beyond the school gates, away from the comfortable and familiar—at the sprawling Vilder Park bordering the school grounds, one of the most popular spots in Southbound Thugwood for accessing the Gubbuh-Plardy River. The distant Thugwood skyscrapers stretched into the faraway cityscape, emblazoning their image upon the scenery—but Rover saw none of it.

"…I want to thank you for the chocolates…and for helping with our paint immobilizer…"

The river shimmered from the glowing, infinite sky. A fresh wind unfurled across the wide, grassy field, giving its charity of outdoor freshness to Rover's overheated body.

"…And I want to say that you seem like an exceptional person, not just with the Super Club at school. I can tell you're genuine through and through…"

Laughter and conversations rang out from the surrounding people enjoying the weather. Dogs barked playfully, birds chirped overhead, and the farthest reaches of the background held traces of traffic noises—but Rover heard none of it.

"That's why—"

Rover pressed his hands together and respectfully bowed before Quinn, his joints and muscles tensed and strained from anxiety, the sweat on his face most likely visible.

"—I want to ask you to go out with me."

A pause dampened the moment as the world inhaled, holding its breath. There was no noise, no light, no movement…only expectancy.

"I will."

Every detail of the environment—from the wisps of the clouds to the veins of the leaves to the creases of the riverbank shore—all spilled back into place as Rover looked up from his bowed position.

He stared at the soft mulberry eyes framed with rose petal lemonade hair.

"H-Huh?"

That was when Quinn, with dazzling compassion and humility, tilted her head and smiled.

"I'll gladly go out with you!"

It was that exact scene that replayed millions of times over and over in the boy's head. The commute home on the bus was like riding through a dream.

His family spoke to him when he arrived. Their words and faces were like changing television channels, incomplete and forgotten once switched. He might've replied to them. It didn't matter.

He drifted through the house and floated up the stairs to his room. The first real contact he made with reality again happened when he collapsed facedown onto his bed, still fully dressed, even with his shoes on.

Hugging his pillow, it was impossible not to smile.

3!3@3#3$3%3^3&3*3(3)3_3+3

"You have a pervy look in your eyes," Adele said when she walked into Rover's room.

Rover was sitting in his gaming chair, staring at the TV turned off, feeling too good to watch or play anything. Lumpy sat in the desk chair, battling a Phantom Gorilla in *Glove Alien Fight*.

"I do not have a pervy look!" Rover shot back at his sister.

"Well, you're drooling."

Rover wiped his mouth with his hand.

"He's been like this since I got here," Lumpy told Adele, not looking away from the game on his phone. "I want to try the multiplayer feature in *Glove Alien Fight* with him. The game manual was updated today, and it explains the new feature. It sounds awesome! It uses augmented reality!"

"Fuuunnn…" Rover moaned with a distant, dreamy face.

"I can practically smell the testosterone from here." Adele waved at the air with a scrunched expression. "Seriously, are you in heat?"

"Uh…" Rover began, wiping his mouth again.

"*Stop!*" Adele held out her hands. "Please don't answer that…"

"Rover has a good reason," Lumpy said, defeating the Phantom Gorilla with an in-game item called an Exorcising Banana Peel. He looked up and grinned. "Isn't that right?"

"I do," Rover told his sister, crossing his arms with a smug smirk. "To tell you the truth…I asked that girl out today."

"I knew it," Adele groaned, tossing her head back.

"Quinn agreed to be my girlfriend!" Rover stood tall with his hands on his hips, looking like an action hero posing by a cliff side.

Adele's face stretched into a devious grin, and Rover regretted telling his sister about Quinn.

"Welllll…" Adele placed her finger on her chin, pretending to think. "If that's the case, then I'll just have to play my role as your little sister in this situation."

Rover slouched. "I can only pray about what that could *possibly* mean."

"Mwa-ha-ha-haa!" Adele pranced around Rover, mocking him with a singsong voice. "Rover's got a girly-friend! No telling how it'll end! Hope she helps him grow a spine! Or he'll be sad and, uh, (something that rhymes)!"

"Whatever. You're just jealous that I got a girlfriend before you got a boyfriend."

"Hmm, who says I want a *boy*friend?"

"Wh-What...?"

"Just kidding," Adele said. "But,"—she leapt across the room and put her finger right in Rover's face while wearing a murderous look— "if you make fun of my status as single...I'll *end you*, Big Bro."

"Terrifying," Rover muttered, rolling his eyes.

"Anyway," Adele said, "just remember to uphold *your* relationship duties."

"What do you mean?"

Adele shrugged. "You need to do your part, be your half of the deal. And I think you'll need to really 'level up' in order to do that. Quinn is over-powered by default. Her stats and abilities are waaay over the limit for operating normally in life."

"Don't talk about my relationship like it's a video game," Rover grunted.

"Meh, just trying to make it easier to understand, because you're a dimwit."

"It was an effective metaphor, Adele," Lumpy added, equipping his character with the Ape Laser Armor dropped by the Phantom Gorilla. "So, Rover...since we're on the subject, there's a question I've been wanting to ask."

"What?"

Lumpy paused the game to look at his friend.

"Where is she?" he asked.

A coldness fell into Rover's gut. "What do you mean by that?"

"Uh, exactly what I said," Lumpy told him. "If you're dating, why aren't you with her?"

"Um, uhhh..."

"Dude." Lumpy became serious as he confronted Rover. "You asked her out, she said 'yes,' and then you left her alone?"

"Er..."

"*Gasp!*" Adele shouted melodramatically, clutching her heart in one hand. "How could you leave a woman hanging like that?" She sneered. "Well, I guess you just aren't cut out to be there for her."

"It's fine!" Rover told them, raising his voice. "It's only the first day, and it's only been an hour."

"Double *gasp!*" Adele shouted, both hands now over her heart.

"Here you are," Lumpy added, "hanging out with me while your girlfriend is off somewhere by herself."

"You're the one who wanted to hang out, Lumpy," Rover muttered. "And don't say 'girlfriend' so casually..." He blushed. "It's embarrassing."

Lumpy and Adele looked at each other and nodded, their expressions hard and dutiful—the sight made Rover nervous.

"It's settled," Lumpy told Rover.

"*What's* settled?"

"Don't worry," Adele snickered, "we'll make sure you don't crash and burn on the first day of your romantic endeavors!"

"I'm not crashing and burning!"

"Not *yet*, my friend." Lumpy socked Rover's arm with a confident smile. "We'll help you out."

"That's quite all right," Rover muttered.

"I just emailed Quinn," Adele said, holding up her smartphone. "I said you'll meet her at the Icarus Centre."

"HOW DO YOU HAVE QUINN'S NUMBER?!"

"I get things done." Adele shrugged. "I traded phone numbers with her the day she was over here...in your room." Her ringtone went off. "Oh, Quinn said okay."

"WAHHH!!!"

"Don't be a louse," Adele said. "For real, we're trying to help you out."

"Yeah, Rover," Lumpy said. "The hard part's over, asking her out. Now you're good to go."

Rover's breathing grew heavy. "Haa...gaahhh..."

Nodding at each other again, Lumpy and Adele each grabbed one of Rover's arms and dragged him out of his room, down the stairs, and out the door.

LUMPY FREEB

AGE: 18
HEIGHT: 193 CM (6' 4")
HAIR COLOR: EXPLODED PUMPKINS
EYE COLOR: WET SAND
OCCUPATION: SENIOR AT SOUTHBOUND THUGWOOD HIGH SCHOOL
FAVE FOODS: TAKOYAKI FETTUCCINE, TURDUCKEN NUGGETS
FAVE HOBBIES: FISHING, VIDEO GAMES

ROVER'S BEST FRIEND SINCE CHILDHOOD. HIS PERSONALITY IS THE OPPOSITE OF HIS FRIEND'S, BEING MORE MODEST AND FRIENDLIER. BECAUSE HE'S DATED BEFORE, HE TENDS TO GIVE ROVER SOLID "MAN TALKS" AND SPEAKS FROM EXPERIENCE. WHEN ROVER WALLOWS IN DESPAIR DUE TO GIRL PROBLEMS, LUMPY IS THERE TO WALK HIM THROUGH IT.

DESPITE HIS HEIGHT AND PHYSIQUE, HE IS NOT VERY ATHLETIC AND HAS DIFFICULTY KEEPING UP WITH ROVER AT TIMES. WHILE HE IS OFTEN THE VOICE OF REASON, HE CAN BECOME IMPULSIVE AND CRASS WHEN PROVOKED TOO MUCH.

ROVER… Lvl 675

Allowance… {T}38,000

<<EXPENSE GOALS>>

Anti-Grav Skateboard… {T}499,999

<<CURRENT EQUIPMENT>>

Gloves… Butler
Armor… Brick Jacket
Acc.1… Yeet-Line Skates
Acc.2… Farm Equipment

LIMITS ARE FOR BABIES!

THE Icarus Centre in Southbound Thugwood was a bustling shopping district with an overactive nightlife and hyper highway system. Frequent motorcar accidents and traffic congestion resulted in hundreds of auxiliary roads and bypasses being constructed. As a result, the district became a chaotic paradise for shoppers who were bored of safe, practical trips to the market. Danger shopping was *in style*.

This was where Adele had arranged for the meetup with Quinn. She exited the bus with Rover and Lumpy, and they stood on the sidewalk by the busy street.

"She's waiting in front of the Nu Clear R-Cade," Adele said while in the middle of an email frenzy with Rover's girlfriend.

Lumpy slapped Rover on the back, smiling. "Ease up, don't be so tense!"

"Right..." Rover's shoulders automatically lowered. "Let's get going, then..."

When they approached the Nu Clear R-Cade, Quinn was nowhere to be seen. They stopped by the entrance and looked around.

"*Found you!*" Quinn landed behind Rover and hugged him from behind. She spun him around and beamed at his sweaty face. "I couldn't resist hiding and ambushing you. Hee-hee!"

Seeing Rover stiff as a board, Lumpy spoke for him. "Do you always ambush your dates?"

"This is actually my first date," Quinn replied, "but I can always do this from now on if you want, Rover."

Utter fear gripped Rover from inside, rendering his bones frozen.

Say something! His mind screamed at himself. *The hard part's over! Just talk to her!!!*

"Hi."

It was a start.

"Hi!" Quinn replied with a bright smile.

Lumpy faked a cough.

Rover understood that cough. "Ah, yeah!" He swallowed his nervousness, but his jelly legs still jiggled. "Uh...I r-really don't w-wanna be ambushed like that."

Quinn giggled. "I figured."

She repeatedly snapped her fingers in time, doing a slight bob from side to side, as if ready to break into a song.

"Soooo...whatcha wanna do, Rover? It's our first date!"

Her modest movements were orchestrated and perfectly fluid, the groovy music in her head puppeteering her hands and feet.

"Well..." Rover looked at the arcade entrance, blushing from the girl's outgoingness. "Let's go in here. Umm...they have a pretty cool snack bar that has slushies and ice cream, and we can hang out there if you don't wanna play any games."

"That sounds delicious!" Quinn replied. "And it'd be a good idea if I don't play the games. I'll snap the joysticks right off! Heh-heh!"

She mimed the snapping of a joystick with her hand, wearing a menacing expression before giggling.

Adele whispered to Lumpy, "Is she a bonehead?"

Lumpy just shrugged.

Still bobbing rhythmically left and right, Quinn held her hands behind her back.

"Before we go in, I have one thing I want to ask you," she said to Rover. "...It's weird, though."

She appeared somewhat timid as she fidgeted, which Rover couldn't interpret.

"What is it?" he asked.

Is she nervous, too?

"Because we're dating now...I want you to call me 'Quintegrity.'"

Staring at her, Rover said, "...'Quintegrity'?"

"Mm-hmm."

"Uh, okay. But why?"

"It's a portmanteau of my first and last names."

"I get that," Rover replied, scratching his head, "but *why?*"

"Pleeeease? It's something I've always imagined my 'special somebody' would do."

"Your s-special s-somebody..." Rover's jelly legs jiggled again. However, looking into his girlfriend's eyes, he was met with her full-on stare of hope.

The lion in the boy's heart awoke, its proud mane fluffing Rover's arteries with courage. Rover's legs stopped shaking as he poised his next sentence.

"Very well, Quintegrity!"

"*Yay!*"

He was not ready for the hug. He was not ready for the warm softness pressing into him as his heavy breathing kicked in. Unlike the first hug, this was face-to-face with his man-motor already running hot.

"Ahh...gaahh...haaa..."

However, Rover's overheated loss for words was short-lived when he noticed a group walking toward him. He recognized the four teenagers from school, collecting his composure in a heartbeat as he understood what was coming:

A fight.

Quintegrity, sensing the tension of opposition in her boyfriend, released her hug and looked at the group of other teenagers, three boys and a girl.

One of the approaching boys stepped up to Rover, grimacing from disgust. He had messy hayfield hair and graphite-toned eyes...eyes that he was named after.

"Rover Chork," the boy said, his hands in his jeans pockets.

"Graphite Condor," Rover replied.

Lumpy clenched his fists and glared at Graphite and his lackeys.

"Um, Lumpy...?" Adele was worried—she'd never seen Lumpy show such animosity. "Who are they?"

"The competition," Lumpy replied in a low voice. "Rover and Graphite have been rivals forever...usually for stupid stuff, though."

Adele wrinkled her forehead, annoyed. "This is the first I've heard of this playpen war my brother's been having... Not that I care."

Graphite Condor spit out his bubblegum at Rover's feet and stared at him. "What are you doing here?"

A smirk cracked on Rover's lips. "I'm on a date with my *girlfriend.*"

Looking at Quintegrity, Graphite was taken by surprise. "*Qu-Quinn Integrity*?! You scored the legendary babe?!" The other three in his group gawked as well.

"Watch what you say about her!" Rover growled.

However, Quintegrity's face lit up.

"Aww...I'm a *legend*?" she cooed. With her hands on her hips, she stood tall and laughed out loud. "I always try my most bestest! It seems my hard work is appreciated!" She looked at Rover and blushed, making *him* blush with thrice the embarrassment. "I'm so happy my effort isn't going to waste and is contributing to people's happiness..."

Her little dance moves became more emphasized and elaborate, swaying her hips, swinging her arms, and snapping her fingers louder to whatever upbeat song was stuck in her head.

"Huh?" Graphite gawked at Quintegrity's spontaneous dancing before he focused back on Rover. "Whatever. Seeing *we're* here, let's get down to business!"

"State your bullshit, Graphite," Rover grunted.

"*Glove Alien Fight* has that new player-versus-player feature." Graphite brandished his smartphone. "I challenge you to a duel!"

Rover made eye contact with Quintegrity. She'd stopped dancing, freezing in an awkward position on one foot, curious as to what Rover's reaction would be.

This is my chance to prove to Quintegrity what I can do...and to put Graphite in his place.

Smirking, Rover turned to his challenger. "You know what happens to the loser, right?"

"Other than *public humiliation?*" Graphite raised his voice, deliberately drawing the attention of the crowd—they'd yet to see such a blatant public standoff with *Glove Alien Fight*'s new feature.

Lumpy and Adele glanced around, seeing people congregating. Excited whispers flittered among the spectators.

"I see you haven't read the rules." Rover yanked his smartphone from his pocket and twirled it in his hand. "The winner receives some hefty experience points and coins. Not surprising. However, that's not all." His cocky grin widened at his opponent. "The winner also takes all the *consumable items* in the loser's inventory."

Graphite raised an eyebrow. "I don't believe you."

"Take a look in the manual," Rover told him, loading *Glove Alien Fight*. "It's all in there. I think the manual was updated when the game was updated today."

Taking a moment to read the rules of the player-versus-player feature on their phones, Graphite and his cronies confirmed Rover's words.

The crow-haired, dark-skinned, ninja-looking girl in Graphite's group wore a worried expression...and she also wore an ensemble of belts comprising over seventy percent of her clothes. Her name was Tallyhawk Kusumegido.

"Hey, Graphite," she said, lowering her phone, "are you sure this is what you wanna do? It's one thing to lose a battle and not get anything...but to lose all of your consumable items..."

Graphite grunted at her. "I understand the risk, Tallyhawk."

"Just remember," Rover added, messing with his character's Glove Alien weapon, armor, and accessories on his phone, "you won't lose your equipment or accessories, but all of your in-game potions, ammunition, tax fraud vouchers, baits, lock picks, desserts, monster feces, and such are collateral." He gazed over the top of his smartphone, satisfied with his character's battle configurations. "Are you willing to put all that on the line?"

Graphite gritted his teeth. "I said I challenge you, Rover." He looked around, seeing the growing crowd that he'd purposely attracted was now recording the encounter on dozens of phones—public humiliation would indeed still be a result of failure. "I'm not backing down."

"I ain't so sure," said the cross-eyed boy in Graphite's group, Hodge Dipcringle. He adjusted the goggles on his forehead (which he only wore as a steampunk fashion statement). "It took you weeks to find those Bone-Lip Lures in the Bloodbean Forest..."

"And the Unicorn Dung Sushi in Curmudgeon's Dungeon," Tallyhawk chimed in.

"Shut up!" Graphite yelled. "I won't lose! Even if it's *Rover Chork*." He scowled at his opponent. "No...especially *because* it's him."

With some taps on his phone screen, Graphite commenced the setup for the player-versus-player battle. Watching their phone screens, Rover and Graphite were surprised to see their in-game character avatars projected into the real-world environment.

"Whoa!" Rover moved his phone around, seeing some of the game's elements displayed around him. "The manual mentioned augmented reality, but actually seeing it is awesome!"

"Ha-ha, yeah!" Lumpy looked at Rover's and Graphite's avatars through his phone, both standing one metre tall. "AR technology is the next big thing!"

A three-option roulette appeared on their screens, quickly toggling through "Deathmatch," "Ring Finder," and "Strongest Hero."

"The match type is random," Rover said as the roulette slowed down. "This determines the rules of the match."

"That's lame," Graphite muttered as the "Ring Finder" option was selected and the instructions were presented. "So...we gotta find the gold rings, and the player with the most rings in the 40-minute time limit wins? That's *super* lame!"

Lumpy and Adele received a notification on their phones from *Glove Alien Fight*. In fact, every bystander received it.

"It's asking us to participate?" Adele selected "Yes" on her phone with a smirk. "Sure, I'll see what's up."

"Me too," Lumpy said, opting in as well.

Rover and Graphite saw the "Ring Hiders" number on their phone screens increase as more bystanders chose to participate. As each person did so, their in-game avatars were also displayed in the AR environment.

"The Ring Hiders each get one ring." Rover read the onscreen instructions aloud, assuming Graphite was too dumb to do so. "They have two minutes to choose the locations. When placed, the rings will be invisible to us, and we'll need to use our characters' Clairvoyant Radar to guide us to them. It's just like hunting treasure chests and hidden objects."

Graphite chuckled. "Excellent. My Clairvoyant Radar is maxed out. This'll be easy!"

Not saying anything, Rover sneered in response.

My Clairvoyant Radar is only level six out of ten. Four levels makes a big difference. This is gonna be tough...

Lumpy watched through his phone as his avatar had a gold ring appear in its hands—a fat, dull, somewhat irregular gold ring.

"Huh?" He looked closer at the virtual object. "It looks...like a bagel."

"Yeah," Adele added, looking at the one her avatar held. "I was expecting something shiny and pretty, like the ones from *Chronic the Sledgehog*."

In total, thirty-one spectators opted in as Ring Hiders. After a quick countdown, each Ring Hider ran off in different directions, physically chasing their own avatars through the real world to deposit their gold rings in various places.

"This is hard," Lumpy grumbled, following behind his avatar and watching it through his phone. "You can't see where your character's going unless you go with it and watch it through an AR-capable device."

A car honked its horn as another Ring Hider dove out of traffic, having followed his avatar into the street.

Lumpy's eyebrow twitched. "And, uh...it's dangerous, too... Maybe augmented reality isn't *that* great..."

He had his character drop its ring in an alley, hiding it behind a salad dressing vending machine where it vanished from the phone screen. Seconds later, when his character's Clairvoyant Radar pulsed, he caught a fleeting glimpse of the ring.

"I hope Rover doesn't get beat," he said to himself, looking down the alley toward the street. "Graphite said his Clairvoyant Radar was maxed out, meaning his character has the farthest possible detection range for hidden treasures."

"You should have more faith in your friend!"

Lumpy jumped from fright when Quintegrity was suddenly next to him, being even sneakier than Adele.

"It's not like I don't have faith in him," Lumpy said, catching his breath from the shock. "Rover's the best *Glove Alien Fight* player I've ever met. He's completed tons of in-game missions recommended for players at higher levels."

Quintegrity smiled, her cheeks brightening. "That's wonderful. He's talented, then." She tapped her toes on the ground and snapped her fingers in a funky rhythm, doing a subtle dance and swinging her assault rifle-shaped purse. "We all have talents inside us. I hope to someday share what's inside me with him."

"Uhhh...don't word it like that in front of him," Lumpy chuckled. "He'd...like, die. Come on, let's go watch the match."

"Yeah!"

Before following Lumpy out of the alley, Quintegrity looked at the spot where Lumpy's character hid the ring, and she smiled.

4!4@4#4$4%4^4&4*4(4)4_4+4

Looks like I'll need to adjust my settings again. Rover went through his character's equipment and configured his setup. *This isn't a normal battle, so I'll trade the kick-butt stuff for speed and agility.*

He equipped the Shyster's Shoes, which increased his character's movement speed and jumping distance, but at the cost of lowering its defense—not being a battle, the defense stat was meaningless.

And to make up for my inferior Clairvoyant Radar, I'll need something to boost my detection abilities.

With that, he equipped the Hound Doggo Shnozz, which boosted his Clairvoyant Radar by one point.

Graphite's goofy guffawing made Rover's skin crawl. "I bet you're equipping the Hound Doggo Shnozz, Rover. For your information, so am I!" He tapped on his phone screen. "That puts my Clairvoyant Radar at level eleven out of ten. That's practically omniscient treasure detection! I bet you didn't think about going over the level cap."

Level caps have actually been on my mind these past few days.

Rover bit his lip in contempt, but two arms wrapped around him as a heavenly softness pushed into his back. His every body hair stood on end to better detect the lush sensation.

"I know where a ring is," Quintegrity whispered into Rover's ear, revving his brain with primal urges.

"Ahh...haahh....y-yeahh?" he stammered.

His girlfriend let go, giving him control of his body again.

"You'll win this, no problem!" she told him, grinning big while pumping her fists into the air and holding a muscleman pose.

"Of course I'll win this," Rover replied, giving Graphite a dirty look.

The two-minute ring-hiding session ended, and a countdown started on Rover's and Graphite's screens. They clutched their phones, gearing up for the competition. Every spectator watched the AR through their phones and tablets—there were now far more people in the crowd than just the thirty-one Ring Hiders.

5...4...3...2...1...

START!

The crowd erupted into cheers and shouts.

"That alleyway down yonder!" Quintegrity pointed to where Lumpy had dropped his ring.

"Got it!" Rover replied, heading to the alley with his in-game avatar. Through his phone, he watched the digital character dart off and leave him behind. He broke into a sprint, trying to keep up.

Dude! It's so fast! I knew I had the right equipment configuration!

The Clairvoyant Radar pulsed on his screen, creating a vague compass-like indicator on Rover's screen and pointing in the direction of each ring within range—the closer the ring, the bolder and brighter the indicator.

It works just like in the original game, Rover thought, chasing after his avatar into the alley.

With the Clairvoyant Radar, he saw the ring flicker on the screen.

Here it is!

Now close enough, the gold ring fully presented itself onscreen behind the vending machine. Rover watched the avatar grab the bulky, irregular ring, split it in half, smear a creamy substance on both halves, and devour it with comically animated bites.

"It...really *is* a bagel," Rover muttered. "Like an anime-style bread-eating race on steroids..."

The "Rings" counter on his screen showed he had one ring. He wheeled around and darted from the alley, meeting Quintegrity, Lumpy, and Adele.

"Thanks for the tip!" Rover said to his girlfriend. He stopped on the sidewalk, assessing the other rings' locations with the Clairvoyant Radar.

"Yeah," Lumpy said with a grin, "she must've seen me drop that ring there." He gave a thumbs-up to Quintegrity.

Quintegrity beamed with her hands on her hips.

"There're a few over here." Rover hurried down the sidewalk, eyes glued to his phone. "I gotta get 'em!"

Quintegrity watched her boyfriend take off with Lumpy and Adele. Some spectators tagged along with them, watching the augmented reality action through their phones and tablets.

"Everyone's having so much fun," she said aloud, clasping her hands together. Seeing Graphite in the other direction, she skipped over to him through the crowd of spectators.

"Got another one!" Graphite said as his avatar devoured a gold bagel. Some bystanders clapped.

The cross-eyed boy chuckled. "With your level eleven Clairvoyant Radar, you can partially see the paths taken by the Ring Hiders. Your victory is guaranteed!"

"*That's* how it works, huh?" Quintegrity pushed her dazzling face in between Graphite and Hodge.

"Ack!" Graphite sputtered. "Where'd you come from?!"

Quintegrity looked at Graphite's screen for a split second before the boy yanked it away from her gaze.

"Interesting," she said, full of curiosity.

"Hey!" Graphite stuck his finger in Quintegrity's face. "No screen peeking!"

The third lackey, Isho Eep—a bald meathead teen boy with a pierced lip—moved in front of Quintegrity.

"You can't be relaying info back to the other player, girlie," he grunted, crossing his arms.

"It says so in the rules?"

"Th-That's beside the point," the meathead muttered. "It's about sportsmanship. Know your limits."

Quintegrity snorted with laughter, and the glow on her face and gorgeous smile captivated the four rivals.

"And *that* is our advantage!" Quintegrity declared, drawing the attention of every bystander recording her through their phones' or tablets' AR-capable video recorders.

"*What's* your advantage?" Graphite demanded.

"The meathead telling me to know my limits," she chortled.

Isho scowled. "M-Meathead…?"

The radiant girl laughed again and leapt at Graphite. Landing directly in front of him, she hunched over and pointed up at the boy, giving him a very distracting view down her shirt.

Her grin was a tad devious as she said, "Because…*limits are for babies*!!!"

Then she pranced off.

Graphite gaped, forgetting he was competing in a game.

"Dammit…" he growled, squeezing his smartphone. "*How?* How did Rover hook up with such a *hot babe* like her?!"

He turned toward his avatar and ran across the street, dodging a speeding Florist Delivery dozer.

4!4@4#4$4%4^4&4*4(4)4_4+4

"Five bagels down!" Adele cheered as Rover's avatar scarfed down another gold ring. "I bet you're doing this faster than that mongrel!"

"I'm sure I am." Rover watched his onscreen ring-count indicator tick up another point. "It'd be nice if the game told me how many rings the opponent had." He clenched his fist with a cocky smirk. "But...this makes it more thrilling! Mwa-ha-haaa!"

"I love how diabolical you get, dude," Lumpy snickered, looking around through his phone's AR. He noticed Quintegrity barreling toward them with a big smile.

"Ahoy, Rover!" She wrapped her arms around Rover, making the boy shiver in ecstasy before she saluted him. "I bring recon!"

"Recon?" Rover asked, rubbing away his goosebumps.

"Down Jarepli Boulevard, there are four rings to the east and two to the west. And if you take Zooloo Street north, there are six more you can get to. All twelve of them are in or around the Icarus Centre's open-air shopping mall."

"That mall is practically a whole village by itself," Lumpy chuckled. "It's huge."

Rover was skeptical. "How do you know about the rings, Quintegrity?"

"I have my ways." She pointed to a horizontal flagpole jutting out of the building above the Nu Clear R-Cade entrance, displaying the flag for the arcade's logo. "That flagpole is where I was hiding to ambush you. I'll scurry back up and scout things out!"

"But...wait!" Rover called, but Quintegrity already took off.

"She's a lunatic," Adele muttered, watching the girl scale the side of the building like a lizard and perch atop the horizontal flagpole.

"Let her be," Lumpy said. "She seems to be having fun."

Lumpy and Adele followed Rover as they hurried to the corner of Jarepli Boulevard.

"If I get all those rings she mentioned," Rover mused, looking up and down the street, "then I'll have seventeen, more than half of the thirty-one total." He nodded. "I think I know the fastest route."

"How'd Quinn figure out where those rings are?" Lumpy asked. "I really wanna know..."

"Screen peeking," Adele replied, huffing from the running. "I saw her seduce that mongrel to get a look at his phone. His Clairvoyant Radar is at level eleven, and Quinn must've seen the rings' locations."

"That's kinda cheating, though," Lumpy said, "but...the rules don't say you can't do it."

"This could make some interesting competitions," Adele added. "I wonder if CEO Claudius intended for it to be like—"

Rover cut her off. "His mandate will over done soon, so whatever."

He gazed up at his girlfriend still on the flagpole. She waved at him, and he waved back with a smirk.

"She's a devious one," he said, snickering. "Heh-heh...I like it."

"And she isn't using her phone right now." Adele kept a close eye on the girl. "Either she's still pretending not to play *Glove Alien Fight*, or..."

Rover ran off before she could finish speaking, and the three hurried down Jarepli Boulevard as Quintegrity looked on.

ADELE CHORK

AGE... 16
HEIGHT... 160 CM (5' 3")
HAIR COLOR... FRESHLY MINED COAL
EYE COLOR... YOUNG, BUDDING PINE NEEDLES
OCCUPATION... SOPHOMORE AT SOUTHBOUND THUGWOOD HIGH SCHOOL
FAVE FOODS... PEACH SUNDAE ROCKET ROLLS, CRAB CAKE BURGERS
FAVE HOBBIES... WATCHING *MAGICAL POODLE SNICKERDOODLE*, ANTI-GRAV SKATEBOARDING

ROVER'S YOUNGER SISTER. LIKE ROVER, SHE IS HOTHEADED AND DEVIOUS. SHE'S ALSO A BIT OF A MONEY-GRUBBER AS SHE'S OBSESSED WITH SAVING UP FOR AN ANTI-GRAV SKATEBOARD (A SKATEBOARD THAT USES THE LATEST ANTI-GRAVITY TECH).

ADELE IS SUSPICIOUS OF QUINN, EVEN AS SHE WARMS UP TO HER. SHE LOVES MAKING LIFE HARD FOR ROVER AND TEASES HIM FOR GETTING NERVOUS AROUND HIS OWN GIRLFRIEND. IS AN AVID COLLECTOR OF *MAGICAL POODLE SNICKERDOODLE* MERCH. DESPITE BEING A TOMBOY, SHE HAS A SOFT SPOT FOR CUTE THINGS.

ROVER… Lvl 675

Allowance… {T}38,000

<<EXPENSE GOALS>>

Anti-Grav Skateboard… {T}499,999

<<CURRENT EQUIPMENT>>

Gloves… Butler
Armor… Brick Jacket
Acc.1… Shyster's Shoes
Acc.2… Hound Doggo Shnozz

"Impossible" Is Another Word for "Dare You to Try"

ROVER **sprinted down the sidewalk**, failing to keep up with his AR avatar, bumping into several pedestrians and calling out quick apologies.

But he never slowed down.

This is a race, so common courtesy can suck it!

Lumpy and Adele hurried behind, their lungs burning from running.

"I can't..." Adele stopped and clutched a streetlamp post. "I'm beat!"

The Clairvoyant Radar pulsed on Rover's phone screen, updating his hints to the ring locations. He skidded to a halt, looking up a big stairway leading to the second level of the Icarus Centre's enormous open-air shopping mall.

I'm close to one, he thought, jogging up the steps alongside his virtual character.

The bagel was stowed within some hedges planted around an artificial grass patch in the wide walkway. As Rover caught his breath, he watched his avatar smear something akin to cream cheese on the sixth gold bagel and chomp it down.

Lumpy stumbled up to his friend, sweaty and tired.

"How far...are the rings?" he panted.

"Most aren't actually too far," Rover replied, watching another radar pulse on his phone. He wiped his sweaty brow. "Follow me!"

"Go on," Lumpy said breathlessly. "I'll tag along. Adele died somewhere behind us..."

"Okay, I'll find you guys later!"

Lumpy laughed, pushing himself to follow Rover. "Where's the dude get his stamina?"

5!5@5#5$5%5^5&5*5(5)5_5+5

Rover reached the 120-metre-tall shatinum archway to the enormous commons area in the Icarus Centre's heart, and he stood underneath it to wait for his Clairvoyant Radar to update. Numerous street vendors filled the place with tantalizing aromas of grilled, sizzling goodness and bubbly refreshments. Merry chatter from hundreds of shoppers rose above the buildings, riding the heat from the sun-soaked walkways.

He stared at his phone, looking around through the AR camera.

"It's around here somewhere..."

However, Rover spotted Quintegrity's grin—upside down—through the phone. She had climbed the nearby palmaple tree and dangled in front of the phone's camera.

Gripping the tree branch with her feet interlocked, she said, "What's up, buttercup?"

Rover chuckled. "You sure like flashy entrances, huh?"

"Ha-ha-ha! Yep!"

Quintegrity dropped from the branch, landed with a handstand, and sprang back to her feet.

"Hey..." She approached Rover, giving him a warm smile.

"Wh-What?" he asked.

What is she doing? Why is she getting so close?!

"There's one right there."

With an outstretched finger tipped with autumn-colored fingernail polish, Quintegrity directed Rover's attention to the base of the archway.

"There is?" Rover peeked through the phone camera into a nook between the archway's base and a building wall. "Oh, in the back! I can see a bagel in there."

The AR avatar had no problem accessing the narrow quarters, and another gold ring was claimed, seven total for Rover. He smiled, giving Quintegrity a high-five.

"Nice!" he shouted. "You're making this way easier!"

The girl cackled (actually *cackled*) with her hands on her hips.

"'Tis nothing!" she replied. "There's nothing against helping the competitors, right?"

"This is fine. The rules say you can't *physically* help or hinder the players by transporting them or getting in their way, but what you're doing probably doesn't count."

"Then I'll make sure you win!" she said with a thumbs-up.

A tender, serene smile found Quintegrity's lips, and she danced and bobbed her head to the funky song playing inside her mind.

Why is she always doing that? Rover wondered, watching the girl's enticing moves. *For some reason, it makes me wanna dance, too. But...I can't dance. The heck am I thinking?*

5!5@5#5$5%5^5&5*5(5)5_5+5

Their next ring was on top of the awning in front of Ulrich's Weather Shoppe. Among the dozens of weather shoppes in the Icarus Centre, only Ulrich's sold weathervanes made from metals mined from the wastelands outside Thugwood.

Rover viewed the awning through his phone and narrowed his eyes. "They put it up *there*?"

"Can the characters fly?" Quintegrity asked.

"Not without special items, but...they can climb."

He directed his AR character toward the awning. With the tap of an onscreen button, Rover's character grabbed on to the awning post and shimmied up.

"It works!" Rover exclaimed, controlling his avatar to pull itself to the top of the awning. "Wow...the precision of mapping the game elements to the real world is *really* impressive!"

After a few steps, the avatar fell to the ground.

"Tch." Rover gritted his teeth. "It's hard controlling it from this angle. This really is a pain compared to the original *Glove Alien Fight*."

"Hmm..." Quintegrity thought for a second. "But, is it *better* than the original game?"

"Oh, heck yeah," Rover replied, having his character latch on to the awning post again. "It's way more fun like this!"

5!5@5#5$5%5^5&5*5(5)5_5+5

After the eighth bagel was collected, Rover and Quintegrity headed into the subterra locomotive canals. The echoing locomotive engines muffled his phone's in-game sound effects as they passed the ticket gate with their prepaid passes. Down the brick stairway, they descended into the industrial scent of electrical exhaust.

On the platform, Quintegrity smiled as she reminisced. "I haven't been down in the sub canals since *forever*."

"How do you get to the other prefectures, then?" Rover asked, raising his voice over the clanging bells and howling horn of the departing locomotive. "Buses?"

He spotted the next ring in the high ceiling trusses, tucked next to the light fixtures over the locomotive tracks.

"I go mostly everywhere on foot," she said.

"That's a lot of running around, but you can *haul ass* like nobody I know! Are you really not half-goddess, or something???"

"Nope, I'm just me."

"That's a terrible answer," Rover said, lowering his phone and cracking a smile, "but I'm glad you're on my side."

Quintegrity snapped her fingers and put both thumbs up. Near the top of the stairs heading to the station's exit, something caught her eye.

"Oh, somebody's joining us," she said happily.

Through his phone, Rover saw another person's *Glove Alien Fight* avatar. Its shell armor indicated the Tortoise Spacesuit was equipped.

The Tortoise Spacesuit, Rover thought. *That person's character has its gravity effects cut in half...meaning it can jump twice as high, has half the weight to climb faster, and is resistant to falling damage. I bet they were the one who placed that ring up there. But...there are too many people here to see who's controlling it.*

"That's clever." Rover smirked, looking back at the distant ring when his Clairvoyant Radar pulsed again. "Some of the Ring Hiders might have better maneuverability than the competitors. That could potentially make some of the rings impossible to reach..."

"Can you find a way to climb up there?" Quintegrity asked.

Rover sighed, surveying the area through the AR camera first, then with his eyes.

"It doesn't seem likely," he replied. "It's not worth wasting time on it. I should get the other rings first."

Quintegrity didn't respond, but instead fixed her gaze toward the sub canal station ceiling trusses.

Seeing his girlfriend's lack of reaction, Rover told her, "Sorry our first date turned out like this. It's not what we planned."

Yet, she smiled right away. "Don't be sorry. I'm having fun! I never get to do this."

He returned that smile. "Glad to hear! C'mon, I think there are some other rings close by!"

"Three about that-a-way." The girl pointed, most likely to some above-ground point in the distance, then redirected her finger in a second direction. "And the rest are about thems-a-ways!"

Rover hesitated for a moment, looking at the shining girl.

"You really know where they are?" he asked.

"I do." She pouted. "What...you don't believe me?"

"...It's not that I doubt you," Rover said, "but I'm impressed by your screen peeking skills."

The girl blinked. "I really don't know what 'screen peeking' means, but it made Graphite mad. You mean you can't look at each other's phones during the game?"

"Well, kinda," Rover answered. "It's more of a courtesy thing, but I guess doing it isn't breaking the rules."

"Aye-aye!" She saluted him. "Then no problem. We should hurry, though."

They rushed out of the station and up to the ground level, leaving the uneaten virtual gold bagel in the trusses over the locomotive boarding area.

5!5@5#5$5%5^5&5*5(5)5_5+5

Rover's character clung with both hands to a powerline strung over the open-air mall's ground level. The virtual person had no weight as it traversed, so the cable didn't sag. Mostly everyone had no idea what was happening above them as they went about their shopping and errands.

A ring was tied to the powerline using another in-game item, a Steam-Powered Extension Cord—an intuitive way to make the ring harder to get.

People can be pretty creative with this ring-hiding business, Rover thought. He watched from the ground through his phone, moving his character closer to the ring.

"You're good at this game," Quintegrity told him, peering over his shoulder at his screen.

"It's tricky when I'm far away from the avatar," Rover said as his character snagged the ninth ring with its mouth. "I'm getting used to it, though."

While moving his character back across the powerline, he was distracted by Quintegrity's groovy footwork. It was subtle, but she was nonetheless dancing in place.

"You know..." he said, focusing back on his dangling avatar, "I still don't know how you get away with not meeting the daily quota for *Glove Alien Fight*."

The girl stopped dancing. She gave Rover an adorable smile.

"Because I'm *awesome*."

Rover sighed. "Well...I can't argue with that, but it's impossible to avoid it forever. No one can evade the law for as long as you claim to."

"'Impossible' is another word for 'dare you to try!'" she replied, flexing her biceps. "Ain't no stoppin' this! Ha-ha!"

"...Okay?"

His character leapt from the wire and landed on a second-level footbridge.

"The next ring is that-a-way!" Quintegrity said, pointing. "In the big fountain over there."

She's been spot-on with the ring locations, Rover thought as he made his character hop down from the higher walkway. *How much screen peeking has she done? Or...she's gotta have a photographic memory.*

The boy smirked as his girlfriend began to boogie with her hips again, absolute joy on her face.

Am I dating a mythical creature? Yeah...as if!

Rover turned his phone to see Graphite's avatar run into the open. It headed down the large outdoor strip of the open-air mall and straight for the fountain where the next ring was.

"Gotta go!" Rover chased after his own avatar, but was getting tired from all the running he'd done.

Although Rover's character was faster, Graphite's character was much closer and beat Rover to the ring. The sound of Graphite's guffaws rang through the open shopping district.

"I don't think so, Rover!" Graphite was on the second level of the open-air mall, controlling his character from afar. "That's another one for me!"

"Don't let his crap-talk hold you back!" Quintegrity announced while running behind Rover. She gave him a playful smack between his shoulder blades, then pointed to yet another ring. "The next one is in a palmaple tree over there. You could get it first!"

Through his phone, Rover's Clairvoyant Radar gave a glimpse of virtual gold tucked away in a palmaple tree up on the second-level walkway. He stopped running, deftly scrutinizing a nearby wall formation—it would provide climbable access for his character to reach the tree.

And he looked at his girlfriend, who cheered for his sprinting character.

Does she really have a photographic memory? Graphite is way over there on that different walkway. Did she look at his screen again? No, I don't think so...

Quintegrity's dance moves stayed in the rhythm, but her moves grew and motions evolved, putting more of her body into each step, each twist. Her finger snaps were accompanied by claps, and her heels and toes tapped harder on the ground.

When the two made eye contact, Rover sensed her rhythmic energy's beat. The motions of her hands seemed to weave a jazzy, soulful melody, and her feet played a groovy bassline that pumped down through the earth. It was as if imaginary music was dancing to *her*, not the other way around—and Rover could hear it...and it relaxed him.

Pay attention to the game!!!

Rover popped out of his funky daze, making his virtual avatar leap toward the climbable wall and latch on.

"All right!" Quintegrity laughed as Rover's character scurried up toward the higher walkway.

She's not looking at my screen, Rover thought, giving his distracted attention to his character. *A photographic memory and screen peeking wouldn't really help her, either. The Clairvoyant Radar only points toward the rings, so...*

Rover's avatar pulled itself up onto the walkway.

"Go, Rover's little game dude!" she shouted, pumping her fist into the air. "You've got this!"

But...what if it's not a photographic memory...?

He glanced back at Quintegrity. She looked on, watching the game and cheering.

It's almost like she's watching my avatar the way she's—wait!!! That avatar wearing the Tortoise Spacesuit in the sub canal—how'd she know it was there if she didn't use an AR-capable device...?

Quintegrity looked at him, grinning, transmitting her funky-jam vibes straight into him.

His heart raced, but not because of the brilliant smile and beautiful face.

Something else was now implanted in his thoughts...

"H-Hey..." Rover said, overcome by his sudden revelation and the girl's undeniable energy. "...Can you *see*...the augmented reality...?"

She didn't reply.

Her dance moves continued to sway to the rhythm in her mind.

Step. Clap.

Step-step. Clap.

Step. Clap.

Step-step. Clap.

But, Rover could tell what she was thinking. He knew by the way her eyes sparkled and lips curled, as if she was relishing the excitement of sharing a secret.

"Get it, Graphite!" the crow-haired, dark-skinned girl called out through the crowded area.

"Yeah! Get it!" the cross-eyed boy hollered.

Rover turned back to the game on his smartphone.

Questions can wait until I beat Graphite at this!

He controlled his character to shimmy up the tree just before Graphite's character reached the trunk. The angle and distance from which Rover stood made the task difficult, but with a much swifter character, he claimed his tenth ring.

"Yes!" Quintegrity applauded. "Another bagel! Nom nom nom..."

"That's ten," Rover stated, keeping his concentration. His Clairvoyant Radar revealed the direction of more rings, and he directed the avatar accordingly. "Gotta go this way!"

Graphite Condor squeezed his phone with frustration.

"Whatever," he sneered. "You can run, Rover...but you can't *fly!*"

He used one of his consumable items on his AR character, a Goosepack. His character donned a jetpack with goose wings and a goose head helmet. With the tap of an onscreen button, Graphite launched his avatar into the air, steering it like a remote control airplane.

Through his phone, Rover heard the jet engine and honking goose calls from the soaring Goosepack while he ran. He hesitated to slow down his own avatar, although he was falling behind it.

Quintegrity laughed at the overhead honking character as she ran alongside Rover. "Oh! A goose! That's adorable!"

"Wrong!" Rover shouted, flustered. "It's *deplorable*! The Goosepack grants temporary abilities of a rocket-powered goose!"

And if Graphite's been using Goosepacks this whole time, then he might have the lead right now. Grr...I should've saved mine!

The girl giggled, then dashed ahead as if they'd been standing still and not already sprinting. Rover watched in awe as she leapt like a mountain lion to the second-level walkway.

Clinging to the outside of the guardrail, she held out her hand for Rover to grab.

"Have no fear!" Quintegrity told Rover with gigantic encouragement. "Your little game dude is a ruthless, goose-less bagel-snatcher!"

But, he didn't take her hand.

Instead, he leapt onto the back of a nearby bench, deftly hoisted himself up, and climbed over the guardrail.

"You bet it is," Rover sneered as he landed on the second level, some of the sweat falling off his body. They hurried off without a moment to spare. "Also, I *told* you that physically assisting or hindering a player is against the rules!"

"Got it! No hoisting or inhibiting from me, then!"

Rover flicked his eyes through his phone screen's AR, seeing his character and the Clairvoyant Radar—he was still right on track.

ROVER… Lvl 675

Allowance… {T}38,000

<<EXPENSE GOALS>>

Anti-Grav Skateboard… {T}499,999

<<CURRENT EQUIPMENT>>

Gloves… Butler
Armor… Brick Jacket
Acc.1… Shyster's Shoes
Acc.2… Hound Doggo Shnozz

GRADUATED FROM SUPREMACY

GRAPHITE'S Goosepack reached its time limit, and he griped when his avatar fell from midflight, taking falling damage.

"I thought I had more time with it!" he snarled at his phone screen with what little breath he had from chasing his avatar.

I misjudged, he thought as he ran along the second-level walkway, *and my HP went down a little from the fall. My character can get hurt during this match, so I wonder if zero HP means I'll be disqualified...*

He slowed to a trot, catching his breath and taking a gander to find his avatar, peering over a guardrail.

"I didn't see where it landed!" he whined. "I can't keep up with a Goosepack on foot!"

His three lackeys hobbled up to him, equally winded from running.

Isho pointed while still looking through his phone. "It fell to the ground level way over there. I can't see it from here, though." His lip piercing caught the sunlight as he frowned.

Frustrated, Graphite growled and dashed off to find his avatar.

6!6@6#6$6%6^6&6*6(6)6_6+6

Shoppers and commonfolk were catching on to the event, watching through their phones and tablets. They moved aside as Rover and Quintegrity rushed past, understanding why the two were in a hurry. Some even cheered the couple on.

Rover noticed Graphite's avatar below on the lower walkway.

Graphite's character! But, it isn't moving. Is he too far away for it to work? No, he probably just can't see it, so he's not controlling it.

Rover had his character climb another part of the guardrail and leap to a picnic area below. It landed on a table's parasol with a gold bagel resting on top, then devoured the item.

"Yeah!" Rover yelled. People who'd been watching applauded him. "That's eleven rings. Five more, and I'll have more than half." However, he saw Graphite's avatar moving again. "Oh man, gotta keep going!"

Hodge had purchased a novelty telescope and held it up for Graphite to aim his phone's AR camera through. It was a novelty item, but offered enough magnification for Graphite to see his character from farther away…yet, he didn't like what he saw. Rover was already on the move, his avatar much too fast to catch.

"Damn…" He lowered his phone, looking on with his own two eyes.

"What's wrong, dude?" Hodge asked.

Graphite bit his lip. "I can't catch Rover." He looked around through his phone again and spotted something peculiar with his Clairvoyant Radar. "Hmm?"

"What's up?" the dark-skinned girl asked.

"There's a ring Rover passed up, Tallyhawk," Graphite replied. "If I can't get the other rings over there, then I might as well get one more over this way!"

6!6@6#6$6%6^6&6*6(6)6_6+6

Underneath a porcelain statue of a giant folding chair, Rover claimed his twelfth ring.

His thirteenth was inside a sabretooth koi tank, one of many aquatic displays glamming up the shopping district. Controlling the character to swim was challenging while Rover stood outside the tank, but the ring was his in the end.

Thankfully, the sabretooth koi aren't part of the game and don't notice the character, Rover thought as a couple of the large, bright fish stared at him, dragging their protruding fangs against the fish-proof glass. He flicked his eyes at Quintegrity, who hadn't stopped smiling and dancing. *Or can they see the AR and just not care…?*

"Found you," came a weary voice. Lumpy jogged up to Rover, Adele panting loudly behind him.

Rover wiped his sweaty forehead on his sleeve.

"I'm on a roll!" he told them, already heading for the next ring.

"Onward and upward!" Quintegrity chimed in as she jogged away.

As Rover and Quintegrity pushed on, Lumpy chuckled while his body felt ready to collapse.

"Where…do they get…their frickin' stamina?!"

The fourteenth ring was on the ground in front of a sleuth store. The fifteenth was hanging from a karaoke parlor's sign, tied with another in-game item called a Rope.

"One more, one more to have over half of the thirty-one…" Rover waited for his Clairvoyant Radar to show him the direction of the next ring. When it pulsed, he groaned. "I gotta *backtrack* for it! Wow, what a sham…"

He thought for a moment, then laughed, piquing Quintegrity's curiosity.

"I see what's going on here," he said with a snicker. "It's the one I couldn't reach before. In the subterra locomotive canal station." He checked the countdown timer on his screen. "Only a few minutes left…"

"Do you need to go back to it?" the girl asked.

Rover grinned and watched Graphite's avatar running in that direction. "Yeah, but not to get it."

When he and Quintegrity made it to the locomotive station platform, Graphite was already on the scene, making a scene, shaking his fist angrily at the light fixtures and trusses.

"Who did this?!" he roared. "I can't reach that one!"

"Oh yeah?"

Graphite turned to see Rover approaching, wearing a sly smirk, Quintegrity by his side. One by one, Lumpy, Adele, Tallyhawk, Hodge, and Isho staggered down the stairway to the station.

"Out of Goosepacks, Graphite?" Rover mocked.

"Grr…" Graphite glared at the out-of-reach ring. "I am, but it was worth using them all to get as many rings as I did."

"How many did ya get?"

"You'll see when the match ends. We're in the last seconds."

Many of the bystanders and Ring Hiders had followed into the subterra station, awaiting the final results. When the timer ran down, Rover, Graphite, and the Ring Hiders had the words "TIME UP" appear on their screens.

The results were tallied:

[PLAINTIFF] Graphite Condor: 15 Rings.
[DEFENDANT] Rover Chork: 15 Rings.
STARTING SUDDEN DEATH ROUND!!!

Gasps and murmurs were aplenty. Both characters' health were reduced to one HP.

It was now a battle, one-on-one.

"*Crap!*" Rover swung his phone to focus on his opponent. "I don't have time to change my equipment!"

Graphite moved and aimed his phone, capturing his and Rover's avatars on his screen at once. "Now *this* is what I wanted from the beginning! A *battle*! Even if it's one shot, it'll be a much-earned defeat, *Rover*!"

Rover watched the opposing character raise both hands. Its fists ignited above its helmeted head, showcasing the effects of its equipped weapons.

It has the Flaming Glove Aliens equipped. Not good, it has great long-range attacking.

Among the speculating crowd, Adele chugged a bottle of water and dried her sweaty face on her handkerchief. She and Lumpy watched the sudden death round unfold from almost nowhere.

"Graphite's fireballs are fast," Lumpy said, watching Rover's AR avatar run, flip, and climb to avoid the attacks. "They're also setting the AR place on fire."

"Crazy…" Adele breathed, transfixed on her phone as the virtual flames overtook the action.

Rover stayed close to his own avatar, trying to keep all of the incoming fireballs onscreen at all times.

I can't hit him with my Butler Glove Aliens on, he thought. *And there's an AR fire spreading in here. If I take the slightest burn damage, it'll knock me out.*

Adrenaline loosened his fingertips, making his sweaty thumbs struggle with the slippery touchscreen controls. All exits from the sub canals were blocked by virtual fire, forcing him to retreat farther into a dead end. There, he scrolled through his equipment settings as the flames encroached.

I have to change my weapon!

The equipped Butler Glove Aliens were wonderful close-quarters weapons, specializing in Mach-speed slaps, backhands, and intimidating finger gestures. They also increased dexterity, which was the speed of Rover's character's arms and hands, quickening many in-game actions. However, that advantage was purposeless now.

I didn't want to use my best Glove Aliens like this and let people know I have them…but it's either spill the beans or lose them all to Graphite!

He replaced his weapon with the Beelzebub Glove Aliens, steering clear of the spreading fire from Graphite's character, who remained at a safe distance. Three new onscreen buttons appeared on Rover's smartphone—his actions provided by the equipped weapon.

There's my chance! Rover thought, seeing a small clearing through the virtual blaze. *I just gotta get a* tiny *bit* closer!

Rover's character charged toward the opponent, its weapons appearing as skeletal matter clumped around both hands with extra-boney knuckles and spurred fingers.

He tapped an action button labeled "Winter's Sepulcher."

And Quintegrity stood in place, trapped in astonishment. Her breath caught, eyes widening while utterly speechless.

Every person whose AR device was tuned in to the event saw the same thing: a screen entirely full of ice crystals—they had burst up from the virtual floor and occupied over half of the locomotive platform.

The glistening weaves of winter-hued ice crystals branched in all directions. Up close, they were quite detailed for the mobile video game's graphics, but the *size of its entirety* was the real spectacle to behold.

All those serenely cold, perfectly carved daggers...

The thunderous rattle still reverberating through the AR station...

Glimmering, glittering, flittering flurries of snow and frozen mist...

...Those had taken Quintegrity's breath away, anchored her feet to the ground, and tethered her mind to stupefaction.

I knew it, Rover thought as he saw his girlfriend react to being engulfed amid the virtual cluster of wintry splendor. *You really* can *see the augmented reality!*

"Hey."

Rover's voice pulled Quintegrity out of the moment. He offered a smile. She gawked at him, speechless...frozen from surprise—very fitting for the virtual icescape around her.

His grin stretched from ear to ear. "You like that?"

Dazzling, mesmerized eyes were her answer, the expression on her face replacing the need for a vocal reply.

"What the???" Adele's hands shook as she stared at her phone. "What'd he do?!"

Lumpy found his voice. "I...I don't know." He looked up, seeing how everyone was equally dumbfounded. "Rover was already, like, the supreme *Glove Alien Fight* player, but now...I'd say he just *graduated* from supremacy!"

Inside the ice, above Graphite's avatar, a bloody number appeared, referring to the damage the crystalline eruption had dealt (a number more than twice that character's maximum HP).

"WINNER: ROVER CHORK!!!" appeared on everyone's screens.

The onscreen message conjured a robust ovation with cheering and chanting of Rover's name. Total strangers swarmed him, shaking his hand and exchanging online gamebuddy requests.

"That...was...*cool!*" Quintegrity applauded her way through the crowd. She stopped in front of Rover and stared with fascination. "And you won!!!"

Rover grinned. "I'm just a ruthless, goose-less bagel-snatcher!"

Quintegrity's laughter was hearty. "Wrong! Your little game dude was *that!*"

"Meh."

"But you're something even better."

Her smile softened as she stepped up to Rover, keeping eye contact. Rover really tried to reply, but his speech was clocking out for the moment. Quintegrity scooped him up in a hug, then hoisted him over her head with both hands.

"You're my *boyfriend*!!! Ha-ha-ha-haaa!"

"H-Hey! P-Put me d-down!"

6!6@6#6$6%6^6&6*6(6)6_6+6

"Hey there, Lumpy's little game dude!" Quintegrity waved at Lumpy's augmented reality avatar as he had it run and jump around an alleyway. "And Adele's, too!"

Adele almost choked on air. "I-I can't believe it... She really sees the AR objects?!"

"That's crazy," Lumpy said under his breath. "How do you do that, Quinn???"

"The power of *funk* compels me!" she replied, grinning and snapping her fingers to the rhythm in her soul.

Rover gave her a serious look. "Really, tell us. You gotta have some kind of cybernetic enhancements in your eyes."

"Nope!"

"Then...you're a mutant...?"

"I'm just a regular human."

Rover deadpanned toward Lumpy and Adele. They shrugged.

"Ugh," Rover grunted. "It's hard to believe you, Quintegrity."

"It must be." Nodding, she said in a quiet voice, "I very well know why you don't believe me."

Lumpy chuckled. "I'd say it's mutual, Rover. She won't tell us how she sees the augmented reality, and you won't tell us where you got those Beelzebub Glove Aliens."

"I wanted them to be a secret," Rover replied. After a moment, he added, "I can't have people knowing...especially with this player-versus-player feature. I never planned on using them like this..." His voice trailed off. "Now people know I have them..."

"So be it." Adele gave a shrug of reluctant acceptance. "You both have your secrets. When the time is right, you'll let each other know. Just leave it at that."

Rover and Quintegrity looked at each other—Lumpy and Adele could see their agreement in that silent exchange.

"Kinda suspicious," Lumpy whispered to Adele, "don't ya think?"

Adele's face flattened. "Honestly...whatever my brother does and who he dates is none of my business. But yes, it's still suspicious as hell."

"Suspicious, but proud!" Quintegrity exclaimed haughtily.

"Wah!" Adele jumped back. "She heard us..."

6!6@6#6$6%6^6&6*6(6)6_6+6

After Graphite's defeat, public humiliation, and forfeiture of all in-game consumable items, Rover and Quintegrity continued their date as originally intended. With Lumpy and Adele, they killed the next few hours at Nu Clear R-Cade, munching on cheese-char popcorn, snacking on turducken nuggets, and sipping Fizzy Nifty soda pop, all while making the rounds on arcade games of all varieties ranging from cutting-edge to prehistoric.

"I wanna see the games you like best, Rover!" Quintegrity told the boy.

As Rover's anxiety put the squeeze on his sweat glands, Lumpy patted him on the back.

"Here's your chance to spend some more one-on-one time with her," Lumpy whispered to his friend.

Rover gulped. Without the thrill of a *Glove Alien Fight* match, his nervousness was given free range to wreck his mental state.

"R-Right," Rover replied, quelling his jitters to some degree.

His girlfriend was happy and eager to watch him play, although she didn't seem to understand the games' concepts. She refused to participate in playing, claiming she'd break the machines if she got too involved.

As the sun set and the blanket of night skies was pulled over the horizons, the teens caught the bus back to their residential area before the Curfew Crusade began their patrol. Rover had learned firsthand that the Curfew Crusaders packed painful teenager prods, which were basically cattle prods with adolescent-strength reconfigurations (Rover's acne had practically been singed off from the zap).

They exited the bus at their stop and took to the neighborhood on foot, chattering about Rover's triumph in the AR match. The houses were closing up for the night, electric glows of TVs peeking out from the hundreds upon hundreds of windows as the residents settled in with their favorite shows and video games.

Coming up to the Chorks' house, Quintegrity, grinning wide, wrapped her arms around Rover.

The boy broke out in an instant sweat, which shone in the bright moonlight.

"Goodnight, Rover," she said sweetly. Even her voice, not just her breath, was warm and steamy...or perhaps that was just Rover's *reaction* to her voice.

"G-G-Googoo..." Rover sputtered. Being pressed against the girl's body unplugged his tongue.

"Awww!" Quintegrity cooed, squeezing Rover tighter. "You're babbling like a baby." She laughed. "You're so goofy. I'll see you all tomorrow morning, then. Goodnight, peeps!"

Rover still had no control over his words when Quintegrity let go. She skipped away without him telling her goodnight.

Adele, however, hunched over in laughter.

"Gawd, what a chump, Big Bro!" she chortled as mirthful tears filled her eyes. "What *was* that baby babbling you just did? Ha-ha-ha! You really were so worked up over that hug that it bitch-slapped the vocabulary right outta you."

"Shut up, Adele!"

Rover looked down the street in the direction Quintegrity had left, seeing her pirouetting beneath a streetlamp down the hill before she skipped into the darkness.

A breeze blew up, making him shiver. "Brrr! It's chilly."

"Well, you're covered in sweat." Lumpy grinned. "Dude, you turned the color of a baboon butt when Quinn hugged you! Liked it, didn't you?"

"Heh-heh…" Rover did like it. He really did. "It w-was…cool."

Adele stepped in front of Rover, resting the back of her head against both of her hands, snickering.

"You better apologize to your girlfriend for not telling her 'goodnight'!" she said. "After blowing three thousand thuggoons at that arcade, you better not let her down by forgetting simple, important things."

"I did tell her!"

"Not in plain Anglo-Thugwoodian. We've already lost five thousand thuggoons to her, and you've only progressed this far!"

"Will you drop it?!"

Another mild breeze passed by, carrying Adele's and Lumpy's laughter down the hillside street and into the skies above the neighborhood. Those jubilant voices were the last to be heard in the streets that night before the bedtime hour.

ROVER... Lvl 686

Allowance... {T}35,000

<<EXPENSE GOALS>>

Anti-Grav Skateboard... {T}499,999

<<CURRENT EQUIPMENT>>

Gloves... Beelzebub
Armor... Brick Jacket
Acc.1... Shyster's Shoes
Acc.2... Hound Doggo Shnozz

IMPROVING PERFECTION

ROVER **couldn't concentrate** in class the next day. Tsu-*day* was typically the most boring day of the week, and Mr. Geography Teacher yammered on about continents. Geography just seemed pointless as life was practically nonexistent outside Thugwood. Also, the boy's mind was preoccupied with video games and, especially, Quintegrity.

Rover felt his phone vibrate from an email. He stealthily checked it under his desk as Mr. Geography Teacher slapped his metre stick stylus against the globe displayed on the touchscreen chalkboard.

Quintegrity sent me an email? She wants me, Lumpy, and Adele to meet her after school.

"And remember, children!" the teacher told the class. "Leaving Thugwood and going outside the surrounding Jerry Co. Walls is basically suicide, unless you're on Militia duty or some other hogwash. Anyway, that's it for today."

He unfolded his metre stick stylus into a stylus gavel and struck his podium with it, making a hollow, woody sound that knocked on each students' eardrums.

7!7@7#7$7%7^7&7*7(7)7_7+7

To alleviate the long distances between classes, the school rented out Rollabouts to students and faculty members, which were small, electric-powered carts that a single person could stand on—they were convenient for getting around and quicker than running.

Unfortunately, the Rollabouts were also great for campus-wide racing, which had two consequences: (1) Many of them were wrecked, lost, or stolen by feral bear-tigers; and (2) the school's headmaster jacked up the rental fees and Rollabout insurance as a result of the first consequence.

Therefore, Rover, Quintegrity, Lumpy, and Adele took the trek on foot through the campus Courtmeadows to the Clubhaus High-Rise building.

The Courtmeadows filled most of the space between the school buildings, carpeted with springy, shiny lilygrass that glossed the capaciously spacious outdoor grounds, dotted with coves of trees and the occasional drinking fountain oasis (to probably stem off dehydration when weary students got lost between classes).

Sunlight glared off the lilygrass lawn, an effect known as "fieldlight," and Rover shielded his eyes with his hands.

"Ugh, stupid shiny grass. This is why I hate the Courtmeadows when it's sunny…"

"Yeah," Adele said, putting on her shades and hopping a little with each step on the lilygrass, "but I love the way it feels to walk on! It's like a big trampoline field."

"It isn't as springy as a trampoline," Lumpy told her, tapping his toes on the grass as he put on his shades, "but it is kinda weird."

"I should've brought my shades, too," Rover said, turning away from the sun to reduce the grassy glare.

Quintegrity bounced on her heels, alternating between each foot as they walked. She wore a toothy grin while taking in the brilliant weather without eye protection.

"Hey," Rover said to her, "isn't it too bright out here for you? You should wear shades…or, like, squint."

Quintegrity pressed her ankles together and bounced on both heels at once, preserving the same tempo from her steps. She turned to Rover with a soft giggle.

"Nope. I loooove sunshine."

After a couple midair spins with her arms straight out sideways, she switched to bouncing on her toes, again alternating between feet.

"I don't think your love of sunshine matters," Rover muttered, still shielding his eyes. "This fieldlight can be dangerous to your retinas."

The girl bounced closer to Rover until she was bouncing directly in front of him. His forehead sweat matched the shiny sheen of lilygrass as he felt Quintegrity's bouncing through the lawn under him. However, certain aspects of her bouncing were harder for a boy to ignore, and Rover cursed the bright surroundings for blinding his view of said up-close bouncing.

She removed a tiny, flexible fabric pad from her pocket, put it on her index fingertip, then pressed it onto Rover's nose bridge between his eyes.

"Boop!" Quintegrity booped as she did so, still bouncing.

The pad gently stuck to Rover's nose and displayed a dark screen that covered his eyes.

"Whoa…" Rover gazed around the Courtmeadows. "You had holoshades this entire time…and you aren't using them???"

"I told ya I don't need them," the girl replied. Her smile made her close her eyes for the longest time since stepping outside, and her cheeks glowed brighter than the twinkling, breeze-swept fieldlight.

Lumpy leaned in to admire the holoshades on Rover's face. "Solar-blocking holograms are highly advanced technology. Man, those holoshades must've been expensive."

"They were, but I got 'em for a bargain!" Quintegrity sped up the tempo of her bouncing as she picked up the pace. "Now let's go, slowpokes! To the Clubhaus, where mystical wonders await!"

The others chased after her, clumsy at first as their strides were increased by several centimetres due to the springy lilygrass, but eventually picking up speed as each bound propelled them ever farther.

"Whoa!" Adele cried as she dashed forward. "I-I didn't know lilygrass could be this bouncy!"

"Of course!" Quintegrity laughed from ahead. "Lilygrass gets mega boing-a-rific after it soaks up a bunch of sunshine! People never bother with it because of the fieldlight."

The other students in the Courtmeadows stayed on the pathways. Although bouncing on the lilygrass was considered a sin against maturity, they couldn't help but envy the gall to do what Rover and the others were doing.

"For real?" one girl muttered to her friends. "Bouncing on lilygrass? Are they trying to go blind?!"

"They have shades," another girl replied, "and it looks like fun."

"But it's sooo childish," a third girl droned.

"Meh, growing up is overrated," a fourth girl said, shrugging.

7!7@7#7$7%7^7&7*7(7)7_7+7

Each Thugwood high school provided significant accommodations for school clubs in the form of a Clubhaus High-Rise building. There, every club had its own apartment consisting of a main activity space, two offices, and one storage room.

Well, *almost* every club. While floors one through four were identical with multiple, matching club apartments, the fifth floor was an exception. That was where Quintegrity led Rover, Lumpy, and Adele.

The elevator stopped and opened, and Rover stared straight out down a short hallway with a single door at the opposite end. Aside from that simple layout, the drab hallway was decorated just like the others on the lower floors.

"There's only one club apartment up here?" Rover asked as they followed Quintegrity's high-step march to the sole door.

"Sure is!" she replied, stopping in front of the unimpressionable door at the end of the hall.

She lifted her foot (higher than her high-steps had been), and...

WHAM!

...kicked the door down with a single blow. It remained perfectly upright for the first two metres it traveled, then fell flat on the floor.

Grinning happily in the doorway, she turned to her confounded, jaw-dropped guests.

"The entire top floor belongs to the Super Club!" she told them.

Lumpy and Adele entered, instantly captivated by the penthouse overflowing with luxurious amenities and lavish commodities. Rover was speechless for a moment as he stepped inside, but quickly focused on the busted door.

"But..." he said to his girlfriend, grimacing, "why'd you kick the door down...?"

Quintegrity stood the door upright and pointed to the hinges.

"I installed special kick-in hinges that just pop right outta the doorjamb," she answered. "I don't want to install new hinges each time I enter."

"Then *anyone* can enter!" Rover argued.

"Nah, the hinges are tough, and the deadbolt is still legit."

The girl pointed to the busted part of the doorjamb where the deadbolt had been ripped out of the wood. She set the door back in place, snapped the hinges in, and reached into a cardboard box by the doorway—a box full of new deadbolts pre-installed inside portions of replacement doorframes.

"This way," she added, "I only need to replace the deadbolt each time. And since each deadbolt has its own pre-installed, removable portion of the doorframe built in, the only part that gets damaged is this pre-installed part, leaving the rest of the doorframe unharmed by my brazen entrances."

Her smile was too sincere for such absurdity.

Rover's eye twitched as he stared at her. "But...whyyyyy???"

"Because I want to have fun every time I come here!" Quintegrity boasted, juggling seven new deadbolts at once.

In seconds, she cleaned out the doorframe notch using a scraper, slathered it with a fresh coat of Hercules Glue, and inserted the new deadbolt. With a snap of her fingers, an automatic vacuum cleaner scurried out of a doghouse in the living room, cleaned up the remaining debris by the entrance, and returned to its home with the name "Ryuumba-*chan*" painted over the little door.

Quintegrity complimented the vacuum cleaner. "Good job, Ryuumba-*chan*!"

With a relaxed sigh, Adele stretched out on a couch by the huge windows that made up nearly the entire wall. "This place is freaking awesome! You could live here! The living room alone is *huge*...and the TV takes up the whole wall!"

"And you can see almost half of the school campus from up here," Lumpy said, looking out the windows. He ran his hands along the sea-marble coffee table with a tea set on it, and he smiled at the human skull-shaped teacups and unicorn skull-shaped teapot.

"Step into my kitchen," Quintegrity told them, impersonating a phantom butler, or something. "My purpose for bringing you here awaits in there."

The kitchen was around the corner from the living room. Glistening stone countertops, grovenut wood cabinets, and shiny appliances were abundant. Quintegrity's guests were left in awe. Everything was beautiful...including the hanging light fixtures.

"For *real*???" Adele squealed, marveling over every aspect of the immaculate accommodations. "I-It's a nicer kitchen than the home economics classroom's! Or even the Culinary Club's!"

"Well," Quintegrity said, somewhat embarrassed as she scratched her cheek with one finger, "the Culinary Club had way more appliances to start with, and their actual cooking space is four times larger."

"But there's a lot of stuff in here." Lumpy looked around before leaning in close to a nearby...*thing*. "Like, I don't even know what this is."

The thing on the counter was smaller than a microwave, had three dials, an antenna, a mechanical arm, and something that looked like a pottery wheel.

"That's the flavor enhance-a-roony," Quintegrity explained, petting the machine. Its mechanical arm reached out to her, and she gave it a "handshake."

Rover snorted. "I've never heard of one of those."

"I had to procure it myself," his girlfriend said, "along with most of the stuff in here. I use this place to make my sweets and treats for fundraisers, and only the most exquisite, eccentric, and extraterrestrial appliances are sufficient."

Skeptical, Rover asked, "You don't get in trouble for bringing, uh, *extraterrestrial* equipment into the Clubhaus? Does Headmaster approve of it?"

"He does," she replied, "as long as it's for the Super Club, anything is possible. When I informed Headmaster that this stuff was for the Super Club, he totally understood. There's nothing to worry about!"

"What's the Super Club even do?" Lumpy asked Quintegrity. "Nobody really seems to know."

"Well..." She thought about her answer. "Right now, I'm selling chocolates as a fundraiser. All the proceedings go to the school."

"Okay, I know about the fundraiser," Lumpy said, "but what's the *main point* of the Super Club? You're its president."

Quintegrity put her finger on her chin to think.

"I basically just do whatever I want," she said with an innocent smile.

The others stared at her.

"What do you mean by that?" Lumpy asked, his eyes half-lidded.

"I mean just that," Quintegrity replied. "Headmaster and the school faculty trust what I'll do, so they let me do it."

"Wait a minute!" Rover shouted. "You mean they let you do whatever you want as long as you say it's for the Super Club?!"

Quintegrity giggled. "Yep!"

"That's pretty cool!" Lumpy chortled. "What about the other members of the club? Do they get away with it, too?"

Nodding, Quintegrity replied, "That's right. As long as you tell them you're doing something in the name of the Super Club, you won't get in trouble."

"That..." Rover grumbled, "...is the most *preposterous* thing I've ever heard..."

"But it's true," Quintegrity told Rover, "so remember that when you carry out future Super Club duties."

A moment was needed for Quintegrity's statement to soak in.

"Uh..." Rover grinned nervously. "You said that like we're all in the Super Club here."

"That's right," Quintegrity said with a happy smile. "Rover, Lumpy, and Adele—you're my first members! I'm so happy to have others in the Super Club with me now!"

Rover panicked. "SINCE WHEN DID WE JOIN?!?"

Quintegrity was confused by Rover's reaction.

"When you asked me out and I agreed," she said nonchalantly, giving Rover a curious look.

"Waaaiiit..." Lumpy's gears turned in his head. "Does that mean...I can do whatever I want at school...?"

"Only in the name of the Super Club," Quintegrity told Lumpy with a cute salute.

"Anything?" Adele asked, her eyes widening. "Like *anything* anything?"

"Things of any!" Quintegrity cheered.

The power. The freedom.

Lumpy and Adele were gleefully thunderstruck. Rover, however, was a tad worried.

"Are you really sure about this?" Rover asked Quintegrity. "I mean, is it a good idea to let students do whatever they want?"

"I already told you the school trusts me." She spoke with sincerity.

"It makes *no sense* that Headmaster would just trust you with so much!"

Quintegrity assured him with a smile. "I instilled the notions of my capabilities into Headmaster when he felt the funky clockwork ticking within my spirit. As a smart man, he understood my jams and my jellies just by being in the same room as me!"

"Balderdash," Rover murmured.

"Is it, Rover?" The girl winked.

As if that wink had been laced with hypnotherapeutic power, Rover understood that he himself had probably experienced similar, uncanny moments of wanting to put his trust in Quintegrity just by being close to her. It also could've been his hormones rattling around. Or just a false memory altogether.

This girl is frickin' persuasive, he thought.

Quintegrity continued with enthusiastic, open-arm poses, "Now you three will have those club membership perks! Only because you, my members, will be acting under my supervision. I'm your president, after all!" She winked again. "So, let's do our best! Tee-hee!"

"But...*what* are we doing?" Rover grunted, sidestepping that second wink.

"Making chocolates!"

She opened the triple-door refrigerator, removed a large sheet tray, and discarded the plastic wrap to reveal a large assortment of chocolates.

"Here's my sample batch of chocolates. There are ten varieties on this tray, and they're all included in the *Shamelessly Massacred by Chocolate* airdropped pallet with the other ninety varieties I make."

"A hundred varieties???" Rover was lost for words.

"Two of each," Quintegrity said, placing the tray of chocolates on a nearby table. "Please help yourselves!"

"*Two hundred* pieces of chocolate?" Adele drooled at the fantasy. "Haaahh...it almost would've been worth buying that huge box. Big Bro...think about it."

"...About what?" Rover muttered.

Adele drooled with a dreamy look on her face. "Split among you, me, Mom, and Dad...fifty pieces of chocolate each..."

"You're the one who talked me out of it!" Rover snapped.

Adele pouted. "Don't go blaming me if you make poor decisions."

Rover looked at the chocolates on the tray. Each one was perfectly shaped, molded flawlessly.

"You make all of these yourself?" Rover asked Quintegrity. "For the entire fundraiser?"

"I do! All made by hand from scratch."

What could Rover say to that? It was too amazing, too shocking for him to comprehend.

"That's incredible." Lumpy picked up a piece of chocolate and popped it into his mouth. "Wow, this is really good!"

Quintegrity grinned. "Thank you so much! I work hard to make sure every piece is consistent and just right, so I inspect each of the three thousand pieces I make every day."

Lumpy choked, narrowly avoiding a literal death by chocolate by gulping it down.

"*Three thousand*?!" Rover exclaimed. "How the heck do you make *three thousand* pieces a day???"

"I just do, I guess," Quintegrity replied with overflowing innocence.

"But, that's insane! You'll burn yourself out if you don't be careful!"

"Oh, don't be silly," Quintegrity chuckled with a confident grin and her hands on her hips. "With you guys with me, we'll *squelch* the concept of 'burnout' together! I already had a perfect operation going by myself, but with you three, I plan on improving perfection...together!"

The glorious commodities, the unrivaled chocolate flavor, and the cosmic magnificence of Quintegrity's attitude... They threatened to consume Rover, but it was a necessary overabundance, he realized, that he needed more than anything in the world.

He ate a piece of chocolate, his sugary lips spreading into a smirk.

"Then," he said to his girlfriend, "let's make this the most super Super Club possible."

"Yeah!!!" Quintegrity cheered.

"Yeah!!!" Lumpy and Adele added, their hands and mouths chocolatey from eating more samples.

I could get used to this, Rover thought as he watched his girlfriend and sister dance around the fascinating kitchen with each other, hand-in-hand.

"This chocolate is so good!" Adele popped the last chocolate into her mouth. "I bet you're a good cook."

"Yes, I try to be," Quintegrity said.

"You should make dinner at our house," Adele told her with a big smile.

"I should!"

Rover's heart skipped a beat.

"Like, tomorrow!" Adele added. "You can meet our parents."

"Absolutely!"

"Adele!" Rover barked. "Stop setting up things with my girlfriend!"

"Oh, get over it!" The younger sister swatted Rover on the back with a sly smirk and laughed.

Then again, Rover thought, blushing as Quintegrity clasped her hands together and smiled at him, *even though I could get used to this, I might have a long way to go before I do...and I'm willing to take that journey.*

ROVER... Lvl 686

Allowance... {T}35,000

<<EXPENSE GOALS>>

Anti-Grav Skateboard... {T}499,999

<<CURRENT EQUIPMENT>>

Gloves... Beelzebub
Armor... Brick Jacket
Acc.1... Shyster's Shoes
Acc.2... Hound Doggo Shnozz

<< 8 >>
EVERY SONG IN THE WORLD ON YOUR PLAYLIST

CRICKE†S **chirped their chipper songs** to the stars over Thugwood. Rover and Quintegrity walked down the street through the residential neighborhood on their way to the local grocer.

Dinner would be a grandiose affair that Wenno-*day* evening.

The couple crossed the cable bridge over the Gubbuh-Plardy River. Their path was illuminated by the bridge's streetlamps, as well as the headlamps of passing vehicles.

"You'll get to meet my parents tonight," Rover said, watching his phone as he played *Glove Alien Fight*; the standard game, not using the augmented reality.

In front of Rover, Quintegrity's slow high-step marching and exaggerated arm swings kept to a steady, funky groove that bumped its beat through her brain.

"I'm looking forward to it very much," she replied, not altering her forward march.

"To be honest," Rover told her, gripping his phone tighter as he defeated a Boogeyman Drunkard in the game, earning magnesium coins, "I'm a little worried. My family is full of picky eaters."

"It won't be a problem."

"You don't understand how my family is."

"Hey."

Quintegrity stopped walking. She turned around and blasted Rover with the energy from her most powerful "thumbs-up and bold smile" combo. It halted the boy in his tracks.

"I told you we've got this!" Her sunniness beamed through the boy. "Their socks shall be knocked right off."

The attitude shockwave from the girl's confidence alone was enough to chase away rifle-toting vultures from a roadkill buffet. However, Rover was no vulture...he was a Chork, and he wasn't backing down.

He pocketed his phone. "Mom is happy she won't be cooking tonight, that's for sure. I'm not saying this'll be a *bad* thing."

Continuing with her high-step march to the funk music in her head, Quintegrity gestured toward the sky, bridge, river below, all of Thugwood, and pretty much everything...all with sweeping arm motions that appeared almost like she was stretching after a lazy nap.

Step. Step. Step. Step.

"Take a look around," she told Rover in a serene voice, her multiple shadows stretching as they passed the last streetlamp on the bridge. "Feel the rhythm of the world as reality's favorite band strikes up a funky beat. That's how you know which dance to do and which beat to step to."

The sidewalk widened past the bridge, and Rover took the opportunity to move next to Quintegrity as she continued her in-tempo strides.

He gave her a flat look. "Is that your way of saying to just go with the flow?"

"It is." She smiled at him as they approached the grocery store parking lot. "You just gotta tune in to the rhythm of life, and go with the funk-a-tronic boogie that flows through everything!"

Rover listened to the crickets. He looked at the starlit sky. Quintegrity's words kinda made sense to him, though, as if he could sense this "boogie" in the scenery around him.

He chuckled. "I always knew each member of my family had their own ways of going through life. Their own 'songs,' as you might say, never made much sense to me, or to each other...but sometimes I think there's a common theme among our tunes."

They stopped walking, the glow of the grocery store's signs painting their faces with iridescent florescence, their neon hums adding to the symphonic cricket cacophony.

Curious and intrigued, Quintegrity looked at Rover.

"What do you mean?" she asked.

The boy thought for a moment. "Well, it's like how everyone is different. That would mean that everyone has their own groove, right?"

She nodded. "Mm-hmm."

"But there are people who have the same songs on their playlists as other people," Rover continued. "Like, they listen to some of the same stuff. Like this funky groove you talk about. It's unique for some, but many of us share the same tunes from time to time...ya know?"

"Yeah, I think I understand." Quintegrity grinned. "You get it!"

"If so," Rover added, "with my knowledge of my family, and you, uh...being *you*...then we'll cook them up something that matches everyone's dinner rhythm!"

All this talk about the funky boogie throughout the universe was hard for Rover to comprehend, and he still held skepticism toward pleasing his family's palate.

I think I'm not just spouting nonsense, and that I'm actually offering insight to what Quintegrity's saying.

Yet, amid his doubt and nervousness, he held out his hand for his girlfriend to take.

Without missing a beat, Quintegrity took her boyfriend's hand.

"For sure!" she replied happily. "Just imagine...every song in the world on your playlist! Then there will never be a moment of misunderstanding!"

At that, they hurried toward the grocery store entrance.

The automatic doors slid open.

Rows of possibilities were lined up before them where arrays of ingredients and foodstuffs were waiting. Quintegrity danced in the aisles, twirling and springing as she grabbed the items and placed them in their shopping baskets, her assault rifle-shaped pursed swinging and swaying at her side.

Parsnips and parsley! Arugula and artichokes! Beef flanks and beet filling! Chicken and chutney! Potatoes and tomatoes! Carrots! Onions! Garlic! Thugwoodian allspice!

More...

More!

"MOARRR!!!" Quintegrity cackled as she raided and paraded, stuffing and stashing nary a missed ingredient into their baskets. Really, they each carried three baskets on each arm, filled to spilling at any moment.

Rover offered to pay with the Adamantite credit card his parents lent to him for the occasion, but Quintegrity swiftly beat him to the punch with her superior Mythril credit card.

The cashier man scanned each item like the good robot he was paid to be.

Beep

Beep

Beep

Quintegrity didn't even flinch at the total price racking up as she brandished her Mythril card.

Swipe

[Payment Approved]

And they hurried back to Rover's home.

8!8@8#8$8%8^8&8*8(8)8_8+8

Chop chop chop!

Grate. Grate. Grate.

Quintegrity's knife-work showcased her remarkable sleight of hand. The blade caught the lights in the Chork household kitchen, appearing as flickering glints of radiance in the midst of fillet-slaying, veggie-eviscerating movements.

Rover sped around, matching the girl's movements, sorting through the prepped food and throwing them into appropriate skillets, pots, pans, ice baths, and wave-cookers. His skills at motion-capture arcade games were very handy around the kitchen.

The steaks and chicken fillets hit the hot oil in the pans, searing the marinated scents right out of them and into the air.

"Mmm, smells good!" Dad commented as he passed by the kitchen.

Juices and spices dripped from the skewers and into the mini charcoal grill, sending their olfactory previews wafting about the house.

"There are *great things* happening in here," Mom sang as she passed by the kitchen.

The top crusts of multiple pies and pastries crisped and flaked in the oven, pumping the sweet aromas of caramel and berries and cocoa into the environment.

"Oh wow, I can't wait!" Adele remarked as she passed by the kitchen.

And that was only half of the feast!

Rover and Quintegrity scrambled, flambéed, and fricasseed. Confits of garlic and duck and pork belly were assembled in ways Rover had never seen on plates as Quintegrity stacked towers of gravity-defying entrées. Medleys of greens and peppers and gourds were drizzled with rivulets of seasoned oils Quintegrity had never imagined would make complimentary pairings as Rover blended and upended daring vinaigrettes with chilled villainy of tasty treasures.

Thus, the full spread of fixings were completed within minutes of each other. Nothing hot had gone cold; nothing cold had melted. The timing was perfect.

The couple high-fived, and then they set the dinner table.

One-by-one, everything was laid out in front of the wide-eyed, water-mouthed family.

Feeling triumphant and proud, Rover took his seat.

However, Dad watched as Quintegrity sat next to Rover, and he smirked at his son.

"So, tell me," Dad said to Rover, his face loaded with more mischief than the baked potatoes were loaded with bacon, chives, bourbon salt, black pepper, and garlic oil, "...how far have you gone with Quinn to learn how to cook food fitting for a king?"

Rover's face imploded as if he'd eaten the leftover lemons not used in the lemon-lime tart-strudels.

"*Hrrk*!" He choked on his embarrassment. "Wh-What d-do you mean 'how far'?!"

"*Gross*, Dad," Adele muttered. "Please don't assassinate my appetite with your pervy crap."

"Oh, don't tease Rover," Mom said, hitting Dad on the shoulder. "He's already a hormonal ball of fire. Don't pour kerosene on it."

"You'll understand, son," Dad said with a devious smirk. "Sometimes, the best moments *sneak up* on you. Heh-heh-hehhh!"

"Gah!" Rover was lost for words, his hands quaking too much to handle his silverware.

A shadow suddenly did sneak up behind him.

Startled, he turned to see Quintegrity's smiling face only centimetres away. She reached around behind Rover, put her index and middle fingers on the table, walked her hand up to the salad spoon protruding from the salad bowl, and catapulted a cherry tomato from the greens—it landed perfectly in her mouth.

Sweating at the table was uncomfortable, but Rover couldn't prevent it.

Is Quintegrity thinking about Dad's comment?! he wondered as the heat rose from under his collar.

Quintegrity said nothing about it, though, which made dinner very awkward for the boy. At the least, his family of picky eaters was utterly enchanted by the meal, so he was grateful for that.

Together, he and Quintegrity had successfully found (and *nailed*) his family's common tune...a song in the key of F (for "food").

Food Major.

As Dad consumed his helping of duck confit like a savage animal, a blissful expression washed over him.

"This is stupendous!" he said between bites. "What's for dinner next time, Quinn?"

Quintegrity responded with an entertained smile. "Oh, you know, the usual. It's a simple formula: 'Maximum' plus 'Most' equals 'What's for Dinner.' Remember that, and you'll be whipping up something like this every single meal!"

"I don't think we can *afford* 'Maximum' plus 'Most'!" Dad's face and voice were jubilant, but the tear streaming down his face was probably more from sadness than joy.

"And talk about a caloric overload," Mom added, sipping her wine with a thin smile. "If we do every meal like this one, then they won't be special anymore."

"You're right," Quintegrity giggled. "We don't want to lose that specialness. Right, Rover?"

"Uh, right!"

Throughout dinner, Adele shot the occasional glance at her brother and his girlfriend. There was still that telltale nervousness on his face, as his smiles were too frequent and overdone. However, Adele noticed there was something else inside him. Alongside his jittery idiocy was sincerity...a true kind of happiness that played well with Quintegrity's vigorous positivity.

Perhaps, Adele thought as she chewed on a piece of succulent yellow snapper sashimi, something she normally despised any other time, *they really are a better match than I'd originally thought.*

8!8@8#8$8%8^8&8*8(8)8_8+8

After Quintegrity had gone home, Rover lazed around with his family in the living room. A ditzball game was on TV as the boy leaned back on the couch next to his father, feeling heavy and sleepy from the meal.

During a commercial break, Dad said, "That was the best meal we've had in a long time! Not just because of the food, but as a family."

"I agree," Mom replied. "Quinn really brought us together, didn't she?"

"Yeah." Rover smiled, proud of his girlfriend. "She's awesome."

Adele sighed. "Too bad you're only dating her for shallow purposes."

"I am not!" Rover told her.

"You're a boy," Adele added, "so your motives are obvious. At the very least, you want to enlist her for your cause."

"Shut up, Adele!"

"Your 'cause'?" Dad gave Rover a curious look.

Rover crossed his arms over his full belly. "Adele's talking about my plan to defeat CEO Claudius at *Glove Alien Fight* so I can lift the daily playtime mandate."

Dad laughed. "Well, go get 'em, son! Just be careful."

"About what?"

"You're going against the government. Even if this all seems fair and looks like a game on the surface, it's most likely rigged against anyone who wants to make a stand." Dad's smile weakened. "I don't want you getting over your head."

I'm already over my head, Rover thought. *Quintegrity's abilities make me uneasy, and then there's her claim that she doesn't play* Glove Alien Fight...

"Or...are you already over your head?" Dad asked, his smile strengthening with deviousness. "I can see it on your face."

"I'll be fine," Rover told them, staring at the TV.

Again, Dad's expression become concerned, sharing it with Mom as they both looked at their son.

"As long as you're careful, Rover," Mom said.

Rover's last line of defense in the discussion was to merely repeat what he'd said. "I'll be fine."

ROVER… Lvl 689

Allowance… {T}35,000

<<EXPENSE GOALS>>

Anti-Grav Skateboard… {T}499,999

<<CURRENT EQUIPMENT>>

Gloves… Butler
Armor… Ape Laser
Acc.1… Yeet-Line Skates
Acc.2… Farm Equipment

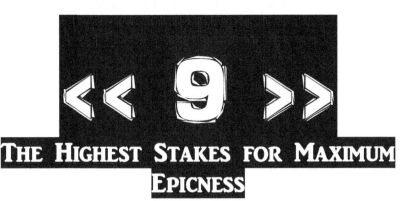

THE HIGHEST STAKES FOR MAXIMUM EPICNESS

WHAM!

The Super Club members entered the club penthouse after school on Thurdur-*day*, stepping past the kicked-in door lying flat on the carpet. Quintegrity promptly repaired the replaceable deadbolt, having the automatic vacuum cleaner suck up the extra dust and debris.

"Good job, Ryuumba-*chan*!" she said, petting the little vacuum before it scurried back to the doghouse in the living room. "All right, team. The first order of business is to brainstorm the Super Club's next fundraiser. The chocolate fundraiser Operation Chocolatier Action Punch is nearly over, so we need to start planning."

Rover, Lumpy, and Adele made themselves comfortable on the couches around the sea-marble coffee table. Although they were in a luxurious setting, the school required the club to perform constructive tasks, so the members each held their own notebooks and writing utensils—this was still work, after all.

Quintegrity stood by the coffee table as she addressed her members.

"I'll let you three decide what kind of fundraiser it'll be," she continued with zest. "Also, we need to decide where the proceeds will go."

Lumpy raised his hand. "The money we raise goes to the school, right?"

"It can," Quintegrity replied, "but, as the Super Club, we have full control over our income. We can pocket every thuggoon for ourselves if we desire!"

The prospect of money made Adele fuzzy inside. "No way... We can *keep* it all???" She rubbed her greedy palms together, snickering.

"Easy there, killer," Rover told his sister, worried about the evil gleam in her eyes. He put his pen to his notebook. "Okay, let's list off our options."

A few minutes into the session, the doorbell rang. Quintegrity hopped up from her cushy chair.

"A visitor! I wonder if a student has a request or a bone to pick."

"Let's hope it's the former," Rover said.

Quintegrity strode to the door, unlocked the deadbolt, and met the guest with a robust greeting.

"Hi there, Graphite!"

Rover scowled. "Damn, it's the *latter*."

Graphite Condor entered the penthouse, wearing a serious face that amplified his pencil lead-colored eyes. He looked at the three Super Club members sitting in the open living room, giving Rover an especially curt and crass glance.

Rover scoffed, twirling the pen in his hand. "You come to lose more items in *Glove Alien Fight*?"

Furrowing his brow, Graphite said, "Actually, I'm here to request the services of the Super Club."

"Certainly!" Quintegrity hopped onto her chair, crouching on the cushion with her knees pulled to her body. "Have a seat. Would you like some sparkling tea?" She gestured to the unicorn skull-shaped teapot on the sea-marble coffee table.

"No thank you." Graphite sat in the other chair identical to Quintegrity's and faced the four members. "Actually, it *is* about *Glove Alien Fight*."

Rover placed his notebook and pen on the coffee table. He was intrigued by the solidity in Graphite's tone—peculiar, serious behavior for a request involving something as menial as a video game...although it was the *mandatory* one.

The guest looked at Rover. "Have you played any more of the game's player-versus-player mode?"

"No." Rover shook his head. "It's a lot of fun, but I haven't bothered with it much."

"Then, I suggest making time for it," Graphite said. "The competition between us the other day was significant for Thugwood, and I thought you should know."

"What do you mean?" Rover asked.

"It went viral. A lot of people posted a lot of videos online of that match. Because of it, a lot of people have been getting serious about *Glove Alien Fight*, but that's not all." He paused, looking at everyone. "Yesterday, I was contacted by a man named Benedict Torrent."

"Benedict Torrent!" Rover's eyes got wide. "He's one of the most famous livestream hosts for video games."

Graphite nodded. "He applauded me for my bravery for challenging you, which is neither here nor there, I suppose. Anyway, he wanted to help me because I'd lost."

"What'd he do to help?" Lumpy asked, leaning into the conversation.

"He gave me a piece of info," Graphite said. "Benedict Torrent, first of all, has logged more playtime in *Glove Alien Fight* than most people. Because of that, his character reached the highest level: nine hundred ninety-nine."

Rover leaned back in his chair while thinking. "Then…nine hundred ninety-nine is the level cap."

"That's super impressive," Adele told Graphite. "To think that someone is already maxed out…"

"Yes," Graphite said with a nod, "but that's not the important thing. He told me he acquired an item called 'Special Number 1' when he reached that level."

Now Rover was all ears. "What's it do?"

A smile crept onto Graphite's lips.

"That's where it gets interesting," he said. "Although the Special Number 1 item couldn't be used or equipped, it's listed under the consumable items."

"Meaning it's key for something," Rover said, crossing one leg over the other as he sat on the couch. "Maybe there's some way to use it after certain conditions have been met—those kinds of things have happened in the game before. And, if it's a consumable item, then it can be taken by someone who wins a player-versus-player match."

"I think that's *exactly* the point," Graphite said. "The in-game description is 'Collect all ten for a real cash prize, and *Glove Alien Fight* will proceed to the Next Phase.'" He dropped his voice, adding, "Ten people will need to reach level nine hundred ninety-nine and battle it out to acquire all ten Special Number items."

"Whoa…" Adele's money-grubbing smirk returned. "A real cash prize… I wonder how much it'll be."

"What I don't understand," Lumpy said, "is the part about *Glove Alien Fight* proceeding to the 'Next Phase.'" He looked around at the others. "What's that about?"

"No idea," Graphite grumbled. "Benedict didn't know what the Next Phase is."

Rover stood up, pacing with his arms crossed. "I really wonder…if this has something to do with CEO Claudius' broadcast the other day. Remember? When he announced the player-versus-player feature, he also said that if someone defeats him in the game, then the daily quota mandate will be lifted."

"That's right," Lumpy pointed at Rover. "He *did* say that, and he said he'll only accept challenges from people who have met the prerequisites or something. That really might have something to do with the game moving to the Next Phase."

"Yeah..." Rubbing his chin, Rover continued to pace. "From what this sounds like, CEO Claudius is providing incentives for people to get badass in the game, hoping someone will step up to challenge him and lift the mandate." He bit his thumbnail with a firm expression on his face. "And I plan to be on the frontlines of that effort. To hell with the stupid daily quota."

Adele shook her head. "But, that doesn't make sense. Why would he egg us on to lift the mandate? Doesn't he *want* everyone playing his favorite game every day? Why go through all this trouble just for him to play with other people? I bet thousands of people would want to challenge him right now, even just for fun."

"Hmm, good point." Rover stopped pacing and looked at Quintegrity. "What do you think, Quintegrity?"

The boy saw his girlfriend staring at the floor while she remained crouched in her chair. She let go of her pants, which is when Rover realized she had been gripping them rather tightly.

Yet, her face lit up as she replied to Rover's question.

"It's a mystery, indeed!" she sang.

"Anyway," Graphite continued, "now for why I came here. I want to ask to team up with you guys." He smirked, looking at the club members. "With the Super Club, we can take the ten Special Numbers for ourselves, and we can split the cash prize. We'll be unstoppable!"

"Request denied!" Quintegrity declared, grinning. She stood up tall on the cushy chair, her hands on her hips, raining her gorgeously happy expression down on the crushed Graphite below.

"Wh-Why?!" Graphite stood and clenched his fists. "Denied?!"

"Because *Rover* will win that cash prize!!! And he ain't splittin' it with anyone! Unless he desires..."

Graphite gritted his teeth as Rover chuckled.

"Thanks for the tip, Graphite," he said with a smug smile. "You heard the girl, though."

"Then...then..." Graphite shook with anger, trying to contain himself. "Just team up with me, anyway! It doesn't have to be a Super Club request! I'm actually swallowing my pride and willing to put aside my jealousy! You're the best *Glove Alien Fight* player I know, Rover! I need you..."

Rover thought about it for a moment, or at least pretended to.

"Nah."

"WHAT?!? You petty little—"

"It's settled, then!" Quintegrity leapt from her chair and landed on the floor, sending funky-vibe quakes through the carpet, up the walls, and around the ceiling. "Your request has been denied." She tilted her head to the side with a giggle, holding her hands behind herself as if she was asking Graphite for an extra lollipop. "Now, is there anything else you need?"

Graphite hung his head and basically wept. "No…that was it…"

"In that case," Quintegrity told him, "we'll be resuming our Super Club duties. Sorry, but it's a private session."

The defeated boy dragged his feet toward the door. "Then, I'll be on my way…"

Before he reached the exit, Quintegrity approached him. She offered a paper cup with a plastic lid, gentle wisps of steam rising from the sip hole.

"Here." Her voice was like soft silk against Graphite's eardrums, her smile warmer than the cup she presented. "Take some sparkling tea. It's my very own blend, and I want you to have some."

The boy stared for a second, confused, but unable to turn down such a generous, sincere offer. He took the paper cup in both hands, feeling his soul heating up from his fingers until it reached his heart…and he hadn't even tasted the tea yet.

"Uh, thank you," he told her with a small smile.

"Feel free to ask if you have any other request for the Super Club."

"Yeah, I will."

Graphite closed the door behind him, and Quintegrity locked the deadbolt. The penthouse sank into a less-than-peaceful quietness.

"Soooo…" Adele attempted to break the awkward silence. She put her pen to her notebook. "Fundraiser?"

However, as soon as Rover sat back down on the couch, he got on his phone to do some internet searches.

"Benedict Torrent, eh?" he muttered, looking at his phone. A few searches showed Rover the results he'd been looking for. "Aha! Check this out." He held up his phone for the others to see the screen. "He does livestream video game stuff online and has other videos and blogs all centered on games."

"Your point?" Adele asked, impatient.

"Two points," Rover replied. "For one, he's a very skilled gamer, so beating him in a *Glove Alien Fight* match for that Special Number item will be tough. Secondly, he's doing a Q&A session right now for fans to call in and talk, so it should be easy to contact him and see if Graphite is full of taco turds about these Special Numbers."

Lumpy searched for the livestream session on his phone. "I'm checking out his Q&A session now."

Sure enough, there was a live video of Benedict Torrent taking calls and answering fans. He was a skinny guy in his early thirties wearing a baggy, bright polo shirt with big glasses and even bigger headphones over his neat, beach-colored hair. His outfit and chill attitude made him appear to be on a permanent vacation.

A phone number was provided in the video's description, and Rover immediately called it, watching Benedict on Lumpy's phone.

Within a few rings, there was an answer.

"Thank you for calling Torrential Talk! You are live!!!"

"Holy crap, I got through!" Rover was surprised, letting his excitement slip for the hundreds of livestream viewers to hear.

"I would say crap isn't anything less than utterly holy," Benedict chuckled.

"Huh? O-Oh, I get it! Ha! Ha-ha-ha!" Rover began to sweat. "I've never been on a show before... This is crazy!"

"All righty then," Benedict said, "I'm answering each callers' three questions. What secrets do you want me to spill?"

Raising an eyebrow at the live video, Adele said, "This guy has balls to be doing this in front of a live audience. Or just dumb."

Rover took a deep breath. "I heard a rumor just now, and I wanna confirm it with you. Is it true that you obtained a special item when you reached level nine hundred ninety-nine in *Glove Alien Fight*?"

Benedict froze for a second, as if in thought, then smiled with an airy chuckle.

"Yep, it's true," he answered confidently. "Not only did I learn that that is the game's level cap, but I was rewarded with something unexpected. Just a moment, I'll show you."

Rover, as well as the other few hundred viewers, focused on the livestream video, watching Benedict Torrent bring up *Glove Alien Fight* on his tablet. After a moment, he held the tablet up to the camera.

There, at the bottom of the consumable item list, was the Special Number 1 item. Its in-game description was just as Graphite had said.

"Apparently," Benedict said, still holding the tablet to the camera, "when a person reaches the maximum level in *Glove Alien Fight*, they get one of these Special Numbers, but probably only the first ten people. As consumable items, they can change hands among players through winning the AR matches."

"Yeah...that's what I was told."

The number of viewers watching the video was indicated at the bottom of the screen, and that number had nearly doubled before Benedict pulled the tablet away from the camera.

Rover sure had a knack for creating viral content.

Benedict smiled. "I think it'll make things super interesting in *Glove Alien Fight*! Don't ya think?" He reached off camera, seemingly tinkering with something that nobody could see before resuming the session. "All right, two more questions!"

"Well…" Rover took another deep breath and boldly clenched his fist. "Will you accept my challenge to a match in *Glove Alien Fight*?!"

Lumpy and Adele were stunned. They looked at each other.

"But, Rover," Lumpy hissed, "your character's level isn't close to maximum!"

With a quiet laugh, Benedict turned his gaze off-camera toward where he'd reached just seconds ago. He nodded, a firm smile on his face as he sighed.

"Well, well, well," he finally said. "It seems your voiceprint matches the voiceprint of one of the competitors in those popular videos of an AR match. I'd spoken with Graphite yesterday, so I suspected it was you, Rover Chork."

Rover's breath seized, and he stared at Lumpy's phone, at the sly smirk on Benedict's face.

"What kind of call-screening tech does this dude have?" Adele asked, her hands on her hips.

Quintegrity looked at Rover, seeing how being called out only spurred him on as he replied with his own smug grin.

"Yep," Rover said, "seems like the polecat is out of the bag."

"Then, the answer is no," Benedict replied.

"*Hey!*"

"After analyzing the troves of footage between your match with Graphite Condor," Benedict continued, leaning back in his gaming chair and adjusting the massive headphones on his beachy head, "I've concluded that you're a hell of a *Glove Alien Fight* player. Your wits are quick and your control over your in-game avatar is amazing. Because of that, if I were to face you in an AR *Glove Alien Fight* match…we'd need the highest stakes for maximum epicness. That way, my viewers will get some major entertainment!"

Rover clicked his tongue in frustration, watching the number of viewers for this livestream video skyrocket. For sure, Benedict was riling up his fanbase.

I should've known something like this would happen, Rover thought. *This is a show I'm on, after all.*

"Therefore," Benedict added, "I'll only accept your challenge under certain circumstances."

"Then," Rover said, hesitant, knowing he was backed into a corner, "what are those circumstances?"

"There are three," Benedict answered. "First, you must be at level nine hundred ninety-nine in *Glove Alien Fight* so it'll be equal. Second, you must also possess at least one of the Special Numbers to make things more high-risk. Third, because this basically acts as my livestreaming business doing you a *service of exposure* within the gaming community"—he paused, nonchalantly picking his fingernails as if he wasn't on camera— "I'll need one hundred thousand thuggoons."

"Say what?!" Rover shouted into the phone. "I gotta pay you to do this?"

"Ooh, sorry." Benedict obviously feigned the apology. "You already had your three questions answered. Thank you for calling, Rover. I'll leave this deal open exclusively for you, but only for a limited time before I accept the challenge from somebody else. I hope to hear from you again."

The phone call ended as Benedict answered the next call. Lumpy stopped the video, watching Rover squeeze his phone and stare at the carpet.

"Quintegrity," Rover said, not looking up.

"Rover!" she replied with an innocent smile that suggested she didn't know what the hell was happening.

"I have an idea for the Super Club's next fundraiser." Rover leaned back on the couch, a huge sneer stretching across his face. "Let's raise enough money for me to whoop Benedict Torrent's ass at *Glove Alien Fight...in front of his entire fanbase!*"

ROVER… Lvl 689

All Money… {T}35,000

Allowance… {T}35,000
Fundraiser… {T}0

<<EXPENSE GOALS>>

Benedict's Payment… {T}100,000
Anti-Grav Skateboard… {T}499,999

<<CURRENT EQUIPMENT>>

Gloves… Butler
Armor… Ape Laser
Acc.1… Yeet-Line Skates
Acc.2… Farm Equipment

<<SPECIAL NUMBERS>>

① ② ③ ④ ⑤

⑥ ⑦ ⑧ ⑨ ⑩

THE UNIVERSE REALLY IS REVOLVING AROUND ME

AS Rover sank to the bottom of the school swimming pool, the dull, low, muffled sounds of the underwater environment gave him a short period to think. He watched the trail of bubbles behind Jinkies Clayfast, their local mermaid, as she put torpedoes to shame while darting from end to end.

The water currents rocked Rover as he sat on the pool's bottom.

Jinkies is kinda inspirational, he thought. *I wonder if she or Quintegrity would win in a swimming match against each other.*

After pushing himself to make some quick laps, he crawled out of the water, feeling every muscle burn from the workout. Checking himself out, he realized his body was getting toned all over as the dripping water ran along newly sculpted muscle formations.

"Damn," he snickered, massaging the budding six-pack on his abdomen, "I'm looking good."

"You were killing it out there, Rover!" Mr. Pool Coach approached the boy with a grin. "Training hard for the Interschool AthletaCom?"

"Yeah," Rover replied, stretching his arms and legs. "I gotta be in top shape for anything during the AthletaCom, and I feel like swimming is a great all-around workout."

"Just by watching you, someone would think you were on the swimming team." Mr. Pool Coach sighed. "You would've done great, but you never signed up, and you're a senior now."

"Yeah." Rover shrugged it off. "I have other things to focus on, though."

"Like the Super Club?" the coach said, smiling. "I heard you and your sister and Lumpy Freeb were accepted into it."

Returning the smile with a thumbs-up, Rover replied, "Yep! That's gonna keep me busy, for sure! We're actually about to start a new fundraiser..."—his eye twitched as his smile began to hurt— "...and I'll be pretty *swamped* with that soon."

10!10@10#10$10%10^10&10*10(10)10_10+10

"One hundred thousand thuggoons," Adele whined as she walked down the school hallways with Rover, Lumpy, and Quintegrity. "Dude...that's more than what's in our savings for that Anti-Grav skateboard, and we've been saving up for a while."

"Yeah," Rover said, directing his bored gaze toward the ceiling as they walked, "but we also didn't have the Super Club on our side, and now we do."

"I know, but still..." Seeing her brother wasn't yielding to her concern, Adele grunted. "Why not wait for Benedict Torrent to lose his Special Number to another player, then beat *that* person at it? It'd be *free*."

"Who's to say Benedict will lose to anyone?" Lumpy pointed out.

"That includes Rover!" Adele retorted. "If he loses, then we'll waste that money!" Her fingers writhed like snakes as her lips slithered into a drooling smile. "Precious, luscious money..."

Lumpy shook his head. "But, Benedict might not play against anyone else to make sure he keeps the Special Number. He seems pretty serious about his livestreaming business, so the match against Rover might be more important to him than advancing further in *Glove Alien Fight*."

Rover shrugged. "I'll have to get to level nine hundred ninety-nine before all ten Special Numbers are in play. That'll be the easiest way to meet two of the three requirements. I know I can do it! I'm already leveled up pretty far, so I have an advantage! I even squeezed in some extra hours playing last night after bedtime."

"Ugh." Adele buried her face into her palms, smothering the flame of her greedy grimace. "Do you know how many people are aware of these Special Numbers because of your phone call with Benedict? I'm worried there're probably thousands of people skipping school and work right now to get to the max level and get their own Special Number."

"I've got this," Rover replied with a grin. "I'm not scared! Ha-ha! Not scared at all! Ha-haa-haaa!!!"

"Ha-haa-haaa!!!" Quintegrity mimicked.

"He's totally pissing himself," Lumpy whispered to Adele. "He told me this morning."

"Yeah, I figured," she said.

"Hey," they overheard someone whisper, "Daremont and Olaf are always hanging out together. Do you think they're...f-friends?"

"*Gasp!* No way! I pray they aren't..."

"Oh no," Lumpy muttered, pulling Rover closer. "Did you hear that?"

"A friendship? So what?" Rover asked.

Lumpy stared at Rover with dead seriousness. "Dude. Daremont and Olaf as good friends: think about it."

In fact, Daremont Radclaft and Olaf Thumdiggles were nearby with several other students. Daremont was a short boy with slicked, banana bunch-like hair and always wore creamy, collared shirts. Olaf had a strong jaw, crooked nose, and hair that looked like a sleeping fox was curled up on his head.

Sure enough, the two looked friendly with each other.

"Wait…" A gloom bubbled up in Rover's gut. "Olaf Thumdiggles: The King of Sarcasm…and Daremont Radclaft: The King of Puns…"

Rover and Lumpy stood firmly in place, immediately aiming their ears toward the two students in question.

"Oh yeahhh, Shawna," Olaf spouted, rolling his eyes, "Me and Daremont make such greaaat enemies, because we get along sooo well. Geeeez!"

"The *root* of our friendship can't be *beet!*" Daremont exclaimed happily. "So, it'll *turnip* everywhere!"

Rover trembled with fright.

Oh nooo…

"Okay, guys." Rover had his game face on to issue orders to Lumpy, Quintegrity, and Adele. "The King of Sarcasm has formed a partnership with the King of Puns." He kept his voice low. "Do you know what this means?"

"Oh!" Quintegrity's eyes lit up, idea-stricken. "We should have them join our group!"

"*NO!!!*" Rover pulled the four of them into a huddle. "We need to stay *far away* from them. Everyone got it?"

Quintegrity, Lumpy, and Adele nodded.

An excruciatingly fake laugh came from behind Rover. It was none other than Olaf Thumdiggles.

And he was walking toward them.

"Just so you knooow," Olaf droned with a massive shrug, "you'll have sooo much luck staying faaar away from us, because we *only* come to the *same* school together a fewww times a year."

Daremont beamed, pointing at himself with his thumb. "And distance can't protect you from my *far-fetched* puns!"

Rover just stared, his ears twitching in misery from the conversational assault. Adele made a gagging face. Lumpy shivered from chills. Quintegrity smiled at the sight of new friendships being forged.

When the duo walked away, another person approached, shaking her head.

"It was destiny for those two to team up," the dark-skinned girl said.

Rover recognized her—the hair like crow feathers and the ninja outfit covered with straps and belts were always the dead giveaway.

"You're one of Graphite's lackeys," Rover said in a flat tone. "Did I forget my weirdo repellant today?"

"I have a name," she replied, irritated, "and I'm not a lackey. I'm Tallyhawk Kusumegido." When nobody said anything, she crossed her arms. "I heard you spoke with Graphite about the Special Number items."

"Yes, I did." An impudent grin spread on Rover's face. "He was groveling like a little bitch because we won't team up with him."

Tallyhawk smirked, shifting her weight from one leg to the other. "Groveling sounds like him. Anyway, the internet is buzzing about your livestream call with Benedict Torrent."

"Let 'em," Rover said. "What's it matter?"

"They're making you a target."

Rover looked at the belt-clad girl. "A target?"

"They wanna know about those Glove Aliens you used to defeat Graphite," Tallyhawk explained. "With Benedict talking so highly of you, his followers started analyzing the footage of your match against Graphite with more scrutiny. Word of mouth about that match has been going strong, but after yesterday, it's become a full-blown internet sensation."

She brought up an online video on her smartphone, just one video of dozens showing the famed match. Rover felt his skin crawl.

"Over half a million views already..." His voice was small as he took the phone from Tallyhawk. He wasn't interested in watching the video and instead checked the comments. "They...they're all going nuts about my Glove Aliens... Some of them actually sound really pissed that they don't know what they are, accusing me of cheating..."

I knew I should've kept the Beelzebub Glove Aliens a secret. Now everyone knows about my trump card.

Tallyhawk took her phone back. "Even though weapons aren't traded through the player-versus-player matches, people are claiming they want to fight you just to get a better understanding of those Glove Aliens. Honestly, I think this is good news for you."

"You do?" Rover asked, narrowing his eyes at the crow-haired girl. He wrinkled his forehead in thought. "Actually...thinking about it, you gain a lot more experience through the player-versus-player AR matches than in the regular game...and it's a lot more fun to play."

He chuckled, then laughed heartily enough for other students to look his way.

"Ah...all right, then! I was gonna dive right into more AR matches after school, anyway. Now, it seems I won't need to look for opponents because they'll be lining up instead!"

"See what I mean?" Tallyhawk smiled (and was rather cute when she did so). "You'll have a good chance of reaching the max level and getting one of the Special Numbers that way."

"The universe really is revolving around me." Rover rubbed his hands, snickering in a dastardly fashion. "Gwa-ha-haa!"

"Gwa-ha-haa!" Quintegrity mimicked, but far more adorable than Rover.

Adele frowned at her brother. "*Someone's* full of himself."

"There's one more thing." Tallyhawk's smirk segued into a flatter, more serious expression.

"Oh yeah?" Rover looked at her.

"I challenge you to an AR match in *Glove Alien Fight*. I want to see those crazy Glove Aliens of yours."

The statement was nowhere close to a grand proclamation, but some students had been listening to the conversation between Tallyhawk and Rover, the star of the latest internet sensation. Rover looked around, annoyed by the eager faces awaiting his response to the challenge.

I've been getting a lot of attention these days, and it's gonna keep getting worse. What a pain...but I guess it isn't too bad.

He snickered. "You'll lose all of your consumable items just to get another look at my weapon? I might not even use it."

"Believe what you want."

"Sure. I'll accept. Five o'clock today at Gwoid Park."

"Consider it done," she said.

Right away, the excited whispers kicked up around them:

"Rover's doing another match!"

"Gwoid Park at five!"

"I'm gonna be there!"

Hearing the buzz made Lumpy chuckle. "Dude, sounds like you already have an audience."

"Whatever," Rover replied, shrugging. "Let's go, or we'll be late for authenticity class."

"Isn't this just greeeaat?" Olaf's spear of sarcasm pierced straight through the flurry of whispers as he walked up to Rover, his eyes rolling like they were about to be unscrewed from their sockets. "Joining the Super Club really *doesn't* make you into a celebrity, I guess."

When Rover caught a glimpse of Daremont's beaming face through the crowd, he winced in anticipation for what was coming next.

"Ack!" He grabbed Quintegrity's arm. "Run away! Pun incoming!"

Luckily, they made their escape before Daremont could ruin their lives with wordplay punishment.

10!10@10#10$10%10^10&10*10(10)10_10+10

"You gotta be getting worried," Lumpy told Rover while they were in the Super Club penthouse. With Adele, they played standard three-player co-op *Glove Alien Fight* in the living room.

"About what?" Rover asked, having his character dodge a boulder thrown by the large Troll they battled. "About Tallyhawk? She's going down after this meeting."

"I'm talking about the attention you're getting," Lumpy said.

"Not really. It's a little annoying, but I think I'll get used to it. I only got famous because my match against Graphite was the first big AR battle that a lot of people recorded."

Lumpy charged a pillow attack with his character's Snoozing Glove Aliens and pummeled the Troll in the face, putting it to sleep.

"Don't sell yourself short, man," he told Rover. "Even Benedict said you were really good. If not for him saying that, your popularity wouldn't have gotten so big. And it's gonna keep going, I think."

"Yeah, maybe."

Using the Hardboiled Glove Aliens, Adele landed the final blow on the Troll, earning the three of them experience points and glass coins. She looked toward the kitchen, seeing Quintegrity rushing around, her movements like a blur while finishing the last batch of chocolates for the previous fundraiser, Operation Chocolatier Action Punch.

"She really doesn't need our help," Adele said. "It's like we're wasting our time here." Running her hand along the couch cushions she sat on, she smiled. "Not like I'm mad about easy club credits, though."

Lumpy put his phone down, rubbing his eyes. "Man, that Troll was a heck of a boss we just beat." He looked at Rover. "We need to think of a fundraiser idea now. Something that'll make enough money to challenge Benedict."

With his phone on his lap, gazing at the high ceiling full of pretty chandeliers, Rover said, "We don't need to raise it all with just one fundraiser."

"True." Lumpy stretched and yawned. "It'd save us time if we did, though."

"We should do a café thing!" Adele suggested, getting fired up. "Something like what you and Quinn did for dinner the other night, but do it restaurant-style here at school!"

Rover grunted. "The Buffoon Club did that last year and almost burned down half the commissary building. The lunch lady strike happened because of that! Those ladies get *scary* when the hairnets come off!"

"Yeah," Lumpy said, feeling queasy, "that lunch lady strike was *tragic*."

"Oh, we're better than those buffoonish goons," Adele chuckled, waving her hand dismissively. "Besides, Quinn will be with us."

Quintegrity ran into the living room, appearing before them practically like a lightning strike.

"I think it's a lovely idea!" she told them, her hands in the air over her head. "Let's do it!"

Rover and Lumpy waved away the ozone from Quintegrity's shocking appearance, and they looked at each other with shrugs.

"Sure," they said in unison, smiling.

Quintegrity brandished a notebook and pen from nowhere and slammed them on the sea-marble coffee table. She gave the other club members a big smile.

"Come up with some menu ideas. I gotta finish these chocolates before the radiation levels get too high."

"*R-Radiation?*" Rover peeked into the kitchen where strange machines were, like, machining.

The girl nodded. "Yep! Like I said, only the wackiest and potentially deadly equipment can handle the workload required to make my candies!"

With Quintegrity back in the kitchen, Rover looked at the notebook she'd placed on the coffee table.

"Uh, let's stick to normal food cooked normally," he said, a single bead of sweat running down his face. "Those appliances scare me..."

"Come on." Adele pouted. "Just *one* weird item that requires some of the crazy things in our kitchen here."

"Lunch lady strike," Rover muttered. "I don't wanna piss them off again."

"We won't burn the place down!"

"Lunch. Lady. Strike."

Adele crossed her arms. However, during her flashbacks, she realized Rover had a point. So much Worcestershire sauce everywhere...so many cinnamon rolls laid out in various places for unsuspecting students...all the egg yolk chokers and butter bombs and carrot catacombs and muffin missiles...

"Okay," Adele said as her spine turned to ice, "normal cooking appliances will be fine. Hey, TV-*chan!*"

The 254-cm television winked on, responding with an irate female voice that squawked, "What?"

"Play the new episode of *Magical Poodle Snickerdoodle*," Adele told TV-*chan.* "I need to get caught up on it."

"Fine."

"Hey!" Rover gave Adele a dirty look. "Don't watch TV. We're doing more co-op after this meeting so I can level up before my match."

Adele propped her feet up on the clover-plaid ottoman. "You leveled up three times from that Troll. I think you're making good progress." She turned up the volume on TV-*chan*.

"Uh, hey," Lumpy said, holding up his notebook, "we're not playing games or watching TV, guys."

Rover ignored him. He gripped his phone, trying to keep his head in the game. "You know what, Adele? Let me—"

"'He's the number one poodle in all the woooorld!'" Adele drowned out Rover's words by reciting the show's introduction as it blared through the thirty-four speakers in the living room. "'Magical Poodle Snickerdoodle is the poodle to know! Together with his trusty owner, Goober McDubious, *things wiiiiill get done!*'"

"I love this show," Lumpy said.

"I guess it's okay," Rover muttered as he battled a Demon Dinosaur by himself.

"But, we're in a club meeting right now!"

Rover ignored Lumpy again.

I gotta level up more, he thought, using his coveted Beelzebub Glove Aliens to quickly bring down the Demon Dinosaur. *If I'm gonna be this widely known...then I gotta be the best I can be.*

He took a second to wipe his palms on his pants—they were sweaty.

ROVER... Lvl 701

All Money... {T}35,000

Allowance... {T}35,000
Fundraiser... {T}0

<<EXPENSE GOALS>>

Benedict's Payment... {T}100,000
Anti-Grav Skateboard... {T}499,999

<<CURRENT EQUIPMENT>>

Gloves... Beelzebub
Armor... Ape Laser
Acc.1... Dowdy Cape
Acc.2... Meme Template

<<SPECIAL NUMBERS>>

① ② ③ ④ ⑤

⑥ ⑦ ⑧ ⑨ ⑩

SURVIVAL OF THE MOST BADASS

GWOID **Park** was one of the many forgettable parks throughout Thugwood, complete with all of the obligatory features that parks come with: a children's playground, a laser tennis court, a cricket palace, a concession booth, a grassy field, and a riverside dock (along the Megms River in this case).

Rover, Quintegrity, Lumpy, and Adele took the bus to the Gwoid Park stop. Through the bus window, Lumpy saw the congregation of people ready with their phones and tablets.

"There's a crowd," Lumpy told the others. "Looks like...um, about forty or fifty people. I know parks get crowded on weekends, but it's only Feefee-*day*."

"Hmph." Rover shrugged, only glancing out the window.

Something soft and warm grabbed his hand. He looked at Quintegrity sitting next to him as she gave his fingers a gentle squeeze. When she brushed aside her rose petal lemonade hair, the boy made a connection with her soft mulberry eyes.

Sensing the spark from this connection, she said, "Don't be scared, Rover!"

"I-I'm not scared."

"You look nervous, though." The girl pulled him closer, pressing her soft body against his arm.

That's because you're rubbing all up on me!!! Rover thought as his face got hot.

"I'm fine, really," he told her, looking away.

She gripped his biceps. "Ooh...have you always been in this good of shape?"

"Uhh..."

Then she squeezed very, *very* hard.

"*Ow!*"

"Mwa-ha-ha-haa! You're still a softy, though."

As soon as Rover, Quintegrity, Lumpy, and Adele got off the bus, they were approached by two teenagers they had never met before.

"Hey, it's Rover Chork!" the tubby teen boy said. "We heard about your match against that belt-suited ninja chick, Tallyhawk, so we came all the way from Northish to check it out."

Rover raised his eyebrows, somewhat surprised. "All the way from the Northish Prefecture to Southbound? That's pretty far."

The stick-necked teen patted his tubby buddy on the shoulder, saying, "We wanted to see you in action, Rover. Anything to get a glimpse of those wild Glove Aliens you had."

A group of all ages flocked up. Among them, minus the starstruck expression, was Tallyhawk Kusumegido. She walked up to Rover, her smartphone in her hand.

"You're late," she said, traces of a scowl on her face.

Rover glanced at the nearby street clock. "Meh, by less than ten minutes." He started up *Glove Alien Fight* on his phone. "All the more reason to get this underway quickly, I guess."

The bystanders activated their augmented reality functions on their devices, letting them see Rover's and Tallyhawk's game avatars in the environment. Rover held his breath as he watched the onscreen roulette toggle through "Deathmatch," "Ring Finder," and "Strongest Hero."

"'Ring Finder' has been selected," Tallyhawk said when the roulette stopped.

"Again, huh?" Rover mumbled. He heard the whispering chatter from the crowd. "There are a lot more people here for this match. I wonder how many Ring Hiders will participate this time."

"We'll see," Lumpy said, tapping the "Yes" button on his phone screen to opt in as a Ring Hider. The bagel-like gold ring appeared in his avatar's hands. "Anyway, I'll just drop mine right here next to you."

"We can't," Adele told him as she read the game instructions on her phone. "We can't drop them within twenty metres of the players' starting position."

Lumpy sighed. "Sorry, man, I tried to make it easier for you."

"It's a good rule," Rover replied, "otherwise it'd be too easy."

Looking at his girlfriend, however, Rover thought of their advantage: Quintegrity could somehow see the AR elements without the proper technology.

The game developers didn't want it to be too easy...but here I am with Quintegrity...and...

Oblivious to Rover's unease, Quintegrity smiled at him, alleviating some of his doubt. While the onscreen number of Ring Hiders ticked up (over forty at this point), she moved closer to him, getting his attention with her calming expression.

"You know," she said in a delicate, soothing voice only Rover could hear, "if people find out my secret, they'll think you're cheating."

Rover's lips pursed into a thin line. "Way to ease my worries."

"You said on the bus you weren't scared."

"...That was on the *bus*..."

"You'll do fine, babe."

Cheating, huh? Rover opened his character's equipment setup, seeing his Beelzebub Glove Aliens. *People are gonna have their suspicions, no doubt.*

Fifty-six Ring Hiders altogether joined in. Rover scanned the bystanders, trying to memorize as many of them as he could as the first countdown started. The crowd scattered as the fifty-six Ring Hiders chased after their avatars, Lumpy and Adele included. Both Rover and Tallyhawk kept their eyes on as many of them as possible, watching where they were going.

"Good luck, bud!" Lumpy called as he took off.

"Kick her butt, Big Bro!" Adele chimed in before dashing off in her own direction.

It seems pretty easy to rig these Ring Finder matches beforehand, Rover thought, taking a mental note of the Ring Hiders' directions. *If I got a group of supporters, we could determine the ring locations ahead of time, giving me an idea of what route to take when the match starts.*

He looked at Tallyhawk, whose blank expression surveyed the area.

I don't know anything about Tallyhawk's character... She's not a blabbermouth like Graphite, so I don't know how her Clairvoyant Radar compares to mine. Since that last match, I only leveled mine up once, putting it at seven out of ten without the Hound Doggo Shnozz equipped, and level eight with it.

Quintegrity watched over Rover's shoulder as he equipped his game character with equipment to boost his speed, dexterity, and clairvoyance. The carefree look on the girl's face annoyed the boy more than it relaxed him.

"Just so you know," he said to his girlfriend, "I don't plan to show my Beelzebub Glove Aliens this time. We need to make sure to get as many rings as possible and avoid another tie. I don't want another sudden death round again."

"You can count on me!" she replied, standing tall and proud, thumping her chest once with her fist. She ran to a tall ashafras tree and climbed it with remarkable elegance and nimbleness, perching on the highest branch to get a look around.

"What is she doing?" Tallyhawk asked, looking at Quintegrity with suspicion.

Sneering, Rover replied, "Being my girlfriend."

The belt-clad girl stared at Rover. "I think there's more to it than that."

"Our relationship is our own," Rover told her with an upturned nose. "What it means for her being my girlfriend isn't your business."

Tallyhawk chuckled, running her hand through her crow-feathered hair and toying with her ear.

"It's obvious that she's checking things out for you," she said, keeping her eyes on Rover. "Probably watching the Ring Hiders to tell you where they went."

Rover didn't say anything, only smiling and shrugging. He watched Quintegrity leap from the ashafras top branch, land on one foot, and point toward the children's playground.

5...4...3...2...1...

START!

The remaining spectators cheered, and the match began.

As expected, Tallyhawk's avatar headed in the direction where Quintegrity had pointed. Her avatar was fast, but not quite as fast as Rover's. Immediately, Rover scrolled through his list of consumable items.

I only have one of these, he thought, selecting the item, *so I gotta make it count!*

Through her phone screen, Tallyhawk watched Rover's character don a winged jetpack and a goose head helmet before it blasted off into the sky.

"Tch!" Tallyhawk clutched her phone with irritation. "He has a Goosepack."

Rover sprinted after his soaring character, doing his best to control it from his disadvantageous position on the ground. Through his phone, he saw the first gold bagel on top of a slide and clumsily swooped his character down to nab it, making the character smash facedown into the ground. After the character made a comical face-smash animation, Rover noticed some of his HP had been depleted from the rough landing.

"Damn, that hurt me," he grunted as he ran to catch up with the avatar. He controlled it to scamper up the slide where it munched on the bagel. "I still got it, though."

"Yeah, Rover!" Adele cheered, having made it back from hiding her ring. The other bystanders cheered as well.

Seeing Tallyhawk's avatar lagging behind, Rover had his own avatar blast off again before he could catch up to it. Another radar pulse gave him a glimpse of a ring resting on top of the playground's jungle gym, and he steered his flying character toward it.

It's hard to steer the Goosepack from my perspective...but I think I got the hang of this now!

People watched the goose-powered character fly in a stable trajectory overhead, its honking heard through the dozens of phones and tablets tuned in to the event. Rover's lungs warmed up as he sprinted, but his body didn't feel tired, instead embracing the workout.

All that aggressive training in the pool is paying off...

Tallyhawk lagged behind her slower character, jogging to save her stamina. As she watched Rover's avatar descend and cling to the side of the jungle gym, a rush of adrenaline pushed a grin onto her face.

She steadied her finger, ready to tap an onscreen button.

"Wait for it..." she said to herself. "And...got you!"

She tapped her phone screen. Her character stopped running, its hands sparking with electricity, indicating the Zappy Glove Aliens were equipped, and it shot a ball of glowing light straight into the sky.

In a second, a virtual lightning bolt struck the jungle gym. Although the real-life metal bars and poles didn't conduct the AR lightning, Rover's character was close enough to be blasted to the ground.

"Crap!" Rover saw his character's HP damage. However, the *true* damage was the Paralysis status effect inflicted by the electrical attack. "My character's paralyzed from that! It can't move!"

Up close, Rover spotted the tiny in-game object sticking up from the ground in the middle of the jungle gym—a Frightening Rod. After its one use, it disappeared.

He clenched his teeth, seeing Tallyhawk's avatar leap onto the jungle gym and climb toward the gold ring. He glared at the crow-haired girl who wore a small smirk.

"You set this up ahead of time, didn't you?" he snapped. "Whoever put that ring up there told you they were going to, and you knew to put your Frightening Rod there!"

Tallyhawk didn't say anything, only shrugging and smiling, mimicking Rover's smug response for her earlier accusation that Quintegrity was helping him locate rings.

11!11@11#11$11%11^11&11*11(11)11_11+11

Across Gwoid Park, a mustachioed man watched Rover's avatar take the lightning hit. He had a novelty telescope held up to his phone's camera, watching the augmented reality action from afar.

Laughing, he pulled his fake mustache off to readjust it, then toyed with the small communication device in his ear.

"Good call, Tallyhawk," he said, adjusting the wig on his head. "Setting up those Frightening Rods and having us place the rings by them was a good idea."

Tallyhawk's voice came through the disguised guy's earpiece. "Your suspicions might be correct, Graphite. Rover's girlfriend seems to play dirty...so we're gonna do the same."

"It ain't dirty because it's not against the rules," Graphite replied, watching Tallyhawk's avatar devour the gold bagel on the jungle gym. "It's strategy and survival of the most badass. We're just giving them a taste of their own piss."

"Right you are."

Graphite directed his telescope to another corner of Gwoid Park. The meathead boy, Isho Eep, was wearing a similar fake mustache and wig, and he indicated to Graphite with a thumbs-up. From the top of the large Gwoid Park Welcome Centre, another similarly disguised person—the cross-eyed boy Hodge Dipcringle—also gave Graphite a thumbs-up.

"I saw some people drop their rings southeast of you, Tallyhawk," Hodge said through the communication earpieces, holding his tablet camera up to his own novelty telescope. "You'll be able to get a few in a short timeframe."

"I'm on it," Tallyhawk replied, her avatar hopping down from the jungle gym. "With my Clairvoyant Radar only at level 3, you guys need to lead me to victory."

"We've got eyes and ears all over this park," Graphite said, sending his message to his three pals. "Quinn Integrity isn't gonna give Rover the upper hand this time."

He knelt and grabbed his cup of sparkling tea purchased from a tea and bacon vending machine, then took a sip, frowning.

"Although...her sparkling tea is way better than this sludge."

11!11@11#11$11%11^11&11*11(11)11_11+11

"Aww, your little game dude is all twitchy, Rover."

"It's the Paralysis status effect," Rover growled, not looking at his girlfriend. His hands trembled from anger. "I can't do anything until it wears off after a minute, and my Goosepack will be out of time before that happens. Until then, I need a favor from you."

Quintegrity's face lit up. "Sure! Anything at all!"

"Before that lightning attack hit me," Rover told her, "there was an in-game object under the jungle gym called a Frightening Rod. Do you remember seeing it?"

"Yep! I didn't know what it was."

"I need you to find as many as you can. They're probably close to other rings, just like this one was." He glanced around, irritated. "I bet Graphite's crew rigged this. If that's the case, then there're probably more Frightening Rods."

"Aye! I'll keep my eye out for them!"

"Ha-ha! That's why I can count on you, Quintegrity."

To Rover's surprise, the girl became bashful, kicking at the dirt under her feet as she clasped her hands behind her back.

"Oh gawrsh!" she replied, giving Rover big doe eyes that made him temporarily forget the match he was in. "You flatter me, Rover!"

She hugged him, making him slump in her embrace as his joints failed to keep him upright.

"Pathetic," Adele snickered from behind.

Lumpy said to Rover, "So, Tallyhawk must've had things arranged before the match. That was a nasty trick."

"Not 'nasty,'" Rover told him, smirking, "but 'clever.' If I wanna stand a chance to keep winning these matches, then we'll need to up our cleverness, too."

Lumpy smiled at Rover's devious expression. "I knew you'd say something like that."

A small sound effect came from Rover's phone, alerting him that the Paralysis effect on his character had worn off.

"Time to go!" he said as his character hopped to its feet.

"This way!" Quintegrity said, leading the way. "I'll tell you when you get to a booby-trapped ring, so just go after them as usual!"

"Got it!" Rover replied.

They chased after Rover's character as the crowd cheered on.

ROVER... Lvl 703

All Money... {T}35,000

Allowance... {T}35,000
Fundraiser... {T}0

<<EXPENSE GOALS>>

Benedict's Payment... {T}100,000
Anti-Grav Skateboard... {T}499,999

<<CURRENT EQUIPMENT>>

Gloves... Butler
Armor... Ape Laser
Acc.1... Shyster's Shoes
Acc.2... Hound Doggo Shnozz

<<SPECIAL NUMBERS>>

① ② ③ ④ ⑤

⑥ ⑦ ⑧ ⑨ ⑩

NUCLEAR REACTOR HEART

"SEVEN rings down." Tallyhawk snickered as her character gobbled another bagel. She spoke into her communication earpiece, "Rover may be faster, but if he doesn't know which rings are booby-trapped, then two more paralyzing strikes should keep him behind me. If he's careful to look for Frightening Rods by each ring, that'll also slow him down."

Hiding on top of the Welcome Centre, Hodge used his cheap telescope to watch Rover's actions across the park.

"Rover's heading into the tightest cluster of rings by the dockside souvenir strip," he said to the others through his communication earpiece. "He also hasn't used any more Goosepacks, so I think he's out."

Isho stalked Rover and his team, staying close to the park buildings and shrubbery, using his own cheap telescope with his phone's AR camera.

"Quinn must've tipped him off to those rings' locations," Isho said. "She was running all around, but I can't imagine she'd remember the details of that many Ring Hiders. The three of us versus *only her* works in our favor."

"What about Rover's friend and sister?" Hodge asked, seeing them tagging alongside Rover.

"Clueless nitwits," Isho replied. "They probably left the ring scouting up to Quinn. Bystanders and Ring Hiders can't use their Clairvoyant Radar to find the rings—only the competitors can. If the friend and sister know what we're up to, they still can't do anything if they don't know where the rings are."

"Excellent," Graphite replied, following Rover and staying just out of sight. "The other two Frightening Rods are that way, too. We'll let you know when he gets close to one, Tallyhawk."

"Roger that," she said. She controlled her character to climb a streetlamp where another ring was tied with an in-game item called a Heavy Duty Licorice. "I have a nearly unlimited attack range to hit him with the lightning. With him out, I'll circle around and get most of the rings from where he is."

Her avatar split the eighth ring, smearing the cream cheese-like stuff on it and devouring it.

"You know," Graphite said through the earpiece, "that plan is a stretch. I know how Rover is...and he'll be tough to predict."

"I know that." Tallyhawk's character leapt from the streetlamp, and she chased it to the next ring. "That's why I'm sticking with my original goal...even if I lose the match, I want to see Rover's crazy Glove Aliens again."

"That's bold," Graphite told her, "but it's *your* consumable items on the line."

After a moment of silence, Tallyhawk answered, "Yeah, but whatever. In the end, Rover's the one who'll be facing Benedict Torrent. No way am I bothering with *that* guy in a match."

12!12@12#12$12%12^12&12*12(12)12_12+12

"Avast!"

Quintegrity's shout caught Rover off guard. She leapt in front of him from around a corner, nearly making the boy drop his phone.

"What?" he demanded, clutching his chest. "Don't scare me like that!"

She pointed, keeping her voice low as not to be heard by the bystanders. "The ring by the drinking fountains has one of those Frightening Rods by it. You can't see it from here, but you can save time if you skip that one."

"Awesome," Rover replied.

Lumpy looked around them. There were over twenty people watching Rover, but nobody who looked like Graphite's crew.

"They'll suspect something after this," Lumpy muttered to the others as they hurried to the next ring.

"Let 'em," Rover told him. "We'll just have to stay one step ahead of them!"

The Clairvoyant Radar indicated a hefty number of rings were inside the Gwoid Park cricket palace. Being a simple cricket palace open to the public for people to play cricket games, it was a much smaller field than the professional palaces. By no means, though, was it a very small place.

"Onward!" Quintegrity shouted from in front; she hadn't even broken a sweat from running. "To that big building up ahead, ye scurvy scoundrels! There be hidden treasures aplenty! Nineteen rings, but one is booby-trapped—the last rigged ring!"

Despite the physical strain, Rover pushed to run even faster as he, Quintegrity, Lumpy, and Adele hurried to the cricket palace.

12!12@12#12$12%12^12&12*12(12)12_12+12

Isho kept his distance behind Rover's group, not only to stay hidden (despite wearing a half-convincing fake mustache and wig), but because he was getting tired. He gasped and wheezed, slowing his pace to a trudging gallop as he caught his breath.

"How...the...hell...?" he choked, wiping his sweaty, bald head with his handkerchief. "...They're *fast*..."

"Isho and Graphite, we need you to keep a visual on them," Hodge said, peering through his novelty telescope and tablet camera. "Even from my position up here, I can't see everything. I lost them right now."

Isho gulped down a few breaths before replying. "They're heading...to the cricket palace." His shoes dragged on the ground with every tired step.

"The cricket palace?" Graphite jogged across the park, his cup of sparkling tea sloshing under the lid. "Wait...does that mean...?"

"They avoided the rigged ring by the drinking fountains," Isho said, wiping the sweat from his brow. "I saw them stop, talk about something really quick, and Quinn pointed to the drinking fountain...and then they headed away from it."

"Completely avoided it, huh?" Graphite clicked his tongue.

"Yeah," Isho continued, "and I'm pretty sure they couldn't get a visual on the well-hidden Frightening Rod next to it from their position...almost like they already knew..."

Grunting, Graphite shouted, "The hell does that mean?!" Some people looked at him questioningly, not seeing the small communication earpiece he spoke into. "Hmm...do you copy that, Tallyhawk?"

Tallyhawk controlled her avatar to swim across a small artificial pond where a ring was "floating on" the water.

"I heard..." she muttered, claiming the bagel. Turning her gaze toward the big cricket palace building, she shook her head. "It doesn't make any sense."

"Very strange," Hodge added. From atop the Welcome Centre, he saw Rover and Quintegrity sprinting toward the palace, Lumpy and Adele struggling to keep up behind them. "I see Rover's group. They're heading there now."

"We'll see how they react to the last booby-trapped ring in there," Graphite said, stopping for a moment to catch his breath. "If we can't learn anything new about Rover's crazy Glove Aliens...then we might learn something else about how he operates!"

12!12@12#12$12%12^12&12*12(12)12_12+12

The Gwoid Park cricket palace was unmentionable in comparison to other park cricket palaces. The playing field was mostly hard dirt with well-kept grass around the sides, all surrounded by bleachers with a maximum seating capacity of five thousand people.

Rover nabbed a ring close to the palace's main entrance.

"Go that way!" Quintegrity told him, pointing down the walkway along the top of the bleachers. "Get the three down there, then head into the bleachers for a bunch more. I'll go scout the place to find them all."

When Rover took off, Quintegrity turned to the entrance. Lumpy was leaning against the wall, gasping for air. Adele was lying flat on her back.

"Poor things!" Quintegrity said. "Let me get you something to drink before the dehydration monster claims your lives."

"Thanks…" Lumpy's voice was practically a dusty rasp.

A nearby vending machine dispensed two big bottles of artificial water after Quintegrity swiped her Mythril credit card. She handed them to Lumpy and Adele, who gulped the water down.

"How's Rover doing?" Lumpy asked, looking toward the cricket palace interior.

Quintegrity held her hands behind her back, looking into the palace from the main entrance.

"He's doing wonderful," she said. Turning back to Lumpy, she tilted her head as her smile widened. "I gotta go help him out. You two should take it easy."

"Don't worry about us," Lumpy said, forcing a grin on his burning, sweating face. "We'll just stay *right here…*"

12!12@12#12$12%12^12&12*12(12)12_12+12

"Got that one!" Rover pumped his fist in the air as his avatar munched another gold bagel in the bleachers.

"The next ones are in different rows all around there!" Quintegrity told him, gesturing toward the bleachers with dramatic, theatrical arm movements, as if she was confessing her undying loyalty to the remaining rings in the seating area.

Rover scanned the seats with his phone's AR camera, seeing numerous twinkles with the Clairvoyant Radar. "A lot of people sure aren't original with their hiding spots, huh?"

Quintegrity hopped from seat to seat, row to row, like a ballerina dancing to funky, jiggy concertos.

Hop. Spin. Hop. Spin.

Clap! Clap! Stomp!

Hop. Spin. Hop. Spin.

Stomp! Stomp! Chomp!

Jazz hands!

While she did this, Rover rushed from one ring to the next, taking the bleacher stairs and aisles while commanding his game character to nimbly jump and flip over the chairs. It was like the character was inspired by the groovy vibes Quintegrity filled the place with.

He looked around as his character ate another ring. Among the few dozen spectators cheering him on, he couldn't see Tallyhawk or anyone else in Graphite's crew.

"Hey, Quintegrity!" he called.

"Hmm?" The girl stopped in the middle of a pirouette, balancing perfectly on her toes atop a bleacher seat.

Rover beckoned to her, and she ran along the top of the seats, making her way to him.

"Where's that rigged ring?" he asked her.

"In front of the men's restroom on the northwest side," she replied, pointing across the cricket palace field. "Save yourself the trip of going all the way over there."

"Sweet. Are there any others in here?"

"One other, by the side entrance with the butterfly cage."

"That's pretty close." He wiped the sweat from his forehead. "Man…I'm getting worn out."

"Forge forth, Rover!"

"Ha! Didn't plan on doing otherwise. Let's go!"

A large cage full of exotic butterflies known as Mondo Butters was by the cricket palace's side entrance. Their wingspans measured over seventy centimetres across as they fluttered around as delicately as the big-ass bugs could for something their size.

When Rover reached the entrance, he looked around through his phone camera, his throat parched from the workout.

"I don't see it," he said. "Are you sure it's here?"

Quintegrity put her finger on her chin as she thought. "Yes. It was right here."

A girl's shout broke the silence. "That's because I got it first!"

Movement appeared on Rover's screen—Tallyhawk's avatar slid in from the side entrance. Gunshots rang from numerous AR devices as the spectators watched Rover lose most of his HP.

He had his character duck and take cover inside the restroom vestibule.

"Dual pistols," Rover murmured, using an in-game Potion to restore his HP. He glanced at his girlfriend. "Tallyhawk has the Hardboiled Glove Aliens."

"Are they egg-launching pistols?"

"N-No...they use six-shot revolvers." He used a consumable item called a Ramen Candle Firework, staving off his opponent with sparkly booms. "Her weapon has a strong attack and long range, but has limited ammo and is hard to aim...thankfully, she missed over half her shots."

Tallyhawk rounded the corner, holding an ice cold bottle of Suki Yuki Snow Juice to her sweaty face, which was flushed enough to be noticed on her dark skin. She had her character stand back to avoid the raucous razzle dazzle from Rover's item.

"Well then," Rover sneered, standing in the middle of the in-game fireworks. "You caught up to me."

The belt-clad girl popped the tab on her Suki Yuki Snow Juice and chugged some of the refreshing drink.

"I was collecting my own rings somewhere else," she replied, speaking over the firework sound effects coming from everyone's phones and tablets, "so don't act like you're winning."

Rover checked the number of rings he had.

Under half of the total. Damn...I really might be losing, depending on how many Tallyhawk has. But there are more than ten minutes left.

Rover's Clairvoyant Radar detected some more rings outside the cricket palace. Before the Ramen Candle Firework animation slowed and dimmed, Rover selected another consumable item. His avatar darted from the restroom and threw it at the opponent.

An AR explosion knocked Tallyhawk's avatar away. Deadly digital flares of every color ricocheted throughout the cricket palace walkway, growing faster, their numbers multiplying by the second.

Tallyhawk squeaked from terror, instinctively running herself out of the palace alongside her avatar, fleeing from the firework finale. "Nope! I ain't messing with a Mortar Kombat Surprise!"

Meanwhile, Rover's character was trapped in a bathroom stall as the raging firework storm thundered around it. Along the palace walkway, Quintegrity was prancing and rave dancing in the colorful storm.

"Well, this plan *backfired*." Rover sighed as he stood outside the restroom stall where his character took shelter. "I'm wasting precious time here!"

When the raving ricochets waned, he hurried on to continue the match.

12!12@12#12$12%12^12&12*12(12)12_12+12

Isho's voice came through Tallyhawk's communication earpiece. "He left one in the palace."

"I know," she replied, glancing back at the cricket palace as she jogged away.

"Quinn knew where it was," Isho said into the communicator as he stood in the bleachers. "She told him when Rover asked where the 'rigged' one was."

"Damn them..." Graphite said, listening in on the conversation from outside. He watched Rover and Quintegrity hurry out of the cricket palace. "That Quinn Integrity is *good...*"

"That's not all," Isho said, heading back up the bleacher steps toward the walkway through the cricket palace. By now, the Mortar Kombat Surprise effect had expired. "I got here in time to see her run around to look for the rings."

"But," Hodge said, "she shouldn't be able to see them with her device. She's not a competitor in the match."

Graphite thought for a second. "Jailbroken or hacked devices *might* make that possible. *Might.*"

"Maybe." Isho stopped walking, as if preparing himself for what he was about to say. "But...she wasn't using a phone or tablet...or anything else, from what I could tell."

"Maybe she had AR holovision goggles," Hodge said. Through his cheap telescope, he noticed Rover and Quintegrity running across the park. "The newest ones use hologram technology to display the augmented reality. They can be pretty discreet. Apparently, standard VR headsets can be used, too, and are preferable because they're cheaper than AR holovision goggles and provide a behind-the-character third-person view of the game."

"I don't know..." Isho replied, making it to the top of the bleacher steps. "I didn't see her use anything like that..."

Outside, Graphite leaned against a chain link fence to adjust his wig and fake mustache.

"Maybe we're missing something," he said almost in a whisper, losing sight of Rover and Quintegrity as they continued the game, "...because seeing the AR without a device is impossible."

Frustrated, he tossed his empty paper cup in a waste bin.

12!12@12#12$12%12^12&12*12(12)12_12+12

Outside Gwoid Park, just across the street, the warm breeze blew Quintegrity's long, rose petal lemonade-colored hair as she occupied the top of the tall building of Ed's Alphabet Pet Store. When Rover claimed the last ring in the immediate area, she hopped from the roof and bounced off the awning, scaring two elderly ladies who were pushing shopping carts full of alphabet pets and grammar crackers.

When the girl approached her boyfriend, he was staring at his phone, grumbling.

"That's all for this area, Rover!" Quintegrity told him.

"Hrrrmm...I still have under half of the rings."

Quintegrity saw the boy's downtrodden reaction.

"Sorry," she said. "It's a lot for me to keep track of. I don't want to scare people by moving too fast."

"Uh...it's too late for that..."

"*But!*" Her grin widened as she pushed her face so close to Rover's that his eyelashes fluttered from her unrestrained peppiness. She pointed her finger toward the distance. "There's one more ring I could find from my spot on the alphabet pet store!"

Rover looked through his phone. "Up in that tree?"

"Nope. Beyond that."

Using both his phone and just his eyes, Rover followed Quintegrity's finger.

"But...the only thing farther than that...is that skyscraper...waaay across town."

"Yep! It's got that pointy peak on the top. I see there's a gold ring dangling from it."

"*Are you frickin' kidding me*?!"

She giggled. "Frick no!"

"Gah!"

The Clairvoyant Radar pulsed on Rover's phone, but it did no good.

"Yeah," he grunted, scowling at his phone, "of course it's too far to see with my Clairvoyant Radar." He stared at the skyscraper and scratched his head of freshly mined coal-colored hair. "Never mind getting up there, but someone actually made it that far in the two-minute time limit given to Ring Hiders! Unless they drove...or something...but their game characters would need a vehicle, too...which isn't impossible..."

"I'll do better to keep track of the Ring Hiders next time," Quintegrity said, flexing her biceps. "Now I know how much effort must go into these matches! I'll unleash my nuclear reactor heart!"

Although her biceps looked average as she flexed, Rover suspected she could fold a crowbar between her arm muscles.

He smiled at her, swept away by her unwavering motivation.

Her determination reminds me of how I get when playing video games, he thought.

12!12@12#12$12%12^12&12*12(12)12_12+12

Gasping for breath, Rover jogged toward the laser tennis court where Quintegrity had found two more rings. His shoes dragged in the grass while his avatar was far ahead and climbing the chain link fence to get inside the court.

Time's almost up. If I can just get two more, that'll give me twenty-five of the fifty-six rings. Not quite half, but it's possible Tallyhawk didn't get the others. Maybe I'll have a shot at winning...

However, Tallyhawk was already in the laser tennis court, and through his phone, Rover saw the crow-haired girl's avatar munching on the gold ring.

"Dammit!" Rover spat, hardly having the breath to curse out loud.

There are a lot of people around. I don't want to give them any more footage of my Beelzebub Glove Aliens, but one ring might make the difference!

A realization dawned on him.

Actually, I might benefit from this exposure. Many of these people are here to see me in action. If I use the same attack as last time, then I'm not showing anyone anything new, but still giving them what they want. Damn show business!

Rover's character climbed over the fence and landed in the court. Tallyhawk noticed.

The Clairvoyant Radar gave Rover a fleeting glimpse of the ring's location.

I can see the ring! It's closer to her than me. Her character is slower than mine, but that won't help me now.

His shaky, sweaty right index finger soared across his phone screen and scrolled through his equipment list, and his left thumb pushed the onscreen button to have his character charge toward the ring.

While running alongside Rover, Quintegrity watched his quick fingers on his screen. Rover selected the Beelzebub Glove Aliens, and his onscreen buttons changed to his new weapon's abilities, including Winter's Sepulcher.

Tap

Quintegrity stopped running, planting herself in place, her eyes wide and dazzled from the game effects. All of the spectators reacted similarly, some gasping, some cheering, but all mesmerized as their phone or tablet screens filled with virtual ice stalagmites and digital flurries of swirling glitter.

The crystalline icescape of Winter's Sepulcher lingered for several seconds, as if boasting and showing off its eye-catching glory before disappearing into AR nothingness. On the ground, in the virtual overlay of the laser tennis court, Tallyhawk's character lay as its health had been reduced to zero in a single hit of overkill.

Tallyhawk growled, staring at the onscreen aftermath in her trembling hands. She saw Rover's character with skeletal matter clumped around both hands with extra-boney knuckles and spurred fingers.

Still, she forced a smile. "Well…at least I got to see Rover's Glove Aliens up close again…"

The spectating crowd cheered Rover on as his character hurried to the final ring during the last few seconds of the match. He propped himself against the chain link fence, having a decent view from there, too tired to take another step. Sweat from his face dripped to the fence and grass.

While his character munched on the gold bagel-like ring, he fell to his knees with a grin just as the timer counted down and the match ended.

ROVER… Lvl 703

All Money… {T}35,000

Allowance… {T}35,000
Fundraiser… {T}0

<<EXPENSE GOALS>>

Benedict's Payment… {T}100,000
Anti-Grav Skateboard… {T}499,999

<<CURRENT EQUIPMENT>>

Gloves… Beelzebub
Armor… Ape Laser
Acc.1… Shyster's Shoes
Acc.2… Hound Doggo Shnozz

<<SPECIAL NUMBERS>>

① ② ③ ④ ⑤

⑥ ⑦ ⑧ ⑨ ⑩

<< 13 >>

CURB STOMPED BY DELICIOUSNESS

"**YOU** *lost*?!" Adele clutched her head. "How did you lose?!"

Rover sat on a swing in the Gwoid Park playground, staring at the dirt beneath him and gripping a bottle of mango-flavored Wisewater he'd bought. His hair and clothes were matted with sweat. Quintegrity stood behind him, massaging his shoulders, alleviating his woes.

"Tallyhawk had one more ring than me," he said with a sigh. "I knocked her character out, but it didn't end the match because no matter what, the player with the most rings after forty minutes wins."

Lumpy sat on the swing next to Rover, pushing himself back and forth with his feet on the ground. "Now you know to work that into your strategy."

"Yeah."

"Man," Adele murmured, "not only did you lose all your consumable items, but you didn't get any experience for the match."

"I know." Rover stared at his phone, the screen off. "Pretty much a huge waste of time. I need to reach level nine hundred ninety-nine as soon as possible to get a Special Number item...and face Benedict Torrent."

"So," Lumpy said, "that means you'll need to play as much *Glove Alien Fight* as possible at pretty much all times."

"No worries." Rover cracked his knuckles. "I have a plan to reach the maximum level as fast as I can." He stood up from the swing, straightening his back and clenching his fist, staring bravely into the distance. "I'm dropping out of school!!!"

That earned him a swift punch in the arm from his younger sister.

"*Hey!*"

"Don't be a dingleberry," Adele said in a flat tone. "School's more important."

"Maybe we can cheat the system," Lumpy suggested. "I'll face you in a bunch of AR matches and let you win each time."

"Won't work," Rover said, shaking his head. "You can only face the same person every ten matches." He chugged the rest of his Wisewater, letting out a refreshed, mango-scented breath. "Let's get something to eat. I worked up an appetite."

Quintegrity hopped with excitement. "Ooh! My favorite deli is close to here, so let's go there!"

Lumpy agreed. "Yeah, sounds good. You should take a break, Rover. You played hard today."

Smiling at the late afternoon-painted sky, Rover said, "I sure did. If anything, I give myself props for that."

13!13@13#13$13%13^13&13*13(13)13_13+13

Quintegrity showed Rover, Lumpy, and Adele the way to Me Luv Good Stuff Deli. Tantalizing aromas wafted out to the sidewalk as they entered, luring them in with the smells of baked bread, sliced meats, cut cheeses, coffee pies, spice-stuffed crumpet rolls, and cream-filled melon jellies. Long, glass cases were loaded with assorted goodies Rover had never heard of, many with names he couldn't pronounce. When he looked at the customers dining in the cozy chairs filling the quaint interior, he realized how fresh and tasty everything appeared.

"Prepare yourselves to be *curb stomped* by deliciousness!" Quintegrity told them. With a twisted grin, her face was scary enough to send shivers down the spine of people who weren't even in the building (which actually happened). "Put your mouth on the sandwich... Now say goodnight..."

She chomped down, making sure her bite was audible, then giggled.

"Uh..." Rover felt a drop of sweat roll down his cheek. "You aren't selling me on this place..." He looked at Adele and Lumpy, who each had their own single bead of sweat run down their cheeks.

The man behind the counter had hair like wilted ferns and a cleft chin, and he greeted Quintegrity with a big smile.

"Hey there, Miss Integrity! I was wondering when I'd see you again."

"Ahoy there, scalawag!" she replied, aiming her assault rifle-shaped purse at the man. "Keeping the business afloat?"

"Haven't burned it down, yet!"

"That'd be a disaster!"

"Don't tempt me!"

They laughed heartily.

Adele stared at them. "Um...is this their usual relationship?"

Lumpy shrugged. "Guess so."

"What'll it be, Quinn?" the deli worker asked.

"The usual sandwich, please!" She was way too excited and...*proud*?

The man sighed. "Really? I can't get you to try my other stuff?"

"Nope. You'll fail like the jabroni you are. I know what I want."

"Not even a *slight* change? You might discover a new favorite."

Quintegrity swung her hips in a rhythm as she rapped her answer:

"Turkey and bologna
In a deli matrimony
And no phony mortadella
You jabroni deli fella!"

The man chuckled and shook his head, rustling his wilted-fern hair. "Only you're allowed to insult me, Quinn."

Quintegrity cackled with her hands on her hips. "I have that kind of authority!"

They laughed heartily again.

The girl turned to Rover and the others.

"Get what you want, guys," she told them with a smile, unsheathing her Mythril credit card. "It's on me!"

"Thanks, Quintegrity," Rover replied, returning the smile.

Quintegrity pulled him close in a one-arm hug, giving him a flare-up of anxiety.

"I'm treating my boyfriend," she told the deli man. Her smile faded. "He needs to eat his sorrows away; he's suffering from a loss."

The man gave Rover a slight bow of solemn condolences. "I'm very sorry to hear that."

Rover's face twitched. "Hehhh... I-It's really not that serious..."

"Not all losses are created equal," the man replied. "It's best to take it for what it is—all of its pains and lessons—and keep moving on. That's how we get stronger."

Rover considered that.

It's totally out of context, he thought, turning back to Quintegrity's beaming expression as Adele and Lumpy placed their orders. *But even so, he's right.*

He smiled at the deli worker and pulled Quintegrity closer. "I'll have what my girlfriend is having."

ROVER… Lvl 703

All Money… {T}34,700

Allowance… {T}34,700
Fundraiser… {T}0

<<EXPENSE GOALS>>

Benedict's Payment… {T}100,000
Anti-Grav Skateboard… {T}499,999

<<CURRENT EQUIPMENT>>

Gloves… Beelzebub
Armor… Ape Laser
Acc.1… Shyster's Shoes
Acc.2… Hound Doggo Shnozz

<<SPECIAL NUMBERS>>

① ② ③ ④ ⑤

⑥ ⑦ ⑧ ⑨ ⑩

BULLETPROOF SKIN & A SOUL MADE OF GALAXIES

"I heard you did a greeeaat job in that match against Tallyhawk yesterday."

"Shove it, Olaf," Rover grunted as he walked down the school hallway on his way to the Super Club penthouse on Satty-*day*. He was playing *Glove Alien Fight*, which he did at every possible moment since getting home last night.

"You knocked her out, but she won by *ringing* you out!"

"Dammit, Daremont!"

Olaf Thumdiggles' sarcasm and Daremont Radclaft's puns bombarded Rover, and the other students snickered at the verbal abuse.

Luckily, Olaf and Daremont parted ways at the next hallway junction, although the walk still wasn't entirely peaceful. Rover could see and hear the quiet, under-the-breath comments being made as he passed his fellow classmates.

"Heeey," came a mocking voice from behind.

Rover sighed, keeping his eyes on his phone and not changing his pace.

"What's up, Graphite?" Oh, Rover knew what was up, though.

The other boy walked alongside him. "How's it taste to be defeated?"

"It's fine," Rover replied, not looking at him.

Graphite chuckled. "You were getting too popular too quickly, being the star of those videos and being in the Super Club and..."—he choked down a lump in his throat— "...and dating Quinn Integrity. Now you know that you ain't invincible."

Still concentrating on the game, Rover said, "It's not over yet. This won't slow me down."

The rock-solid resolve was something Graphite easily picked up on. He narrowed his eyes at Rover playing the video game.

"Tallyhawk told me she didn't get many items when she beat you," Graphite said, his tone softer and more casual, "and they were all normal items, too."

Rover didn't reply. He was too busy pushing an anvil off an ice cream truck to squash a Werewolf enemy below him, a move that earned him extra technicality experience points and velvet coins. Also, his character leveled up.

"If you've been hauling normal items the whole time," Graphite continued, "then you must be damn good to be as far in the game as you are."

"Is this a surprise?"

"That would mean you haven't been hanging around any special dungeons and enemy bases lately, which provide better items and stuff."

"That's not true. I just use a lot of the higher-end stuff because I need them. I also make sure my opponents don't get anything good if I lose a match."

"I don't think I trust that answer, Rover."

"A brilliant conclusion, probably."

Graphite put his hand on Rover's shoulder, stopping him. "How the *hell* did you get those special Glove Aliens, then?!"

A grin spread on Rover's face as he finally looked at Graphite. Several students had overheard the question and were listening in.

"I found them," Rover said.

"*Where*???"

"Up your ass and around the corner."

Rover kept walking. The students trying to eavesdrop snickered as Graphite stood there, fuming.

14!14@14#14$14%14^14&14*14(14)14_14+14

The Super Club members sat around the sea-marble coffee table in the posh penthouse living room and discussed their upcoming fundraiser, known now as Operation Maid Invasion, a maid café-style restaurant. Quintegrity took a sip of homemade honeycrest sparkling tea from a skull-shaped teacup, then reviewed the list of menu ideas they'd devised together.

"Crab cake burgers with citrus aioli and cilantro pesto—sounds bright and fishy, like electric eels!"

Adele scratched her head with the top of her pen. "It was my idea…but 'electric eels'…?" Her finger brushed something papery between the couch cushions, and she removed a crinkled school food slip worth one thousand thuggoons. "Oh, score! I found something."

Quintegrity continued, "Jillfruit lemonade with crushed, fresh mint—sounds refreshing and exquisite, like passing a test you *knew* you were gonna flunk!"

"Um, thank you? (Question mark?)" Lumpy asked. He retrieved a pen from his tank top's breast pocket. "I just really like jillfruit."

As Quintegrity went down the list, Rover had been engrossed in *Glove Alien Fight* the entire time, determined to keep leveling up. The fundraiser was an afterthought to him.

An incoming call alert popped up on his smartphone. He had configured his phone to only alert him of phone calls while playing *Glove Alien Fight*, as not to interrupt the gameplay during potentially crucial in-game moments.

"Somebody's calling me?" He paused the game and accepted the call. "Hello?"

A familiar, somewhat smug voice came through the phone.

"Rover Chork, I take it?" Benedict Torrent asked.

Rover tightened his grip on his phone. "Yeah, it's me, Benedict."

Lumpy and Adele became attentive, watching Rover. Quintegrity, however, kept working on the café menu for Operation Maid Invasion.

"Hmm…" Quintegrity scribbled in the notebook. "There's an idea. Deviled eggs benedict…with a *torrent* of hollandaise! Bwa-ha-ha! *Snort!* Make it demonically spicy, too…"

Benedict told Rover, "I saw some new online videos about you. You lost to that ninja-looking girl dressed in, um…*belts*. Her name was Tallyhawk Kusumegido, if I'm not mistaken."

"What of it?" Rover said.

"If you couldn't defeat her, then are you sure you can defeat me?"

With a snicker, Rover leaned back, resting his left arm across the back of the couch. "What's it matter to you? You should be happy that you *think* you have the upper hand. I'll be at the same level as you when we square off, so my character will be a lot stronger and faster than it is now. I'll be better at the game, too."

Benedict laughed. "I like that about you, kid. Not willing to back down. But don't forget about the hundred thousand thuggoons I'll need from you. It's the price of business and all that, since it'll be part of my livestreaming series."

"I haven't forgotten how you're bamboozling and extorting me." Rover looked at the other three around the sea-marble coffee table; Quintegrity was now listening intently. "You'll have your payment in full. I have my *dream team* backing me up on that."

He smiled at them. Lumpy and Adele didn't offer much of a response, but Quintegrity smiled back with a dutiful nod.

Although, my dream team is more like only one other person, specifically.

"Good to hear," Benedict said. "I assume you'll be competing in more AR matches. Therefore, I'll be staying up to date on them. Videos of these matches are getting popular—you aren't the only one in the limelight. However, you are the *main star*, mostly thanks to your Glove Aliens...but you should know that your ratings have suffered from losing yesterday's match."

"I don't care about popularity and rankings or whatever," Rover told him, crossing one leg over the other as he stretched out more on the couch, "but I should feel flattered that you're keeping track of those things for me." Grinning with a devious glint in his eye, Rover added, "It's almost like you're my biggest fan."

More laughter came through the phone.

"Right, right," Benedict chortled. "As I said, I like you, kid. I look forward to this match of ours."

"Likewise."

"Until next time, Rover."

"Yep."

As soon as the phone call ended, Adele leaned forward and asked, "So? What'd he want?"

Rover shrugged. "Just a phone call from my biggest fan."

"Ya know," Lumpy said, "it's really cool that you're doing this. You really are like an online celebrity. Getting this much attention from a high-profile gaming icon like Benedict Torrent is...well, *cool!*"

"Except for the extortion bit," Rover grumbled.

"I've been wondering, though..." Adele said, crossing her arms, "if Benedict also has the Beelzebub Glove Aliens...or something similar...or better."

"I'm not worried about it," Rover replied, chuckling and resuming *Glove Alien Fight*. "Not worried at all. N-Not one bit."

Quintegrity, Lumpy, and Adele all watched the sweat form on Rover's twitchy face.

"Cut the tough guy act," Adele told him with a chastising scowl. "We know you're scared shitless."

"Heh-heh...ha-ha-haaa...n-nooo..."

"Don't be scared, babe!" Quintegrity popped up from behind the couch Rover sat on and wrapped her arms around him. "You've got me on your side! Victory shall be yours!"

"Gaahhh! S-Stop it! I'm fighting the Lurky Turkey Bandits' leader!"

Quintegrity laughed before she leapt over the couch, soared through the air, and landed back on her chair.

"Maybe that was the wrong approach," she tittered as she sat properly in her seat. "I had to pick on you, seeing you so vulnerable. Just count on me, though. Benedict won't know what hit him!"

"W-Well," Rover said, "at least people don't know that you can see the augmented reality. That'll give us an advantage."

"Until they *do* find out," Adele said, tapping her pen on her notebook. "Be real, guys, can we keep it a secret forever?"

"Quinn will have to be sneaky about it," Lumpy added, "while also keeping better track of the Ring Hiders, which we can help with."

"I'm your girl for this task!" Quintegrity boasted with a convincing smile.

Rover held some skepticism, though, and set his phone on the sea-marble coffee table.

"Hey, Quintegrity…" he said, his tone low, "why don't you just tell us how you do it?"

She looked at him, her joyous expression diminishing somewhat.

"How I…can see the augmented reality game elements?"

"Yeah." Rover gave his girlfriend a hard stare. "It goes without saying that that ability is far beyond normal or even possible, especially if what you claim is true, saying you don't have any cybernetic enhancements…and that you're a *regular human*."

He hesitated to say that last part about being a regular human, feeling it was especially rude and rather unsettling. Quintegrity placed her notebook on her lap, looking down at it for a moment.

"Remember, Rover," Lumpy said, "that wasn't your agreement. If she told us how she's the way she is, then you'd tell us how you got your Beelzebub Glove Aliens."

"It's okay, Lumpy," Quintegrity said. "My secret is much bigger than Rover's…so it's right if I say something." She looked at Rover. "I've had some, shall I say, *extraordinary* experiences during my life." Her speech was soft—not necessarily timid or hesitant, but confident and open. "Sorry, but I'm not very comfortable talking about it in *full* detail, but I understand why it's hard to comprehend why I am the way I am."

Rover had never before encountered so much heartfelt resistance from Quinn Integrity.

"If you really don't feel comfortable talking about it," he told her, "then I'll respect that and won't push you. I just hope you understand our suspicions about your, uh…*abilities*."

The girl nodded at him. "I do understand. I was expecting this conversation at some point."

She gazed out the large penthouse windows at the lilygrass sheen across the school's Courtmeadows. As she collected her thoughts to string into words, Rover watched the way she pulled her feet closer to her chair, the way she hunched forward a bit as the uncertainty crept onto her face.

She continued, "The world beyond the Jerry Co. Walls changes people, and the effect of my life spent out there has had the most extreme impact on me, far more than anyone else I know of."

Rover, Lumpy, and Adele tensed up.

"Wait, *whaaat*?!" Adele shrieked. "You were *outside* the Jerry Co. Walls?!"

"For how long?" Lumpy asked, raising his voice a little. "It isn't fit for human survival out there! It couldn't have been for *too* long."

Shaking her head, Quintegrity replied, "I don't know. I have no frame of reference to confirm the rumors about time being different beyond the Walls, so I have no idea."

A bang rang out. Rover had stood up, his knees colliding with the coffee table and scooting it back as he did so, rattling the skull-shaped tea set placed on it.

"That's impossible!" he shouted. "The only way anyone can go outside the Walls is for highly-specialized Militia duty, which you're too young to be in the Militia at all! Or...or if—"

"I was exiled."

Silence fell upon the Super Club penthouse, filling it from the high, light fixture-laden ceiling down to the squishy carpet. It was the kind of silence that saturated the furniture, the air, the spirit...taking away the coziness and leaving nothing but emptiness. It seeped down through all of the lower levels of the Clubhaus building.

Adele looked at Lumpy, whose open mouth and dazed eyes showed he had no answer to give. When she looked at Rover, though, she saw his jaw clench, his fists balling tightly, and an edge in his eyes drilling directly into the president sitting in her chair...the girl who wasn't the same person without her signature glow and overflowing bravado.

"You're a liar." Rover's accusation was the most unwelcome break to the unnerving silence. His words were sharpened by anger, even without raising his voice. "*Nobody* comes back from exile."

Unfazed by Rover's reaction, Quintegrity told him, "But I did." Her expression wasn't serious...only blank.

"The Substantial Board of Exile is supposed to maintain their permanent verdict of all exiled people," Rover said, keeping his tone in check, although his stiff posture and glare gave away his thoughts. "Never mind that the Thugforce Militia should be hunting you down to *de-rationalize* you for not playing *Glove Alien Fight*." His hands trembled as he narrowed his eyes, which did nothing to reduce his glare's potency. "The

Substantial Board of Exile has their policies enforced by the Cohort Squadron, who works directly for CEO Claudius. If they catch you..."

"I'll be put to death." Quintegrity grinned, clasping her hands together. "Don't worry about me, I know the dangers."

"*HOW THE HELL ARE YOU SO CALM ABOUT THAT*?!?!" Rover thundered, flailing his arms in a frenetic frenzy.

"Because I'm tough. I have *bulletproof* skin and a soul made of *galaxies*!"

Rover scowled. "Meaning...?"

Standing up from her chair, the most delicate, sincere, uplifting, soul-soothing smile found its way to Quintegrity's lips as she flexed her biceps on both arms...

She took a deep breath, sucking in the melancholy atmosphere itself...

"*MEANING I'M FAR TOO SUPER AWESOME TO BE CAUGHT*!!!"

Her declaration did more than negate Rover's doubt—it downright obliterated it, vaporizing the chilly silence away from every surface inside and outside the Clubhaus building, scrubbing the scariness away with purifying, funky vibes.

The three Super Club members were at ground zero for this exultant wave of Quintegrity's affirmation, such that they literally heard the brassy, concussive jazz blast of her energy—and they took it straight to their faces! Into their hearts! Their bones!

Rover crumbled onto the couch behind him, a result of being hit by his girlfriend's words. He tried to look up at Quintegrity...but his neck was like old celery, limp and sad. Instead, he leaned forward, massaging his forehead in his hand with a raspy sigh.

Taking a seat on the couch next to Rover, Quintegrity leaned against him and placed her head on his shoulder. She kept the position for a moment before looking up at him.

"You gotta believe me, Rover."

In that moment, the boy noticed a fundamental quality Quintegrity held. Her lightness weighed against his shoulder and, when paired with her gentleness, brought out the humanly frailty she hid beneath her strength.

Yes, he had seen this quality when they first met. It had revealed itself to him while he'd been lost in her soft mulberry eyes, just as he was now.

She's a girl. A person.

Letting his mind tumble and bumble, Rover put his arm around her.

"Only because you've already proven yourself as a super awesome badass, I only partially doubt your story...but I'm still skeptical." He turned away with a displeased face. "I'll try to believe you."

She smiled at him and nodded. "Thank you." Jumping up, she grabbed her notebook with the list of Operation Maid Invasion menu items. "All right, let's get down to business."

Lumpy and Rover glanced at each other. Almost like telepathy, they both knew to go along with Quintegrity.

Adele, on the other hand, stared at the girl and ignored her comments on the list of menu items.

Returned from exile... Not playing Glove Alien Fight *is a harsh (although idiotic) crime, but going against a top-level government body like the Substantial Board of Exile is a whole different thing. Quinn isn't just a criminal—she's a full-blown felon; tried and sentenced, now escaped from her punishment. Wow, Big Bro...you've really gotten yourself into something.*

14!14@14#14$14%14^14&14*14(14)14_14+14

After the Super Club meeting, Quintegrity tagged along as Rover and Adele went home. Before Rover followed his sister inside the house, he turned to his girlfriend.

"You know," he said, making eye contact, "I don't even know where you live."

Quintegrity smiled and looked away for a second, then met Rover's eyes again. "My living conditions are a spectacle and a miracle!"

His eyes narrowed. "So, where do you live?"

"The Super Club penthouse." Her peppiness suffered no loss.

"I somehow expected that answer." Rover sighed, running his hand through his hair. "Well...I better get inside. I'm gonna have a long night playing *Glove Alien Fight* and leveling up."

"Go get 'em, Rover!" She hugged him, making him warm. "I'll see ya tomorrow."

"...Yeah... Have a good night, babe..."

"You too!"

Rover stood on his porch, watching the girl trot off through the neighborhood. When she was out of sight, he looked at the ground, then looked around, and then headed inside.

14!14@14#14$14%14^14&14*14(14)14_14+14

On the outskirts of the residential area, a helicopter flew overhead. Its exceptionally bright searchlights and loud, deep-rumbling propellers indicated it belonged to the Thugforce Militia, being bigger and more powerful than private or commercial helicopters, yet lacking the stealth and precision of the ones used by the elite, secretive Cohort Squadron.

Quintegrity zipped across the quiet street and hid in a small residential alleyway, avoiding the searchlight's watchful beam scouring the neighborhood. She had learned to identify the different vehicles used by all of Thugwood's law enforcement and government agencies—it was important to have a solid understanding of one's predators.

There are more of them these days. Not surprising as I'm in most of those online videos for that game.

Moving as if she was an appendage of the shadows, she snuck all the way back to Southbound Thugwood High School. As president of the Super Club, she had rights to access the school grounds and its facilities at all times. She decided to bypass the main gate (which she had a key to) and hopped the fence instead.

ROVER... Lvl 722

All Money... {T}35,700

Allowance... {T}34,700
Fundraiser... {T}0
Food Slip... {T}1,000

<<EXPENSE GOALS>>

Benedict's Payment... {T}100,000
Anti-Grav Skateboard... {T}499,999

<<CURRENT EQUIPMENT>>

Gloves... Beelzebub
Armor... Jinnin Tunic
Acc.1... Bug Repellant
Acc.2... Pension Extender

<<SPECIAL NUMBERS>>

① ② ③ ④ ⑤

⑥ ⑦ ⑧ ⑨ ⑩

MAKE YOUR MAXIMUM YOUR NEW MINIMUM!

ROVER **was up late**, playing *Glove Alien Fight* in his bedroom, when he heard his door creak open.

"What do you want?" he muttered, not looking.

Adele walked in, seeing her brother sitting at his desk with his back turned to her and looking at his phone.

"I went to the bathroom and saw your light on," she said, sounding slightly groggy. "What are you doing?"

Rover didn't budge. "Leveling up."

"Ah." She watched Rover for a few seconds as he remained hunched over his phone, the game's sound effects filling the quiet room. "Say...how do you feel about Quinn? I mean, you're dating her, so..."

The game sounds stopped. Rover gazed at his wall, then swiveled in his chair to face his sister.

"Worried," he said, "and...confused, I guess."

"You realize if she's telling the truth about that exile stuff, then that makes her a felon."

Rover gave some small nods in quick succession, looking at the floor. "A felon...facing a death sentence."

"It could all be crap, though."

"I know, and it probably is," he replied, leaning back in his chair. "Really, part of me thinks it's true, but the rest of me thinks she's lying. I *hope* she's lying."

Closing the bedroom door, Adele asked, "What if you find out she really is lying?"

"Then, I'll confront her," Rover answered right away. "I'll ask her why she lied. Depending on what she says, I might break up with her or drop out of the Super Club. It would suck, but it'd be hard to trust her."

"That'd be the easy route. But, theoretically...what if she *isn't* lying?"

Rover swiveled back around. "I don't wanna think about it."

As the sounds of the game resumed, Adele glanced around the room, eventually landing her eyes on the bookshelf.

"Anyway," she said, "can I borrow a manga? I want my friend Gale to read *I Was an Attorney, but I Woke Up as a Jug of Coolant in My Defendant's Garage, and I Am Now My Own Evidence against My Case.*"

"No way! The last time Gale borrowed my manga, she lost it."

"It wasn't her fault," Adele said, walking to Rover's bookshelf. "That was during the lunch lady strike. We *all* lost something that day."

Rover grabbed a shot put ball replica off his desk and hurled it at Adele, hitting her in the stomach.

"*Poouuhhh*!!!" The wind was knocked out of her, and she doubled over, holding her belly. "Ugghh... Y-You got me right in the gut..."

"Don't just come into my room and go through my stuff."

"You can't give me that crap." Adele straightened up and shot Rover a contemptuous glower. "Dad said you were in my room, sniffing my perfume before asking Quinn out."

"Uhhh..."

"Pretty weird, man."

Smirking, Rover said, "At least I waited until you weren't home. You just came in here without knocking, knowing I was here."

Adele crossed her arms. "Waiting until I wasn't home to go into my bedroom makes it less creepy *how*?"

"You're lucky I'm just playing a game now," he said. "Considering what time it is, it's very possible you could have caught me yanking my yeti."

"*Ew!*" Adele cringed and covered her ears. "Okay, okay, I'll leave!"

She promptly skedaddled and slammed the door shut, leaving Rover in peace.

Continuing the game, he snickered. "I knew that'd get her out."

15!15@15#15$15%15^15&15*15(15)15_15+15

Rover spent his entire weekend playing *Glove Alien Fight* to level up, going straight through Sundun-*day* and Nundinum-*day* without doing much else.

"How's Quinn?" Dad asked Rover at dinner Nundinum-*day* evening. "I haven't seen her around lately. Does she still like cooking?"

Mom gave Dad a sad look. "Do you dislike my chicken fried rice, dear? All the best market deals are on Nundinum-*days*, and it was mostly chicken and rice this week."

"Um...y-your fried rice is exquisite, dear."

"You'd rather have Rover's girlfriend cook?"

Dad took too long to answer, earning him an icy stare from Mom.

"I'm mostly curious about Rover's first love," he said, smirking. "A young boy has his needs!"

Adele already had her hands over her ears, but Rover spoke before Dad could add to the fire.

"She's just doing her own thing," Rover answered, not looking up from his bowl. "I guess I need to figure out if I want to be a part of it. Until then, we'll give each other some space."

Mom and Dad both dropped their forks at once, their eyes tearing up as they smiled at their son.

"You sound so grown up!" they said in unison.

Rover grimaced, thinking, *It's annoying when they sync up like that.*

Mom told him, "Relationships come with very important decisions. If the other person leads a life you don't agree with, then you aren't obligated to stay with them. That decision is much easier to make before marriage, though, so remember that."

"You might get pinned down for life!" Dad added with a grin. Mom gave him another icy look, and he cleared his throat. "Talk to Quinn about it to reach a mutual ground between you two."

"I did talk to her...kinda."

"Good," Dad said with a satisfied nod. "Make things clear for both of you."

"Is this about those internet videos you're in?" Mom asked Rover. "You've been getting a lot of attention lately. Are you okay with it?"

"It's not really about the videos," Rover answered, pushing the rice around his bowl. "That isn't a problem."

"Any sort of fame or recognition comes with potential problems," Dad warned. "Don't let your guard down just because you're comfortable with it."

That thought lingered with Rover even as dinner resumed without further talk on the matter.

15!15@15#15$15%15^15&15*15(15)15_15+15

The pursuit continued to reach level nine hundred ninety-nine. Throughout school on Mondee-*day*, Rover struggled not to nod off at any random moment. His head bobbed and eyelids flickered while sitting in class. He would snore himself awake while riding the escalators between floors. At the lunch table, he would have face-planted into his own food if Lumpy hadn't caught him.

Gotta level up, Rover kept telling himself, playing *Glove Alien Fight* at all times between classes.

The four Super Club members trekked across the Courtmeadows to the Clubhaus, keeping to the paved pathway so Rover wouldn't fall over on the springy lawn. Keeping his eyes open was easier as the sun wasn't out, reducing the glare from the lilygrass.

Quintegrity massaged Rover's shoulders as they walked, an entertained grin plastered on her face.

"You're feeling a little slumpish there, Rover," she chortled. "Those all-nighters chipping away at you? I don't hear from you for two days, and look at what's become of you! Ha-ha-ha-ha!"

"I'm chipper as a chipper!" Rover slurred as he walked, playing *Glove Alien Fight* on his phone.

"Dude, that made no sense," Lumpy said, raising his eyebrows, "and you haven't slept the last few nights...or *days*, for that matter. You should really get some sleep."

Rover shook his head, not to disagree with Lumpy, but to shake the sleepiness out of him—it wasn't very effective.

"I gotta keep playing *Glove Alien Fight*," he replied, straightening his back as his vision vibrated from the lack of shuteye. "At thish rate...I'll reach the maxshimum level by some night...or night..."

"Onward and upward!" Quintegrity cheered, high-stepping while exaggerating her arm swings with each stride. "Use your passion as a rocket-powered battery pack to achieve your maximum, Rover! Achieve *beyond* maximum!! Make your maximum your *new minimum*!!!"

Rover pumped his fist into the air like it was a rock tied to a rubber band, and his arm flopped back to his side where it dangled like an untied shoelace.

"For real, Big Bro," Adele said with a sigh, "be careful. They say brain damage starts after about three straight days of being awake. Because your brain was already defective right out of the package, you'd best wrangle in your remaining neurons before they get taken out to pasture."

"Is that because it's *pasture* bedtime, Rover?" Daremont called as he ran past, laughing into the overcast skies.

"Sleep deprivation is sooo good for your grades!" Olaf added monotonously, running alongside Daremont.

Lumpy groaned, dragging his hand down his face. "Somebody should put those kids away."

"I think they're targeting me..." Rover grunted, dragging his feet on the paved path. He commanded his onscreen character to throw a Bomb into a nest of Mutant Ants, killing dozens of them and earning him magnetic coins as he leveled up.

15!15@15#15$15%15^15&15*15(15)15_15+15

They entered the Super Club penthouse, stepping over the kicked-down door. Dragging his feet through the living room, Rover paused his game, dropped his phone on the couch, and then plopped down onto the cushions. By the time Quintegrity repaired the door ("Good job, Ryuumba-*chan*!"), Rover was curled up on the couch with his eyes closed.

"Hey!" Adele barked at her brother. When he didn't respond, she groaned. "Well, better to sleep now than never, I guess."

"I'll go prepare the sparkling tea," Quintegrity told them, dancing across the living room. "It's my new flavor, and you get to be my guinea rats! Chrysanthemum with lemon grass and *extra* serendipity. Trust me, that last one makes all the difference!"

She skipped to the kitchen. Lumpy and Adele leaned in close to whisper to each other.

Adele asked, "What if those weird appliances are stolen government machines?"

"I don't know." Lumpy shrugged. "I was gonna ask what 'serendipity' tastes like..."

A citrusy, floral aroma wafted around the room as Quintegrity brought the tray of human skull-shaped teacups and unicorn skull-shaped teapot. The clinking sound of her placing the tray on the sea-marble coffee table jarred Rover awake.

"H-Huh?!" He glanced around with bloodshot eyes and a panicked expression. "How long was I out???"

"You still are," Adele told him straightforwardly.

"Oh no!" Rover jumped up. "I-I'm wasting time sleeping! I gotta level up!"

Adele snickered. "Punch yourself in the face. That'll wake you up."

Rover threw a punch at his own face, but Quintegrity caught his fist just before the hit. Confused, he looked at his girlfriend who smiled and shook her head.

"Adele!" Rover snapped. "Nice try."

"Mwa-ha-haaa! Almost got you."

"Now that we're all present and conscious," Quintegrity said, clapping her hands together, "I want to show you all something! Wait right here."

In five seconds, she retrieved a cardboard box from the next room, placed it on the floor by the coffee table, and removed some of its contents for the others to see.

Lumpy scratched his head at what Quintegrity was holding.

"Uh...fake mustaches?" he asked. "And wigs. And communication earpieces..."

"This is how I'll be better at helping Rover," Quintegrity said with a big smile. "During his video game matches, I'll disguise myself and communicate with these little gadgets that fit right over our ears."

"That's pretty smart," Rover said, taking one of the earpieces and examining it.

"It wasn't my idea," Quintegrity said, sticking a fake mustache under her nose. "I learned this tactic after interrogating Graphite."

Adele peered at her. "When you say 'interrogate,' what did you do...?"

"O-ho-ho-ho-ho!" Quintegrity twirled her mustache with a villainous laugh. "I knew something was suspicious during that match with Belt Girl. Come to find out, her friends were wearing these kinds of disguises and communicating with similar earpieces. They watched where the Ring Hiders stashed their goods and relayed that info to Belt Girl!"

"Tch." Rover clicked his tongue, holding the earpiece in his fist. "Those bastards. Tallyhawk wouldn't have won."

"But we have the greatest secret weapon." Quintegrity put on a wig which was dreadlocks with a top hat, and she put her hands on her hips. "*Me!*"

Rover sneered, putting the earpiece on. "All right! Whoever faces me next won't know what him 'em!"

Quintegrity ran around the living room with her arms straight out at her sides, making airplane noises, the fake dreadlocks fluttering behind her. Lumpy and Adele tried on some of the different wigs for themselves, seeing how goofy they could look and taking pictures with their phones. Rover resumed playing *Glove Alien Fight*.

Somehow, amid the shenanigans, they got a lot done for planning the Operation Maid Invasion café fundraiser. At the end of the meeting, after Lumpy and Adele packed up their notes, they noticed Quintegrity was still sitting and writing in her notebook.

"Aren't you done, Quinn?" Lumpy asked her. "We're heading out."

Adele looked at Rover who was busy playing his game as he shuffled toward the door; she knew he was paying attention, only pretending to ignore the conversation as everyone awaited Quintegrity's answer.

The club president smiled at the other members.

"Very well," she said, her voice soft and sweet like the sparkling tea she'd been sipping. "I still have some things to do. You all go on ahead."

"Okay..." Adele said, grabbing the doorknob. "Good day, Quinn."

"And good day to you all, as well."

However, Rover stayed in the room. He looked up from his phone, Lumpy and Adele watching him.

"Quinn," he said.

She giggled. "I thought I asked you to call me 'Quintegrity.'"

"Quintegrity…" Lost for words, Rover wondered why he'd chosen to say anything at all. He gazed at the gorgeous girl sitting in her cushy chair with her notebook. "…Have a good night."

Quintegrity's smile widened. "You too, Rover!"

Rover was the last one out, closing the door behind him. The three of them headed down the fifth floor's sole hallway and entered the elevator—he kept playing the game.

"Do you think," Lumpy asked on their way down, "Quinn got those disguises to, ya know…hide from the law?"

"I think so." Adele nodded. "Probably to hide from the government people looking for her, assuming she really is back from exile and on the run and not playing *Glove Alien Fight*."

Rover defeated an in-game enemy, not saying anything.

"But," Lumpy said, "it doesn't make sense for her to come back. Right, Rover?"

"I guess."

Lumpy studied his unenthusiastic best friend, seeing his face was already worn down from sleepiness.

"However," Rover added, pausing his game, "you know what's really bothering me the most about it?" He slid the phone into his pants pocket as the elevator reached the ground floor. "I wonder what she did to get exiled in the first place."

"Assuming she's telling the truth," Adele said, stepping out of the elevator in the Clubhaus lobby.

"Yeah," Rover muttered, "assuming that."

"Honestly," Adele said, "she's dumb for telling us all that. How does she know we won't turn her in?" When Rover glared at her, she held up her hands. "Not saying I will! Jeez, if looks could kill…"

"She trusts us," Rover told them as they walked through the lobby. "And until I learn more about whether or not she's lying, then I'm gonna trust her, too."

Lumpy laughed. "I know you, dude. You really mean that, and not just because she helps you for *Glove Alien Fight*. You really like her."

"Y-Yeah." Rover blushed. "I do really like her. It's weird, but I feel I can really understand her…like we're communicating without communicating."

"Are you talking about those weird, funky, danceable vibes that she gives off?" Adele asked. "I swear I get music stuck in my head—or in my entire *body*—when she starts groovin' and feelin' the moment."

"She does have that effect," Rover said with a faint smile.

They exited the Clubhaus building, feeling the late afternoon air approach the perfect temperature under cloudy conditions.

ROVER… Lvl 790

All Money… {T}35,700

Allowance… {T}34,700
Fundraiser… {T}0
Food Slip… {T}1,000

<<EXPENSE GOALS>>

Benedict's Payment… {T}100,000
Anti-Grav Skateboard… {T}499,999

<<CURRENT EQUIPMENT>>

Gloves… Beelzebub
Armor… Jinnin Tunic
Acc.1… Bug Repellant
Acc.2… Yakuza Tools

<<SPECIAL NUMBERS>>

① ② ③ ④ ⑤

⑥ ⑦ ⑧ ⑨ ⑩

<< 16 >>

DECLARE YOUR CONFESSION TO THE CRIMINAL GODDESS!

In the back yard behind the Chork household, Rover and Lumpy prepared for a player-versus-player *Glove Alien Fight* AR match. Adele sat on the wooden parapet of the deck overlooking the yard, snacking on a plate of peach sundae-flavored Rocket Rolls. School was out that Tsuday to celebrate Saint Persnickety Day, a prime opportunity for Rover to gain some extra levels.

"Don't go easy on me just because we're friends, Lumpy," Rover said. "No holds barred."

"It might not make a difference. You're at a way higher level than me in the game right now."

"These matches are the fastest way to level up." Rover watched the roulette on his phone toggle through the three match types. "You're doing me a big favor, pal!"

"H-Hey! Don't already assume I'm gonna lose..."

The onscreen toggle stopped on "Deathmatch," in which the players fight each other as they would fight AI enemies in the original game. The main difference was the augmented reality projections.

Lumpy chuckled under his breath. "Ugh...Deathmatch. I was actually hoping for this one, but..."

"You still have those Hippo Sparklers?" Rover asked, not bothering to conceal his smirk. "I could use some more."

"Beat me and find out."

Deathmatch games had a two-minute period for the combatants to configure their characters' Glove Aliens, armor, accessories, and other skills. As the timer counted down, Lumpy stared at his character's setup on his phone screen.

Rover typically favors speed and agility when playing the regular game, but his offensive settings during big battles make him a force from Hell. I should balance my defense with speed and evasion. Yeah...I think this setup is good.

The match began. Lumpy's phone screen instantly became an arctic explosion. His character collapsed. The match ended.

"*Grrrr!*" Lumpy clenched his teeth and waved his phone in protest. "Dammit, Rover! That was unfair!"

Rover stretched his arms as if he had just exercised (or was yawning from boredom).

"No holds barred," he said, looking at the list of consumable items he'd taken from Lumpy. "You should've prepared yourself for the worst."

"If I'd configured the highest defense available at my level," Lumpy grunted, "that attack still would've killed me in one hit! Or even with my speed all the way up, I wouldn't have gotten away from that!" He ruffled his exploded-pumpkin hair in frustration. "Like, did you even *see* how much damage that attack did to me? You would've killed me four times over! Those Beelzebub Glove Aliens were already way over-powered when you fought Graphite...but now it's just *asshole-ish!*"

"I leveled up fifteen times from that," Rover said, ignoring Lumpy while viewing the battle results. "You were worth more experience points than Graphite. Thanks for playing, Lumpy! Heh-heh-hehhh!"

"Screw you..."

Rover continued scrolling through the list of items he'd won.

"You had a lot of good stuff," he said. "Seven Goosepacks? How'd you have *seven*???"

"I don't use them often, like it matters now. They're all yours."

"Remember when you offered to lose a bunch of matches against me to raise my level? You said that before knowing you can't challenge the same person until after nine other AR battles. What happened to *that* mindset, huh?"

"...Yeah."

Looking at the deck, Rover noticed Adele had gone back inside the house. As Lumpy still cursed under his breath, Rover set out to find his next AR match victim.

16!16@16#16$16%16^16&16*16(16)16_16+16

"Hey, Adele!" Rover trapped his sister on the living room couch.

She shrank back, scared by the look on Rover's face.

"Uh, what?" she asked with a crooked scowl. "I'm trying to watch *Magical Poodle Snickerdoodle*."

Rover held up his phone. "I challenge you to—"

"No."

"You don't even know what—"

"I want to keep all of my items, thank you very much."

"C'mon, you'd be helping me out a ton."

"Bite me."

"Which part?"

"Get out of my way!" Adele yelled, kicking Rover back. "I'm watching TV."

"Fine, fine. Be that way."

Rover's hunt for another victim continued.

16!16@16#16$16%16^16&16*16(16)16_16+16

When Dad and Mom sat side-by-side while giving their own parental stares, Rover realized how intimidating they could be, especially when he tried voicing his unpopular opinions. He'd sat down with them at the dinner table to have this awkward talk, now regretting his decision to even *think* they would make great AR match victims.

"Son," Dad said, resting his elbows on the table with his fingers interlocked—he wore his classic Dad smile, "I don't see why this is so important to you."

Not backing down, Rover clenched his fist with a bold grin.

"To defeat CEO Claudius and free Thugwood from the mandate!!!" he replied, attempting to hide behind his gusto. He thought he'd done quite well, as the air around him seemed to rumble from his announcement. Maybe he was delusional, though.

"For glory?" Dad asked.

"Uh, well, a little...but mostly because the daily quota mandate is crap."

"What you're asking," Dad continued, unfazed by his son's ambition, "is for Mom and me to sacrifice our *Glove Alien Fight* consumable items for your gain?"

"It's not really like that," Rover said. "If you win, then you'd get all *my* consumable items. And...I really want to get rid of the mandate."

"We've seen your gameplay footage online," Dad said. "We know about your special Glove Aliens and the advantage they give you."

"Um..."

Dad and Mom exchanged glances. Rover recognized that exchange—he was about to fail at his attempt to convince them.

"How are your studies?" Mom asked. Her ability to sound and behave like a soulless puppet when scolding her children was frightening in the most visceral ways.

"Uh...they're fine..."

"We won't get any surprises when your report card comes in?" she asked. "Despite all the time you've spent playing video games?"

Rover had to take a moment (without appearing to take a moment) to think about his answer. He didn't remember failing enough assignments to earn a disgraceful grade in any class, but *Glove Alien Fight* had dampened his ability to keep track of those things.

Mom and Dad raised their eyebrows in unison, a sign of being a perfect pair, as well as a sign that Rover actually appeared to take a moment to think of his answer.

"Uh…I don't think so…" he said.

"Aside from the mandatory one hour of playing each day," Dad told Rover, "Mom and I don't focus on much else in *Glove Alien Fight*. We don't stand a chance in a match against you. Also, we're not putting our consumable items on the line for your, erm, 'glory' and heroic deeds like freeing Thugwood. We need those items! Right, Mom?"

Mom smiled and nodded. "Yes. That Lich Queen in the Marsh of Itchiness won't stand a chance against us this time. We have all those Smoothie Bombs now!"

"Gwa-ha-haaa!" Dad guffawed. "She's got it comin'!"

"Uh…" Rover tried not to grimace, "the Lich Queen is only the first boss. You still haven't beat her?"

"We have other things to worry about than a video game," Dad replied, standing up. "Isn't that right, dear?"

"Yes," Mom said, also standing, "such as keeping two teenagers in line."

They both smiled at him, holding that pose like a couple of dolls with evil spirits behind their eyes and teeth. Rover accepted that as his cue to flee. Leaving the dining room, he heard his parents snickering.

"Finding people to play against sucks," he grumbled.

16!16@16#16\$16%16^16&16*16(16)16_16+16

Rover, Lumpy, and Adele spent a few hours on hardcore *Glove Alien Fight* adventuring. Rover leaned back on his mattress and stretched, getting the blood circulating to his numbed toes. Sitting in one place for too long was challenging in and of itself, after all.

Lumpy set his phone down and rubbed his eyes. "I need a break. My joints are stiff."

"Yeah," Rover said, setting his phone on the mattress next to him. "I leveled up a lot today, so I can take the rest of the night off from *Glove Alien Fight*."

"You're welcome for that," Lumpy muttered.

"What do you wanna do next?" Adele asked. "I tried making plans with Gale or Lorelei tonight, but they've both got dates tonight." She sighed, running her finger across the carpet she sat on. "Must be nice…"

Rover gazed at the ceiling for a moment.

"I'll call Quintegrity," he said, using his phone. "She might wanna do something."

Lumpy gave Rover a mocking grin. "Ah, doing boyfriend-type stuff for once, eh?"

"Whaddaya mean 'for once'?" Rover shot Lumpy a dirty look. "I mean…" He paused for a moment, going through his list of contacts on his smartphone. "I just need to spend more time with her…"

"And learn about her *crimes*!" Adele held her arm across her forehead in a dramatic fashion. "Even though your lives drive you apart, your hearts fight to bridge that divide!"

Rover heard the phone ringing on the other end. His pulse quickened. What would he say when she answered?

"Rover!" Quintegrity's beaming face practically came through the phone.

"H-Hi, babe," Rover said, his face warm. "How are you?"

"Lonely." Now her pouting face came through the phone. "You never call me, and I was so happy seeing your name on my caller ID."

"Well, it's time to make that up to you."

"Excellent! I'll be at your place in no time."

"Whoa, wait…" The call ended, and Rover looked at Lumpy and Adele. "Um, she's coming over here, I guess…"

"Heh, makes it easy for us," Adele said, seeming satisfied. "I'll make some more Rocket Rolls."

When Adele opened the door, she was met by Quintegrity standing in the hallway with her hand up, as if about to knock on the door.

"I shouldn't be surprised you're already here," Adele chuckled, "but I am."

"I was already in the neighborhood," the vibrant girl said.

"Stalking your boyfriend?" Adele asked with a rude smirk.

"Not without his permission!" She winked at Rover, who shivered. "I just dropped off the last orders of the chocolate fundraiser. Having over eighty thousand orders during the course of only four weeks is pushing it, even for me."

Those statistics literally scared the other three in the room.

Rover found his voice, saying, "Come on in, babe. We finished playing a bunch of *Glove Alien Fight*, so we're looking for something else to do." He felt bashful, turning away for a moment. "Uh, I thought it'd be nice to include you."

Like she'd used teleportation, Quintegrity was on the other side of the bedroom and wrapping Rover in a huge hug.

"That's so sweet! Thank you for including me!"

"Gahh…haahhhh…n-no p-p-problem!"

"Whatever you wanna do, I'm fine with it, Rover. Let's enjoy our youth to the fullest!"

She lifted Rover off the bed, using him like a barbell to do a few deadlifts, laughing all the while.

"*Stop*! P-Put me down!" Rover cried.

She dropped him on his bed, giggling as he nearly bounced off. "Sorry, I forgot you don't like being manhandled like exercise equipment. Hee-hee-hee!"

Rover sat up, shaking. "You gotta stop doing that…"

"We're about to make some Rocket Rolls for a snack," Adele told Quintegrity, "and then we'll figure out what to do for the rest of the day. We have a lot of time before the curfew."

"I've never made Rocket Rolls before." Quintegrity approached Adele with so much enthusiasm that Adele instinctively stepped back. "Please let me help."

"O-Okay."

When the two girls left the room, Lumpy snickered.

"Quintegrity could provide power to a power plant," he said, standing up to stretch.

"I wouldn't be surprised if she was Thugwood's source of energy," Rover chuckled, standing up as well.

Lumpy watched Rover stretch his legs by walking around his bedroom.

"So, Rover," he said, "you're really going all in as her boyfriend?"

After a few seconds, Rover nodded. "Yeah, I am. I told you this. I'm gonna trust her for now. It's the only way I'll ever learn more about her…and whatever situation she's in now. I know it isn't the smartest or safest choice, but…yeah."

"Hmm." Lumpy thought about that. "If that's so, you gotta step up your role."

Rover stopped pacing and stared at Lumpy with a raised eyebrow.

"What do you mean by stepping up my role?" he asked.

"You know," Lumpy said, shrugging, "be more active in your relationship."

Commence the sweating—Rover felt his fingers twitch. "Be more active…?"

"Yeah. Do more things that couples do."

"…Like what…?"

"Well," Lumpy said, "for starters…there's the *obvious thing*."

Rover's heart skipped a beat. "You mean…like…uh…"

A sinister grin stretched on Lumpy's face as he did groping motions with his hands. "Like getting reeeaaal close to each other. Heh-heh!"

147

Cue Rover's panting.

"But, there's no need to jump the gun," Lumpy continued, holding up his index finger. He cleared his throat. "Simply by spending more time with her, you'll be showing your affection."

"That's why I called her today!" Rover said, getting defensive.

"Good, good. Keep it up, but do it more. Do it at all times. Shower her with the unshakeable notion that you are dedicated to her."

"I *am* dedicated, Lumpy! What more do I have to do?!"

Lumpy groaned. "Man, I'm not gonna hold your hand all the way through this…"

"But, you've had a girlfriend before. I need your advice."

"You mean when I dated Iori Hajima? Dude, she left me to elope with that assistant janitor at school! I don't have the best advice for you dating *Quinn Integrity.*"

"Well, ya know…" Rover said, "it's hard to *always* be there for someone. I'm busy and stuff…"

"You're in *high school.* You ain't that busy."

"I'm very busy with *Glove Alien Fight.*"

Lumpy shook his head. "Tsk, tsk, Rover. Letting your girlfriend go to the wayside over a video game…"

Appalled, Rover clenched his fists. "It's important to me! And…it's not like it's *more* important than Quintegrity!"

"I don't knoooow," Lumpy said with a mocking grin, trying to get under Rover's skin. "Last I checked, you spend a lot more time playing *Glove Alien Fight* than you spend with Quinn…"

"Er…gahhh…"

Lumpy switched to a serious demeanor so quickly that Rover jumped.

"Look, bro," he told Rover, stepping up to him, "you gotta stop making excuses. You gotta get over your fear of girls."

"B-But—"

"No 'buts'!" Lumpy pointed at Rover's face. "Man up and face the disco. You'll need to stop getting all tongue-tied around her."

"I don't *always* get tongue-tied!"

"Go for a zero percent tongue-tying rate," Lumpy told him.

Rover pursed his lips. "But…"

"*No 'buts'*! This is a but-less zone!"

"In my defense…" Rover replied through clenched teeth, making Lumpy roll his eyes, "I'm doing my best! It takes time!"

"Time is the enemy, Mr. Sir!" Lumpy announced, holding out his arms. He moved in closer to Rover, seeing his friend's sweat glistening on his forehead. "Think about it. You're here being all wishy-washy on whether to spend more time with a video game or your *girlfriend*. I'm saying you need to *show* your love for her!"

"I *do* love her!"

"Then, at least *tell* her!"

"*Ack*!"

Astounded, with his mouth agape, Lumpy stared at Rover. "You mean...you haven't told her you love her?"

Rover's quivering lip answered before he could speak.

"What the hell, dude?!" Lumpy grabbed Rover's shoulders and shook him. "Girls need that affirmation from boys! Boys need it too! In your case, the girl needs the boy to step up and be a man! Declare your confession to the criminal goddess! Like a *man*!"

Backed into an emotional corner, Rover cried, "Don't gender-shame me!"

"*I'm not shaming your gender*!!!" Lumpy shook Rover harder. "I'm telling you that Quinn is waiting for *you* to take the relationship further! Waiting for you to be a *man*! She's done her part as the woman, so it's your turn!" Lumpy got centimetres from Rover's face. "You're a *man*, aren't you?!"

"Eegeegeegee..."

"...*What'd you say*?!"

"..."

"ARE YOU A MAN, ROVER CHORK?!?"

Rover sucked in a whiny breath, scrunching his entire face into the most pitiful expression Lumpy had ever seen in his life.

"...I'm a *worm*!"

SLAP!

The sting from Lumpy's slap transferred from Rover's left cheek all the way to his right one.

"She will *leave* you, Worm Boy!" Lumpy again latched on to Rover's shoulders, shaking harder than before.

Rover gasped, his face drained of color as shivers struck his spine. "Wah! Wh-What are you saying?!"

"I'm saying you could get *dumped* for another guy!"

"**Gasp!** Nooo..."

"There are tons of other boys who already had their eyes on her," Lumpy said, "like *Graphite*."

"..."

"You could lose out to any of them if you don't step up!" He dropped his voice, adding, "Plus, there's all her sketchy stuff she's been talking about. Chances are she'll have her hands too full to bother with a bumbling bloke who *claims* to be dating her."

Taking a moment to let Lumpy's message soak in, Rover pushed back from his friend.

"Then..." he said, fighting the trembling in his tone, "I-I'll do my part...as a *man*."

"And you'll do that," Lumpy said, stabbing his index finger into Rover's breastbone, "by telling her you love her."

"Y-Yeah..."

"Got it?"

"I said 'yeah'!"

"Say 'yes.'"

"*Yes!*"

Rover's bedroom door opened as Quintegrity stepped inside.

"Hey, Rover?"

Like a statue on a rotating base, Rover turned his body around to look at his girlfriend. Lumpy could swear he heard the sound of stone grinding on stone as Rover swiveled, spine stiff, arms straight down and rock solid, his face unmoving like a busted sculpture carved out by a drunken stonemason.

"I-Love-You."

The words were flatter than steamrolled flapjacks.

Quintegrity stared, dazed, her eyes wide and mouth open.

Then she laughed, her cheeks glowing. "Aww!!! I love you too, Rover!" She pranced into the room and squeezed Rover the Statue in a hug. "Oh my...you're hard as a rock!"

"Giggity," Lumpy commented with a smirk.

Quintegrity laughed again. "I suppose that sounded a little dirty, didn't it?"

Rocky shuddering was the only sign of life coming from Rover the Statue. When released from Quintegrity's hug, the boy rocked in place, still locked up from head to toe.

"Anyway," Quintegrity said, "Adele asked if I can put my unique spin on the Rocket Rolls. Now that I know how to make them, I feel like I can *conquer* them!"

"Conquer away," Lumpy replied, seeing how Rover was incapacitated and unable to speak for himself.

"Yay! You won't regret it!"

When the girl left and closed the door, Rover the Statue toppled straight over onto the floor.

"You should be a mime," Lumpy told Rover, amused. "You do a perfect impression of an inanimate object."

"Leave me alone," Rover said from the floor, speaking into the carpet.

"She also said you were 'hard as a rock.'"

"It almost killed me…"

"But it didn't," Lumpy told him, taking a seat in the chair he'd been sitting in while playing *Glove Alien Fight*. "That means you got stronger today. Twice, actually…both times because of me. And this time, it didn't cost me my consumable items."

"It only cost me my pride," Rover squawked into the carpet.

"Payback's a bitch," Lumpy mocked. "Hope you enjoy those Goosepacks and Hippo Sparklers I'd been hording."

"Thanks, Lumpy." Rover rolled over to look at him. "You're a good friend."

"Dude…are you crying?"

"Yes."

"Oh. I was afraid I was hallucinating."

"You're not." Rover rolled back onto his stomach and buried his soggy face into his carpet.

ROVER… Lvl 827

All Money… {T}35,700

Allowance… {T}34,700
Fundraiser… {T}0
Food Slip… {T}1,000

<<EXPENSE GOALS>>

Benedict's Payment… {T}100,000
Anti-Grav Skateboard… {T}499,999

<<CURRENT EQUIPMENT>>

Gloves… Beelzebub
Armor… Jinnin Tunic
Acc.1… Farm Equipment
Acc.2… Yakuza Tools

<<SPECIAL NUMBERS>>

① ② ③ ④ ⑤

⑥ ⑦ ⑧ ⑨ ⑩

CRASH!

Wenno-*day*'s historical vandalism class had been in session for only twenty minutes when the first disruption burst through the window—a large albatross with a mail delivery satchel hanging around its neck came crashing through the glass.

As the beleaguered teacher tried to wrestle the bird, the students' zippy whispers breezed around the classroom.

"I didn't know anyone actually used carrier pigeons these days."

"That's not a pigeon! It's a pterodactyl!"

"With the uproar it's caused, it's more like a *terror-dactyl*!"

"Shut up, Daremont!!!"

Mrs. Historical Vandalism Teacher was a bulky, musclebound woman who had served sixteen years in the Vast Penitentiary, so she was able to pin the feathered messenger onto her desk with ease. As the large, squawking albatross flapped its huge wings, the teacher clutched the delivery satchel and removed its contents: a single letter.

"Well, what do we have here?" Mrs. Historical Vandalism Teacher smirked as she examined the letter in one hand while holding the albatross' neck in the other. "Passing notes like civilized students is *too much to ask* these days, eh?" She looked up at her students, who were paralyzed by her prison-hardened glare. "It's for Rover Chork."

Rover stiffened up as the muscular woman approached his desk. The big bird in her hand had given up on life, slumping over as the teacher held the letter out for Rover.

"Why don't you read it out loud for the class to hear?" she growled, the lines on her face deeper than the ocean's trenches.

Wanting to survive class that day, Rover gulped, taking the letter from the murderous teacher with forearms the size of his thighs. Standing up, he read the letter aloud to his fellow classmates:

"'Oi, prick! I mean you, Rover Chork. You think you're some kinda hotshot in *Glove Alien Fight*, I bet. I'll have you know, just because you're the whore of the game's augmented reality matches, that doesn't make you a champ. Benedict Torrent has taken a liking to you, but I want to see what you're really about, and maybe I'll prove Benedict wrong. I challenge you to a *Glove Alien Fight* AR match! Meet me at Coldshoulder Square tomorrow at 6:00 PM. XOXO, Captain Pretentious.'"

Feeling the eyes of every student, the teacher, and the albatross on him, Rover scoffed at the message, gripping the paper in both hands. He slammed the letter onto his desk, then tore a blank page from his notebook.

"I accept!" Wearing a cocky grin, he wrote those two words in huge letters on the page.

Everyone clapped as he stuffed his reply into the albatross' delivery satchel. Mrs. Historical Vandalism Teacher freed the bird from her grasp, and it immediately flew out the broken window.

"If you lose, Rover," the teacher told the boy, gutting him alive with her soulless eyes, "you will pay for my broken window with *more than money.* Understand me?"

Shrinking into his desk, Rover replied with a small voice, "Yes, ma'am."

"Good." Mrs. Historical Vandalism Teacher walked toward the front of the classroom. "Now, on page twelve hundred eighty-four, we'll begin the lesson on Count Earlstadt Shuxang, known as 'The Toad-Faced Disgrace,' the influential pioneer of putting underwear on the heads of public statues..."

17!17@17#17$17%17^17&17*17(17)17_17+17

During lunch, Rover made more progress in the regular *Glove Alien Fight* at the table while Quintegrity spoon fed him slamberry applesauce. His Clairvoyant Radar detected an invisible treasure chest he almost missed, so he made sure to open it.

"Oh, cool!" His discovery earned him a new weapon: the Infantry Glove Aliens. "I made the mistake of selling these earlier in the game, but now I'll level them up and see what they can do."

Clank!

Across the table, Lumpy deliberately set his food tray down loud enough to get Rover's attention.

"I heard you got challenged by *Captain Pretentious*!" Lumpy put his hands on the table and leaned forward. "Is it true???"

"Uh, yeah," Rover replied before taking another spoonful of food from Quintegrity.

"Was it *really* with an albatross? That's how Captain Pretentious likes to communicate."

"Sure was," Rover muttered. "Crashed right through the window with the letter in a satchel around its neck."

Lumpy sat down, laughing. "So, the legends are true!"

"Who the hell is Captain Pretentious?!" Rover barked, putting his phone on the table. "Is he famous or something?"

"*She* is kinda known among the gaming community," Lumpy said, doing an internet search on his phone. "I'm on her website now. It says that Captain Pretentious has made a name for herself with video game blogging, has appeared in a bunch of magazine and online interviews, and... Wow, the list goes on and on. She's got a lot of influence behind the scenes of the video game industry. Also, it says that despite her horribly pretentious personality and condescending demeanor, she is a leading donator and activist of dozens of charities...and even owns an animal shelter for abandoned and abused animals." Lumpy looked up from his phone at Rover. "She's like...a *real somebody!*"

"Hmm..." Rover tapped his finger on the table. "It still feels weird getting all this attention from people who are kinda big." He sneered, rubbing his hands together. "People must actually fear me as a force to be reckoned with in *Glove Alien Fight!*"

Lumpy shrugged, putting his phone away. "Probably. I mean, even though you lost to Tallyhawk Kusumegido in a Ring Finder game...it's obvious that your Beelzebub Glove Aliens make you *super over-powered* in Deathmatch fights, Strongest Hero matches, and even the regular, non-AR game itself. All of the message boards and forums I've looked at online have people up in arms about your Glove Aliens, and nobody seems to know anything about them or of anything stronger."

"All part of my grand plan, Lumpy," Rover told him with a sly smirk.

Staring at him, Lumpy asked, "And...what is your grand plan?"

"Even as my friend, I can't tell you."

"I can't ask you where you found those Glove Aliens, can I?"

Rover shrugged. "You can."

"And let me guess," Lumpy said, frowning, "you'll keep telling me you found them 'up my ass and around the corner.'"

Rover nodded. "That's my standard answer for *everyone* who asks."

"What if *I* ask you, Rover?" Quintegrity leaned in close, giving her boyfriend big puppy dog eyes.

"Errr...umm...r-right... E-Even you..."

Quintegrity giggled, patting Rover on the back. "A man of your word! Willing to keep your most important secrets from everyone, including your *betrothed!*"

The entire table shook from Rover's nervous, janky twitches.

"M-M-My b-b-be-betro—?!?"

"Just joking!"

Rover clutched his chest, his face getting hot.

"I...uh, think I'm done with my applesauce," he said in a weak voice.

"Mwa-ha-ha-haa!" Quintegrity shoveled the rest of the slamberry applesauce into her mouth and washed it down with a full litre of juicy, red-hot tea. "Anyway, are you gonna accept the challenge by,"—a literal drumroll came from *somewhere* as she paused to build the suspense—"*Captain Pretentious*?!"

"Ha!" Rover picked up his phone and resumed the game. "Of course! I already replied that I accept. It'll be tomorrow at six at Coldshoulder Square."

"All right!" his girlfriend cheered. "We'll rally the Super Club after school tomorrow." She pounded her right fist into her left palm, resulting in a small crack of thunder that a third of the cafeteria heard. Her lips stretched into a pointy, devious grin. "Together as a club, we'll *slaughter* the opponent, Rover!"

"Hell yeah, we will!"

A drop of sweat ran down Lumpy's face as he watched both Rover and Quintegrity cackle like a couple of mad scientists.

However, he'd always known how Rover got riled up with video games. In fact, Lumpy envied that passion and dedication, and as he wiped the drop of sweat from his cheek, he couldn't help but smile before biting into his mutton skewer.

17!17@17#17$17%17^17&17*17(17)17_17+17

Nary a cloud lingered overhead as the sunbathed vicinity of Coldshoulder Square filled with eager spectators on Thurdur-*day*. In only one day, news had spread far and wide of the *Glove Alien Fight* match between rising star Rover Chork and established video game enthusiast Captain Pretentious.

Coldshoulder Square was a versatile district in the Easterly Thugwood Prefecture, featuring plenty of eclectic shops, restaurants, and purportedly vague revenue-amassing business operations for drug lords and the filthy rich. At least the high elevation created some beautiful scenery and photogenic destination spots.

Rover adjusted the communication earpiece on his right ear and looked around at the gathering crowd. The parking lot and nearby outdoor cliff-side observatory were perfect for open-area gameplay.

"There must be over a hundred people here," he said in a hushed tone to Lumpy. "Some of them are even holding handmade signs."

"'Move over for Rover,'" Lumpy said, reading one of the signs. "That one says 'Only wenches love Pretentious.' But...there seem to be a lot more signs supporting Captain Pretentious than for you."

"It's to be expected," Rover replied with a shrug. "She's been doing things for a while now and already had a following." He made eye contact with several groups of students he recognized from Southbound Thugwood High School, and he waved at them—some of them held signs cheering him on. "At least I've got my own local mini-following!"

Quintegrity's voice came through Rover's and Lumpy's earpieces.

"This is Q. Do you read, R and L?"

"Loud and clear, Q," Rover replied.

"This is A," Adele added through the earpieces. "I'm in position."

"I have a visual on Captain Pretentious," Quintegrity told them.

The din of a helicopter grew louder from the distance, and Rover grimaced at the incoming aircraft.

"Don't tell me," he muttered, "but she's in that helicopter?"

On the roof of a building several hundred metres away, Quintegrity nestled into a nook between some ventilation ducts. Her brunette, long-haired wig swayed in the wind as she peered at the approaching helicopter through her holoshades' magnification ability.

Wriggling her fake mustache, she said, "No. She's not in the helicopter. She's strapped to the underside of it."

"*Huh???*"

Rover couldn't see well without a telescope or binoculars. Sure enough, though, as the helicopter grew nearer, he and Lumpy saw something drop from its underside. It freefell for a bit, then deployed a parachute with the word "PRETENTIOUS" in glowing neon lights on the underside for all the people on the ground to witness. An eruption of applause and cheering followed as dozens of Captain Pretentious' fans chanted her moniker.

"I guess her website didn't lie," Lumpy snickered. "She really is full of herself."

Not replying, Rover merely watched his incoming opponent swoop down from the cloudless sky. Her shadow darted across Coldshoulder Square, eventually coming into contact with her feet when she reached the ground.

Her landing was inappropriately graceful. She touched down first with her right foot, then her left knee, and finally her left hand. As she held the position, her cute patchwork-laden cape (yes, she had a *cape*) draped down behind her across the ground, flat with CGI-level perfection.

Also, she was, like, twelve years old.

In a heartbeat, three boys with immaculate hair wearing ruffled tuxedo shirts dashed to her side and caught the parachute before it could fall and ruin the flawless choreography. Holding the parachute above and behind them with the neon "PRETENTIOUS" as their backdrop, the boys themselves also held their own poses of well-formed showmanship.

To make things worse, the crowd went wild. Boys and girls cooed and shrilled as the minority of spectators responded with disgusted looks.

This had to be staged, Rover thought, feeling the need to gag at the sheer ostentatious display.

The three groomed boys disconnected the parachute from Captain Pretentious and removed her harness, then the little girl slowly rose to an upright position, sweeping her arms in ballet dance movements before she finally brought her highlighter-flamingo-colored eyes up to greet Rover.

Her button-bombarded jacket was like a ceremonial knight's from a fairytale and was starched to a stiffness that rivaled drywall. Her shirt was a flowery turtleneck blouse thing that was tucked into her tight, polka dotted dress pants. She wore knee-high boots and silky gloves with a kitty ear headband on her head of frosty, shoulder-length hair to complete the look. As for the color scheme of the entire ensemble...imagine a disemboweled rainbow being the victim of a paintballing massacre.

The ruffled-tuxedo boys quickly folded up her parachute and returned to her side. Instantly breaking out of her graceful stance, she thrust her silky, touchscreen-capable glove-clad finger at Rover.

"Oi, prick!"

Rover glanced around, then smiled and shrugged.

"Sorry," he said, "but I must've mistaken you for somebody else. The person I'm waiting for knows my name."

Captain Pretentious narrowed her highlighter-flamingo-colored eyes at Rover, then held out her right hand to her side, palm up. One of her boys presented to her a tablet and placed it in her grasp.

"Very well, *Rover Chork*," she said, looking down at her tablet as she operated it. "I had expected your low-class rudeness, you being an everyday pleeber...but I'll honor your miniscule pride by referring to you by your birth name."

She preened herself, fluffing her hair and adjusting her starchy jacket. With her tablet held out at arm's length, her flat expression quickly changed to a glowing smile to take a selfie, only to revert back to the flat, bored countenance after the shutter sound effect.

"Ugh, great..." Rover groaned, starting *Glove Alien Fight* on his smartphone. "Getting insulted by a spoiled, bratty kid is all I needed today."

There was a gasp among Captain Pretentious' fans, and a double gasp among her three ruffled-tuxedo boys. Captain Pretentious, though, bared her teeth and shook her fist at Rover.

"You have *balls* to call me a kid!" she hollered. "Don't you know *anything* about me?!"

Adele was posted on the rooftop across the street from where Quintegrity kept watch, and she listened in on the competitors' conversation through the communication earpieces. She peered over the side of the building, glaring at Captain Pretentious from afar.

"Oooh…" Her fists trembled with anger. "I really wanna punch that bitch in the face."

"Easy there, A," Lumpy muttered as he stood next to Rover. "Hitting children is, uh, frowned upon."

"Then, let the frowning rain upon me!" Adele hollered.

Rover sneered at Captain Pretentious. "I think the more I know about you, the more I'll need dementia to clear my brain of your idiocy." He furrowed his brow and took a demeaning step forward. "Actually, I never heard of you until your albatross crashed into my school yesterday…so I guess you're not *that* famous!"

More gasps accompanied the bulging veins on Captain Pretentious' face.

"If you had a shred of intellect," she said through gritted teeth, "you'd know that I'm a full-grown woman. I'm almost twice your age, so *you're* the brat here!"

"Oh-ho-ho!" Adele snickered. "She's not a child, she's just a legal loli. Hitting adults is less frowned upon than hitting children, right?!"

The low buffeting of more aircraft propellers came from the distance. Adele squinted, seeing another helicopter that appeared barely larger than a speck over the horizon.

"Don't tell me," she grumbled, straining her eyes to watch the aircraft. "She has *another* helicopter? Ugh…it looks like it's coming this way."

Somebody appeared next to Adele, and she jumped as Quintegrity's smiling face came within centimetres of her own.

"Ack!" Adele shouted, thrashing her arms in fright. "Q?! You can really freak people out with how fast you move! You're better at sudden appearances than I am!"

Not answering, still smiling, Quintegrity pushed her finger onto the bridge of Adele's nose between the eyes.

"Boop!"

A little pad stuck to Adele's skin, which projected the solar-blocking hologram directly in front of her face.

"You're letting me use your holoshades?" Adele asked, looking around.

"It's bright out here," Quintegrity told her. "It'll protect your eyes from the sun." She imitated using binoculars with her hands, making rings with her fingers in front of her eyes. "They have a zooming function to see far away. They don't have an AR function, though, because I don't need a device for that."

"This is perfect, thank you." Adele took a gander at the approaching helicopter, zooming in automatically. "Huh? How'd they know I wanted to zoom in? Do they have Brainlink technology???"

"Yep!" Quintegrity replied.

"Wild..." Adele was in awe. Zooming in more on the approaching helicopter, she could see it in great detail. "Wow, these zoom in far! And...okay, it's probably not Captain Pretentious' helicopter. It looks like..."—her stomach felt cold— "a Thugforce Militia chopper..."

She turned to Quintegrity. The older girl stood there, her hands held behind her back, keeping a serene smile on her face behind the fake mustache and brunette wig hair. However, her eyes appeared less vibrant than usual...inconsistent with her smile.

"Hey, Q...?" Adele noticed something was amiss in the girl's expression—a distraught visage masked by a smile. "What are you thinking about?"

Slowly, Quintegrity's grin filled with her telltale vibrancy as she looked at Adele, eyes now crinkling along with her upturned lips.

She swayed her hips, shifting her weight from one foot to the other. Her hands were raised halfway, snapping her fingers in time with every other motion of her body.

Snap, snap, snap, snap

"I'll be spending more time on the ground for this event," Quintegrity replied, her voice laced with tranquil traces. "R has a match to win, and I'll do whatever I can to help him."

Adele glanced back at the cliff-side parking lot overlooking most of Easterly Thugwood. Her brother and his friend were there, surrounded by a crowd with Captain Pretentious and her boys. The crap-talking banter still came through Adele's earpiece.

She turned down the earpiece volume.

"Yeah, he has a match to win," she said, "but..." Looking at Quintegrity, who continued to sway and snap her fingers, Adele realized she had nothing to say, no point to make. Quintegrity's groove answered whatever question Adele couldn't put into words.

Snap, snap, snap, snap

The deep roar of the powerful helicopter grew louder.

Quintegrity suddenly stopped her dance. She turned around and looked up, reaching out toward the sun burning bright and hot in its cloudless domain. Her fingers cast their shadows upon her skin, but did not block her face—she wanted the sun to see the calm, quiet smile she had to offer it.

"Even from the ground," she said softly, still reaching for the sun, "I'll be able to *touch the sky*."

And for several seconds, Quintegrity looked directly into the sun, not flinching, not squinting, and not blinking. Adele felt the need to talk Quintegrity out of such a retina-searing act, but deep down, she knew not to say anything—not to ruin this moment of heart-to-heart between the burning sun and the extraordinary girl, both of which were shining with equal dazzle.

A crescendo of cheers caught Adele's attention, and she whirled around to see down into the crowd, zooming in with the holoshades.

"…—ey…?" She turned the volume on her earpiece back up, hearing her brother's disgruntled voice through it. "Hey! R to A???"

"Yeah, A here, I hear ya."

"Are you even listening? What are you doing?!"

Adele looked back at Quintegrity still reaching toward the sun…touching the sky.

"Um, I was just staring at the sun, sorry," Adele replied absentmindedly, staring at Quintegrity.

"What? How unevolved are you to do *that*?!"

"Don't worry, R," she said, smiling as she watched Quintegrity lower her arm, inhale deeply, and leap from the rooftop. "I'm wearing your girlfriend's holoshades for this heart-to-heart with the sun."

"Listen to what I was trying to tell you," Rover grunted as he configured his character's settings and equipment. "The match is a Strongest Hero one. That means I'll be competing alongside Captain Pretentious against hordes of enemies. The one who kills the most will be the winner."

"Got it," Adele confirmed. "What do you want us to do?"

"The two players will be confined to a limited area. Do you see the AR wall around us?"

Adele looked through her phone screen. "I do. It's a see-through barrier around you, like a big dome."

"Our avatars can't leave this area," Rover explained, scrolling through his list of character's accessories. "The enemies will appear all around us outside the barrier and come at us. Unlike the hidden rings, everyone can see the enemies with AR. I'll need you to keep a lookout and tell me what's coming. I'm sending L to assist you."

Lumpy received a nod from Rover, and he hurried out of the cliff-side parking lot and crossed the street. Overhead, the Thugforce Militia helicopter soared past and slowed down, changing its course.

"Tch." Rover spit on the ground and muttered into his communication earpiece. "It *really is* a Thugforce Militia chopper."

"Do you think it's here for...ya know?" Lumpy asked through the communicator.

The helicopter lowered its altitude, circling around in a slow, wide arc.

Rover kept his eye on it. "They're probably curious about this crowd. They often take care of riots and largescale disruptions of peace, and it's common for them to supervise big public gatherings."

"Hopefully, that's the case," Adele said from the rooftop, zooming in on the chopper as it nudged closer to the crowd. She scanned the area, but had lost Quintegrity. "Although...Q took off. She said she's sticking to the ground."

Rover replied, "It's possible the Thugforce Militia is here because of me... They could've seen in all those online videos that Q was with me—"

"Ixnay on the etailsday," Lumpy warned as he jogged into an alley. "Our communicators are prone to wiretapping..."

"What gives here?!" Captain Pretentious shouted, shaking her little silk-covered fist at the helicopter as it circled around again. "That is sooo distracting and unnecessary! This is a peaceful event, dammit."

Rover laughed, mocking her. "Coming from the person who parachuted from her *own* helicopter just to get here!"

"Yeah, that's right, you pleeber," she retorted, standing akimbo, a smug grin on her childish face. "I aim for *extreme pretentiousness*! It's in the name, after all."

"Call her Gertrude," Lumpy said, looking for a ladder to climb onto a building. "I found out online it's her real name. Gertrude Flubberbulge."

Sneering at his opponent, Rover said in a droning voice, "Yeah, whatever, *Gertrude*."

The crowd went silent. Even the helicopter overhead stopped in place. The girl (woman?) dropped her jaw, her bright eyes going colder and darker than a dead fish's. Murderous vibes crackled out from her, like an insidious aura of contempt and malice. With a corpse-like expression and words like the leaking stench from the underworld, Captain Pretentious stared at Rover as the onlookers shivered.

"People only address me by that name..." she said darkly before clenching her fists with rage and screaming, "when they WISH FOR DEEEAAATH!!!"

"Too bad it's the wrong match for that!" Rover shot back as the pre-match timer counted closer to zero. "We're fighting side-by-side, and there's no friendly fire!"

More than a hundred spectators had their AR devices tuned in to the match as it kicked off, many of them recording the footage or livestreaming the video online.

In his studio, some tens of kilometres away, Benedict Torrent leaned back in his chair, a small smile on his face as he watched the live feed of the match beginning, sipping a mug of steaming chocolate malt milk.

"*Raawwrrrr*!!!" Captain Pretentious' war cry (or whatever that shriek was) carried into the surrounding district, down the streets, and off the buildings.

17!17@17#17$17%17^17&17*17(17)17_17+17

Half a block away, Quintegrity pressed her back against a brick fence, staying out of sight of the loud Thugforce Militia helicopter. At the sound of Rover's opponent already screaming in frustration, she could only smirk.

A delicate *whoosh* rushed by from overhead, something anyone would think was a gust of wind. However, Quintegrity had already ducked into a pear-bean bush, knowing that whooshing sound very well.

Even with my disguise, I still should hide. Those Militia fighters may be easily fooled, but that Cohort Squadron chopper isn't piloted by sharp-eyed, quick-witted geniuses for nothing. As I thought, they're on my tail...which is very unfortunate for them!

She giggled to herself before hearing the Cohort Squadron chopper whoosh by again, a little farther off this time. Her sharp footsteps echoed as she sped down the alleyways at half the speed of sound, yet she still failed to get a visual of the stealthy helicopter...and she knew they had failed to see her, as well.

Captain Pretentious

AGE: 31
HEIGHT: 145cm (4' 9")
HAIR COLOR: Frosty
EYE COLOR: Highlighter–flamingo
OCCUPATION: Entrepreneur, online celebrity, and charity organizer.
FAVE FOODS: Chardonnay–glazed seaweed mushroom casserole.
FAVE HOBBIES: Alcoholic tea parties, video games by the pool.

A well-known online celebrity with her own media production company. She is very prolific, providing various coverage and information for her viewers. Her other entrepreneurial ventures include tech development and various business services.

To her despair, her childish appearance and horrible personality were mostly what propelled her celebrity career. She also hates her real name, Gertrude Flubberbulge, and lashes out at all who utter it. Despite her downsides, she is a charity activist and donates much of her wealth. She is also a significant influencer, and many people become wealthy or successful from partnerships with her.

ROVER... Lvl 853

All Money... {T}35,700

Allowance... {T}34,700
Fundraiser... {T}0
Food Slip... {T}1,000

<<EXPENSE GOALS>>

Benedict's Payment... {T}100,000
Anti-Grav Skateboard... {T}499,999

<<CURRENT EQUIPMENT>>

Gloves... Infantry
Armor... Jinnin Tunic
Acc.1... Farm Equipment
Acc.2... Yakuza Tools

<<SPECIAL NUMBERS>>

① ② ③ ④ ⑤

⑥ ⑦ ⑧ ⑨ ⑩

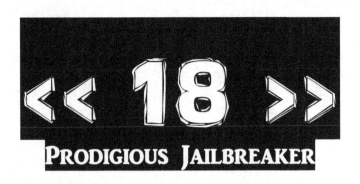

PRODIGIOUS JAILBREAKER

THROUGH the augmented reality cameras, spheres of virtual light flashed where each in-game enemy spawned, giving only a one-second warning before their arrival. The spawns seemed random in both timing and location, although they adhered to the real-world environment and only spawned on the ground.

The random appearances made it difficult for Rover's scouting party to spot the oncoming danger, and the AR monsters emerged from any side street, alleyway, and tunnel to swarm the two competitors.

Lumpy rounded a street corner, watching through his phone, when some enemies spawned in front of him.

"Four more Goblins and one Gull Hornet are coming from the northwest down Retcho Avenue," Lumpy broadcasted through the communication earpieces.

"They're pretty much flocking from the southwest, too" Adele said, spotting the enemies through her phone. She was near the top of a utility pole, scanning the area around her. "Goblins, Zombies, and Bugbears."

"Got it!" Rover replied. He watched the approaching horde come from all directions. Overhead, the Thugforce Militia helicopter kept a slow, low orbit around the area.

I don't want to rely on the Beelzebub Glove Aliens just yet, he thought. *My Infantry Glove Aliens should do just fine for now, and I have the Knitted Glove Aliens if I need some extra variety in my attacks.*

His character stuck both arms out straight ahead, firing simple energy bullets from its fists, a standard Infantry Glove Aliens attack. The spray of fully-automatic projectiles could damage the monsters beyond the transparent barrier enclosing his and Captain Pretentious' avatars. As such, Rover began getting kills before the enemies had reached them.

"Well-played, prick!" Captain Pretentious called out with blatantly patronizing intent. "Thanks for the idea!"

She equipped her avatar with the Flaming Glove Aliens and commanded it to launch fireballs at the swarm charging from the opposite direction. Virtual flames spread around the cliff-side parking lot's AR environment, igniting the enemies and dealing continual damage. Onlookers cheered at the digital, burning carnage.

Her Flaming Glove Aliens don't reach as far as my Infantry Glove Aliens, Rover thought while taking out enemies in rapid succession. *Her fireballs are the only long-range attack that weapon has, and the rest are close-quarters. Still, she can inflict widespread burning damage to compensate for—*

His thoughts were interrupted when Captain Pretentious whirled around and redirected her flames. Some Gull Hornets and Beagle Eagles had flown up from the cliff's ledge. She caught them on fire, and her avatar rushed in to defeat them with some blazing punch combinations.

She knew they were coming up over the cliff?

"Hey, guys!" Rover called to his team through his earpiece. "There are enemies coming up over the cliff. I think one of Captain Pretentious' boys are down there keeping an eye on things for her, so check it out!"

"I'm on it!" Adele pocketed her phone and hurried down the utility pole, hopping two ladder rungs at a time, then dashed toward the cliff side. She kicked off her sandals to more easily climb the tall chain link fence barefoot, and she peered over with the magnifying holoshades. There was a small footpath along the rock face, and sure enough, one of the ruffled tuxedo-shirt boys was down there with a tablet.

She wedged her feet into the chain link fence, getting a good grip with her toes, and leaned over the top to examine the area through her phone's AR camera.

"Yep, there's a guy down there. Some monsters are spawning on the footpath below. The flyers are flying up, and the others are climbing. You've got a lot of them coming, so keep watching the ledge, R!"

"Right!"

Rover's character held both fists together, gathering energy for a flickering ball of light, then launched it at the monsters across the parking lot. It exploded on impact with a Goblin, taking it and eight surrounding enemies out at once.

I have a limited number of those Beam Grenades, so I gotta save them...

With the nearest threats eliminated, he turned to the Beagle Eagles swooping over the ledge. They entered through the barrier before Rover shot them down with the full-auto energy bullets.

Captain Pretentious laughed like a child who had stolen a hundred cookies while she roasted enemies coming through the barrier, their virtual screams of agony coming through her tablet's speakers. However, the burning enemies continued to attack, swinging their rusty sawblades and shooting their crooked nails from rickety nail guns. Eventually, their HP dwindled either from burning damage or Captain Pretentious' character's fist strikes.

Still, the monsters had infiltrated the playing field.

"Theeey're heeere!" the tiny woman sang maniacally.

She pummeled flaming Goblins and Zombies alike, both of which were highly susceptible to Fire Elemental damage. This gave Captain Pretentious an advantage as enemies fell to digital ash around her character.

Rover resorted to the best close-quarters attacks for the Infantry Glove Aliens: a cavalry sabre.

"About ten more Trolls and Zombies coming from the northwest," Lumpy warned. "Plenty more behind that."

The single-handed sword's strikes were stronger than the Flaming Glove Aliens' punches. Rover chopped down the surrounding foes and lobbed another Beam Grenade into a group of monsters. With no more enemies on his side within the barrier, he directed more full-auto energy bullets into the horde around Captain Pretentious' character, taking some out.

With a jagged sneer, she derided Rover's quickness at stealing her kills. "Ooh, that's how it is! Can't get your own enemies, eh?!"

"Beggars can't be choosers!" Rover retorted, flashing an arrogant smirk.

"Two Gull Hornets behind you, R!" Adele called.

"And a swarm of all kinds of enemies from the northwest!" Lumpy added.

Rover shot down the Gull Hornets coming over the ledge, and then directed his energy bullets to the approaching horde across the parking lot, thinning the flood of oncoming attackers. Some of the enemies' nail gun attacks hit his character from afar, but the equipped Jinnin Tunic armor happened to have piercing resistance, which greatly lessened the damage.

"Listen up," Rover said into the communicator as his energy bullets continued flying, "I need you guys to keep an eye out for the Goblins, Zombies, and any other enemies weak to the Fire Elemental. I'll try to take them out at long-range before they get close. Captain Pretentious is favoring her flame attacks, and I'm pretty sure she might have more kills than me by now because of it."

"Right!" Lumpy and Adele replied in unison over the communicators.

Rover clicked his tongue. "Q? What's the word? I haven't heard from you in a while."

"I hear you loud and clear!" Quintegrity's zesty voice came from Rover's earpiece.

"What have you been doing?" Rover grunted, suppressing the monsters' advancement. "L and A have their hands full watching my back!"

"They certainly do!" she replied. "In fact, they're doing such a good job that there's nothing more I can do right now. Don't worry, I've been waiting for a moment when I need to step in. Until then, I have my hands full as well."

"Huh? Doing *what*?"

"I'm going to capture one of Captain Pretentious' boys! Hee-hee-hee!"

"Wh-What??? Capture?!" Rover heard a warning from Adele, and he spun around, readied his character's sabre, and then slashed at a Bugbear that had climbed over the fence by the cliff ledge. "J-Just don't hurt him, Q!"

"Gwa-ha-ha-haaa!"

Then she went silent.

"Q? Q???"

No reply.

"Hrrrm…" Rover mumbled to himself. "Actually, I'm kinda looking forward to what she's about to do."

18!18@18#18$18%18^18&18*18(18)18_18+18

One of the ruffled tuxedo-shirt boys hung from a second-story window outside a throw rug tailor store, his right hand gripping the window molding while his left hand held up his tablet to scout for virtual monsters.

"Three Trolls and two Bugbears approach from the southwest, Captain," he said into his communication earpiece.

With great agility, he pushed off the building, grabbed a tree branch with his free hand, and descended to the lower branches and to the ground…

…And right into Quintegrity's arms.

"Caught you!" she chortled.

"WAAHHH!!!" The frightened boy leapt from Quintegrity's arms like a scared cat jumping straight up, landing on his feet. "Where the heck did you come from?!"

"Not from nowhere!" she replied, practically cheering about it. "I've been *stalking you*!"

"Ehhh…" The boy demurred, shrinking away from the mustachioed, glowing face.

Quintegrity looked around, seeing the high fences, surrounding buildings, and building overhang that blocked the sky.

"Mm-hmm!" She gave a single, resolute nod, appearing satisfied. "This is a good spot to talk."

"Talk about what?" the boy asked, keeping his distrustful eyes on her.

"It's about the helicopters around here." Holding her hand up to her ear, she said, "Hear that?"

"Huh?" The boy listened for a few seconds. "Oh, the Thugforce Militia helicopter? They've been monitoring the AR matches lately. We see them at all of the matches Captain has attended or participated in the last few days."

"Why are they monitoring the matches?"

Shrugging, the boy said, "I dunno. Probably making sure no trouble happens. They always monitor big group events, anyway. Concerts, sports, and all that stuff. Keeps the peace."

"Oh?" Quintegrity was intrigued, tilting her head and grinning. "That makes sense! But...what about the *other* helicopter?"

The boy glanced around—he had to get back to the game.

"Well...Captain likes to make flashy entrances, ya know? That's her own personal chopper. I think it's really cool! I can't believe I get paid to do the stuff I do!" He smiled a happy, handsome smile.

"No, no, no, no." Quintegrity shook her head and waved her hand. "I'm talking about the *other* helicopter flying around with the Thugforce Militia one."

Confused, the boy asked, "What other one?"

Quintegrity smiled softly, pointing at the boy's tablet. "Look around the sky with your augmented reality camera."

With half-lidded eyes, the boy told Quintegrity, "Come on. I have a game to get back to. If I don't—"

He didn't even see the girl move...but she was suddenly by his side. Giggling, she gave him a playful shove hard enough to push him against the throw rug tailor building.

"Hey!" The boy puffed out his chest. He seemed quite muscular under his shirt, despite his average build. "What the hell's the matter with you? I don't care who—"

Again, he failed to see Quintegrity move. Before he knew it, she had rushed over, stopped directly in front of him, and pounded both of her fists into the cement wall on each side of the boy's body, trapping him in place.

Already startled, his blood ran cold when he noticed Quintegrity's fists had literally gone *into* the cement wall, halfway up her forearms.

Her cute smile moved closer to his panicked face.

"It's just a small request." Her voice was still soft, but loaded with danger, like a pincushion full of dynamite needles. "Can you do that for me?"

"...I th-think I just p-p-peed myself, ma'am..."

"Use your AR camera to find the phantom helicopter. I just wanna know how many lights are on its underside." Her smile broadened and cheeks blushed, putting a sparkle in her eyes. "Tell me, and I'll get you a fresh pair of undies!"

"Y-Yes!"

The boy stumbled on wobbly legs out from under the building's overhang and stood in the open. Quintegrity twirled her fake mustache and watched him aim his tablet around, searching the skies. Nearly half a minute passed when he noticed something.

"Oh!" He followed it with his tablet—the speed at which he moved indicated how fast what he'd seen was traveling. "I saw something!"

"You did?" Quintegrity clasped her hands together and grinned. "What'd it look like?"

"I took a video of it…"

The boy walked back (his legs still shaking) and showed Quintegrity the recording. In the two seconds it was onscreen, she could clearly make out its distinct futuristic shape and dark color.

"It really is a helicopter," the boy said, replaying the video on repeat multiple times, "and…it only appears on the augmented reality?"

"That's correct," Quintegrity told him, patting him on the back, laughing as the boy tensed up from the touch. If she could punch through a building, she could turn him into pudding, after all.

"It has one light on the bottom," the boy added. "Weird…I've never heard of this in *Glove Alien Fight*. Are there even helicopters in the regular non-AR game…?"

"Thank you so much!" The girl reached down her shirt and removed a clean pair of briefs. "I gotta go help Rover now!"

"R-Rover?!"

Stupefied by confusion and fear, the boy hardly had the will to take the gift. The underwear smelled like peanut brittle mousse pie when he hooked the garment on his finger.

Then, the girl skipped away, sticking to the alley while she glanced at the sky.

Holding the underwear at arm's length between his finger and thumb, the boy's face twitched.

"I…don't know if I should put these on…" He rubbed his thighs together. "But…I should…"

18!18@18#18$18%18^18&18*18(18)18_18+18

Having made it across the street, Quintegrity hid between two vending machines, one selling fried fish and the other selling anti-motion sickness kits. She switched on her communication earpiece.

"Captain Pretentious uses jailbroken tablets," she broadcasted through the communicators. "She or someone she knows is a prodigious jailbreaker who's risking being trodden by the law."

"Huh?" Rover asked. "How do you know?"

"Because I'm awesome!"

"…Right…" He sounded flustered, being in the heat of a match.

Lumpy chimed in, "There are rumors on the internet about her using jailbroken tablets."

"And I confirmed it!" Quintegrity boasted.

"Really?" Rover wondered aloud. "I wonder if I'll be able to use that information in this match, though."

"You can do it, R!"

Peeking out of her hiding spot, Quintegrity didn't see anything else worth acknowledging, so she took a moment to evaluate her discovery.

Normal tablets used for games wouldn't be able to detect the AR cloaking on government vehicles. Their tablets clearly were store-bought models available to the public, but illegally jailbreaking them would upgrade their specifications to near-Militia-grade ability. Doing so is dangerous because they could get caught, but it's also quite…pretentious!

She glanced at the cloudless sky again. No danger.

More importantly, it's only a one-light Cohort Squadron chopper… They aren't that serious yet.

She giggled.

Well, at least as unserious as the Cohort Squadron can be. I'd better change my wig, though.

18!18@18#18$18%18^18&18*18(18)18_18+18

"Forgive me for correcting you, Captain, but I know what I saw. It was, without a doubt, an in-game helicopter! A girl with a mustache told me! I have it on video."

"Now isn't the time for this discussion!" Captain Pretentious' voice blared through the groomed boy's earpiece. "After this match, I demand to see your video!"

"Yes, ma'am."

He staggered out of the restroom stall where he'd changed into the underwear Quintegrity had been carrying in her bra. He tucked his ruffled tuxedo shirt into his cotton dress pants.

How'd that girl know what size I wore? he wondered, lifting his legs high a few times, testing the undergarment's fit.

"And what the hell have you been doing?" Captain Pretentious hollered at him. "You haven't updated me in a while, and when you do, it's about some dumb *helicopter!*"

"I-I apologize!" Shoving the door with his shoulder, he remembered it swung the other way, so he flung it open and barged into the noodle restaurant he'd ducked into after meeting Quintegrity. "I had to use the restroom! You know I have a weak bladder!"

"You'd best quit confusing your bladder for your brain. Next thing, you'll be pissing your mind straight out! Your worth rests in your loyalty, and even the most loyal dogs won't stop the sled for a piss break! *Understand*?!"

"Yes, ma'am!"

The restaurant patrons, all elderly, gave him disapproving glowers as he made for the exit. He wore a distraught look while he bumped into several occupied chairs and tables, apologizing more to the person over his communication earpiece than to the people whose noodle meals had been interrupted.

ROVER... Lvl 853

All Money... {T}35,700

Allowance... {T}34,700
Fundraiser... {T}0
Food Slip... {T}1,000

<<EXPENSE GOALS>>

Benedict's Payment... {T}100,000
Anti-Grav Skateboard... {T}499,999

<<CURRENT EQUIPMENT>>

Gloves... Infantry
Armor... Jinnin Tunic
Acc.1... Farm Equipment
Acc.2... Yakuza Tools

<<SPECIAL NUMBERS>>

TOUCH THE SKY

"ZOMBIES from the northeast, R."

"I'm on it, L."

"Goblins are reaching the top of the cliff, too," Adele added.

"Damn," Rover grumbled, "what's with all these fire-vulnerable enemies? Is this match rigged against me?"

"I think you're doing pretty well," Lumpy said. He'd found a lookout spot on top of a tattoo parlor, giving him a wide view to spot augmented reality enemies.

"Oh yeah?" Rover asked. "How do you know how well I'm doing?"

Lumpy shrugged. "Hopeful speculation?"

"Your hopes have never helped my dreams," Rover replied with a frail smirk. "What about you, Q?"

Quintegrity's bubbly voice came through Rover's earpiece. "Everything's peachy! I know what I need to do now for this match to work in your favor."

With a well-aimed Beam Grenade, Rover took down an entire swarm of Zombies before they could enter Captain Pretentious' fiery range.

"And don't worry," Quintegrity added as Rover shot down some Goblin stragglers that had crossed the playing field barrier, "I won't hurt anyone."

"It's bad that you feel the need to assure me of that."

"Hee-hee..."

"Heads up, R," Adele said, leaning over the fence by the ledge and watching the approaching threats. "There are stronger enemies climbing up the cliff: Raptor Mantises."

"That's perfect." An excited, devious glimmer appeared in Rover's eyes. "It's about time some monsters appeared that are in *my* favor."

"Yes," Lumpy agreed, moving along the edge of the rooftop to get a different angle on the action through his phone. "The Raptor Mantises are stronger than these runts, true...but they're fire-resistant. That means Captain Pretentious will lose the effectiveness of her fire attacks."

"Not only that," Rover said, quickly swapping out his character's Glove Aliens. "The Raptor Mantises are weak against Cuddly Elemental attacks, and my Knitted Glove Aliens are perfect for that!"

His onscreen avatar's hands were soon covered in fuzzy, multicolored yarn that hung from its entire body as if it had rolled around in a crafts store. Some of the spectators laughed at the ridiculous appearance, but they also knew that Rover's tactic could potentially alter the tide of the match.

These new foes stood over one metre tall when scaled to the real world, slightly taller than the players' avatars. The first Raptor Mantis climbed the chain link fence and hopped onto the ground, hissing and snapping its claws on the tips of its mantis arms while showing its fangs.

Rover's avatar spun the multicolored yarn over its head, forming a spider web net, then fired it at the charging monster. The attack was slower than the Infantry Glove Aliens, but the stretchy, sticky web covered a wide area at mid-range.

Two Gull Hornets were also caught in the same wide attack, but they were not defeated because the strike was not powerful. The Raptor Mantis also survived, but it had much more HP than the other monsters and had taken by far the most damage Rover had inflicted in a single hit since the start of the match.

One more strike of the same Cuddly Elemental attack killed all three monsters at once. Satisfied, Rover chuckled.

That chuckle was followed by an obnoxious laugh from Captain Pretentious.

"Oh-ho-ho-ho-ho! New enemies have arrived!" Her character stood at the center of a virtual conflagration that burned all of her surrounding enemies to nothingness. "And they're weak to Cuddly Elemental damage!"

Rover scoffed, knowing something was brewing in the miniscule madam's mind.

"Captain," said a boy's voice through her earpiece, "more Raptor Mantises approach from all sides. They're mixed in with the same previous enemies, too."

"So," Captain Pretentious said, seeing the wave of incoming enemies through her tablet, "...this is where the battle gets *really* engaging..." A toothy grin stretched across her small face.

Rover alternated between his Infantry Glove Aliens and Knitted Glove Aliens, taking out fire-vulnerable enemies at a distance before routinely casting out cozy nets to wipe out the Raptor Mantises.

Sweat covered his face; this method was intense, and a single slipup or change in enemy formation could destabilize its effectiveness. Some enemy nails from their nail guns chipped away at Rover's character's HP. The next wave of monsters was nearly there.

With a swath of fireballs, Captain Pretentious eliminated most of the fire-vulnerable Goblins and Zombies as they encircled the playing field barrier. The ignited monsters took continual damage, charging in with agonized roars, swinging their weapons and claws wildly before the little woman's character punched them out. All except for the large Raptor Mantises—they were immune to being caught on fire, and they charged closer.

"Heh." Captain Pretentious chuckled under her breath, switching her Glove Aliens.

Everyone saw Captain Pretentious' character covered in the same colorful yarn as Rover's character, wrapped around the hands and lacing over the body in a messy tangle. The character's new appearance matched the murdered-rainbow color scheme of the person controlling it.

"She has the Knitted Glove Aliens, too," Rover grunted.

Lumpy clenched his jaw, leaning against a ventilation shaft on the rooftop, and he watched the match through his phone.

"So much for that new advantage you thought you had," he said flatly.

When the current wave of enemies passed through the barrier, two large, spoked discs of spiraling energy appeared on both sides of Captain Pretentious' character, resembling yarn spinning wheels. They linked to the character's colorful strands, glowing and whirring as they spun faster.

"What is that?!" Rover saw the action through his phone, trying not to be distracted from the battle. "I don't have that attack... Her Knitted Glove Aliens are more leveled up than mine!"

The opponent's avatar spun in circles, swinging the glowing yarn spinning wheels around it at blinding speed. Extending farther out with each revolution, the wheels mowed down the crowd of surrounding monsters, taking them all down in a single hit, including the Raptor Mantises.

Seconds later, the wheels vanished when the attack ended. With a quick weapon swap, Captain Pretentious followed up with more flames and burned the next wall of fire-vulnerable enemies. She repeated this pattern several times over the next minute.

"Damn!" Rover shouted when his character took a nasty bite from a flying Raptor Mantis. "Her method is way better than mine!"

"Urrghh..." Adele groaned as she watched Captain Pretentious rack up kills at an accelerated rate while Rover's character took hits. "You better think of something quick, R!"

During a brief lull in enemy attacks, Rover opened the onscreen menu to change his Glove Aliens.

He had a last resort, and there was no time to falter.

"Fine! Here we go!"

19!19@19#19$19%19^19&19*19(19)19_19+19

Seven blocks away, Quintegrity swapped her wig to the dreadlocks and top hat. Sneaking around, she located the inconspicuous entrance to an infrastructural command tower, a facility that controlled the district's utilities and automations. A guard stood watch in front of the dark entrance, and most people wouldn't have noticed him due to his uniform purposely camouflaged with the drab concrete walls and ground.

Quintegrity scampered up the tower's wall, using any protrusion from the building to climb it. After listening to the urgent commentary regarding Rover's game, she had her reason to nab a peek at the ruckus.

Just above the surrounding buildings and trees, she took a gander at the parking lot where the AR match took place. The stiff breeze played with her wig dreadlocks.

Jagged pillars of virtual ice, visible from nearly a kilometre away, blasted upward to form a tomb of freezing graphic textures within a settling tempest of digital snow and frigid dust. The entire parking lot was encased along with every spectator, reaching up to the Thugforce Militia chopper hovering just above the icy peaks.

A smile found its way to Quintegrity's mouth. "Backed into a corner, my dear?"

"Shut up," Rover muttered through the earpiece. "I'm not capable of the crazy things you are, so don't make fun of me."

"I'm not making fun of you, silly!" Giggling, she added, "Don't worry. The timing is tight, but still on track. You could even call it perfect."

"I'll just let you do your thing, then..."

"Yeah!"

Alerted by a sudden whooshing sound, Quintegrity scurried alongside the infrastructural command tower, using the minute protrusions, conduit pipes, and maintenance ladders. The sound shot past her.

She turned off her earpiece.

"They still haven't found me!"

Rover hadn't bothered asking Quintegrity what she was doing. Instead, he respected the pause—*his* pause—during the temporary, morose stillness caused by Winter's Sepulcher demolishing every enemy in the playing field's vicinity.

While the crowd broke out of their stupor with cheers and applause (and boos and accusations of cheating from Captain Pretentious' fans), Quintegrity dropped off the tower from over four stories high. She threw a cinder block against a metal panel around the corner, distracting the guard with the sound, and she approached the infrastructural command tower entrance.

The fingerprint scanner recognized her to be authorized personnel in a facility responsible for upholding the mechanical stability within Coldshoulder Square and the other surrounding districts, letting her inside before the aggravated guard came back.

Simple mechanical security can't withstand my destiny, she thought as the door slid shut behind her, *nor withstand the funk of my soul!*

A middle-aged man yawned as he monitored the feedback equipment in the control room on the top floor. From behind him, the swish of the automatic sliding door startled him, and he snapped around in his chair to face his visitor.

Standing in the doorway was a mustachioed girl with long dreadlocks and a top hat. She spoke up while the operator fumbled and jumbled his stumbling words.

"Good day, sir. I'm here on behalf of the Chloroform Broker Department."

The man regained his sense of duty as the mysterious visitor advanced into the restricted area. He adjusted his glasses with a shaky hand.

"No, you're not," he said, trying to sound firm, but his back was hunched and tense. "Uh, because th-the Chloroform Broker Department would never send someone dressed as an uncouth high schooler to do work. Who are you?"

Blushing, Quintegrity said, "Yes...I suppose you're right. I apologize for this inconvenience."

An explosion came from down the hallway, and the operator's eyes nearly popped out of his face.

"Oh mercy!" he cried. "What *was* that?!"

"The chloroform closet," she answered, upholding professional etiquettes and sagacious calmness armed with uncanny sickly-sweetness.

"*Aahhhh*!!!"

The operator bolted from his station and out the door, Quintegrity hot on his heels down the hallway.

"Wait, mister!" The girl grabbed the man's wrist, stopping him. "It's dangerous!"

"Then, what are we s-s-supposed t-to do???"

Despite the miniscule time required to blink, the man didn't have that chance before the handkerchief covered his mouth and nose.

"Just breathe deep."

The voice...the soft mulberry eyes...the hint of a prankster's contentment in the curls of her smile; such were all the things the man took in and enjoyed as the overwhelming peacefulness pulled his eyelids down and latched them shut.

In no time, he was snoring.

"Sorry for the panic attack, mister," she said as she hoisted the snoozing guy into her arms, carrying him back to the control room while skipping to the beat in her head. "There's no real danger. I'm just good at making noise! Ha-ha!"

With the operator propped upright in the corner, Quintegrity removed her mustache, wig, and hat. She looked over the tower's control dashboards, her finger on her chin as she gawked. Childlike curiosity lit her eyes as the colors, lights, and funk-fueled interface won her over.

Snap-ity! Clap! Snap-snap! Clap!

Snap-ity! Clap! Snap-snap! Stomp!

The lights responded to her sounds, to her motions, and to the groove that fluxed and flowed through and out of her. Each panel, gauge, meter, and indicator surged and receded with her rhythm, turning the entire heads up display into a visual orchestra under her baton.

Oh, yes. The funk was *strong* here.

"I've never used a Disc Jockey User Interface before," she snickered to herself, glancing back to the slumbering, mumbling man in the corner. "You're quite the groovin' dude to be using this every day. I salute you, groovin' dude. And...now that I take a good look at you, your glasses aren't normal prescription glasses. They have AR capabilities."

Quintegrity turned back to the control console and sat in the gaming chair positioned at the helm. She pressed the funny-looking button that stood out, being huge and the color of pretty tropical fish and labeled "Manual Operation."

Every shadow vanished as the room lit up with electronic splendor. Under manual operation, the augmented reality control panels revealed themselves to the master of the chair, and the motion capture cameras watching from every direction mapped the master's movements to the hologram coordinates—Quintegrity could "touch" the AR controls responsible for the heartbeat of one hundred square-kilometres of the Easterly Thugwood Prefecture.

Two AR turntables rimmed with bright lights were side-by-side in front of her. Beyond and around them, various sliders, buttons, and dials completed the interface, all feeding into equipment for recording, looping, and sampling.

...This machine was made for her...

She placed her hands on the holograms. They shimmered and scintillated from her touch. The music began, and the city bowed to her beat.

On the far west end of Coldshoulder Square, a patch of traffic signals went dark. Honking motorcars clogged the streets as road rage and anarchy descended upon the motorists.

But, there needed to be more.

Quintegrity put her entire body into feeling the flow, gracing the console's every AR component with her fingers and palms, twisting her back to reach the farthest equalizers, extending her legs to stomp each floor pedal, transcribing the grooviness from inside her veins into the pulse of the city itself as she laid down the funkiest track in recent memory. The feedback to the master's chair was audible in the soul, bypassing the ears and boogying straight into the brain. Furthermore, this music had always been clear to her, within her, *because* of her...and now the districts' vitals were one with her music as her audience, her stage, her dance partner...

...And as her soul.

She cackled in euphoric delight, taking this soiree to the metaphorical ballroom floor.

"Ya'll ready to open up this *mosh pit*?!" she announced to nobody in particular, yet everybody all at once. Every tooth in her ear-to-ear smile glistened in the electric bonanza, and with both arms laid upon every slider at once, she pushed every setting up past eleven. "*Heeeeere comes the breakdown!!!*"

The water main bubbled and burped. The surveillance systems winked out and whimpered. The thuggoon servers crashed and crinkled. Sprinklers spritzed and spluttered. Automated paint immobilizers let the coatings run wet. Vending machines ran away. Streetlamps activated disco ball mode. As the city let its hair down and gave in to the commanding DJ, the east end of Coldshoulder Square transformed into a rave scene reflecting Quintegrity's quintessential funk.

However, every citizen caught up in the commotion was terrified. Chaos ensued. They couldn't handle the cosmic power of the funk.

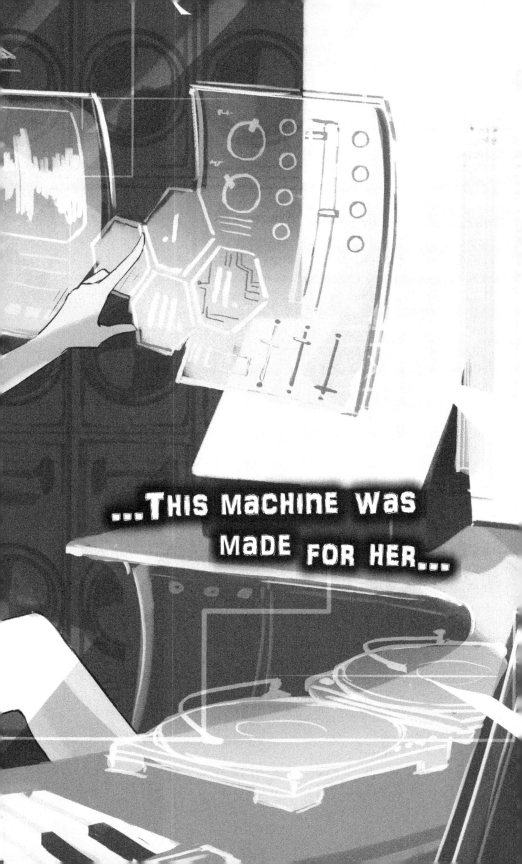

Captain Pretentious howled in anger, stabbing her index finger at Rover. "You think this *ice blast* of yours is something special, don't you?!"

"It holds its own place in my ice-cold heart," Rover said, shrugging.

"I don't know how the hell this isn't cheating!" she hollered.

When the arctic attack finished its animation and slowly vanished to nothingness, the two competitors looked around through their AR devices. Rover could see more monsters approaching from the distance, and he equipped his Infantry Glove Aliens to prepare for more long-range attacking.

"Two minutes left," Rover grunted, seeing the countdown timer on his screen as he waited for the monsters to enter his range. "And I have no idea how many kills she has." He tugged on his shirt collar to release some of the heat, then wiped his sweaty forehead on his arm.

Captain Pretentious growled when she saw Rover's avatar equip the Infantry Glove Aliens again. "He's just *messing* with me, choosing not to go all-out. What a frickin' brat." She narrowed her eyes at him. "No doubt, he'll make a name for himself. It was fate that we met today."

"I thought you didn't believe in fate, Captain," one of her boys replied through her earpiece.

She turned toward the incoming monsters. "I also don't renounce it, either."

"Maybe Rover feels guilty for abusing his special Glove Aliens," another boy said.

"Doubtful," she muttered.

Adele peered over the chain link fence she clung to—she had an unobscured view of the east side of Coldshoulder Square at the bottom of the cliff. Catching her eye from the distance, the colorful lights in the town below were flashing and pumping to a beat she couldn't hear, but could sense.

"What in the world...?" She zoomed in with her holoshades to check it out. "Is there a festival in town?"

"Everyone," Quintegrity said through their earpieces, "let me know how Captain Pretentious reacts next."

"Huh?" Rover fired full-auto energy bullets at the incoming Zombies, keeping them out of his opponent's blaze. "Reacts next to what?"

"It's comiiiing!"

"*What's* coming?!"

Captain Pretentious smeared her fires around in front of her avatar, waiting for the enemies to run into her blaze. As she watched the horde grow closer, something at the top of her tablet's screen grabbed her attention.

"What the...?" She focused on the object; it was airborne, dark as night, and moving quite fast, about to pass overhead not too far from the playing field.

More importantly, she couldn't see it with her eyes.

"That's it!" one of the boys broadcasted through their communicators. "That's the helicopter I saw, Captain!"

"Is that a rare enemy?" Aiming her fireballs up, she unleashed a barrage at the incoming thing. "I'll be taking that one, thank you!"

The spectators turned their devices toward the sky...but saw nothing, exchanging confused whispers and expressions. Even Rover, Lumpy, and Adele couldn't find what Captain Pretentious was going on about.

Is this...what Quintegrity mentioned?

"Q," Rover said, taking out two Raptor Mantises with some well-timed knitted nets, "Captain Pretentious is saying she sees something..."

"Ooh...is it distracting her?"

He looked at the childish woman, seeing her frustration as she aimed her fireballs into the sky.

"Uh, yeah..."

"Splendid!" Quintegrity cheered. "That's your opening!"

"Wh-What are you talking about???"

"Dammit, dammit, dammit!" Captain Pretentious hollered, her avatar being swarmed and damaged by enemies. She was forced to run around and switch to defensive maneuvers for a moment. "My attacks went right through that thing!"

"Maybe it was invulnerable to fire, Captain," one of the boys told her.

"No, that wasn't it..." She mowed down her surrounding enemies with her powerful yarn spinning wheel attack. "It would've showed there was no effect. Instead, the hits didn't even register!"

She growled as the mysterious aircraft headed east over the cliff, which was followed by the Thugforce Militia helicopter. The boy on the walkway along the rock face watched them head in the same direction.

"Captain, it looks like they're going to where all those lights and stuff are happening," he said into the communication earpiece. "I still can't see what's happening down there."

"Whatever!" Captain Pretentious spat. "It's out of my attack range now. What a fine distraction that was!"

Amid the action of the match, Rover's curiosity threatened to generate his own distraction.

"Q!" he said. "What did you do?"

"It ain't over yet, R!"

"H-Hey! Answer me!"

"Not yet..."

In the epicenter of the infrastructural control tower, Quintegrity stood and shoved the gaming chair away with her butt. She cracked her knuckles, took a deep breath, and readied her finale.

Her arms and fingers blurred from the speed of her operations, mixing and looping the funky, bumping beats with the skill and complexity needed by three operators at once. The electric rave lights captured her afterimages, flowering and blossoming as Quintegrity moved the city's lightshow from the east end of Coldshoulder Square to the west and beyond.

"*Maximum overload!*" she called out as she forced the Disc Jockey User Interface to reach breaking capacity.

An earthquake came from the west. Rolling blackouts followed.

Rover and Captain Pretentious were brought to their knees. Adele fell from the fence, landing hard on the shaking ground. From the rooftop he was on, Lumpy wrapped his arms around a post to keep himself upright. People stumbled and collapsed. In an instant, the AR match flickered and lagged on everyone's screens, but soon restored itself.

When the earth calmed down, the people did not. Scared shouts and nervous whispers blew through Coldshoulder Square and the surrounding districts.

Rover glanced around, not seeing any damage to the town.

However, there was still a game to be won.

"Nature can't stop me!" Captain Pretentious yelled, getting back to her feet. "But, it can *stop* with the distractions, please!"

She wiped out another group of enemies with her spinning wheels, then noticed the mysterious helicopter had changed its route, heading west toward the origin of the earthquake and rolling blackouts.

"There it is again!" Still, the fireballs did nothing. "What the hell?! I *know* I hit it!!!"

It was another opportunity for Rover to get kills while his opponent did not. He dropped his last Beam Grenade, slashed through several enemies with his sabre, and squelched plenty more Raptor Mantises with his Cuddly Elemental yarn.

Just as the match reached its climax, the clock ran out.

Rover's breath stopped as he looked at his screen. Everyone held the collective silence, waiting for the results...

It was a tie.

The monsters vanished. The sudden death round began as both players had their characters reduced to one HP each.

Neither he nor Captain Pretentious vocalized anything. In fact, Rover didn't even look to see where his opponent was—his Beelzebub Glove Aliens were equipped instinctively, and his finger was already in motion toward the button labeled Winter's Sepulcher...

Frigid mayhem was all everyone's screens could show.

Rover's knees shook as his body lost its tension so quickly that he almost fell over. His character still stood as the icy tomb surrounded it.

Yet, the match didn't end.

Captain Pretentious laughed an ear-piercing, skin-crawling, nail-biting laugh. Damn, did she look and sound evil at that moment.

"I know your finishing move, prick!" she jeered. "The Antifreeze Bracelet is only good for one hit, but it made me *invincible* against any ice attack you had!"

"Shit!" Rover couldn't see the opposing character—there was too much ice blocking the view. Only the word "Nullified" was visible, indicating how much damage Captain Pretentious' character had taken.

His slippery finger slid across his phone screen.

Swap out the Beelzebub Glove Aliens! Equip the Infantry ones!

He immediately deployed the Stationary Riot Shield, a protective barrier that blocked all attacks for a set time. The Infantry Glove Aliens could use it only once every five minutes, so this would probably be his only chance to deploy it this round.

Fireballs came through the frozen structures, hitting the Stationary Riot Shield as soon as it was up. Rover was spared.

The animation for Winter's Sepulcher ended, and through the vanishing ice graphics, he watched Captain Pretentious' avatar leap into the air with a signature sound effect:

Sproing!

The Froggy Glove Aliens... They let the character jump very high. They also have a lightning-quick, long-range attack with near-perfect accuracy because of its auto-target...The Tongue.

Time chugged to a crawl as the opposing avatar soared toward Rover. Hitting it with the Infantry Glove Aliens' energy bullets would require too much accuracy. Hitting it with the Knitted Glove Aliens' web would require too much time.

There was only one pair of Glove Aliens for the task.

He equipped the Beelzebub Glove Aliens. However, Winter's Sepulcher wasn't usable until after the effects completely vanished, but a split-second margin of error was all Rover had.

He tapped the onscreen button labeled "Infernal Rain."

Everyone watched Rover's character put both fists together, aim straight up, and launch an explosive blast high into the AR airspace. The huge projectile itself was nowhere close to touching the opponent, but the concussive force blew Captain Pretentious' character backward, knocking it out of the air and killing it before it landed on the ground.

However, people were still focused on the shooting projectile, blazing like a meteor trying to escape the world and leave the atmosphere. They watched it through their devices, soaring higher than they thought the AR would allow.

Far, far above the real world, only visible through augmented reality cameras, Rover's giant ball of burning wonder exploded, painting the AR sky with a supernova cloud more beautiful, impressive, and captivating than any real-life firework. Hundreds of smaller fireballs showered the digital environment, pouring flames over the entire AR battlefield and way beyond.

19!19@19#19$19%19^19&19*19(19)19_19+19

Two kilometres away, atop a basic radio tower, hidden inside and between the rungs and bars, Quintegrity watched the apocalyptic inferno lay waste to the virtual land. She let out a soft vocal utterance, mesmerized by the sight.

"Wowww..."

Something fluttered in her heart, tickling her eyes and toying with her goosebumps.

"Rover...you and I are capable of *many* of the same things." Holding her hand to her chest, she closed her eyes and smiled. "Even from the ground, you can touch the sky."

She had already removed her earpiece and turned it off, so nobody heard her say that.

ROVER… Lvl 888

All Money… {T}35,700

Allowance… {T}34,700
Fundraiser… {T}0
Food Slip… {T}1,000

<<EXPENSE GOALS>>

Benedict's Payment… {T}100,000
Anti-Grav Skateboard… {T}499,999

<<CURRENT EQUIPMENT>>

Gloves… Beelzebub
Armor… Jinnin Tunic
Acc.1… Farm Equipment
Acc.2… Yakuza Tools

<<SPECIAL NUMBERS>>

① ② ③ ④ ⑤

⑥ ⑦ ⑧ ⑨ ⑩

<< 20 >>

100 Pages of Stupid, Trolling Comments & Ridiculous Speculation

THE interior of Captain Pretentious' helicopter was swanky and cozy, ordained with nutmeg cream-toned carpet, lavish couches, grove oak paneling with shatinum trim, and tons of other worthless appeals meant to snag the eye and comfort the buttocks.

Captain Pretentious had already changed into her kid-sized bunny onesie pajamas, sitting cross-legged on the couch with her chin resting on her hands, and she stared dolefully at her tablet propped up with its stand on the small table in front of her. Her three servant boys shared the couch across from her, each transfixed on their own tablets.

Every one of them used this time in flight above Thugwood to review separate footage of the match Captain Pretentious had lost to Rover Chork.

"Why is it," the little woman muttered while watching her tablet, "that everyone thought I was crazy for shooting at that...that *UFO*...?"

The first of the boys exhaled a chuckle through his nose. "If I may be honest, ma'am, it's because you *are* crazy."

With a faint smile and almost imperceptible nod, she replied, "You aren't mistaken."

The piss-pants boy wiggled in his seat, feeling the snugness of his new underwear.

"It doesn't make sense," he said, "the more I look at it...that UFO doesn't seem to be part of *Glove Alien Fight*."

"Yes..." Captain Pretentious tapped her finger on her tablet, freezing the video on a clear frame of the mysterious aircraft. "That much seems apparent. It may be because of our jailbroken tablets."

"But, augmented reality objects only appear in their respective apps!" the third boy grumbled, rustling his perfect hair which fell back into perfect formation. "Even if they're jailbroken and capable of unexpectedly advanced features—including the AR—that doesn't explain how this object from another app appeared in the *Glove Alien Fight* app."

"You're right." Captain Pretentious leaned back in her seat and folded one leg over the other, stroking her onesie's right bunny ear between her little fingers. Her highlighter-flamingo-colored eyes narrowed at her tablet. "That's why I think this UFO isn't an AR object or the product of an app."

The boys stared at her from across the small table the way birds on a powerline do.

She turned her tablet and its stand around to show them the still shot of the aircraft.

"See that? It kinda looks like a helicopter, right?"

The boys nodded in unison, like birds cocking their heads.

"That much is obvious—the propellers give it away, but…"—she reached over and used her thumb and index finger to zoom in on the video— "take a closer look. See anything peculiar?"

She pointed to the underside of the helicopter, and although the footage was blurry, there was one bright light near the front. Upon closer inspection, the boys also made out a series of circular lights the color of electric eggplants dotting the entire underside.

"Anti-Grav?" a boy asked, leaning in closer.

"Seems so," she replied. "Also, remember we couldn't hear any noise from this one…although those pricks in the Thugforce Militia chopper made it hard to hear myself *think*. Still, this one doesn't seem to make much sound."

The piss-pants boy held his chin. "But, why would a chopper need Anti-Grav?"

"For extra maneuverability and speed?" Captain Pretentious slumped back, sighing and shrugging. "Maybe the propellers are for auxiliary power, like a hybrid engine. Or maybe just for show."

"Wait," the third boy said, shaking his head, "this would mean it really was a *real* object, not AR!"

"AR cloaking technology isn't just stuff of science fiction anymore," the bunny-clad woman told them. "It's real."

"It's not available to the public, though," the first boy commented.

"As far as I know, it isn't yet." Her eyes narrowed to slits as her grin broadened. "There's only one organization I know who designs and uses AR cloaking."

After some thought, the boys gasped in unison.

"The Cohort Squadron!"

"Bingo! Now, the bloody question is what were *they* doing there at our match today?"

"Hard to say," the third boy said.

"This could be bad for us." Captain Pretentious rubbed her chin. "All this footage of me online could be evidence that we jailbroke our tablets.

We won't be arrested, but could face a steep fine of at least a million thuggoons."

"Should we dispose of the tablets?" the first boy asked.

"Yes. Upload all the important files to the cloud, delete everything else that could be evidence of our jailbreaking, and disintegrate the tablets. Disintegration Centres are government-regulated, so make sure to do it yourselves. Good thing we were prepared for the day when we'd get caught for this." She smiled, content with herself. "Now, it's just strange how the Cohort Squadron would be out. It's not impossible for them to do routine patrols, but I've *never* heard of them being deployed without serious cause."

"It's all weird." The third boy crossed his arms. "Not to mention those special Glove Aliens that kid had. What were they?"

"Meh." The little woman flipped the cover over her tablet, then curled up on the small couch into the fetal position, her bunny ears flopping over her eyelids. "I'll think about it later. I need a nappy."

"Tired already, ma'am?" the first boy asked.

"Yeah…that match was the best one I've had during this whole *Glove Alien Fight* AR fiasco, and it wore me out. It's hell gettin' old, boys." She popped her thumb into her mouth and slept the rest of the flight.

While she slumbered, her boys flipped the covers over their own tablets.

"Who was that kid she played with today?" the third boy asked with a yawn. "Rover Chork?"

"Yeah," the first boy replied. "Word all over the internet is he was challenged to an AR match by Benedict Torrent himself."

"He's great at *Glove Alien Fight*, I gotta say." The piss-pants boy wiggled in his seat again. "And…he has a great support team, too…"

20!20@20#20$20%20^20&20*20(20)20_20+20

The rooftop of the Chork house didn't offer a view any more spectacular than the other rooftops in the neighborhood, but nonetheless offered a better view than the front porch or back deck. Rover rested his back against the outside wall of his bedroom, his socks clinging to the rough shingles beneath his feet. He was joined by Adele and Lumpy, as well as his girlfriend who snuggled against him as they watched the last hues of daylight follow the sun below the horizon—the same hues (when stirred into rose petal lemonade) comprising Quintegrity's natural hair as it caught the delicate breeze.

"Whew!" Lumpy finished the simple side quest he'd undertaken in *Glove Alien Fight* and looked up from his phone with a sigh of relief. "Not playing any *Glove Alien Fight*, for once?" he asked Rover.

Rover felt Quintegrity wrap her arm around him, making his head spin from a rush of primal urges.

"N-No. I, uh…just wanna…you know…"

Quintegrity tightened her hold on Rover. "You wanna spend quality time with your girlfriend!"

Bashful chuckling was Rover's response.

Pocketing his phone, Lumpy gazed toward the darkening western sky. "I still don't get it, Quinn."

The girl lifted her head from Rover's shoulder. "Get what?"

"How you managed to, uh…do that." Lumpy dropped his voice. "How you did what you did earlier in Coldshoulder Square."

"Terrorist!" Adele hissed.

"Watch it!" Rover warned his sister, giving her a sour glower.

Adele shrugged with a meager smile. "I'm kidding. But really…knocking out the power grid and causing earthquakes is probably mega illegal…" She was met with Quintegrity's somewhat curious expression. "As if doing mega illegal things has stopped you before…"

Quintegrity laughed, jumping to her feet. "No need to fear! If it's for justice, it's all good!"

"Hmph." Rover rubbed his temples, irritated. "You gotta be careful, though! People might not see it the same way as you. The *law* might not see it the same!"

"Just answer one thing, Quinn," Lumpy said. "Captain Pretentious acted as if she saw something—a 'rare enemy,' or something—and it looked like she tried shooting it with her fireballs."

"It was a Cohort Squadron helicopter," the girl answered quickly, keeping her eyes toward the west skies.

The other three tensed up.

"A *what*?!" Rover got to his feet and stared at Quintegrity. "You mean to say the Cohort Squadron was there watching the match, too???"

"No," she shook her head and turned to Rover. "The Thugforce Militia was probably there for that. The Cohort Squadron,"—her perky smirk stretched up to her eyes— "was there for *me*."

"*Whaaat*?!" Rover's hands and face became clammy. "B-B-But…"

She put her index finger to his lips, instantly silencing him. As he looked at her peaceful and even *playful* expression, he had to resist the urge to lick that finger—it was soft and smelled like the sugarbutter walcorn cookies she'd baked earlier, but he had a sense of decency to uphold here.

When she lowered her finger, the others waited for her reply.

She said nothing. The horizon grew ever darker as she turned to face it.

"I heard about something called AR cloaking," Lumpy said. "Supposedly, it uses AR technology, but kind of in reverse. It can make physical objects invisible to the naked eye."

"How?" Adele asked. "If it's AR, then you'll need AR devices to see it. Or...un-see it...?"

"I really don't understand it," Lumpy replied. "I guess the Cohort Squadron is rumored to have developed it. With their kind of budget, anything is possible."

"Well," Rover said, mulling it over, "Quintegrity can see the AR without devices. I guess that means *everyone* has some kind of potential to do the same. Like you say, Lumpy, with the government's resources, they could do anything, maybe even create specialized AR that people can see (or un-see) with just their eyes."

"Yep," Quintegrity said with a confirming nod. "I don't know how it works because this strolls smack dab into adventurous legends and jiggery-pokery government secrets,"—she made rubbery gestures with her arms and hands— "but in truth, it isn't impossible to see AR objects without AR devices." She smiled, equally proud and adorable. "I'm living, breathing, conniving, high-fiving proof of that!"

Adele groaned. "I don't wanna pretend I know how that kind of AR technology makes sense..."

"It's probably beyond us." Lumpy checked the time on his phone. "I better get going. Curfew is a ways off, but I have homework." He and Rover bumped fists. "Catch ya tomorrow, dude."

"Yeah," Rover said. "Later, Lumpy."

"We'll prepare for Operation Maid Invasion at the meeting," Quintegrity told Lumpy before he climbed through Rover's bedroom window. She struck a muscleman pose. "It's gonna be *lit*, fam!"

"I'm looking forward to it." Lumpy grinned, then entered the house and closed the window behind him.

Adele yawned and stretched. "Yeah, I'm gonna get inside, too. I need to finish my neurotic aquatics homework. Blech...I hate that class."

That left Rover and Quintegrity alone together, both standing on the roof as the stars above peeked out behind their dark curtain of cosmic swirls. He looked at her back as she stared toward the vanishing sunset, and for the first time that day, Rover felt at peace.

Almost.

"You need to stop breaking the law, Quintegrity."

She turned back to him, her face tranquil, but nothing more.

"Me being in Thugwood is already breaking the law." Why did she always sound so nonchalant about these things? "Breaking it of the highest degree, aside from murder or overthrowing the government."

"That's why you need to stop doing *additional* law-breaking."

With a thumbs-up, she said, "It'll be okay."

"That's not what I'm getting at!"

"Then, what *are* you getting at?"

Rover furrowed his brow. Was she actually showing an attitude toward him?

"If you keep breaking the law," he said, keeping his temper in check, "then you'll stand out more. I don't think you're doing really bad things...I hope...but,"—he sighed— "I want you to be more careful."

With a double thumbs-up, she said, "It'll be okay!"

He gave her a deadpan stare. "That isn't the same as saying you'll stop doing illegal things."

Giggling, she said, "Of course not."

His eye twitched. "Then...tell me you'll stop breaking the law."

"I have to break the law to be here, silly."

"Stop doing it more!"

"*Nope*! Ha-ha-ha!" She sprung her arms and legs outward in cheerleading fashion, her face sparkling with honesty and happiness. "I'm gonna do whatever I wanna do!"

"Uhhh..." Rover's continued deadpan was interrupted by more eye twitchiness as his face sagged from disbelief.

Quintegrity stood with her ankles together, lacing her fingers behind her back. Suddenly, she took on a timid demeanor, looking down at the shingles they stood on.

"I'm gonna do whatever I *have* to do..."

In the blink of an eye, she was right in front of Rover, wrapping him in a hug. His heart raced. However, something pushed his hormonal savagery back down—something suspiciously and inconveniently along the lines of...of woe, as he could only think to put it.

She let go. The night was warm, but suddenly felt much colder without her embrace.

"I'll see ya tomorrow, Rover!" Her voice and expression held no trace of their serious conversation having happened. "Goodnight!"

Rover couldn't answer. Even after Quintegrity cartwheeled from the roof. Even after she dashed into the night, becoming one with the shadows. Rover couldn't answer.

He remained on the roof for some time after, his eyes wandering across the constellations as his mind wandered somewhere farther. Lights from aircrafts moved around the sky, some distant, some close enough to vibrate the glass in his bedroom window. He watched them, wondering what kind of helicopters they were. Surely, they weren't all Thugforce Militia choppers, right? With the rise and advancements of Anti-Grav, conventional propulsion aircrafts were becoming cheaper and more popular as personal vehicles.

"There sure are a lot of them these days," he muttered to himself, sitting with his back against the wall as he watched the aircraft lights.

He received a phone call, and he had a hunch as to who it was before checking his phone.

His hunch was correct.

"Hello?"

"Good evening, Mr. Chork," Benedict Torrent said. "Congratulations on your victory against Captain Pretentious today."

"Thanks."

"You should sound more excited than that. She's a major figure in the gaming and electronic entertainment industry. Not quite as well-known as myself, but our work is too different for a fair comparison."

Rover cracked a sliver of a smile. "I won't apologize for my lackluster tone."

"Ah, yeah, I didn't expect much otherwise from you. Anyway, I'm not sure if you've seen the online reactions to your match today."

"I don't follow that stuff. But, I'm sure you have,"—his smile cracked a little more— "you being my biggest fan."

Benedict chuckled. "It's by far the most talked-about *Glove Alien Fight* AR match, by *far*. Although it's not her first loss, anything featuring Captain Pretentious automatically moves up the trending ranks. Aside from that, I can pinpoint two other reasons why this particular match has people buzzing over it."

"My Glove Aliens," Rover said.

"Yes, that's one reason. This is the first time anybody has seen them do something new. People are going crazy over it. It's sparked new hunting parties to find their own, although they don't know what they're called."

"Very few people know what those Glove Aliens are called."

"Well, it's got people riled up to find out. On the other side of the spectrum, mostly Captain Pretentious' fans, you using those Glove Aliens has caused an outcry."

Rover shrugged. "Let them say whatever they want."

"Anyway...the second reason why this match is going viral is, um, much more peculiar. There's plenty of footage showing Captain Pretentious acting strange near the end of the match. Do you know what I'm referring to?"

"Yeah," Rover replied, unwittingly looking at the aircraft lights moving through the starlit backdrop. "It was like she attacked something in the air, but nobody could see what it was."

"Could you see it?"

"I'm sure you'd like to know," Rover said amusedly.

Benedict laughed. "Well, whatever the case, just know that people are suspecting you."

"Huh? What do you mean?"

"You're already a trending topic. Those crazy Glove Aliens were enough cause for suspicion and all kinds of theories. The haters were already calling you a cheater, and they keep looking for reasons to call you worse things. Simply put, it's easy for people to jump to conclusions regarding things that are popular or mysterious. And jumping to conclusions, they are!"

Keeping his voice low, Rover said, "They think what Captain Pretentious saw... They think I had something to do with it?"

Although I didn't, personally...Quintegrity, though...

"That," Benedict told him, "and pretty much every wild variation of that. Regardless of the truth, this is going to build momentum and carry you with it. I've been in the business of online activity, following and setting trends, and practically studying this kind of behavior for a long time. From what I'm seeing, you're gonna be talked about for a while, especially if you keep getting involved with high-profile people and situations, like our upcoming match together."

"Greeeat," Rover muttered, slouching.

"Don't be bummed out about it. You gotta admit it's kinda cool to be famous because of a video game."

"Uh, kinda." He rubbed his chin. "Sorta wish it was a *different* game, though. Like *Per Sauna 5*."

"You may even find yourself a sponsor."

Rover grinned. "Heh, I didn't even think of that..."

"Anyway," Benedict said, "thought I'd let you know these things. A bit of advice: start paying attention to your online following. See what people are saying and doing. It's up to you how you wanna handle that information, but knowledge is power. A hundred pages of stupid, trolling comments and ridiculous speculation could be worth gleaning through for that one nugget of info that could make or break you."

"Sounds like a pain in the ass."

"It is." Benedict didn't sound like he was smiling, but speaking from hard-earned experience. "Okay, then...that's all I wanted to say."

"Cool, thanks for the tips."

"No problem. I look forward to our match, Rover."

"So do I."

ROVER… Lvl 888

All Money… {T}35,700

Allowance… {T}34,700
Fundraiser… {T}0
Food Slip… {T}1,000

<<EXPENSE GOALS>>

Benedict's Payment… {T}100,000
Anti-Grav Skateboard… {T}499,999

<<CURRENT EQUIPMENT>>

Gloves… Beelzebub
Armor… Jinnin Tunic
Acc.1… Farm Equipment
Acc.2… Yakuza Tools

<<SPECIAL NUMBERS>>

① ② ③ ④ ⑤

⑥ ⑦ ⑧ ⑨ ⑩

KICK ASS & CHANGE LIVES...FOREVER!

THE moment **Rover entered** the classroom for historical vandalism on Feefee-*day*, he was hit by a tank.

Or, at least, the scathing glare he received from Mrs. Historical Vandalism Teacher was equivalent to being hit by heavy artillery.

"Rover Chork!" The muscular woman folded her leg-like arms in front of her, furrowing her gargantuan brow.

Freezing in place, the boy squeaked out some kind of sound indicating compliancy.

Mrs. Historical Vandalism Teacher pointed her thumb at the repaired window. "Good work defeating the one responsible for sending an albatross through my classroom window." Her smile was equally frightening to her other facial expressions, resembling a demon ready to feast on innocent students. Some of her giant teeth were replaced with literal bullets (which were definitely live rounds).

"Th-Thank you, m-ma'am," Rover managed to stutter.

"As such," the giantess said, "you're relieved of your window repair responsibility." Her expression changed again, not smiling nor scowling, but just another look for a beast. "Don't let it happen again, or *you'll be my lunch.*"

"Yes, of course!" Rover saluted, horrified and unable to think of another appropriate response.

21!21@21#21$21%21^21&21*21(21)21_21+21

While walking through the halls of Southbound Thugwood High School, it was impossible not to notice the overflowing abundance of posters announcing the upcoming Interschool AthletaCom.

And those weren't the only reminders. Starting that day, as customary in the weeks leading up to the infamous sporting event, the school deployed thousands of little flying drones that whizzed and buzzed around the entire campus like wasps, flying the AthletaCom banners behind them while shooting everything with suction cup darts inscribed with the AthletaCom emblem.

Rover yanked a suction cup dart off his phone screen, the third that day, as he headed to the Clubhaus.

"Grr..." he grumbled, crushing the dart in his hand and throwing it on the floor. "Stupid, incessant reminders. It's not like anyone could *ever* forget the Interschool AthletaCom is coming up. Every school in Thugwood only hypes it up year-round. It's almost on par with Chrizzlemas and Goldie Week, for cryin' out loud..."

During the Super Club meeting in the luxurious club penthouse, Quintegrity showed a PowerPunch slideshow on the 254-cm TV to discuss the details of their maid café-style fundraiser, Operation Maid Invasion. Rover was only half-present, sitting on the couch in a heated level-grinding session for *Glove Alien Fight*, catching only snippets of the discussion.

"With our final menu decided," Quintegrity explained, "we'll need a day to procure all of our foodstuffs and supplies. Then, we'll need another day to set up our kitchen and café. We should also take some time to practice using the alien-like appliances safely—ya'll don't wanna accidentally roast your soul whilst trying to flip a flapjack! Harr-harr-harrrr!"

Adele let out a nervous chuckle, holding a piece of paper in her hands. "So...*that's* why Headmaster had us sign these waivers..."

Quintegrity displayed the next slide, showing crude drawings of everyone involved in the fundraiser with a job position title under each person.

"I'll be in charge of expediting and executive chef things," she explained, pointing to the TV with a metre stick stylus. "Adele and Lumpy will run the front of house, like the servant servers ya be! Arrr, matey..." She jabbed her metre stick stylus like a sword toward her seated club members.

"Why are you a pirate?" Lumpy asked.

"That means Rover will be on the cooking team," she added.

Rover glanced up from his game. "Oh, okay, I'll work in the kitchen. That's cool with me." He looked at the PowerPunch presentation. "H-Hey! What the hell? *Olaf and Daremont* are the other two cooks???"

"Of course!" Quintegrity beamed. "I predict a busy day for the café. Having three cooks is essential for maintaining an optimum customer turnover rate while balancing a favorable labor cost." She clicked to the next slide, showing her mathematical calculations scrawled across the entire wall-sized screen like hieroglyphics. "I created a financial forecast based on the assumption that all of us will be earning standard hourly wages during this operation."

Rover's brain hurt from just looking at the numbers. "Ummm…but we *won't* be getting paid hourly…"

She giggled. "No, but I like to pretend. Remember, team…everything we do now is practice for our futures! That's why I want Operation Maid Invasion to simulate the workforce environments you may find yourselves in someday." She clenched her fists so powerfully that the room rumbled from her exalted ambition. "Take *every moment* you can to build your experience…"

"…I'm trying to," Rover said, looking back at his game.

While Quintegrity, Adele, and Lumpy offered insight regarding ideal table arrangements and preventing grease fires through the power of prayer, Rover tuned out the meeting entirely. His head was in the game as he leveled up, but his main distractions pertained to his phone call with Benedict Torrent last night.

A lot of people are talking about me, and even more will keep talking about me the more I stay public with Glove Alien Fight. *Beyond being annoying, it's not really a problem…and it's actually really awesome, especially if I do get a sponsor!*

He glanced around at the other club members as they moved to the topic of making a soufflé rise through the heat of funk alone.

My main concern is Quintegrity. I doubt people will connect her to that blackout at Coldshoulder Square yesterday, or connect that to the Cohort Squadron chopper Captain Pretentious saw with her jailbroken tablets…but still… Am I being a worrywart?

"Don't look so worried, Rover-wart!" Quintegrity leapt onto the couch next to Rover, making him jump.

Looking at her beaming face, he had the impulse to protest, but knew it'd be futile to do so.

"Is it *that* obvious that I'm worried…?" he muttered.

She nodded, smiling, then wrapped him in a hug, making his cheeks blush as she smothered him with her softness.

"I know things are stressful," she told him, "but don't worry!" She squeezed him tighter, and he heard things pop inside him that normally don't pop. "Your *girlfriend* will whisk you away from the scary things!"

"Y-You're crushing me…"

"With *love!*"

Pop! Pop! Crack!

"*Hrrrggkkk!!!*"

When she let go, Rover's spine realigned itself.

"I'm concerned about you, you know," Quintegrity said, her soft eyes on him. "I don't want you to get too caught up in *Glove Alien Fight.*"

"I'll be fine," Rover assured her, trying to smile with confidence as his last vertebrae slipped back into place, making him wince.

"Ha-ha-ha-haaa!" Quintegrity cackled, standing on the couch with her hands on her hips, making Rover shrink away in fear. Pointing down at him, she said, "See how it feels?!"

Thinking it over, Rover replied, "You mean how you've been telling me you'll be fine, even though I have my doubts?"

"Yep."

"But, this is totally different! I'm playing a game, and you're...doing what you're doing..."

She gave him an innocent, blank face. "It's interfering with your sleep, which is unhealthy."

"Uhh..."

"And interfering with your eating, which is unhealthy..."

"Well, it's not like—"

"And creating an illogical obsession, which is ambiguously unhealthy depending on your coping mechanisms."

"Wait...what's a *copey mechasm*?"

"And it's making you into a well-known, celebrity-type thing, which can scramble your life and have nonconsensual interactions with your mental fortitude."

"...I don't know what that means...but it sounded creepy."

Quintegrity waved her hands in the air, her cheeks puffed with frustration. "So, the feeling is mutual!"

The couple held each other's gaze.

"Sheesh," Adele whispered to Lumpy. "I bet she wanted to get *that* off her chest for a long time..."

Sighing, Rover turned off the game and put his phone down. His eyes were dry.

"Okay, okay," he said, "I'll take a break from *Glove Alien Fight*..."

The radiant girl smiled, but only after a huffy sigh. Her peppiness returned to her movements as she grabbed the unicorn skull-shaped teapot off the sea-marble coffee table, and she refilled Rover's skull-shaped cup with sparkling fig and lavender tea. He took a sip. It was the perfect temperature.

"Speaking of *Glove Alien Fight*," Lumpy said to Rover, letting Quintegrity top off his cup as well, "are you going to accept any of those challenges?"

"Man," Rover moaned as he leaned back on the couch. "I got, like, *twenty-something* requests from challengers in my email inbox since beating Captain Pretentious, not to mention the ones I had before then."

"That's what you get for letting your email inbox pile up," Adele told him.

"Yeah, yeah...I know..." Rover took a big sip of sparkling tea, a glimmer in his eye. "They're just *lining up* to give me experience and their consumable items. Heh-heh."

He caught Quintegrity giving him another expressionless stare, which he'd come to realize wasn't necessarily *emotionless*—blank on the outside, yet as Rover could see in the girl's eyes, there was a shade of hope...and a tint of anticipation.

"But," he said, placing his cup on the coffee table, "it's also annoying. I'll see who I wanna face because my time is limited." He smiled at Quintegrity. "I got stuff to do here. This maid café fundraiser is gonna kick ass and change lives...forever!"

That seemed to light a torch in the girl's heart. "Yeah!"

21!21@21#21$21%21^21&21*21(21)21_21+21

By the end of the weekend, Rover felt like an old rug that had been left out to dry during a hurricane. Homework, the Super Club fundraiser preparations, and at least one *Glove Alien Fight* AR match had been crammed into each day. The stress was enough to pluck out his sanity and leave it for the wolves.

"But, I'm gaining levels!" he'd explain, often to only himself, as his exhausted smile pushed his weighted cheeks up to his saggy, skittish eyes.

He'd said that to Lumpy (again) that Nundinum-*day* afternoon while they hung out on Rover's back deck. His friend sighed with an unpersuaded grimace.

"Dude," he told Rover, "you're more like gaining levels up the staircase to the big dunce cap in the sky. Don't give yourself a heart attack or die from, like, forgetting to drink water." He blew on his steaming skewer of yakitori Quintegrity had whipped up for lunch. "You *are* drinking water...right?"

Rover looked up from his phone, his shifty eyes darting around the back yard.

"Now that you m-mention it..." he replied.

Lumpy handed his glass of Squirm soda pop to Rover. "Drink this. Save yourself."

Glug, glug, glug, glug

"Aahhh..." Rover wiped his chapped lips on his arm. "I didn't realize how thirsty I was." He laughed hard. Nothing was funny.

Lumpy leaned over the deck's treated wood parapet and took a bite of grilled chicken from his yakitori skewer, letting the tare sauce and seasonings drip into the grass below him.

"You should take the day off, man."

"*Never*!!!" Rover hissed, hunched over his phone while sitting in the wicker chair. "I'm so close...almost to level nine hundred ninety-nine...but these last hundred levels require *so many* experience points..."

"At least slow down from taking on so many AR matches," Lumpy told him. "You've been killing it, winning each one. You'll need to save up your items for the match against Benedict. If you lose now, all of those awesome items you got from the AR matches will be lost, and you'll be going against Benedict emptyhanded."

"That's not a bad idea...actually not bad..." Rover's eyes never left his phone screen. "With how close I am...I don't need more AR matches..."

"Do you know what else isn't a bad idea? Eating and drinking before you keel over."

Rover hissed again, his face becoming a little reptilian. Lumpy, knowing his words were falling upon deaf (and stupid) ears, looked back over the side of the deck and chewed another bite of his yakitori. He caught Quintegrity's eye as she grilled more skewers over the charcoal roasting hearth in the back yard, and she waved at him with a wide smile. Lumpy waved back.

The door leading into the house slid open as Adele stepped out, carrying a glass pitcher full of more cold-brewed Squirm soda pop, a lemon slice tastefully wedged on the rim. She placed the pitcher on the table, making the ice cubes floating inside clink against the glass.

"Hey, Adele," Lumpy said, "wanna do a match together? I've only done a few, and they weren't against you yet."

"Sure." She grabbed a skewer off the plate and sank her teeth into it. "After I eat. I'm dying."

"No, you're not dying," Lumpy chuckled, nodding toward the deranged Rover. "*That's* what dying looks like."

She chewed on her grilled chicken and rolled her eyes in agreement.

21!21@21#21$21%21^21&21*21(21)21_21+21

"Dead Rover, Dead Rover, send vital signs over," Adele said through Rover's bedroom door from the hallway Mondee-*day* morning.

"Leave me alone."

The door opened, and Adele entered the room with a smirk.

"You get any sleep last night?" Adele asked her brother.

"A little," Rover murmured, sitting on his bed in his pajamas. "It's Ad Jingle Day, so we ain't got school today to interfere with my life."

However, Adele could see the visible sheen of sweat on his face as his hands shook and bloodshot eyes bugged out.

"You look like a drug addict," she quipped. "Seriously, get some sleep."

"I'm *so close* to level nine hundred ninety-nine!" Rover declared, sounding a bit loony as his body trembled with every word. "Sooo cloooose…ha-ha…ha-ha-ha…"

His thumbs tapped across his phone screen, doing so with such speed that Adele figured he was in an intense battle…or just cracking up entirely.

"Like, *how* close?" she asked in disbelief.

Suddenly, Rover froze up and his harsh breathing stopped. A wild look was haphazardly welded to his face as the phone slid from his fingers and fell onto his lap.

"Uhh…" Adele took a step back, looking concerned. "You okay?"

"I did it."

Blinking, Adele said, "You…? Don't tell me…"

"I just reached the max level…" His necked popped as he turned his maniacal expression toward his sister. "And…I got a Special Number item…"

"Huh?!"

Adele hurried over, and Rover showed her his phone. There was an onscreen message saying he had acquired Special Number 5 for being the fifth person to ever reach level nine hundred ninety-nine in the game.

She clamped her hands over her mouth, stopping a squeal. "Y-You did it! You *really* did it! You're the fifth one *ever* to hit the level cap!!!"

Rover chuckled weakly, his body swaying as if his bed was on a rowboat. Without a verbal reply, he closed his eyes and fell over onto his mattress. Adele crept away, saving her excited squeal until she was in the hallway.

Nobody saw the boy until dinnertime, his face aglow and a spring in his step.

ROVER… Lvl 999

All Money… {T}35,700

Allowance… {T}34,700
Fundraiser… {T}0
Food Slip… {T}1,000

<<EXPENSE GOALS>>

Benedict's Payment… {T}100,000
Anti-Grav Skateboard… {T}499,999

<<CURRENT EQUIPMENT>>

Gloves… Beelzebub
Armor… Brutal Suit
Acc.1… Yakuza Tools
Acc.2… Unsetting Sun

<<SPECIAL NUMBERS>>

① ② ③ ④ ⑤

⑥ ⑦ ⑧ ⑨ ⑩

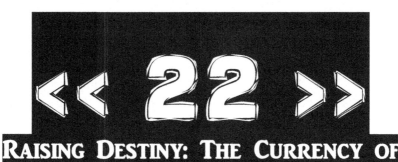

RAISING DESTINY: THE CURRENCY OF ALL THAT EXISTS

BEFORE school the following morning, Rover made it priority to inform Benedict Torrent that the first two conditions had been met for their AR match.

"Special Number 5, huh?" Benedict sounded pleased over the phone. "That's certainly impressive! Now, all that remains is—"

"The hundred thousand thuggoons," Rover grunted. "Yeah, I'm still working on that. And yes, I still think it's a rip-off."

"Such is the price of business," Benedict reminded him.

Oh, that almighty reminder that money is the only way around Thugwood.

And yet, as Rover was met with Quintegrity's hug when he stepped outside onto his doorstep, he almost forgot about the upcoming match while being smothered in his girlfriend's warmth.

"Congratulations on getting to level nine hundred ninety-nine!!!" She squeezed Rover tighter, pushing the blood into his face.

"How'd you know?" he asked when released from the hug.

"You emailed me about it yesterday. Judging by your recent obsessed behavior and the loose tone of your email, I assumed you did so in a mindless, half-asleep daze."

"...Oh. Good enough, I suppose..."

As Rover walked to school with Quintegrity and Adele, admiring his girlfriend's optimism so early in the day, an inkling of a notion seeped into his head: Maybe some people had the means of sidestepping the entrapment of money, not just because they had a lot of it, but because they could exist outside the system altogether.

Exist outside the walls.

Quintegrity said she lived outside the Jerry Co. Walls...in exile...

He zoned out until his sister spoke up.

"Next is paying Benedict the hundred thousand thuggoons," Adele said. She turned to Quintegrity. "Do you really think we'll make that much from our little café fundraiser?"

"Absotively posilutely!" Quintegrity replied, marching down the street with her timely high-steps. "Our school is huge with even huger appetites and a simply hugest addiction for anything the Super Club does. They'll flock, eat, and *pay*! You'll be getting papercuts and finger blisters from all the money-counting at the end of the day! Hee-hee! Not really...because there's no such thing as paper and coin currency anymore."

Quintegrity stopped walking. Rover and Adele also stopped, looking at her.

"Oh, I almost forgot to tell you," she said, grinning. "I informed Headmaster that the Super Club will be procuring provisions today. We won't be going to school so we can shop for groceries and goodies."

Rover's and Adele's faces lit up.

Wide-eyed, Adele said, "You mean...we don't have to go to school today?"

"Correct."

"All right!" Rover cheered. "It's awesome that you got permission to skip school in the name of the Super Club."

"I didn't ask Headmaster for permission," Quintegrity said proudly. "I *told* him."

Being in the Super Club really did have its perks.

22!22@22#22$22%22^22&22*22(22)22_22+22

While every other student in every other school all across the Thugwood Metropolitan Address attended their routine, mundane classes, the four Super Club members journeyed around to various grocery stores and foodstuff suppliers. They bought wiggly puddings and aromatic spices and succulent meatchops and exotic creams and decadent dangers of delicious disarray, checking each item off their sprawling shopping list one-by-one.

Quintegrity paid for all of it, never flinching at the total prices racking up and scaring the clerks with her assault rifle-shaped purse. During checkout at the seventh supermarket they visited, Lumpy whispered into Rover's ear.

"Quinn uses that Mythril credit card like she has infinite funds."

Rover wanted to shrug, but the weight from the grocery bags he carried made that impossible. "Maybe it *is* infinite."

"Like she has no monetary limits..."

"Maybe financially, she's outside the system."

Outside the walls.

22!22@22#22$22%22^22&22*22(22)22_22+22

Later that week on the day of the fundraiser, the Super Club began their preparations for Operation Maid Invasion first thing before school was in session. Every student was given a "Maid Pass" that allowed them to skip one full class of their choosing to attend the maid café.

As such, normal lunch was canceled. The cafeteria was practically handed over to the Super Club, and the scary lunch ladies were given paid leave to embark on whatever the lunch ladies did on their days off. (Cooking children in their homes was an urban legend, but the absence of any evidence *against* the myth was very disturbing.)

Getting the kitchen ready and prepping the food so early in the morning was annoying by itself. However, as Rover slipped the shiny black shoes on his feet and placed the frilly, lacey headband on his noggin, he realized there were many things in life far more awful than manual labor.

He looked at Olaf and Daremont as they assembled the embarrassing outfits—the same outfit Rover had to wear.

"Do we really have to wear..."—Rover gulped, not wanting to hear his own voice say it— "*maid outfits?*"

After a breathy, droning moan, Olaf placed a hand on his hip (and the poofy skirt).

"Wearing a *maid* outfit in a *maid* café?" he said. "Yeah, that makes nooo sense."

"It was Quintegrity's idea, I guess." Rover sighed, realizing he should've left his pride at the door. "She went through the trouble of being her own tailor for these outfits, so it wouldn't be right to let her down."

Daremont's eyes shimmered as he cracked a smile—Rover knew something stupid was coming.

"It's safe to say that Quinn..."

"No!" Rover bared his teeth at Daremont. "Don't you fucking say it!"

"...had these *tailor-maid* for us!!!"

Dragging his palms down his face, Rover *truly* rued not having left his pride at the door.

22!22@22#22$22%22^22&22*22(22)22_22+22

When first class started, the breakfast rush hit the café fast and hard. Despite not having a real breakfast menu (or any specific mealtime menu, for that matter), the students flocked to the maid café, desperate to try whatever kooky concoctions the Super Club's sorcery had sorceled up. Even some teachers, upon finding their entire first period classes empty, joined in the mob.

Adele was quickly overwhelmed, trying to seat the masses and take their orders with a tablet. Her primary source of stress, though, was having to uphold her friendly maid façade while dealing with the unruly customers.

"Nice outfit!" the boys would say, their sneers and snickers rubbing Adele the wrong way. She sensed the underlying motives in their crude leers directed at the tight leggings and short skirt.

"How adorable!" the girls would say, their glowing eyes and blushing cheeks getting under Adele's skin during the waves of questions regarding every possible punitive detail behind the maid costume's design.

"I-It's not like I *wanted* to wear this outfit!" she barked at one point.

"Ooh," a boy said with a sly smirk, "she's a *tsundere* maid!"

"*What'd you call me, bitch?!?*"

The boy laughed with Adele's fist quivering centimetres away from his nose. Suddenly, a gentle hand grabbed her shoulder from behind.

"Now, now," Quintegrity told her with astonishing tenderness, "that's no way to speak to a customer, Adele. They're our masters, after all!"

Adele and everyone around were mesmerized by Quintegrity's grace, and they all fell into order. It was no surprise that Quintegrity looked amazing in a maid outfit, as if it amplified her hospitality and well-meaning personality. Everyone in earshot nodded, happy to oblige with her statement of peace among the students.

Meanwhile, the kitchen was getting its ass kicked.

A small printer wirelessly received the orders from the tablets Lumpy and Adele carried, and it was spitting out order tickets like rapid fire.

"We need three more corndog sundaes!" Rover shouted, ripping the ticket from the printer and hanging it on the ticket rail over the pickup window. By now, he had a curtain comprised of dozens of little pieces of paper listing off the customers' desires.

Every ticket had a customization comment: "Make it funk-a-licious <3 (>.<)"

"Scratch that," Rover said, reading a new ticket, "*five* more corndog sundaes!"

"Like *that'll* be easy!" Olaf replied, his sarcastic tone still monotonous even while shouting. He slammed food onto several plates at once, setting them out for the servers to take.

"Palmaple syrup salad, sub almond butter!" Rover said, reading the next ticket and wiping his sweaty brow on his delicate sleeve. His frilly headband seemed to crinkle in tune with his distress. "And...*another* five orders of chicken wings?!"

"Maybe those wings should be a liiiitle *more* popular!" Olaf said, his hands moving wildly as he plated food at breakneck speed, as if we was a drummer for a heavy metal band during a violent drum solo. The lacey ends of his sleeves seemed to whistle in the wind of his movements.

"These wings are just *flying* outta the kitchen!" Daremont declared as he literally threw order after order of chicken wings through the window (Quintegrity caught them all, even while in the middle of expediting and helping place/deliver orders—she moved very fast).

"You look adorable, Lumpy!" Quintegrity chortled, appearing as a blur while grabbing plates of food. "Your scrawny figure is wonderful for crossdressing!"

"Th-Thanks," he muttered, short-winded as he picked up two deluxe parfaits.

The orders never stopped coming because Quintegrity never stopped seating customers. Adele and Lumpy stumbled toward the kitchen window, collapsing facedown. In the heat of the battle, stuck between punishing puns and snarky sarcasm, Rover forged on.

This is to pay Benedict Torrent! This is to be a king at Glove Alien Fight! *This is to beat CEO Claudius and lift the daily quota mandate! This is...*

Rover caught a fleeting snapshot of Quintegrity's face—she was glowing, sparkling, *shining*. He saw her lost in the thrill of the moment, the exuberance of doing what she does day in and day out.

The boy saw true, honest joy inside her.

This is for her.

For the rest of the day, no matter how grueling the pace Quintegrity set for the café, Rover made sure to match it.

And he did.

22!22@22#22$22%22^22&22*22(22)22_22+22

All six Operation Maid Invasion workers occupied the Super Club penthouse, the highest number of warm bodies to fill the expanse of top-notch accommodations all school year. The club president stood next to the enormous TV as she addressed her team.

"The café ran slower than optimum," Quintegrity told Rover, Olaf, and Daremont, "because the kitchen couldn't keep up."

Rover checked the bandage on his knuckle. Using a chef's knife was nothing new, but the fundraiser had demanded him to utilize one under less-than-comfortable circumstances and in ways he didn't know a knife could or should be used.

The thick adhesive bandage was clotted underneath with a spot of blood, but it looked dry.

It probably won't interfere with my match against Benedict, he thought as he pressed the bandage back down.

"We did fine," Rover told Quintegrity. "We're not superhuman like you."

"So, you're forgiven," she replied with a humble bow. "TV-*chan!*"

"What now?" the irate female voice grumbled from the TV.

"Show the revenue report, pretty please."

"Fine."

A line chart appeared on the wall-sized television, showing the number of customers served and income made each hour, but most importantly, the total amount of money made that day: over eighty-seven thousand thuggoons.

"That's *all* we made?" Rover moaned. "No way! Quintegrity, how much did we charge the customers?"

"A flat rate of a hundred thuggoons," she replied, "no matter what they ordered."

"*What*?!" Rover hollered. "For all that work, that's all you charged?!"

She laughed. "Of course! Lower prices equal easier access for customers. Also, we aren't just raising money...we're raising *destiny*: The currency of all that exists!"

Adele muttered, "But, we fell short of a hundred thousand. If we cut into our savings, we'll have enough...but I don't wanna do that."

"We're still good," Lumpy said. "We didn't have to make all of it from this alone."

"This is a little more than I thought we'd make," Quintegrity said. "Tomorrow, the full moon will be in effect, so when we run the Full Moon Special Entrée, we'll make more money than we did today."

The color drained from everyone else's faces.

"Tomorrow?" Rover asked, his voice small. "You mean...?"

Quintegrity nodded. "Yes. It's a two-day fundraiser."

A lot of staring happened. Quintegrity blinked, then gave a meager smile.

"Uh...I told you that...didn't I?"

"*NO!!!*"

She stuck out her tongue and bonked herself on the head with her fist. "Oops! Aah...I'm sorry, everyone. Tee-hee..."

22!22@22#22$22%22^22&22*22(22)22_22+22

Day two of Operation Maid Invasion was host to the same intensity of work as the first day. Afterward, when the six of them were draped over the chairs and couches in the club penthouse—all but Quintegrity sore and tuckered out—they reviewed the sales report, and had earned more that day than the first.

22!22@22#22$22%22^22&22*22(22)22_22+22

When Benedict received news of Rover's payment being ready, he laughed, pleasantly surprised.

"Not that I was rushing you," he told Rover over the phone, "although, I had expected it to take a little more time."

The six Operation Maid Invasion workers were celebrating their achievement with light snacks at Leche la Orihime-A, the best ice cream pub in Southbound Thugwood.

"Shows you that I'm not holding back." Rover couldn't help but smile as he used his straw to stir his expensive minty allspice lemonade.

"What say we meet somewhere this Sundun-*day*?" Benedict suggested. "The weather should be clear that day, but you know how the weatherman does us sometimes. You can make the payment then, and we'll figure out where to go from there. Sound good?"

"Deal."

"Awesome. I'm thinking we meet at the Icarus Centre at noon."

"Works for me," Rover said.

When the conversation ended, everyone else had their eyes on Rover.

"This Sundun-*day* at noon," he told the others, taking a sip of his drink, "at the Icarus Centre."

"Where it all began with Graphite," Lumpy commented, sniffing his cracker which tasted over-seasoned.

"Benedict *totally* didn't do *that* on purpose, did he?" Olaf pushed his remaining salmon dragon salad around the plate, smearing the balsamic ranch dressing into speckled, creamy whorls. "The Icarus Centre is the leeaast bit ironic."

Daremont had his mouth full of a tapioca ice cream sandwich, but he desperately and vigorously chewed faster to get his imminent pun out. By the gods, Adele seized the moment to punt his pun into the tall grass, never to be heard from.

"You really wanna go through with this, Big Bro?" She looked directly at her brother with a firm and observational stare. "We have all that money from the fundraiser that we busted our booties for. It can go toward *anything*,"—a depraved shadow flashed through her eyes, ever so slight that only Rover had noticed, being familiar with it— "even go straight into our own pockets and toward that *Anti-Grav skateboard*."

Daremont grabbed his head, suffering from brain freeze, his gurgling pun dying from the chill.

"Of course I wanna do this," Rover replied, sighing. "You gotta ask that?" He looked at Quintegrity sitting next to him. She didn't look back, but he knew she was aware of his gaze.

Rover stirred his drink again. "It's actually up to Quintegrity where that money goes, though. Right, Super Club President?"

This time, she looked at him, returning a smile twice as big as his.

"Are you asking me to bail you out of your match against Benedict Torrent?" she joked.

"Ha! Caught in the act."

"Nice try, but I'll *personally drag* you there myself if you get cold feet on me now!"

She turned her body toward Rover, and he found himself drawn into her presence full of jazzy pizzazz.

Rover slurped the rest of his drink and set the glass on the table with a confident twinkle in his eye.

"Then, I better put my wool socks on so I don't get cold feet!"

Daremont clapped, and Rover realized his friends were rubbing off on him, if only a little.

ROVER… Lvl 999

All Money… {T}213,600

Allowance… {T}34,200
Fundraiser… {T}178,400
Food Slip… {T}1,000

<<EXPENSE GOALS>>

Benedict's Payment… {T}100,000
Anti-Grav Skateboard… {T}499,999

<<CURRENT EQUIPMENT>>

Gloves… Beelzebub
Armor… Brutal Suit
Acc.1… Yakuza Tools
Acc.2… Unsetting Sun

<<SPECIAL NUMBERS>>

① ② ③ ④ ❺

⑥ ⑦ ⑧ ⑨ ⑩

DESIGNED TO BE READY BEFORE I WAS BORN!

THE moment Rover stepped off the bus at the Icarus Centre shopping district, he was confronted by an impermeable wall of fans, bloggers, and gaming journalists. With a quick scan of the area, he estimated this crowd was twice as large as the one for the match with Captain Pretentious. There were a couple hundred people, at least, and more were arriving. Being Sundun-*day*, the second busiest market day of the week behind Nundinum-*day*, plenty of potential bystanders were already present and going about their shopping.

A Thugforce Militia helicopter was also present, its deep growls reverberating off every building as it hung overhead, as if to make sure nobody could possibly forget it was there.

Rover was swallowed up by the ravenous paparazzi, slinging his stuttered answers against the onslaught of questions, cameras, and microphones. Adele, Lumpy, and Quintegrity snuck off the bus from the rear exit, wearing disguises.

"And the crowd goes wild," Adele chuckled as she watched Rover get eaten alive by the people. She wore a fake mustache with her hair tucked beneath a backwards baseball cap, complete with baggy clothes to make her appear somewhat boyish.

"Good thing we have these disguises." Lumpy scratched the fake beard on his face and adjusted the little square glasses on his nose. "People might recognize us as Rover's crew, and I don't want that attention. The beard is kinda itchy, though."

The heaviest disguise was worn by Quintegrity. A long brunette wig hung down from under a stocking cap. Dark aviator sunglasses obscured her eyes while a plain scarf around her neck covered part of her chin. Her figure was hidden under a tactical vest and a modest ball gown that reached the ground.

Adele raised her eyebrows at the disguise's ensemble. "Uh...you look really ridiculous like that in broad daylight. Aren't you afraid of drawing *more* attention to yourself?"

Despite the layers of concealment, Quintegrity's sunny response shone through without restraint.

"As long as they don't know it's me, there's no problem!" she declared, making several people look at her. "Ha-ha-haaa!"

Adele and Lumpy made sure their earpieces were functional, and they headed into the ruckus, pretending to be just ordinary spectators. Quintegrity, however, disappeared.

"*Now* where she'd go?" Adele muttered, looking around.

"Let her be," Lumpy said. "I'm sure she'll handle herself."

Another paparazzi swarm crossed the wide walkway of the expansive open-air shopping mall and merged into Rover's swarm. When the sea of people parted, the boy found himself face-to-face with the skinny, bespectacled man with beach-colored hair.

"You're early!" Benedict Torrent said, walking up with his hand extended, wearing a smile bigger than his big glasses. He donned a backpack, his signature, large headphones around his neck. As usual, he appeared to be on a permanent vacation with his sandals and baggy, unbuttoned shirt.

"To be on time is to be late, I say." Rover shook the man's firm hand. For a guy who made a living off playing video games, Benedict's hands were rough, hard, and strong.

Rover started *Glove Alien Fight* and showed Benedict his status screen to prove his character reached the maximum level, then showed his inventory list with the Special Number 5 item in his possession.

"Good, good." Benedict nodded.

"And here's the payment."

Benedict's phone pinged, alerting him that one hundred thousand thuggoons had been deposited to his thuggaccount.

"Excellent," Benedict said, slipping his smartphone into his pocket. "Where and when would you like to get this match underway?"

A small murmur arose from the crowd before Rover had answered.

"Right *here*, right *now*!" he said boldly.

"Heh-heh, I was hoping you'd say that!"

Cheers and whoops followed. People took videos and pictures and held up their signs, the vast majority supporting Benedict. However, as Rover checked out the cluster of signs cheering him on, he noticed more familiar faces showing their support.

Dad, Mom, Graphite Condor, Tallyhawk Kusumegido, Hodge Dipcringle, Isho Eep, Olaf Thumdiggles, Daremont Radclaft, Mr. Pool

Coach, and over a dozen others from school were among the many fans there to support Rover. He made eye contact with Graphite, who gave a single nod and a half-smirk, to which Rover mirrored in response.

Is this what building a following feels like? Rover wondered.

A chubby, but beautiful woman with hair dyed the color of cantaloupe soup slipped the backpack off Benedict, and they pecked each other on the lips. For the first time, Rover noticed the wedding band on Benedict's finger, and it matched the woman's. This was when Rover also noticed he couldn't find Quintegrity anywhere.

Quintegrity's probably keeping her head down somewhere. His tummy got chilly as he looked at the Thugforce Militia chopper. *Is the Cohort Squadron here, too?* Another helicopter loomed nearby as well, which Rover recognized. *Well, well…seems like little Captain Pretentious swung by to check things out, too.*

Mrs. Torrent removed two things from Benedict's backpack: a video game controller and a virtual reality headset. Benedict strapped the headset on, took the controller, and then sat in a folding chair provided by a little boy who looked like a miniature Benedict.

"He has a console controller and a VR headset," Rover muttered into his communication earpiece.

"Yeah, I see that," Lumpy said through the communicator, adjusting his fake, square glasses. He and Adele had taken separate positions on the second-level walkway, giving them both good perspectives from higher up. "The controller will make the game's interface easier to use than a touchscreen, and I've heard of people who play *Glove Alien Fight* AR matches with VR headsets so they don't have to physically follow their avatars through the real environment."

"Just like playing a normal video game," Adele replied, leaning over the second-level walkway's guardrail. She zoomed in on Benedict through the holoshades. "All with the comfort of sitting in your living room." She scoffed. "What a good idea…"

"It's a *great* idea," Rover said, looking at his phone. "After this, what do ya say we invest in some upgraded hardware for ourselves?"

"Blow your *own* money, R!" Adele grunted.

"I think R has a great idea!" Quintegrity broadcasted through the communicators.

"Hey, Q," Rover said, "where are you?"

"Oh, *around.*" Her voice was playful, almost mocking.

Rover sighed, but smiled. "Good enough for me."

Once Benedict wirelessly synched his controller to the gaming tablet held by his wife, he kicked back in his chair and pushed the VR headset visor up so he could look at Rover.

"Well then, Rover Chork. Ready when you are."

"I was born ready," Rover said, brandishing his phone.

"How clichéd to say that," Lumpy snickered.

"I was *designed* to be ready *before I was born*!" Rover added with extra bravado, holding his phone in the air and eliciting cheers from the crowd.

"Atta boy, R!" Quintegrity told him. "Use all that training you did in the womb to lead yourself to victory! Mwa-ha-ha-haa!"

Behind his bravado, the many AR cameras watching the event gave Rover a small pang of anxiety and a touch of stage fright. He gnashed his teeth, forcing a smile to turn that fear into excitement as the onscreen roulette commenced to select the match type...

Every spectator held their breath. Even the Thugforce Militia chopper seemed to stop breathing...because that makes total sense.

When the game selected the match type, Mrs. Torrent folded her metre stick stylus into a stylus megaphone and made the announcement.

"DEATHMATCH!"

Deathmatch: A one-on-one fight to reduce the opponent's HP to zero, knocking them out. There was very little for spectators to do as there were no rings to hide and no enemies to scout for. This was solely between the two competitors. Unlike the sudden death rounds at the end of a tie, there was no guaranteed one-hit win, starting at full health with full preparation for a fight to the death.

"Eh," Lumpy breathed into the communication earpiece, scratching his fake beard, "doesn't look like there's much we can do to help in a Deathmatch."

"Yeah," Rover replied, wasting no time to set up his character's equipment and settings for a true fight.

"All right!" Benedict pulled the VR headset visor over his eyes, essentially putting him into the game. "A real match of strength, wit, and endurance! This is what I wanted! What say you, Rover?"

Was it what Rover wanted?

He answered, "Totally!"

"Oh, one more thing," Benedict said, getting snug in the folding chair. "I won't be holding back. I hope you'll return that favor."

"Depends on my mood."

Benedict chuckled. "If that's the case, then I won't be disappointed..."

The pre-match countdown reached zero.

The fight began.

Every spectator's screen was loaded to the corners with Winter's Sepulcher, accompanied by cheers and boos.

However, Rover didn't take his eyes off his phone screen—he saw the indicator for the damage inflicted on his opponent: "Nullified."

The Antifreeze Bracelet on Benedict's character shattered, sacrificing itself to block the wearer from one hit of Ice Elemental damage.

He anticipated that, Rover thought, his grin cracking across his face, *and I anticipated his anticipation. And I bet his second accessory slot has the Heatshield Bracelet to cancel the Fire Elemental damage from Infernal Rain, so...*

Rover tapped the third attack button for the Beelzebub Glove Aliens before he could see Benedict's character through the icy sarcophagus.

"Belly of the Beast" was this button's name.

Rover's avatar put its hands over its head, holding up a purely dark sphere that formed between both palms. Instantly, a giant vortex of nightly hues opened up as a Darkness Elemental windstorm swamped the AR environment. With the disappearance of the graphics for Winter's Sepulcher, Benedict's character became visible as it was swept away in the swirling currents, taking continual Darkness Elemental damage while spiraling closer to the void held by Rover's character.

"Whoa-ho-hoo!" Benedict laughed out loud, enthralled by the unprecedented fury of Rover's storm. "Now, ain't *this* something?!"

Thanks to the VR headset, Benedict never lost sight of his character, viewing the game through a third-person perspective behind the avatar like in the original game. Additionally, his game controller allowed nimble operation, and he quickly selected the in-game Rope item, using it to lasso a real-life powerline pole. Benedict's character pulled itself along the Rope, then secured itself to the pole to keep from being sucked into Rover's vortex.

Each second, Belly of the Beast unleashed stronger winds over a wider area. Rover rapidly tapped the command button on his phone screen, keeping the attack going and building its strength.

Yet, the continual damage Benedict's character took was paltry, maxing out at two HP damage with each hit. Benedict seized the chance to equip another Antifreeze Bracelet to replace the broken one.

"How high is this dude's defense?" Lumpy grunted, watching Benedict's character use a second Rope item to double its hold on the pole. "It's practically unfazed by...by *whatever the hell this is you're doing, R!!!*"

Adele, on the other hand, shrieked and gasped, confounded by what she witnessed through her phone—she was no help at all.

Rover ignored the distracting commentary from his friend and sister. He ignored the mixed reactions of shock, anger, fear, and jubilance from the crowd.

There wasn't room for losing focus.

Belly of the Beast strikes multiple times, he thought, *and it isn't doing much damage. It's safe to assume Benedict won't feel the need to equip the Smiley Bracelet to negate Darkness Elemental damage.*

The dark storm grew stronger, and Benedict's character began taking upwards of five HP damage with each hit now. Its hands fumed with thick smog while it remained securely fastened to the pole.

"He's charging something up," Adele told Rover, watching Benedict's character. "I see his avatar's hands smoking or something. From the looks of it…"

"Summoning magic," Rover said. He had his own character throw the black hole center of Belly of the Beast, sending out a tornado of Darkness Elemental energy toward his opponent. "From the color of the spell effects, I'd say he has the Legion Lord Glove Aliens equipped." He sneered. "Perfect for countering my Darkness Elemental attack because they add resistance to it. Also, I hope he doesn't have that weapon leveled up to the maximum…"

"Why?" Adele asked. "What happens when the Legion Lord Glove Aliens are maxed out?"

"I don't know," Lumpy said, "but it probably won't be good."

Rover didn't answer.

Three winged Imps spawned around Benedict's character, each wielding a cruddy spear. Immune to Darkness Elemental damage, they soared unhindered through Rover's wicked winds.

"Imps are kinda weak," Lumpy commented.

"Yeah, they're weak, but…"

Rover grunted as one of the Imps threw its cruddy spear, hitting Rover's character and inflicting the Poison status effect, which continually dealt HP damage over time. The Imp promptly pulled another spear from its butt as the other two did the same.

"But, they're frickin' *annoying!*" Rover barked.

He fired Infernal Rain into the air, burning the Imps but not killing them, and kept his character running to dodge their spears. He slid his finger across his item menu, used an Antidote item to cure the Poison status effect that had damaged him, and used a healing Potion to restore his HP. However, another strike from a second wave of Imps reinstated the Poison effect.

Belly of the Beast reached its time limit and disappeared before the black hole core could reach Benedict's avatar. The dark winds died, and Benedict had his avatar hurry into the burning AR environment. His Heatshield Bracelet shattered on contact with part of Rover's raining blaze, but his character quickly caught on fire after another flaming hit and took continual Fire Elemental damage. After equipping a second Antifreeze

Bracelet, Benedict had his character charge through the flames at Rover's character.

Winter's Sepulcher instantly wiped out all of the Imps, but merely broke one of the ice-proof accessories on the opponent. Benedict spawned three more Imps, then launched a barrage of Darkness Elemental energy orbs that locked onto Rover's avatar like homing missiles.

Rover dodged all the poisonous spears and took a hit from one dark orb, taking significant damage. His character was fast, sacrificing defense for speed, and as more homing dark orbs and poisonous Imps swarmed the fiery battlefield, Rover knew it was time to flee.

There doesn't seem to be any barrier to the playing area. Ideal for being the chased one in this match...but damn, that still means I'm on the defensive here!

Using a Goosepack, Rover's character blasted off into the air as his final fireballs fell from above. He healed with a couple Potion items, but it was harder to avoid Benedict's homing orbs in the air than on the ground.

"Benedict is taking decent damage from being on fire!" Adele said. "But, he isn't knocked out yet. How much HP does he *have*?"

"I reckon he has armor that doubles his HP," Rover said, chasing after his avatar through the open-air mall while Benedict sat comfortably in his chair. "That explains how much damage he's able to take before healing."

"Aaaand, he just healed," Lumpy grunted, watching through his phone. "Fire seems to be your best bet, as it's continual and makes any Heatshield Bracelet worthless after the first hit."

"Infernal Rain's strongest hit is the *first* one that shoots straight up," Rover said, guiding some incoming attacks into a third-floor footbridge.

In midflight, Rover's character used Infernal Rain again as additional honking came from his phone's speakers—Benedict also had used a Goosepack, and a goosey chase took place.

Turning around, Rover wanted to keep the match localized to avoid chasing after his avatar and keep his enemies within the burning area. Another blast of Winter's Sepulcher took care of the surrounding Imps and shattered another of Benedict's Antifreeze Bracelets.

Lumpy cheered. "Oh man! In midair, I see that Winter's Sepulcher is actually spherical, but on the ground, only *half* of the attack range is visible! It's *huge*!"

More of Benedict's orbs struck Rover's character, but Benedict had been lit by more falling flame. Swapping to the Infantry Glove Aliens, Rover shot bursts of full-auto energy bullets at his burning opponent. The two characters circled around, filling the virtual airspace with long-range projectiles.

"This is a heck of a dogfight!" Adele watched the aerial action, her fake mustache quivering with excitement. "Benedict is taking half damage from burning now, so he probably just equipped something that halves Fire Elemental damage."

"Immune to Ice and reduced damage from Fire and Darkness," Lumpy mumbled. "He's figured you out, R."

"Just gonna keep burning and shooting 'im!" Rover replied brashly. "And *this*, too!"

Another vortex of Belly of the Beast engulfed the AR environment, and a tornado set out on its own. While it still didn't do much damage, it interfered with Benedict's flight, buying Rover time to heal with a Potion, negate the Poison status effect with an Antidote, and reignite Infernal Rain as soon as the previous one ended. Another round of Winter's Sepulcher wiped out all the Imps and broke yet another of Benedict's Antifreeze Bracelets.

Rover landed his character seconds before his Goosepack vanished, avoiding falling damage. Some stray homing orbs hit him, bringing his HP scarily low, so he took cover under a second-level walkway to avoid further attacks.

When Benedict's Goosepack ran out, his character was caught in the Belly of the Beast tornado, swirling around and around, shooting homing orbs at Rover's character. However, during this time, Benedict noticed something.

"Rover's Darkness Elemental storm is stronger this time," he said casually into the stylus megaphone his wife held, allowing everyone to hear his voice. "In fact, all of his attacks seem to be getting stronger over time. Does that mean Rover's special Glove Aliens inflict more damage as the battle goes on? Stay tuned to find out!"

Lumpy muttered, "He's totally into this whole livestreaming thing. A genuine show host personality."

"Not just that," Rover grunted into his earpiece as his avatar ran into the open, dodging homing attacks, "he suspects my Beelzebub Glove Aliens' passive ability…"

"Huh?" Lumpy asked. "You mean…they get *stronger* as the battle goes on?"

"Not precisely." Rover shot energy bullets at Benedict's storm-trapped character as it also took Fire and Darkness Elemental damage, momentarily inflicting damage faster than Benedict could heal. "I have to keep doing damage with those Glove Aliens' attacks. If I let up, the attack will drop. Also…*all* of my stats are affected, not just my attack. Defense, speed…all of them increase!"

Lumpy chuckled, followed by loud belly laughs. "Truly sinister, my man! I love it!"

Rover used another Goosepack, soaring straight at the opponent. He fired more full-auto energy bullets while taking damage from Imp spears and homing orbs. Soaring past Benedict's character, Rover dealt a quick swipe with his sabre. Benedict was freed from the dark vortex when it vanished, and he immediately used another Goosepack for himself, continuing the midair dogfight.

However, Benedict flew away. Rover was forced to give chase, which meant physically running through the Icarus Centre on foot.

"Dammit!" Rover spat, sprinting after the flying characters.

Rover used Belly of the Beast to slow Benedict's escape, catching the fleeing avatar in the dark winds. This time, Benedict's character was pulled straight into the well-aimed dark sphere core, and not even his Goosepack allowed him to escape. Also, the core inflicted double the damage than the winds alone.

"I'm stuck!" Benedict announced with an excited smile. "Time for a new trick..."

From the ground, giving chase on foot, Rover didn't get a good look at Benedict's character in the air. Its hands fumed again, as if to summon more Imps, but Rover failed to notice how much thicker and viler the character's animation was.

It was a summoning spell, all right. Just not for Imps.

High above the virtual battlefield, a circular pattern of AR light appeared in the sky. Excited chatter broke out among the spectators, many of them seeing this particular effect for the first time.

Rover, though, understood what it meant.

"That's a summoning gate," he murmured, getting short of breath from the sprinting, "and it's the *biggest* one I've ever seen in *Glove Alien Fight*." He tensed up, but pushed himself to run faster.

Damn...Benedict really did max out his Legion Lord Glove Aliens...

A hole opened inside the circular pattern, and through it came a massive being resembling a wolf crossed with a dinosaur. If it had been a physical creature, its winged shadow would've eclipsed a city bus—very large to scale when compared with other in-game *Glove Alien Fight* components, especially the players' avatars.

"Th-That's...!" Adele stuttered, gawking at the huge foe swooping down as the summoning gate closed and vanished.

"Baha Mutt..." Lumpy gulped. "The fabled dragondog king...and reportedly the strongest summon in *Glove Alien Fight*."

Baha Mutt, the dragondog king, used its huge claws and plucked Benedict's avatar out of the Belly of the Beast vortex. It absorbed the

Darkness Elemental damage (which would've healed it if it hadn't been at full health already) and placed Benedict's avatar safely on its back. Benedict, now in control of Baha Mutt, stood unaffected inside the core of Rover's measly storm.

"Q," Rover uttered into his earpiece, his voice rattling, "i-if you've got something up your sleeve...*anything*...now's the time to use it..."

"Sorry," she replied, her tone somewhat disheartened, "but there's nothing I can do in a Deathmatch, so I'm making crepes right now."

"...*CREPES*?!?" Rover howled.

"Ha-ha! Yeah! These people need to eat, and who doesn't love a good crepe? I'm giving them away for free, but people are tipping me, which isn't technically selling and isn't violating solicitation laws!"

At that moment, everyone watching the match through their AR devices heard the mighty roar of Baha Mutt! The beastly proclamation blared from the countless smartphones and tablets across the Icarus Centre's open-air shopping district, making people cheer and shout.

Only Rover didn't share the excitement, nearly paralyzed by the chills running along his spine. He gritted his teeth, staring through his phone at what he had come up against.

BENEDICT TORRENT

AGE... 34
HEIGHT... 188 CM (6' 2")
HAIR COLOR... BEACHY
EYE COLOR... DARK
OCCUPATION... GAME STREAMER & BLOGGER
FAVE FOODS... MUSTARD PIZZA, NACHO PILAF
FAVE HOBBIES... VIDEO GAMES, *DUNGEONS & DRAGSTERS*

THE MOST FAMOUS AND SUCCESSFUL VIDEO GAME STREAMER AND BLOGGER IN THUGWOOD. HE'S VERY KNOWLEDGEABLE ABOUT INTERNET TRENDS AND ONLINE BEHAVIOR, HAVING BEEN IN THE BUSINESS SINCE MIDDLE SCHOOL. HOSTS SEVERAL SHOWS AND PODCASTS, AND HIS SHOW *TORRENTIAL TALK* INVOLVES TAKING CALLS FROM FANS WHO WANT TO ASK QUESTIONS AND DISCUSS NERD CULTURE. HIS WIFE IS HIS BUSINESS PARTNER.

BENEDICT IS ONE OF THE MOST ADVANCED *GLOVE ALIEN FIGHT* PLAYERS, BEING A DIEHARD FAN OF THE GAME BEYOND MEETING THE DAILY GAMEPLAY QUOTA, BUT IS ALSO KNOWN FOR HIS LIVESTREAMS OF EVERY OTHER HIT VIDEO GAME. HE IS ALSO PART OF AN ELITE GROUP OF PLAYERS FOR THE CLASSIC TABLETOP RPG, *DUNGEONS & DRAGSTERS.*

ROVER… Lvl 999

All Money… {T}113,600

Allowance… {T}112,600
Food Slip… {T}1,000

<<EXPENSE GOALS>>

Anti-Grav Skateboard… {T}499,999

<<CURRENT EQUIPMENT>>

Gloves… Beelzebub
Armor… FASCAR Shirt
Acc.1… Yakuza Tools
Acc.2… Heist Hooves

<<SPECIAL NUMBERS>>

① ② ③ ④ ⑤

⑥ ⑦ ⑧ ⑨ ⑩

HISTORY–ALTERING TALENT SCOUTS

"HERE'S your **passionfruit crepe,** mademoiselle!" Quintegrity presented the treat to the next person in the long line at her makeshift crepe stand.

The young woman took the crepe, giving Quintegrity a curious look. "Aren't you...like, *hot* in that outfit? With the stocking cap and scarf and ball gown...and tactical vest?"

"Thank you!" Quintegrity blushed behind her aviator sunglasses. "I always try to look my best, but 'hot' is a new compliment for me!"

"Um...what?"

Rover's panicked shouts blared through Quintegrity's earpiece. She saw, from a distance, Rover's avatar running through the open-air mall with a very savage, winged giant giving chase from above. Deadly beams of energy spouted from its fanged mouth, which Rover's character narrowly dodged every time.

"Sure sounds like an exciting game!" she chortled.

"Q!" Rover wailed through her earpiece. "I need you!"

"Oh, but there's not much I can do..." she replied, a tinge of regret in her voice as she rolled up two mango-spangled crepes. Lowering her tone, she added, "Besides...*they're* here, so I have to stay low-key."

A quick whooshing sound flew overhead as she handed the crepes to an elderly couple with matching spinners on their wheelchair wheels. They used their phones to send a tip to the Digi-Tip jar on the stand, and Quintegrity flicked her eyes to the sky, catching a glimpse of the stealthy helicopter cruising by.

Only one light on it, she thought. *This disguise will be plenty effective in that case!*

`24!24@24#24$24%24^24&24*24(24)24_24+24`

Adele ran along the second-level walkway, keeping up with the augmented reality chase, despite getting short-winded from her laughing. When Rover's character sought shelter under a walkway bridge, Baha Mutt circled around, blasting the hiding spot with its energy beam breath from every possible angle.

"This...is...*great!*" Adele wiped the sweat from her forehead and readjusted her fake mustache, leaning against a guardrail and catching her breath. "Sorry, R, but this is probably the most awesome thing I've ever seen in *Glove Alien Fight*! Even if you lose this match, it was totally worth seeing Baha Mutt in AR action!"

"*Shut up!!!*" Rover barked as he caught up to his hiding avatar under the walkway bridge. "I'm not gonna lose! I need you and L to do something for me."

"What's up?" Lumpy asked, taking his own vantage point from the second level of the Icarus Centre.

Rover swapped his character's all-stat-increasing Yakuza Tools accessory with a 2nd Chance Bangle. He could already see Benedict's maneuverability limitations of controlling such a large summoned creature. However, a misstep earned him a direct hit from one of the beast's beam attacks, bringing his character's HP down to one; the 2nd Chance Bangle accessory on his character shattered, protecting him from a fatal attack, preventing him from losing the game right then.

"Crap!" Rover grunted, equipping another 2nd Chance Bangle in the empty accessory slot. "As I thought, my low defense will get me killed with one hit from Baha Mutt. And I only have this last 2nd Change Bangle..."

"R!" he heard Lumpy call through his earpiece. "What do you need us to do?"

"Get online," Rover replied, watching Baha Mutt's flight and keeping the walkway's cover between the creature and his character. "Look up what weaknesses Baha Mutt has. I need to know everything about it if I wanna get through this."

The next twenty seconds felt like twenty minutes as Rover evaded more energy breath beams from the aerial assailant. Sweat dripped into his eyes, burning them, but he kept them open, not daring to blink as each moment was critical.

"Found Baha Mutt's info!" Adele reported.

"And???"

"It's only weakness is Light Elemental."

"Bah! I don't have any Light attacks!"

"Also," Lumpy added, checking another website with the same data, "it absorbs Darkness. And...uh, it has only two attacks."

Rover saw the towering monster land on the ground about fifteen metres from the sheltering underpass, putting him in direct line of sight. He thought he even felt the ground physically rumble under his feet from the monster's programmed weight.

Instead of its mouth glowing the magical colors of a breath beam, its massive front feet glowed with a sickly aura.

"That's the Wake N' Quake attack!" Lumpy yelled. "Get off the ground!"

Navigating the inventory menu with sweaty, shaky hands was tough. Rover selected the Plunger Pistol and fired it straight up at the underside of the second-level walkway. His avatar left the ground by retracting the rope attached to the plunger. When Baha Mutt slammed down with its glowing front feet, a devastating shockwave rippled across the ground as Rover's avatar dangled over it unharmed.

Rover dropped his avatar, switched to his Infantry Glove Aliens, and deployed the Stationary Riot Shield just in time to block Baha Mutt's breath beam. Imps swarmed the underpass, and Rover quickly reverted back to the Beelzebub Glove Aliens to use Infernal Rain.

The upward meteor hit the underside of the footbridge and exploded on impact, sending a vicious blast of flames out from under the tunnel. With Rover's increased stats from the Beelzebub Glove Aliens, the Imps were toasted in seconds. However, the digital flames obscured everything, and Rover couldn't see the real threat.

He used his last Goosepack, desperate to get out of the blinding inferno. As his avatar took to the sky, a Wake N' Quake shockwave rippled underneath.

That Goosepack was a damn lucky choice.

"Good job, R!" Adele cheered along with the crowd. "You avoided that quake and also caught Baha Mutt on fire!"

"And the fire spread to Benedict's character, too," Lumpy added.

"Hell yeah." Rover had nothing else to say as he used a rare Potion Plus to fully heal his character.

"Hey, listen." Lumpy read more into the article concerning Baha Mutt. "This says Baha Mutt is one of the few special summons that can be controlled, but it's still a summoned thing. That means—"

"It'll be defeated if I defeat the master," Rover replied as he ran after his airborne character, dodging some homing orbs Benedict fired from atop the beast. A sneer found his lips. "Damn...this is gonna be crazy..."

He angled his character around to face his opponent and saw the mighty dragondog king lift off from the digital flames, its body and rider covered in burning animations. Swallowing a dry lump in his throat, Rover flew his character toward the foe.

I only have two of these, he thought, scrolling through his inventory. *Gotta aim this just right!*

Everyone watched Rover's Goosepack disappear in midair, replaced by a bulky jetpack and big antlers on the helmet.

"What?!" Adele squinted at her phone. "Is that a *Moosepack*?"

"Sure is," Lumpy chuckled. "Ever use one? They're badass…and can pack quite a punch, even against the *biggest enemies!*"

Rover's character fell and rammed its antler helmet right into Baha Mutt in midair from above. The huge creature took little damage, but toppled over and crashed to the ground. Benedict's character tumbled from its back.

"*Yeah!!!*" Adele laughed, her maniacal behavior repelling a few nearby spectators. "He knocked Benedict off!"

"Baha Mutt is controlled by the AI without a rider," Lumpy explained, smiling, "and AI enemies are way easier to predict."

Rover whipped up Belly of the Beast, catching Benedict's character point blank as the black hole core dealt the most HP damage it had all match. Then, Rover's avatar charged at the AI-controlled dragondog king.

A direct hit from the beam breath shattered Rover's last 2nd Chance Bangle and reduced him to one HP. As the Darkness Elemental windstorm healed the monster from the burning damage, a tackle from the Moosepack rendered it helpless for only a few seconds.

Luckily, there was an item to buy more time.

The spectators beheld Rover's character smash an hourglass-shaped item against Baha Mutt. When the monster turned a colorless shade and its animation ceased, everyone gasped as they witnessed the use of a very rare item:

The Clockstopper—an item that rendered its target immobile for ten seconds.

In a match such as this, ten seconds was all the difference.

"Now is my only chance!!!" Rover shouted.

Benedict's character was still trapped in the eye of the Darkness vortex when Rover blasted it with Infernal Rain. The continual damage from both attacks was slow to drain the opponent's life…

But, that wasn't the plan.

He's taking almost four times the amount of damage from these attacks, Rover thought. *When it hits four times…the real show begins.*

The Beelzebub Glove Aliens exploded with evil light. Through the dastardly glow, Rover's character sprouted two more arms, each with the glowing, upgraded Glove Aliens, four in total, all extra boney and spurred. All around, jaws were dropped as Rover's cackles echoed throughout the Icarus Centre, and he took delight in the new commands for his weapon's ultimate form.

First, he used Tummy of the Titan.

A hurricane of darkness and filth replaced the previous wimpy vortex, a supermassive black hole at its center, nearly as large as Baha Mutt itself, the entire storm stretching as far as everyone's AR devices would allow them to see from their perspectives. Rover noticed the healing indicators inside the crushing sphere, and he couldn't help but laugh at Benedict's futile attempt to keep his doomed character alive with the rarest, most powerful potions in the game.

Second, he used Stellar Downpour.

There was no upward meteor of might to initiate this flame attack. It began instantly as the AR sky turned to fire, and the rain was of those mighty meteors themselves. Each one exploded on impact with the equivalent to Infernal Rain, and it took little time before the entire AR environment burned in places people hadn't considered were affected by the AR to begin with.

Third was Winter's Hatred, and the entire block of the Icarus Centre became a glacier. Benedict's Antifreeze Bracelet accessory protected against the ice, but unlike Winter's Sepulcher, Winter's Hatred struck thrice...one more time than Benedict's two accessory slots could protect against.

Still, Benedict wasn't defeated.

Rover growled. "Just how much HP does he *have*???" He sneered as Baha Mutt recovered from the Clockstopper. "Ha! Time's about up!"

He glanced at his phone—there was still the fourth ability, only available with the Beelzebub Glove Aliens' upgraded form and after Tummy of the Titan, Stellar Downpour, and Winter's Hatred had been used.

The onscreen button was labeled "Insanity."

No. I need to save it. I can't let anyone know about this one yet...

The beam breath attacks were easier to dodge when Baha Mutt was controlled by AI, and Rover had his character shimmy to the second-level walkway without much problem. From that height, Rover had to guess the angle from his perspective as his character stampeded forward with his final Moosepack. It leapt toward Benedict's character caught in the supermassive black hole.

A direct hit.

And the final blow.

Benedict's avatar was nothing but a computerized corpse amid the dark hurricane and raining hellfire. Baha Mutt disappeared without a trace.

An eruption of cheers shook the enormous shopping district, drowning out the Thugforce Militia chopper and the boos and hisses from Benedict's diehard fans. The roaring ovation alerted Rover of the full size of the audience gathered to witness the legendary match. The realization, being surreal and seemingly impossible, took a moment to settle into his head.

"I won..." A series of laughs escaped from his chest, and he was powerless to hold them back. "I won! I beat *Benedict Torrent*!!!"

His voice echoed far and wide as people rushed at him with high-fives, shoulder pats, congratulations, and joyous praise.

Lumpy emerged from the swarm of people, wrapping Rover in a bear hug from behind and lifting him half a metre off the ground.

"You did it!!!" Lumpy exclaimed, setting his friend down. "That was freakin' *epic*, dude!"

"Hell yeah, it was!" The boys had to literally shout in each other's faces because the uproar was so loud and tightly packed.

Rover saw Adele on the second-level walkway, hanging over the guardrail and cheering her lungs out, and she was joined by dozens of other people who didn't dare enter the rejoicing fray below. There were hundreds of people, and hearing them chant Rover's name was the most exciting thing he had ever experienced.

"That's my *boyfriend!*" Quintegrity cooed through Rover's earpiece. "I knew you could do it!!!"

Yet, Rover didn't see her anywhere. While being smashed in the chanting, cheering crowd, he gazed up, seeing the Thugforce Militia helicopter turn around and head out over the buildings. He also saw Captain Pretentious' helicopter lower itself a little ways from his location, presumably to land in the nearby heliparking lot.

Despite all the attention, something deep inside made him fear there was another helicopter somewhere in the vicinity, scouting the district for his girlfriend.

"I gotta hang low for a while," Quintegrity's voice told him, as if reading his thoughts. "I'll meet you back at your house, okay?"

Multiple hands lifted Rover up, and he was passed along from person to person.

"Uh, y-yeah!" he replied to Quintegrity as he was crowd surfed toward Benedict Torrent.

Rover's feet had barely touched the paved pathway when Benedict took Rover's hand in both of his in a proud handshake, a thrilled grin on his face.

"*Bravo*, Mr. Chork!" Benedict shook Rover's entire arm and gave the boy a solid smack on the back. "Bra-*vo!* That was some mighty fine gaming out there, kid!"

"Thanks!" Rover beamed, returning a playful punch on Benedict's arm. "You really gave me a run for everything I had."

"Told ya I wasn't holding back!"

They both laughed.

"Oi, prick!"

A short, cape-wearing woman with a childish face, frosty hair, kitty-ear headband, and highlighter-flamingo eyes stepped up to Rover.

"Ah, you came, too?" Rover sneered at Captain Pretentious.

"Yeah, I did, ya pleeber." She gave him a thumbs-up. "You deserve my praise. I've never seen *anything* like that! You too, Benedict."

A middle-aged woman approached with a photography tablet, a journalist. "Excuse me. I'm with the Daily Thug, and I'd like to take some pictures for a story."

Rover gawked. *The Daily Thug... That's the biggest news company in Thugwood!*

"Yes, of course!"

She took a picture of Rover, the winner of the biggest *Glove Alien Fight* AR event to date. Then, she took a picture of Rover and Benedict, the two competitors of that event. Finally, she took a picture of Rover, Benedict, and Captain Pretentious, and what a trio they were! Benedict Torrent, the popular video game livestream celebrity; Captain Pretentious, the beloved contributor and philanthropist of the gaming industry and charitable organizations; and Rover Chork, the rising star and new face of *Glove Alien Fight*.

24!24@24#24$24%24^24&24*24(24)24_24+24

Smoky aromas of mesquite wood and marinated steak skewers wafted down the street from the Chork house. The four Super Club members sat on the rooftop as Quintegrity cooked the celebratory snacks on the portable pocket grill. Even with the crowd long gone and the photoshoots over, Rover was still starstruck by his own accomplishments. He bit a chunk off his skewer, gazing at the canvas of clouds painted by the late afternoon daylight.

"Two Special Number items in the bag," Lumpy said as he cracked open a bottle of Vroom Drink, "and eight more to go." He took a sip of the abrasively refreshing beverage, his eyes growing wide from the carbonation before he swallowed. "Think you can do it, Rover?"

"Maybe." Rover fiddled with the half-eaten skewer in his hand. "I already got emails from three other Special Number holders. Numbers 2, 4, and 6."

"Somebody got the sixth one, huh?" Adele contemplated as she took a skewer off the platter. "I wonder how many are in play now."

Rover didn't reply—he was distracted by the obsidian-textured limousine pulling up in front of the house, parking in the street. The back door opened, and a large man emerged. From the distance, it was hard to make out his face and attire, but the extravagance and formality of his fancy suit was obvious.

"Huh?" Adele pointed her skewer at the man walking up their driveway. "Who's that?"

Butterflies flapped in Rover's stomach. He looked at Lumpy, and they both wore the same shocked expression.

"Don't tell me..." Rover said, suppressing a smile. "It's..."

"A *sponsor*?" Lumpy finished the sentence when Rover stalled.

Quintegrity's face was awash with awe. "Ooh... That's a good thing, right?"

"Sure is!" Rover handed his unfinished skewer to Lumpy and opened his bedroom window. "Benedict told me about them!"

"And with the publicity of today's match," Lumpy added, "it's no surprise they're sent to scout you out."

"Yay!" Quintegrity cheered. "History-altering talent scouts make their arrival in a limo! Sounds like a light novel title!"

Rover dashed out of his bedroom, down the stairs, and to the front door. Mom was already greeting the man who had stepped out of the limousine.

"Oh, Rover?" Mom said when her son hurried over with a giddy smile. "This gentleman says he's here to speak with you."

One look at the large man immediately changed Rover's expectations. He wore not a suit, but a Militia dress uniform. With beady, iron-sight eyes under a stern brow, he met Rover not with hospitality...but with something more imposing.

"Rover Chork." The man's voice was strong, fitting for his defined jawline. He never took his beady eyes off the boy.

"Yes, sir."

"I am Sergeant Major Zohar Bloodshank of the Thugforce Militia. I need to have a word with you, Rover Chork."

"I-Is my son...*under arrest*?" Mom asked, looking back and forth from Rover and the man, wringing her hands.

"No, ma'am," Sgt. Maj. Bloodshank said, nary a hint of humanity in his tone. "However, he is being detained for questioning."

"Questions about what?" Rover asked, not wanting to come across as intimidated.

The man's firm expression implied he was sizing up Rover, only to conclude there was no threat.

"We believe you have breached the terms of service for *Glove Alien Fight*, terms which were instated and overseen by CEO Claudius."

The accusation made Rover's muscles and joints stiffen. Sgt. Maj. Bloodshank noticed the boy's reaction, and he gestured out the door toward the limousine parked in the street.

"Follow me, Rover Chork."

Mom was speechless as her son was led outside. The mesquite smoke drifted down from the rooftop, but Rover didn't look back to see if the others were watching—he assumed they were.

"Hey," Adele whispered to Lumpy and Quintegrity as they watched Rover get into the back of the limousine with the big man. "Does something feel...*off*?"

Lumpy nodded. "Yeah. If I'm not mistaken, that guy's outfit looks like a Militia uniform."

"The heck?" Adele swallowed and looked at the car. Nothing seemed to be happening. "What's it mean?"

After a moment, Lumpy muttered, "I don't know."

Quintegrity said nothing. She used the tongs to pluck the charred skewers from the grill grate after burning them. The other two didn't see her fists clench.

Inside the limo, one other person sat on a couch. She was a pretty brunette woman with glasses wearing a milky, single-button suit. While her expression was far softer than the Sergeant Major's, Rover caught the prowling undertones in how she watched him.

When Rover sat on the couch across from these two people, the woman said, "Mr. Chork, I am Lawellen Skofkov."

"Hi." Rover had no other words for the woman.

Lawellen held the boy with her gaze, eyes as dark and soulless as large-aperture camera lenses behind her bifocals. "Have you heard of me?"

Now was not the easiest time for Rover to recall if he had, or had not, heard of this woman.

"No," he replied.

"I am the head of public relations for the *Glove Alien Fight* development team. I speak on behalf of the people who created and maintain the game." She picked up a small television remote and turned on the screen mounted to the side of the limousine's interior. "Do you recognize the contents of these photos?"

Rover did. They were all pictures from his public AR matches, each one capturing the use of his Beelzebub Glove Aliens. There was no mistaking their design: skeletal matter clumped around both hands with extra-boney knuckles and spurred fingers. Given the overhead angle of the shots, it was suggested they were taken from a helicopter.

"I do."

"Explain them," Lawellen said, her small smile a thin mask to hide the deriding motives she took pleasure in.

"These are from the augmented reality matches in *Glove Alien Fight*." Rover kept his voice steady as he gripped his shorts. "Um...they're pictures of me using one type of Glove Aliens."

Lawellen nodded. "Tell us about the Glove Aliens pictured here."

Taking a deep breath, Rover braced himself.

"They're the Beelzebub Glove Aliens."

"Is that what they're called?"

"Yes, ma'am."

Clasping her hands together and lacing her fingers, Lawellen told Rover, "The game's development team told me they never designed such a feature for the final product." Her surveillance-camera eyes darkened as her lips made the subtlest movements to stretch her smile, as if everything she saw through those eyes was being logged in a heartless hard drive inside her.

For a moment, nobody said anything. Rover looked at Sgt. Maj. Bloodshank and immediately regretted meeting the man's firm countenance.

Rover opened his mouth, but Lawellen cut him off.

"I take it you have a theory behind what I'm saying?" she asked him.

Looking down first, Rover nodded. "I made them."

"You *modded* the game," Sgt. Maj. Bloodshank interjected. "Are you aware of the rules on mods and user-created content in *Glove Alien Fight*?"

"They're not allowed," Rover replied, trying to end the conversation quickly by moving it along now.

"Correct," Lawellen said. She turned off the television, placing the remote in its holder with supreme delicacy in her touch. "You were breaking the rules willingly, then."

"I was," Rover said, "but it's just a game." He looked at the Sergeant Major. "Why does the Thugforce Militia care?"

"I, personally, do not care," the solid man replied. "However, *Glove Alien Fight* is not a game. It is *the* 'Augmented Reality Massively Multiplayer Online Role Playing Game of Article Two Hundred Eleven, Section One, Sticky-Note B.'" He took a sip of Holey Water, cleared his throat, and continued, "CEO Claudius has taken it upon himself to construct an entire doctrine based on the ARMMORPG—its *existence and gameplay*—and violating the terms of service surrounding it interlaces with the law and CEO Claudius' rulership as Thugwood's Chief Executive Overlord."

Rover hung his head.

Lawellen Skofkov asked, "Why did you use such a noticeable mod in open view of the public?" Fringes of raw curiosity rimmed her lips. "Did you think this would go unnoticed?"

"Not really…" Rover shrugged, having been backed into a corner. "But…"

"But?" the woman pressed.

"I wanted to do everything I could to beat CEO Claudius and lift the daily quota," he said, looking at her.

The faintest chuckle breathed out her nostrils. "How old are you?"

"Eighteen."

"There's your answer, Ms. Skofkov," Sgt. Maj. Bloodshank said with a chastising raise of his thick eyebrows. "The reckless teenage era of one's life."

"Yes," Lawellen agreed. "While I admit I, too, had my youthful ignorance, I never dreamed of doing something so brazen and foolish. I truly hope somebody rises up to end the daily quota because I hate video games and have to waste an hour each day. But, you took your recklessness too far."

"I didn't expect the consequences to involve the *Militia*," Rover grunted, giving them both a half-lidded scowl. "And it took you guys long enough to catch me."

"We've had our suspicions since your match with Graphite Condor," the woman said, relaxing her shoulders. "The most difficulty and time came from piecing together enough evidence and research to prove this all wasn't a hoax and that somebody *really was* using a mod for all to see. We wanted to give you the benefit of the doubt that you weren't so foolish."

She leaned back in her seat, the new angle revealing her irises weren't dark, but the bright color of a cold computer's glow—even with color, her eyes didn't indicate a human lived behind them.

With nothing left to say, Rover hung his head again. He noticed the softness of the limo couch he sat on; either he'd been too distracted to realize it earlier, or the couch really was too comfortable to be felt.

"Breaching the game's terms of service once is a misdemeanor," Sgt. Maj. Bloodshank told him, "for which you shall be fined."

Rover scowled. "I didn't know it was illegal."

"In many cases," the man explained, "breaching any terms of service is not a crime, but it depends on the product and the nature of the breach. Like I said, this is *Glove Alien Fight* and is the law."

"It's a pity," Lawellen said smugly, "how many people don't read the terms of service for anything. They'd learn a lot."

The Sergeant Major filled out a ticket as he spoke. "With that in mind, I am to inform you that if you breach the game's terms again, you will face *de-rationalization*."

Rover's heart skipped at that last word, and he could only nod and say, "Yes, sir..." He took the ticket and stared at the fine: fifty thousand thuggoons, nine days to pay it or face prosecution.

Lawellen told the boy, "The game's developers have told me they shall await your confession before they take action. Now that you have confessed, your modded Glove Aliens will be deleted, so you'll need to continue participating in the game without them." Her smile stretched into that of a lioness reciting an insulting threnody to its soon-to-be-devoured prey. "Like a good boy who *plays fair* with others."

ROVER... Lvl 999

All Money... {T}150,400

Allowance... {T}112,600
Food Slip... {T}1,000
Crepes Tips... {T}36,800

<<EXPENSE GOALS>>

Fine... {T}50,000
Anti-Grav Skateboard... {T}499,999

<<CURRENT EQUIPMENT>>

Gloves... <None>
Armor... FASCAR Shirt
Acc.1... <None>
Acc.2... Heist Hooves

<<SPECIAL NUMBERS>>

① ② ③ ④ ⑤

⑥ ⑦ ⑧ ⑨ ⑩

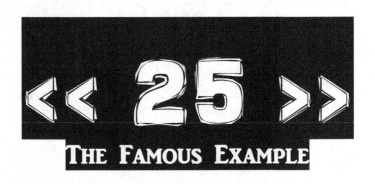

THE FAMOUS EXAMPLE

"**DEaD** Rover, Dead Rover**, send vital signs over," Adele said from the hall through Rover's closed bedroom door that night.

The door swung open, and she was met with her brother's rabid, scruffy appearance, as if he'd been dead for a hundred years and was suddenly zapped back to life.

"Ack!" Adele gasped, covering her face with both arms. "Send them back! Send the vital signs back!"

Rover ignored her, trudging past with his feet dragging on the carpet.

"Hey," she said. "What are you doing...?"

He stopped, making a quarter turn to look at Adele sideways.

"Oh...I don't know." His quavering voice broke through his withered smile. "What's a man to do in my position? Ha-ha. Ha-ha-ha... Perhaps I'll mow the lawn. Yesss..."

Adele raised an eyebrow with a meek grimace. "Uh, it's nighttime."

"The grass grows evermore...even betwixt the hours of day."

"Uugghh..." She sighed and crossed her arms, leaning on the wall. "I know you're mad about losing your Beelzebub Glove Aliens. I get it. I would be, too. But, ya had it coming. You should've stayed low-key with it because it wasn't worth winning those matches."

"It *was* worth it." Rover turned the rest of the way to face his sister. "I wouldn't have two Special Numbers right now without them."

"Yeah, and everyone's pissed because of it. They're calling you a cheater. *I'm* calling you a cheater."

"Lots of people have already been calling me a cheater."

"And now they *know* you are, for sure! I mean, it's hard for me to stick up for you because I think they're right."

"Whatever." Rover turned his back on her. "I'll face the challenge of fighting my way to the top on even ground with everybody."

"Having Quinn help you is also technically cheating."

"No it's not. I made sure to read the *Glove Alien Fight* terms. There's no mention of such a technicality."

"Maybe, but that doesn't mean it's not *cheating*...probably..." Adele shook her head. "Why's it so important to be the best?"

"It isn't about being the best."

"That's not true. You're obsessively competitive, period."

"I know I am," he said. After a moment of serious thought, he added, "I have a real goal, though. I've *always* had one *real* goal with *Glove Alien Fight*. Being interrogated by Sergeant Major Bloodshank and Lawellen Skofkov opened my eyes, and it reminded me of the path I started on from the beginning."

He looked at Adele, who could see the vigor and spirit pour back into him.

"I'm gonna defeat CEO Claudius and free Thugwood of his stupid *Glove Alien Fight* quota."

"Ya know what?" Adele resisted the urge to ridicule Rover, and she smirked. "...That daily quota is a really stupid thing."

"I'm not the only one being oppressed. I'm just the famous example."

"So," Adele said, studying her brother, "you're gonna be the one to rise up against it? Even after this?"

"Yep." Rover's feet shuffled down the hallway.

The next morning, Dad was surprised to the see the entire lawn had been mowed.

25!25@25#25$25%25^25&25*25(25)25_25+25

In the school hallway, while Rover headed to his first class Mondee-*day* morning, a hand grabbed his shoulder from behind.

"Hey!" Graphite barked in Rover's face.

Rover narrowed his eyes. "What?"

After a deep breath, Graphite pointed his finger at Rover and shouted, "*Cheater*!!!" It echoed down the hallway, making everyone gawk their way.

"Yeah, I am."

"Everyone knows. *Everyone.* The topic spread like wildfire on the internet yesterday, but that's not all. That article the *Daily Thug* was gonna write about you beating Benedict Torrent? They still did, but they changed the headline and contents to you being a cheater. It's *front page* news, Rover."

"Every dog has his day."

"How can you be so *smug* about it?!" Graphite spat. "You beat me and stole my consumable items because you cheated!"

Rover looked away. "I'm not proud of it."

"Cram it. You looked all bubbly and stuff when you were being praised for beating Benedict Torrent yesterday! A real soaring underdog posing for photos and answering interview questions."

Rover sighed. "I had to do what I had to do."

The blood pressure in Graphite's face threatened to pop his pencil lead-colored eyes out of his head. "Don't give me that!!! What the hell are you trying to do that warrants cheating your way to the top of *Glove Alien Fight*?!"

"Lifting the damn *Glove Alien Fight* daily quota, that's what!" Rover yelled, clenching his fist. "I'm gonna beat CEO Claudius and wipe out his stupid, idiotic mandate!"

Graphite was taken aback as a zephyr of gasps and "egads" swept through the hallway.

"*For real*???" Graphite's expression screwed up with confusion. "You really *are* shooting for that? Trying to sound all noble to cover your cheater ass?"

Rover nodded, undeterred. "It's been my goal since he first announced a way to lift the quota." He looked around. All the students in earshot were giving him looks of disbelief, skeptical to be on his side. "This isn't stopping me from moving on. The whole publicity and fame thing wasn't intentional, but it sorta happened anyway." He snickered with a flicker of a smirk. "I guess my notoriety as a cheater just brings me back to where I originally expected to be: Doing things my own way, not wanting to be a star, not caring about my public image, but trying my best to end this stupid law."

"You think people are gonna let you be the (cough, cough) 'hero'?" Graphite sneered, making quotation marks with his fingers. "After you blatantly cheated in front of everyone?"

Shrugging, Rover said, "How can they stop me? *Glove Alien Fight* is set to reach the Next Phase when someone collects all ten Special Numbers. I don't know what this 'Next Phase' thing is, but I'm assuming it has something to do with unlocking a way to challenge CEO Claudius. Like Benedict Torrent, CEO Claudius won't accept challenges until certain conditions are met."

"You're just *guessing*," Graphite said.

"We're all just guessing, Graphite! This is a stupid game to him, but it isn't a game, it's actual people and our *lives*...although it's a *game*..."

"What's your point, man?"

"My point is it doesn't matter whether or not people are on my side," he replied, raising his voice to make sure the eavesdroppers could clearly hear. "To move to the Next Phase and get all the Special Numbers, people will have to challenge me because I have two of them. That automatically sets up the possibility to get all ten myself, meaning I might be the one to challenge the CEO."

Graphite clicked his tongue and shook his head. "You're awfully confident, bud. Why not let someone else do it? Nobody's gonna champion a cheater!"

"I'm not riding on being championed."

"But can you *do it*?" Cynical and condescending, Graphite looked Rover in the eyes. "You wouldn't have won any of those matches without those modded Glove Aliens. Your crutch is gone."

"When the crutch is gone, the real strength is built."

Rover walked off, swatting away a drone that hit him with an AthletaCom dart. The other students whispered amongst themselves. Watching Rover's back, Graphite shook with anger and gritted his teeth.

"Dammit," he muttered, "nice punchline." Someone approached him from behind, and he turned to face them, seeing an ensemble of belts. "What, Tallyhawk?"

The dark-skinned, crow-haired girl shrugged. "Ya know what? I'm actually rooting for Rover."

"Urrggh." Graphite rubbed his eyes. "You're not mad because you still beat him in your match."

"That helps." She smirked. "I am still mad at him. Still doesn't mean I don't hope he gets rid of the daily quota."

"But, why *him*?"

Tallyhawk shrugged. "He's got that spark." She crossed her arms. "And he's got Quinn Integrity. He's got the Super Club."

Graphite gazed down the hall, but Rover was gone. A few suction cup darts with the Interschool AthletaCom emblem littered the floor at his feet, and he picked one up.

"I'm not happy about it," he said, toying with the dart between his fingers, "but yeah...if someone's gonna beat the CEO, it *would* be the frickin' Super Club."

25!25@25#25$25%25^25&25*25(25)25_25+25

The Super Club members sat around the sea-marble coffee table, munching on crispy rice cakes. Ryuumba-*chan* swiftly made lap after lap around the seating area, picking up the never-ending dusting of crumbs from the flaky snacks.

"What's our next fundraiser gonna be, team?!" Crumbs fell from Quintegrity's mouth, and she lifted her feet for Ryuumba-*chan* to slip underneath.

"Clearing Rover's name?" Lumpy suggested. When Rover glared at him, he chuckled. "Sorry, man, I couldn't help it."

"These may be trying times, Rover," Quintegrity said, her voice full of wisdom and mouth full of rice cake, "but you mustn't steer from the tasks at hand."

"I ain't steering away," Rover replied, leaning back on the couch. "I'm gonna beat the final boss, CEO Claudius himself."

"Who's to say he's the final boss?" Lumpy asked. "There might be someone else pulling his strings—the *true* final boss!"

"Then, I'll whoop him, too!"

"Fear not!" Quintegrity told them, her hands held out in a gesture of grandeur. "CEO Claudius is, indeed, the top of the fool chain!"

"Uh, *food* chain, you mean?" Adele corrected.

Quintegrity made finger guns at Adele. "I mean *fool*!"

"You really shouldn't badmouth the CEO," Adele whispered, glancing over her shoulder. "You'll be tried for treason." She sighed. "I guess it doesn't make a difference in your position."

Rover swirled the blastberry-lavender sparkling tea in his skull-shaped cup. "I found some new Glove Aliens, so I'm gonna see what they're like and make use of them. Losing my Beelzebub Glove Aliens is my biggest irk, though. I worked hard on modding them and only wanted to use them for fun every now and then."

"But, you *relied* on them for genuine competitions," Lumpy told him. "That was *stupid*, dude. I'm just as mad at you as most of Thugwood."

Rover half-shrugged. "Live and learn."

"Well, *I'm* proud of you, babe!"

"Wahh!"

Quintegrity hugged Rover, some rice cake crumbs falling from her mouth into his tea.

"Never give up!" She stroked his hair, getting close to his ear and whispering, "Never surrender..."

Rover's ear twitched with each breathy syllable. He pushed her off him before his sweat soaked through his clothes and into hers. Quintegrity hopped off the couch, giggling and running around the living room with her arms out, making airplane noises (as she often did).

Lumpy took a sip of his sparkling tea and asked Rover, "Did you contact those people who emailed you? The ones who challenged you to AR matches."

"I did. The guy with Special Number 2 is still on for tomorrow, and he roasted me and said I don't stand a chance without my mods. The people with Special Numbers 4 and 6 haven't responded."

"It's gonna be interesting from here," Lumpy murmured. "I'm sure I'll be lumped in with your status as a cheater because I've been helping you."

"Nice pun, Lumpy!" Quintegrity said.

"...There wasn't a pun."

"We have the disguises," Adele told Lumpy. "We can still hide our identities."

"Actually," Lumpy said, "I've decided against the disguises." He smiled at Rover. "If my best friend is going down this path, then I wanna be there with him, taking the punches, too. No sense hiding."

Rover was surprised, but he grinned. "Thanks, Lumpy. It means a lot."

"I'm still mad at you, though," Lumpy said. "I can't believe you lied to *everyone*, including me."

"...Yeah." Rover stared at the ceiling. "I know...and I'm sorry."

"Even so," Lumpy added, "I owe you my support. Think of all the times you bailed me out of hairy situations. Like when you were my alibi all those times I snuck outta the house to see Iori Hajima when I dated her. Or when you took that hit for me from the teenager prods when we got caught by the Curfew Crusade."

"That *really* hurt," Rover sneered, "a *lot*."

"Hrrmm..." Adele crossed her arms and stared at the floor. "I don't know... I have my dignity to keep."

"It is what it is," Rover said.

"What a copout answer, Big Bro."

Rover took a few gulps of the delicious blastberry-lavender sparkling tea. A shiver accompanied a realization, and he peered into his cup, seeing the floating bits of rice cake that had fallen out of Quintegrity's mouth.

His hairs stood on end. "Oh no, *what'd I do*?!"

"An indirect kiss!" Quintegrity declared, throwing her hands in the air. "I got you, Rover! Mwa-ha-ha-haaa!"

"Aahhh...gaahh...uh..." Rover shook his blushing, sweating head and put the cup on the coffee table with an unsteady hand. "A-Anyway, uh, the fundraiser! Let's talk about the fundraiser!"

"The AthletaCom is coming up," Adele said. "Maybe we can do something for that."

"A power ramen stand?" Lumpy suggested, opening his notebook.

"Ooh, that's a good idea." Quintegrity nodded at the thought. "Yes...power ramen is the best supplementing food for athletes. I can look up some recipes and master the techniques, then pass it along to you guys!"

Rover snorted. "Become a master just like that, huh?"

"It's settled, then!" Quintegrity grabbed the Militia-grade tablet off its charging station. "I'll get to work crunching the numbers and making a PowerPunch presentation for us to review later this week."

"Wait," Lumpy said, "that's it? It was my idea, but we don't have any other ideas?"

No reply.

"I guess power ramen it is," Adele said with a shrug.

Taptaptaptaptaptaptap

Quintegrity's fingers tapped on the tablet screen at lightning speed.

"Don't break that tablet…" Lumpy warned. "I know how you are with electronics."

"It's Militia-grade and bulletproof," Quintegrity explained, her fingers moving faster each second. "I bought it with the tips I made from those crepe transactions yesterday."

"It's crazy you made that much from those free crepes," Adele chuckled.

Quintegrity cackled as she scoured the internet for recipes. "We'll show those Cryptozoology Club members who has the best power ramen! Oh-ho-ho-hooo!"

"Let me guess," Rover muttered, "you liked the power ramen idea because somebody else at school is doing the same thing."

"Correct!"

"And, if it's a competition of any kind," Rover continued, "then it qualifies for the AthletaCom. That's an easy win for you."

"Incorrect!" The vibrant girl shot a determined smirk at Rover. "True, I plan on this power ramen competition being during the AthletaCom. However! I won't be participating! You guys will! After I master the ramen technique, I shall instruct you three on the craft and set you on the path to power ramen conquest."

"Uhhh…" Rover was speechless.

"What'll you be doing in the meantime?" Adele asked Quintegrity.

"Anything! In fact, I plan on entering a footrace because they're always mega popular with tons of participants in the AthletaCom."

"So," Rover grunted, "you plan on trouncing weaklings in a footrace, eh?"

"I'll hold back," she assured him with a teddy bear smile as her fingers assaulted the bulletproof tablet screen.

Nobody believed her.

25!25@25#25$25%25^25&25*25(25)25_25+25

After school the next day on Tsu-*day*, Rover met the holder of Special Number 2, a heavy metal guitarist dude calling himself Jones the Bones. He had a giant Mohawk haircut dyed the color of unripe bananas. Tattoos covered his body.

"I don't care if ya cheated." He sneered at Rover as the Ring Hiders scattered throughout Mooface Park along the Gubbuh-Plardy River. "I want your Special Numbers."

"You'll be going home disappointed," Rover retorted, configuring his character.

Above the park, a Thugforce Militia chopper hung low. Rover tried peering through the windows, but to no avail.

Don't worry, buttheads. I'm gonna play without mods from now on.

Quintegrity crept around a rooftop nook across the street, staying hidden from the Cohort Squadron helicopter. She wore a baggy jersey with basketball shorts, and her jester-like face was painted like a Thuggalo fan of the hip-hip duo Demented Jester Posse.

When the Ring Hiders split up, she noticed a girl in the back of the congregation wait until she was out of sight (or so she believed) to hop on a floating device—an Anti-Grav skateboard—her avatar riding on a little AR scooter. The girl zipped off and Quintegrity followed, sticking to the alleyways.

Far away from the match's starting location, the girl stopped next to a busy highway overpass. Her avatar wore the Tortoise Spacesuit which reduced its weight and increased its jumping capability. She used a Goosepack to soar high above the heavy traffic, and she placed the gold bagel in the beams under the highway bridge.

"It was *you*!!!"

"*Aaahh*!!!"

Quintegrity popped out of nowhere, scaring the girl, making her lose her balance and jump off the Anti-Grav skateboard before falling over.

The girl was dressed in punky skater clothes, a backwards flat bill cap, and Adverse brand shoes. Her irises were like polished copper, and her long, straight hair was naturally colored like sapphire gems and had dyed flares of caesium chloride fires. She trembled as Quintegrity stepped closer.

"Oh no..." she breathed. "I-I've heard of this! Thuggalos jumping people under bridges!"

"Ha-ha-haa!" Quintegrity put her hands on her hips. "That's not true! Thuggalos are only scary-looking misfits. They aren't the devil's minions!"

"...Uhhhh..."

Quintegrity looked at the AR ring in the bridge's trusses. "You're the one placing those rings in hard-to-reach places, aren't you?"

Backing up with an unsure expression, the girl said, "Well...I try to. It makes it more fun."

"Yes...I recognized your little game dude with its turtle armor." She looked at the Anti-Grav skateboard, smiled, and said, "Recon complete!"

"Q!" Rover barked through the earpiece. "What are you doing? Who are you terrorizing now???"

"Just doing my Thuggalo business! *Whomp whomp*! Tee-hee-hee!"

"*Th-Thuggalo*?!"

When Quintegrity dashed off with a gust of wind, the skater girl fell to the ground and sat there for a moment.

"Man..." she muttered, a drop of sweat rolling down her cheek, "there sure are some whackos in this world..."

25!25@25#25$25%25^25&25'25(25)25_25+25

"An Anti-Grav skateboard???" Adele leaned into Quintegrity, her face flushed from inquisitive eagerness. "Where'd she get it? How much did it cost?"

"Sorry, Adele, she didn't say."

The four Super Club members sat side-by-side on a swing set in Mooface Park, looking out at the Gubbuh-Plardy River as they snacked on tangerine-flavored Jabba Cakes they'd bought and reviewed the match against Jones the Bones.

"An Anti-Grav skateboard, huh?" Rover mused as he admired the Special Number 2 item recently added to his inventory list. "And her character used the Tortoise Spacesuit, Scooty-Go-Rounds, and Goosepacks. Yeah, that'll give her everything she needs to put those rings in tough places."

"Scooty-Go-Rounds are super hard to get," Lumpy said, licking the tangerine filling off his fingers. "If she's willing to waste them on hiding rings, then she probably has a lot, meaning she's probably at a pretty high level." He grinned, saying, "Who knows, Rover? You might be facing her someday for a Special Number."

"Foreshadowiiiiing!" Quintegrity hissed in a mysterious, theatrical voice, wiggling her fingers in some "hocus-pocus" gesture. The Thuggalo jester face paint only amplified this act.

Rover chuckled, taking another Jabba Cake out of its package. "Yeah... Foreshadowing."

ROVER… Lvl 999

All Money… {T}113,100

Allowance… {T}112,100
Food Slip… {T}1,000

<<EXPENSE GOALS>>

Fine… {T}50,000
Anti-Grav Skateboard… {T}499,999

<<CURRENT EQUIPMENT>>

Gloves… Scribbly
Armor… FASCAR Shirt
Acc.1… Yakuza Tools
Acc.2… Heist Hooves

<<SPECIAL NUMBERS>>

① ② ③ ④ ⑤

⑥ ⑦ ⑧ ⑨ ⑩

Thank you reader!

But our ending is in another book!

ADVANCE TO VOLUME 2?

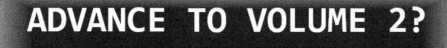 Continue
Screw this

EPIC EQUIPMENT ENLIGHTENMENT

GLOVES	Attack	Defense	Speed	Dexterity	Luck	Elemental	Special
Knitted	500	-	-	-	-	Cuddly	-
Snoozing	550	-	-	-	-	-	Inflict Sleep
Flaming	675	-	-	-	-	Fire, Resist Fire 50%	Inflict Burn
Zappy	700	-	-	-	-	Lightning, Resist Lightning 50%	Inflict Paralysis
Butler	800	-	-	1,000	-	-	-
Froggy	1,000	-	20	40	-	-	High Jump
Hardboiled	1,450	-	-	-	-	Pierce	-
Scribbly	1,450	-	450	-	-	-	-
Infantry	1,700	-	-	-	-	Pierce, Customizable	-
Legion Lord	2,300	-	-	-	-	Darkness, Resist Darkness 50%	Summon Imp, Summon Baha Mutt
Beelzebub	???	???	???	???	???	Ice, Fire, Darkness, ???	Increase All Stats w/Damage, Transform, ???

ARMOR	Attack	Defense	Speed	Dexterity	Luck	Elemental	Special
Brick Jacket	-	500	-	-	-	-	-
Ape Laser	100	615	-	-	-	-	-
Jinnin Tunic	-	680	-	-	-	Resist Pierce 50%	-
Brutal Suit	10	755	10	10	-	-	-
FASCAR Shirt	-	280	200	50	-	-	-
Tortoise Spacesuit	-	200	-	-	-	-	Low-Gravity

ACCESSORY	Attack	Defense	Speed	Dexterity	Luck	Elemental	Special
Yeet-Line Skates	-	-	700	-	-	-	-
Shyster's Shoes	-	-400	2,000	-	-	-	-
Heist Hooves	-	-410	2,300	-	-	-	-

Farm Equipment	100	100	100	100	-		
Yakuza Tools	200	50	300	50	-	-	-
Antifreeze Bracelet	-	-	-	-	-	Nullify Ice	Breaks after 1 use
Heatshield Bracelet	-	-	-	-	-	Nullify Fire	Breaks after 1 use
Smiley Bracelet	-	-	-	-	-	Nullify Darkness	Breaks after 1 use
Dowdy Cape	-	-	-	-	-	Resist All 10%	-
Unsetting Sun	-	-	-	-	-	-	Increase maximum HP 10%
Pension Extender	-	-	-	-	-	-	Increase coins earned 10%
Meme Template	-	-	-	-	8	-	Increase chance to deal Critical Hits
Bug Repellant	-	-	-	-	-	-	Reduce damage from Bug-type enemies 50%
Hound Doggo Shnozz	-	-	-	-	-	-	+1 Clairvoyant Radar
2nd Chance Bangle	-	-	-	-	-	-	Leaves 1 HP after receiving a fatal hit. Breaks after 1 use

THE GLORIOUS GLOSSARY

The Thugwood Metropolitan Address — Often shortened to just "Thugwood." Most likely the only civilized establishment in the world. Has a population of about 100,000,000 citizens. Its structured government, economy, and systems of renewable resources have made it a successful society that has provided safety from the deadly perils of the world for over 2,300 years. It's divided into 5 prefectures: Northish, Southbound, Easterly, Westnook, and Mesial.

Thugwood Governmental Entity — The governing body of Thugwood. A Chief Executive Overlord (CEO) possesses ultimate authority over everything, and multiple responsibilities are designated to other official members. Tons of secrets are kept within their ranks, and don't you dare question what those secrets are.

Thuggoon — The currency of Thugwood. Its symbol is {T̲}. Traditionally, the currency existed as metal coins and eventually paper notes, but all transactions and balances became digital and credit-based several decades ago.

Pleeber/Pleeberz — A derogatory term referring to a person of inferior status or wealth. It's a popular term used by the socially elite to refer to average citizens.

Anti-Grav — Anti-gravity technology is a revolutionary development that allows physical objects to defy gravity without thrust or propulsion. The name "Anti-Grav" refers to a particular brand and manufacturer of this technology, and is by far the most advanced in the field and sees the most widespread use.

Shatinum — An artificial metallic material similar to platinum, but cheaper and more durable. Very popular among people who think chrome is too lame.

Subterra Locomotive Canals — A public rail transportation system that predates gasoline-powered motorcars and roadways. It is the fastest mode of ground transportation. Comprised of a railway network that is mostly underground, it connects to the five prefectures, as well as many rural and remote areas. Originally, the locomotive engines were steam-powered, but they are now all electric-diesel.

Curfew Crusade — A taskforce that upholds the nighttime curfew in Thugwood. They are considered on par with security officers and have significantly less authority than the Thugforce Militia, although they are given complete freedom with their use of teenager prods. Teenager prods are similar to cattle prods, being handheld poles with a shocking tip, but are configured to be most effective on young humans and simeonated (humanlike) species. Special passes are given to children who do certain work or activities after hours.

Thugforce Militia — The primary law enforcement entity in Thugwood. It is also the largest. Low-ranking soldiers are authorized to carry lethal weapons at most times (unless under special conditions), and some of their duties involve patrolling, public services, arresting and detaining criminals, and protecting the peace. High-ranking officers have military abilities, and some of their duties involve amassing armies, exploring the world beyond Thugwood, and submitting official records and reports to the T.G.E.

Cohort Squadron — The elite law enforcement group directly serving the CEO. Their helicopters are thought to be the most advanced vehicles in the world, making use of phenomenal tech for anti-gravity and augmented reality. Every Cohort must pass an IQ test assessment to join the ranks.

Jerry Co. Walls — The largest known manmade structure in the world, they serve as the barrier between the Thugwood Metropolitan Address and the uninhabitable realm beyond. They are also the oldest standing structure in Thugwood because their completion was necessary to establish a colony, and they are thought to have been finished nearly 2,400 years ago. They are constructed mostly from steel and iron, but they are reinforced with mythril, making their durability theoretically invincible. The designer, Jerry, and his company are not well-documented.

Lilygrass — A wild grass that just grows for no reason. It is known for its elasticity which gives it a bouncy property, and it becomes bouncier after photosynthesizing rubbery atoms within its blades. It is also criticized for its reflective properties, often creating a glare from sunlight in a phenomenon known as "fieldlight." Despite its weirdness and annoying existence, it is cultivated for sod and planted in the worst places throughout Thugwood.

Gubbuh-Plardy River — The biggest of two major rivers in Thugwood, the other being the Megms River. It flows from beyond the eastern Jerry Co. Walls, through the eastern mountain ranges in the Easterly Prefecture, and out beyond the western Walls in the Westnook Prefecture. It provides Thugwood's greatest source of fresh water, and it also supplies the most hydroelectric energy. Near the center of Thugwood, it flows underground in a natural aqueduct, allowing it to remain separate from the intersecting Megms River; this intersection is called the Crossduct.

Megms River — The smaller of two major rivers in Thugwood, the other being the Gubbuh-Plardy River. It flows from beyond the northern Jerry Co. Walls, through Thugwood's agricultural epicenter in the Southbound Prefecture, and out beyond the southern Walls. It provides sufficient irrigation to the agricultural regions. Many watersports take place on the Megms because it isn't as deadly to travel down as the Gubbuh-Plardy. Near the center of Thugwood, it flows over the underground segment of the Gubbuh-Plardy River at the Crossduct.

Icarus Centre — The largest shopping district in the Southbound Prefecture, and one of the largest in all of Thugwood. It's home to an enormous open-air shopping mall, and the entire district covers over sixteen square kilometers.

Palmaple Tree — A common tree that is also popular for decoration. The seeds are known as whirly coconuts, and they spiral to the ground with wing-shaped leaves when they fall.

Ashafras Tree — Just another common tree. Probably a combination of other trees.

Idiot Tree — A legendary tree that gained fame online. People claimed to perform poorer on IQ tests if they failed to climb the tree without getting hurt. There is much debate as to if this rumor is true.

Grovenut Wood — A wacky, heavy wood that makes wonderful furniture. It's manufactured from grovenut pulp. Grovenuts grow in cold, mountainous orchards and are edible, containing a rich, bitter flavor.

Jillfruit — Very similar to a jackfruit, but softer and juicier. They are beloved for their sweetness and make popular marinades for poultry and pork.

Pear-Bean Bush — Nobody knows exactly what these bushes are, but their pear-beans are worthy substitutes for both pears and beans in every situation.

Infrastructural Command Tower — A command centre for controlling various utility systems. They are localized for designated regions, and there are many in total all throughout Thugwood. Most of their operations are customizable automations, but a manual override is possible by using the Disc Jockey User Interface.

Disc Jockey User Interface — The manual operating system for controlling the Infrastructural Command Tower. They use an augmented reality user interface; the control panels are projected in 3-D, and motion-capture cameras map the operator's movements to the augmented reality controls. Only the funkiest cats can successfully perform manual operation.

Bear-Tiger — A large, carnivorous mammal native to Thugwood. They are quadrupeds; however, they are very agile on their hind legs alone and are able to stand and walk upright for extended time periods. Because they are literal crossbreeds between bears and tigers, they come in various forms and breeds, resembling many combinations between the two involved species' genomes. Many display excellent skills with reasoning and communication, but they share very dissimilar thinking with humans.

Lunch Lady Strike — You do not speak of the lunch lady strike.

Rollabout — Small, one-person vehicles. There are electric, gasoline, and steam variations for motors. They are common in many schools, public areas, and other places. The operator stands on a wheel-mounted base and controls it with a computerized handlebar.

Sugarbutter Walcorn Cookies — Just like the grandparents used to make! Walcorns are wonderful nuts for baked goods, but they only grow in the most precise environments; most in Thugwood are grown agriculturally. The sugarbutter walcorn cookies are made by mixing crushed walcorns, cinnamon, cloves, molasses, brown sugar, and liquid sentiment into a basic batter.

Jabba Cakes — Small, round cakes named after Jabba tangerines. They contain 3 layers: A sponge cake base, a tangerine jam middle, and a chocolate top.

Cricket Palace — Cricket is a sport involving batting a thrown ball, using a special wood stick to strike the ball. It is almost always held in a cricket palace, and even the most amateur, informal games can become popular to watch. Every palace contains plenty of seating for between 4,000 to 25,000 attendees.

Laser Tennis — Laser tennis doesn't make much sense and is very dangerous. There are no official definitions of the game nor rules, and many matches end in fights between teams who can't decide how to play the game. Many injuries happen accidentally, almost all due to laser burns caused by homemade laser tennis rackets.

Ditzball — An underwater game similar to soccer. Many drownings have occurred. There are no regulations on lung capacity, species of the participants (particularly those of aquatic descent), or bionic breathing modifications to the participants' bodies.

Brainlink — Technology that measures the user's brain activity to perform digital/computerized actions. Most consumer-level products are capable of moderately complex actions, but the most advanced technology is the stuff of nightmares in the wrong hands. Due to its dangerous potential, it is heavily regulated by the government.

Mythril Credit Card — The most coveted line of financial credit with an APR you could just die for. Many of the worst repercussions for debt-devastation are sidestepped with a Mythril credit card. Creditors tremble in the wake of ridiculous legal loopholes during disputes in judiciary courtyards. It's named after the mythril element, a super hard, legendary metal.

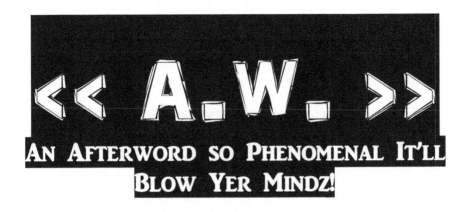

AN AFTERWORD SO PHENOMENAL IT'LL BLOW YER MINDZ!

Iwanted to write a stupid story.

That's the bottom line of what brought this romantic comedy into the world. While it eventually morphed into what I consider to be a rather decent story, I had aimed for something ridiculous foremost.

Before I worked on this story, my last published book was Book 2 of the *ANNO DOMINI ~Allium~* series, titled *Deals with Nature*. I wanted a break from that series and to stretch my creative limbs in a different way. *ANNO DOMINI ~Allium~* is considered a *seinen* story, meaning its demographic is for adult males. Also, I put a lot of inspiration from literary stories and nonfiction into that series. The result gave it a slower, heavier, denser feel than many "true" light novels. This rom com is a much-needed break from the more serious and realistic (in a way) stories I've published.

The funk is very real.

I make soundtracks for all of my stories. Right now, I have playlists on Spotify for many of them. Before I went all in with the writing process of this book, I had to get a "feel" for its mood and atmosphere and find some music that suited it.

Energetic and fun was the idea. I discarded heavy metal and EDM right away because that's in tune with *ANNO DOMINI ~Allium~*. Eventually, I settled on funk, which I'd started enjoying recently. Funk music is fun, upbeat, and danceable, so I injected it into Quinn's philosophy in hopes to amp up the entire story with this funky notion. Also, when I visualize the scenes, I imagine them vividly, and I always imagined this story emphasizing the visuals and soundtrack.

It started with the idea of giving up.

Let's rewind back to when I became addicted to producing original English light novels (OELN).

It started when I completed *ANNO DOMINI ~Allium~ Book 1: Pathology of the Grand Design*. Having a book with illustrations was surreal for me at first, and I loved how it was my first book I would shamelessly parade as being very anime-based. I couldn't wait to crank out the second book, but the idea of a one-shot, standalone light novel instantly appealed to me.

The only rules for this one-shot in the beginning were:

1. Stylized after *shounen* light novels and manga ("shounen" referring to the teenage and young adult male demographic target.)
2. Absolutely goofy.

The aspect of a romantic comedy was not there originally, but came from a different idea. I had planned for *Made From Sapphire* being my last book, a decision made years before it was published. I told myself if I were to ever write another novel, it would be a romantic comedy, kind of as a joke as my last story.

It started with the idea of giving up writing.

However, after publishing *Made From Sapphire* and starting *ANNO DOMINI ~Allium~*, I still clung to the notion of a romantic comedy…like it actually sounded like a fun idea.

I implanted the rom com idea into the standalone light novel idea, and *bam!* As a result, *My Girlfriend is a Super Awesome Badass! With her love of life and affection toward everyone, she and I will be indomitable.* was born.

I renamed it as *The Integrity of the Super Club*, though. The first title was hilarious, but I felt like it didn't really fit the vibe of the story as it grew into something more legitimate.

I was excited to write something goofy, but after I wrote the first page, it became sillier and more carefree than I'd planned. It was now obvious I would have a ton of fun writing it because it hearkened back to a time when *nothing* I wrote was serious (except that secret thing I had going called *Perfect World* to prove my imagination involved more than utter lunacy). Somewhere inside me, my natural writing style was recognized at the start of this project, and it directed this rom com without much restraint.

Not to say there wasn't *some* restraint to writing it. Much of what I learned about storytelling was used. I'm much more experienced with writing now, and I did my best to give this wild project my best shot; it needed a good story to carry all of its immature insanity. I also pushed the budget with the illustrations and time spent on graphic design, as well as pushed myself to create the best thing I could. Book 2 of *ANNO DOMINI ~Allium~* raised the bar for my standards, and I held this rom com to those standards, despite it being very different.

I tell myself I won't have the experience to write the third and fourth books of *ANNO DOMINI ~Allium~* unless I can write something whimsical and fun. I needed to get this rom com out of me, and get it out fast. My only hope is my readers think it's the fun and feel-good story I want it to be.

It wasn't supposed to be a LitRPG, and it kind of isn't one, I guess.

"LitRPG" stories are part of the "Gamelit" genre, and typically involve a video game world or setting in which the characters are highly immersed in a role-playing game scenario. My story is not set in an actual video game-type world, but instead the video game became *part* of the world as augmented reality.

The notion of *Glove Alien Fight* and the daily mandate were there from the beginning. In fact, the first chapter is nearly identical to the super quick rough draft I did when I started the manuscript. The mandatory game was a spur-of-the-moment thing I wrote into the story, all while I was elated by the goofy nature the story had from the very first page.

At first, the game was meant to be an oft-mentioned aspect of Thugwood's lifestyle. Later, while wondering how to make the story more fun, I realized the game could be a great source of entertaining scenes and character interactions, so I devised the idea for multiplayer features. It sounded really cool to have a lot of advanced augmented reality features, too, so the players could use their game characters to interact with the real environment and other AR characters. There weren't supposed to be many details about *Glove Alien Fight*'s gameplay and functionality, but as the game became more pivotal to the plot, the more I was forced to flesh out the world of the game and come up with actual rules and logic (and I say "logic" lightly as hell) for it...because otherwise it would feel cheap or bland.

I needed to be sure the video game aspect was done well to make it good.

With that said, the most important part of *Glove Alien Fight*'s existence had been figured since the beginning of this story's creation. This story's genre had been tweaked to include LitRPG and more action elements, but the story itself remained unchanged, albeit longer.

Rover's stats are not very in-depth and specific. Trust me when I say I spent half a day on a very detailed status system; this decision was late in the process, and the calculations and tracking would've cost a lot of time and energy with high chances for error, so I nixed the thought of the full status system.

Still, *Glove Alien Fight* screwed me. Why? Because...

This could've and should've been one book...

It simply required more written words than I'd anticipated. With the current forecast I have, keeping the story undivided would've yielded a gargantuan, formidable paperback book. I didn't want a formidable book, I wanted a *light novel*...and I ended up with a series...

Because of the spontaneity of this project and the whole *Glove Alien Fight* development, I misjudged its length. I had reached my word count goal for the *entire* story when I'd made it as far as the perceived halfway point in the plot. Based on that, my standalone book was looking to become at least a two-parter, and after a while, at least a trilogy. As the old adage goes, a story needs to be as long as it takes to tell it.

So, finally...

Thank you for reading my romantic comedy!!!

I'm not sorry if it wasn't what you expected lmao. XD

SPECIAL THANKS

I want to thank my friends, family, and readers who continue to support me and my writing. Being a self-published writer is time-consuming, lonely, and filled to the brim with doubt. Commissioned artwork is expensive, too. Hiring a professional editor is even more expensive, so I opt to self-edit. I'm not sure if I would still be writing without your encouragement. You all help me feel like I'm not doing this for nothing.

Many thanks to the very talented artist for this story, SageCamille. Your artwork really breathed life into it! I look forward to working with you on the sequel and hopefully beyond.

A big shout out to everyone who served as a beta reader for this book: My mom, who never lets me down; Alexander McCarty, who plowed through the entire first volume (and then some) and gave me tons of wonderful feedback; Jio Kurenai, who has also been a wonderful commenter and supporter of *ANNO DOMINI ~Allium~* and *Perfect World*; Ine Airlcana, who created my first-ever fan art and contributes so much to the OELN community; Haruto Tonbogiri, who pointed out some flaws in this story that had gone over my head; and everyone else who followed my sporadic online updates. You all provided very valuable feedback!

Lastly, I want to thank everything that is anime, manga, light novels, and general otaku culture...this is my contribution to *that* crowd.

ANNO DOMINI ~ALLIUM~
BOOK 1: PATHOLOGY OF THE GRAND DESIGN

ILLUSTRATIONS BY RUSEMBELL

Chris discovers a holy angel is disguised as his vice principal of a Chicago public high school. He sets on a path to learn why this angel always intervenes with his life. Armed with a purifying handgun and a divine phone app, Chris discovers the darkness that threatens everything.

ANNO DOMINI ~ALLIUM~
BOOK 2: DEALS WITH NATURE

ILLUSTRATIONS BY RUSEMBELL

Food costs begin to spike as Chicago remains in the wake of a contagious epidemic. As Chris explores his mysterious abilities, he meets Sandra, a young woman who has insight into the recent food shortages. Despite unending, malicious forces of nature, Chris struggles with his own values in pursuit of the truth.

Made From Sapphire

Michael wants his college degree. That's the normal American thing to do, right? However, after he partakes in a random magical ritual with his buddies, a beautiful woman appears and presents herself as his demon servant. Shortly after, Michael is introduced to a group who claims to dabble in occult situations. As the doors to the supernatural world keep opening, can Michael balance all of this with his dream of a normal lifestyle?

Perfect World

Krystal suffers from an unknown mental illness. She also has superpowers and lives in Florida. I don't know what else to say about this story anymore. It's a rewritten, republished version of *Perfect World* parts 1 & 2 (my first published story). There's action, creepy shit, psychological bends, and some of my favorite representations of evil in all my stories. Teenagers with superpowers. Enough said.

Made in the USA
Monee, IL
11 September 2020